The Camels Eye

BY
MICHAEL JAMES BALL

Outskirts Press, Inc.
Denver, Colorado

This is a work of fiction. The events and characters described here are imaginary and are not intended to refer to specific places or living persons. The opinions expressed in this manuscript are solely the opinions of the author and do not represent the opinions or thoughts of the publisher. The author represents and warrants that s/he either owns or has the legal right to publish all material in this book. If you believe this to be incorrect, contact the publisher through its website at www.outskirtspress.com.

The Camels Eye
All Rights Reserved
Copyright © 2005 Michael James Ball

This book may not be reproduced, transmitted, or stored in whole or in part by any means, including graphic, electronic, or mechanical without the express written consent of the publisher except in the case of brief quotations embodied in critical articles and reviews.

Outskirts Press
http://www.outskirtspress.com

ISBN-10: 1-59800-080-2
ISBN-13: 978-1-59800-080-1

Outskirts Press and the "OP" logo are trademarks belonging to
Outskirts Press, Inc.

Printed in the United States of America

The Camels Eye is a *Midge and the Kid Series Mystery*

Dedicated to Mary Jean, my wife and editor without whom my books would not be possible.

Cover Art is an original that was designed and created by Jeannie Hoffmeyer

Chapter 1

"Good morning, Mr. President." Jim was alone with the "big guy" in the Oval Office which was very unusual, even at five in the morning.

"Jim, I need your help. This is a tough assignment and you are one of the few people in the world I trust to carry it out. It is a total black operation." The President's eyes were puffy and red. He had the kind of hairdo a college student displays after cramming for exams and taking catnaps at a desk or kitchen table. There would be no photo shoots with this look today.

"Whatever you need, Mr. President. I will do the best I can for you." Jim Featherston had been assigned to lead the Presidential Protection Detail while the President was still running in the presidential primaries. He had been with the president at the elementary school when the news of the events of 9/11 reached them. They had built up such a trust for each other, the President had Jim put on special assignment reporting straight to only him. Jim had been sent to check on the twins, provided transportation for his mother-in-law, talked to a judge on behalf of his wife's nephew who had used poor judgment with some alcohol and a car. He was asked to deliver special messages and sometimes gifts to supporters which would not look good in the press and many other little things when the important man needed discretion. Jim was totally loyal to this plain spoken man who much of the world hated as well as feared.

"I know you will, Jim. Let me give you a brief rundown of the situation." The President rubbed his eyes and reached for his flavored water. Lemon was his favorite.

"We have a life and death situation, and I am not talking metaphorically, if that's a real word. The lives of twenty-three Americans rest on the success of your mission. If you fail, they'll die. Do you understand, Jim?"

"Yes sir, but would it be too much to ask why or what you need me to do?" Jim was not sure how he could save twenty-three American hostages by himself. That is what Delta Force and the CIA are for, he thought. This is way outside his normal type of assignment for this man.

"I'm sorry, Jim, I am getting way ahead of myself. It's just since early last evening, I have not been able to think of anything else. Let me outline the situation for you and it should give you a better understanding of what we are up against." Jim kept silent. You do not interrupt the President of the United States no matter how confused you are.

"Let me say I received this information in strictest confidence from the Jordanian Ambassador yesterday evening. He had received it from his King, via the Jordanian Secret Service. There are twenty-three American civilians being held secretly in a prison in Tehran. He brought me a photograph showing a copy of the New York Times, dated three days ago, next to a picture of the hostages, to prove they are alive. The Persians, or Iranians if that is what they like to be called, want to exchange these prisoners for a ransom." The President paused and took another drink of water.

Jim hesitated to interrupt the President, but decided he had to give him the benefit of his counsel. This man expected at least that much from him. "Mr. President, we cannot deal with terrorist demands for ransom. That will only lead to more kidnappings and more unreasonable demands." There, he had said it. The President had to stand firm, no matter what the short term consequences were. The long term stability of the government and the safety of all Americans depended on it.

"That is what I thought Jim, except these hostages are already dead." The President stared into Jim's wide and confused eyes, enjoying the moment.

"Did you say, dead? You just said the hostages are dead. That doesn't make any sense to me, Mr. President." Jim could not comprehend what the most powerful man in the world was telling him.

Why would anyone pay a ransom for dead hostages?

"I know it sounds crazy, but let me explain. All of the hostages' photographs have been identified by our state department, as people who were assassinated on Arab television in Iraq in the last year. Their families believe they are dead and so does our military. It now appears the executions were staged to shock us into giving concessions or leaving Iraq. Our CIA is in the dark as to when or how these Americans were smuggled out of Iraq and into Iran. This caught us totally off guard." The President took another chug of water.

"The CIA has confirmed the identity of each of these hostages. Their bodies were never recovered and their families have held funerals for several of these people. Jim, I do not want to give these families any more pain. That is why I am sending you on this mission alone. There must be no consultation with the Congress or the FBI. There are too many leaks and it would kill some of the family members to get their hopes up. The news organizations would have hundreds of reporters at the doors of the hostages' homes."

"I agree sir, but I still do not understand what you want me to do for you." He watched as the President pulled a file folder out from his desk drawer and laid it on top of the desk.

"The Iranians' price for the release of all twenty-three hostages is the return of a centuries old emerald called the Camels Eye. It disappeared just before the fall of the Shah and the Iranians think they know the man who has it. That man now lives in the United States near the town of Sault Ste. Marie, Michigan. Do you know where it is, Jim?"

Jim was stunned. Does he know where it is? He served almost two years in the Army guarding the Soo Locks before he joined the Secret Service. "Yes sir, I was stationed in the Soo for almost two years. Of course that was many years ago, but I know the country around there pretty well."

"Excellent. Inside this folder, I have a picture of two men. They are father and son. The Iranians believe these two men are in possession of or know where the Camels Eye is located. The father is the one they believe stole the Camels Eye and took it with him to America."

"How do you know this, Mr. President?"

"I had the CIA man I trust check into it quietly. He believes the Father was head of their museum and defected from Iran just before the fall of the Shah. More details are in here about him and the emerald which is now mounted in a necklace by the famous Harry Winston. This necklace is what they want in exchange for the hostages. Normally I would refuse to deal with these Islamic scum, but under International Antiquities Agreements, that necklace with the emerald belongs to the Iranian government."

"What is it exactly you want me to do, sir?"

"I want you to locate these men, get them to tell you the location of the Camels Eye and retrieve it so we can exchange it for the hostages. I will leave the details up to you, Jim." The President took another drink of water and checked his watch.

"What about the FBI, police, army, or anyone else who may want to get involved?"

"This is black ops, but you may need help. I have a Delta Team assigned to you for this operation. I have also had the Navy dispatch a Seal Team to Lake Superior. NSA is cleared to assist you with communications and top priority information as you request it. Anything else you need, all you have to do is call me. You know my secret number. Your call sign is Rose Garden. You are to call me direct, not any of my staff. No one else in this government is to know about your mission. Do you have any other questions?"

"Yes sir, when do I leave?"

"Now, my helicopter is waiting on the lawn to take you to Andrews. Good luck Jim, and keep me informed."

"Yes Mr. President, you can count on me." Jim shook hands with the great man and left the Oval Office.

Chapter 2

"Uncle Midge, wake up I need some help," the boy said as he shook Midge by the shoulder trying to wake him from his nap.

"What is it Ryan?" Midge grunted as he tried to roll over on the couch to face the cushions on the back while pulling one of the cushions over his head.

"Uncle Midge, my friend needs your help. Please wake up and talk to me about it. Come on, Jacob needs our help." Ryan kept shaking his left shoulder.

Uncle Midge rolled over, stretched his arms over his head and groaned as he opened his eyes. "Okay Ryan, what is the big emergency?"

"My friend Jacob is all upset. Someone has killed his favorite pet."

"Oh man, Ryan, it is up to his parents to take care of that kind of stuff. Maybe someone accidentally hit his dog or cat with a car when it ran into the road or something." Midge was sort of mumbling in that half sleep manner people have as they are just waking up.

"No Uncle Midge, this was no accident." Ryan knew this was just the opening volley with his uncle. His uncle was a gruff acting guy and if you wanted to fight, he was as tough as they come. He would just as soon blast you in the mouth as look at you if you were trying to take advantage of him or someone he cared about. But he was easy to persuade and Ryan would just have to keep asking. He knew his uncle would give in eventually just like with television or candy. He was a soft touch for a kid.

"How does your friend know that, Ryan? Dogs or cats are always running into the road and cars travel too fast." Midge was looking at Ryan with 'bed hair' from napping with his head in a cushion.

"It did not run into the road, someone cut its head off and stuck it on a post by his barn." Ryan knew his Uncle Midge was going to give in now, he had his interest.

Midge sat up and looked at Ryan. "Sounds like a cat hater or something. They should call the police and have the cops check into it."

"It is not a cat. It is a camel, a big brown camel." Ryan was spinning the web now.

"A camel? Who in the world owns a camel in the Soo?" Midge must admit he was getting curious now.

"They own four camels, but Kourosh was his favorite of them all. And they do not live in the Soo. They live on a farm out Nine Mile Road on the way to Brimley."

"What kind of a name is Kourosh?" Sounded like some kind of sneezing sound to him.

"Jacob says it means King, and he was the fastest of all their camels." This sale was almost complete. His uncle really was an easy touch for a kid.

"Well Ryan, what do you want me to do about it? I don't know anything about camels and I am not with the police force anymore. I'm retired, remember?" And glad of it, Midge thought.

"Can we go out to their farm and look around? You used to be a detective and maybe you can see something that will help catch the people who did this to my friend." He was getting close, but Uncle Midge needed a little more information before he would get involved.

"I am a retired detective, and I am not sure how I can help. That is what the police are paid to do, so have Jacob's parents call the police." That should shut the kid up for awhile.

"Jacob says they do not want the police involved." He was slipping a little.

"Why?" No cops, what are they drug dealers or maybe ex-cons?

"I don't know Uncle Midge, but can we at least go out and see my friend, Jacob?" Ryan knew his uncle was weakening and would do it. It worked every time if Ryan wanted to do something, as long as it was not too dangerous.

The Camels Eye

"Fine, but let me get cleaned up first. I was out late last night trying to locate a truck I have been chasing. I just missed him at a bar down in Kinross." Midge got up, went into the bathroom and closed the door. An adult outsmarted by a kid again.

Ryan heard the shower turn on and the water flow. He still had the skill. Uncle Midge was going to take him to Jacob's farm.

Midgely Gregory was 56 years old. He was twice divorced and not looking to make that mistake again. He had retired from the Detroit Police department after twenty-five years of service. The last six years he had served as a homicide detective at downtown headquarters. The job wore him down and was probably responsible, to a large extent, for his second divorce. His first divorce was just the result of his wife and him not liking each other. After he retired, he decided to move to the U.P., better known as the Upper Peninsula to non-Michigan people. The locals called themselves "Yoopers" and there were many "Yooper" jokes floating around the state, something like hillbilly jokes for other states.

Sault Ste. Marie, Michigan is the third oldest city in the United States. It was established in 1668 by the legendary Jesuit missionary and explorer Fr. Jacques Marquette. He named it in honor of the Virgin Mary. The native tribes had been gathering at this spot for hundreds of years around the "Bahweting Drum" for pow-wows of the Sault tribes. The Chippewa still carry on this sacred ceremony in Sault Ste. Marie today.

The St. Mary's River connects Lake Superior to the lower great lakes at the "Sault" where the famous Locks were later constructed to allow ships to move between lakes. Lake Superior is twenty feet higher than the lower great lakes and the St. Mary's rapids were impassable except by portage along the shore of the St. Mary's River for centuries. The tribes as well as the fur traders would have to empty their canoes or boats and portage everything along the banks of the St. Mary's to pass from the lower lakes to Superior, or vice versa. That path is now a road named Portage and today runs along the river and next to the locks. Today some people call it 'fudge avenue' for all the tourist shops selling that sweet chocolate treat to people who come to visit the amazing Locks.

Midge liked this part of the state. It had few people and little traffic. After spending a career in Detroit, he did not want to live in a big city. He liked the water, ships passing through the Locks, tourist season, casinos, and Canada being right across the bridge just like in Detroit. The people were friendly yet not pushy. They were not all trying to keep up with the Joneses. He thought about moving to Florida where it was warm, but he hated the hot and humid summers there when he was younger and opted for the northern cold weather instead.

He did not want to do police work anymore, where he had to bust heads or investigate murders where some druggie had killed women and children. He was sick of that life. He had a pension and insurance for the rest of his life so he did not need to work.

The fact is he wanted to work some. After a couple of false starts as a salesman and truck driver, he found a job that suited his lifestyle. He was a locator for a national repossession company. He could use his computer skill and detective training to locate people who usually had not made their payments on time. He was the only agent the company had in the Upper Peninsula and he liked it that way. It was not really lucrative but paid pretty good for part time work. His pay was strictly based on performance. If he could locate the property for the "repo" guy, he received one percent of the MSRP of the car, boat, motorcycle, or property they recovered. If he actually repossessed the property himself, he received two percent minus a flat four hundred that the company took off the top for its profit. On a $40,000 SUV or a $250,000 boat, that was a good chuck of change. He left the money in the bank and used it for fun or Ryan's education and other 'I want' needs.

He enjoyed the challenge of the hunt. He had become an expert skip tracer, which just meant he could find where people were located when they thought they had disappeared from the world. He helped the local police once in a while because he had all the computer access via satellite through his company, but he never tried to help make an arrest. He had done enough of that in his life. At this point in his life, he did not want to have to shoot anybody, or worse, have them shoot him. Once in a while a local attorney would hire Midge to find a husband or wife who had skipped town. Usually it was the husband and he had taken all their money. Many times they had fled the state. Midge would give the attorney the address where they could be found, but Midge did not leave the state to bring them back. He was not a bounty hunter, just a locator and occasional repossession agent.

Midge had no children, and he was still trying to get used to having Ryan in the house. Ryan was the son of his niece Tanya, who was killed along with her husband, in a car crash outside of Detroit last year. Midge was her closest living relative and the will gave everything to Ryan with Midge as the executor of the estate, including the custody and care of Ryan until age eighteen. Ryan did not know it, but his parents had left him well over a million dollars with the insurance and assets they had accumulated. Midge had invested it in Mutual funds and hoped it would grow until Ryan reached the age of eighteen. Midge took no money for any expenses from the accounts. It was all to be used for Ryan and he would make sure the kid got every penny.

Ryan was now ten years old. He was a skinny boy with short light brown hair and big blue eyes like his mother. He was built on the small side. He had been home schooled by his mother because he was ADHD and did not fit into the school system well. He was a well behaved boy for the most part, but did things that bugged Midge. Midge had managed to get him in a small private school run by the St. Joseph nuns in the Sault. Although neither he nor Ryan was Catholic, Midge thought the close attention and discipline would help Ryan learn better. Public schools had too many distractions and problems as far as Midge was concerned even though he himself was a product of the Detroit public school system. Of course that was many years ago, and the city schools were the crown jewels of the public education system in those days. Today, the Detroit public school system is rampant with crime, guns, drugs, and corruption. He would not wish anyone to attend school there now.

Midge led a simple and organized life. He hated clutter and was something of a neat nick. He kept his counters and desk cleaned and always cleaned and put the dishes in the dishwasher immediately after eating. He did his laundry up every morning and put his clothes away as soon as they were dry and folded. Midge did not want a dog, cat, or even a goldfish for that matter. It was just another thing to care for and clean up after.

Ryan on the other hand, left his dishes on the table or in the sink with leftover food on them. He never rinsed and put them in the dishwasher unless Midge told him to do so every time. He never put the DVD's away or back in the holders. He never made his bed if Midge was not there to help. He left wrappers on the floor from candy bars and ice cream, or whatever he had eaten. It seemed to Midge his mother must have taken care of everything for the boy. He was a typical ten year old, Midge thought. Ryan never caused him any trouble really, he was just messy and not as neat in his habits as Midge would have liked.

Ryan had only one close friend at school, a boy named Jacob. Midge had met Jacob at school when he went to pick up Ryan. Jacob was a dark haired boy and he was on the small side also. They looked similar in stature. They both usually had on back packs, though Ryan's came from a discount store and had cartoon characters on it, while Jacob carried a full leather bag that looked like Coach or Louis Vuitton had designed it. Well, his folks must have a lot of money and a desire to show the world who they are, he guessed. Midge would be afraid Ryan would lose such an expensive bag, so why give a kid such a well made item like that? He did not get it.

Jacob and Ryan got along well and were always together. Jacob was a quiet boy and only spoke if you asked him a question. When he and Ryan were out of earshot, they talked to each other a lot and seemed very happy in each other's company. A dark red Ford Expedition was waiting for Jacob everyday after school to take him home. A man with silver hair and dark complexion was always driving the vehicle. Midge thought the boy's parents must have money to have a full time chauffer, but he never pried into other peoples business unless it was his job assignment.

Ryan loved to read science fiction and enjoyed working on mechanical things. He had read all the Lord of the Rings and Harry Potter books and he had all the DVD's of all those and Star War movies. He was a fast and accurate reader, but seemed to have a mental block with writing things down. If you asked him a question, he would machine gun you back an answer. If you asked him to write it down, he would take hours. You would have to stay with him every minute and force him to write it on paper. Hence was the reason why he was in private school with nuns who would push him to do the work and give him personal attention. Midge did not know how else to get Ryan the help he needed. Ryan said Jacob had the same problems. Maybe that is why they got along so well.

The bathroom door swung open and Midge came out, followed by a bellow of steam from the room. Midge headed for his bedroom to get dressed.

"I should be ready to go in ten minutes, Ryan. Do you have the address of Jacob's house?" He knew the kid never knew an address of any place he wanted to go.

"He said we can't miss it. It is on the south side of Nine Mile Road about three miles this side of Brimley. It is the only farm with a big barn and camels in the corral." An address, why did adults always ask for an address?

"That makes it about fourteen miles out, I guess. Grab some cold pops and put them in the van cooler. I will be right out." Well, at least it was a nice day.

Chapter 3

Midge locked the house up, set the alarm then walked down the driveway to the van. He also had a pick-up truck but chose the van for this trip. Midge had chosen his typical uniform for a spring day. He was wearing blue jeans with a black belt and a dark blue polo shirt with the top button undone. He wore a light blue Lands End jacket that zipped up the front. He had on sun glasses and a U of M ball cap. His shoes were dark brown high tops, size thirteen.

Midge stood six feet tall, and now weighed just over 220 pounds. He had added ten pounds since retiring, but was still strong and muscular. Women found him attractive with his blue eyes and dark brown hair, which was now flecked with a little gray. He smiled easily unless he was working a case. Then he was all business until the case was over. He had a quick wit and a 'Don Rickles' sense of humor, biting and quick with the comebacks. He did not lift weights much anymore, just enough to stay toned, since he no longer had to fight street thugs. He still liked to walk everyday down by the water. It kept his legs and heart in good shape. When there was no school, Ryan liked to walk with his uncle. They would stop and eat breakfast if possible and say hello to Midge's police friends at the station. Midge still had all his hair and his blue eyes were sharp, but he did need glasses to see much of any distance now.

As Midge climbed into the van, Ryan handed him a diet Pepsi. That was how he got his caffeine and usually consumed about six big twenty-four ounce ones in a day.

"Thanks, Ryan. Let's get moving." Midge put the key in the ignition and fired up the Chevy. The van was plain white on the outside with the exception of some large dark tinted windows on both sides and two small ones in the rear. The only other telltale sign this was not a "plain-jane" working van was a glass dome in the top and an arrow like antennae with a small round satellite disc mounted on the rear of the roof.

Inside the van was a different story. It was a full eight passenger length van built with a custom floor plan. The front seats were custom dark blue leather captain chairs that both reclined and swiveled, with big arm rests containing drink holders on the inside. The dark blue full length carpet was very plush with extra padding for insulation. It was so plush you could sleep on it like a mattress, if you chose. The next row of seats contained two captain chairs that also swiveled and reclined, located in the middle of large windows so you could look out on the world. The very rear of the interior was quite different. On the floor, in the middle of the rear doors was mounted a computer desk with a console containing a state of the art nineteen inch flat screen computer monitor. There was a large tower under the desk and recording equipment for both audio and video feeds. It also had a matching dark blue leather captain chair.

If anyone examined the exterior of the van roof carefully, they would notice three round small domes mounted down each side of the roof. These were power audio sensors which at the push of a button on the console, would open up about two inches. They were capable of picking up sound anywhere within two hundred feet of the van.

The large dome in the center of the van contained a state of the art 3D spy camera with a power magnifier lens capable of reading a newspaper at three hundred feet. The camera could swivel three hundred and sixty degrees on a turntable mounted in the dome. The camera was connected to the recording deck and computer in the console. It was a powerful set of tools for a locator or skip tracer. Midge had to send the van to a spy ware facility in Chicago to have it fitted, but it was worth it.

The equipment could be operated from the control console or the front seat with the use of the wireless control panel that fed back to the console. The van was equipped with front and rear heat and air conditioning, a small generator, and a disc heater for long term stakeouts in cold weather.

"Why did we bring the van instead of the pick up, Uncle Midge?" Ryan loved to be inside the van, but Uncle Midge was fussy about not eating or getting the inside dirty.

"I don't know, I just thought it would be nicer to drive today." Midge turned right onto Nine Mile Road, known as M28 on the map, and headed out of town.

"Are you sure your friend knows we're coming, Ryan?" Sometimes Ryan would think someone knew he was coming, but never did. At least it was a nice day in May for a drive.

"I told him we were." For sure he told Jacob he would try.

"I hope his parents approve. If they do not want the police checking things out, I am not sure how we'll be welcomed." They could always turn around and leave, he figured.

"I want to see my friend Jacob and his camels." He would love to ride a camel just like he did once at Potter's Zoo in Lansing with his parents.

"Fine, we should see the farm any minute." We would soon know if the kid was right.

As the van cruised westward over the rolling and windswept land, Midge wondered how the homesteaders felt the first time they saw this land. They would see strands of pine in places that farmers must have planted them for wind protection. It was a sandy soil and would not support crops very well, of that he was sure. The wind blew off Superior and kept the stringy prairie type grass in constant motion. A man tying to homestead this land was betting his life against the government promise of 160 acres of free land. Most never could make a go of it, but a few hardy souls succeeded. They were the people who made this country great he thought, not the whiny lawyers and criminals he had to deal with when he was a cop.

"There it is on the left, Uncle Midge." Man, it looked big, not like the old farm houses you normally saw in this area.

"Sure looks like a farm, but I do not see any camels." It was a great looking barn though.

"They will be behind the barn. Turn in and go up to the barn please." He wondered if Jacob would be there.

Midge pulled into the long driveway and stopped. He looked at the mail box and noticed it contained only the street number. No name was on the box. The farm was nice for this part of Michigan. As a matter of fact, it was large and beautiful. It was certainly not a working farm. He did not see plowed fields anywhere on the farm.

The main house had to be about half a mile off the highway. It was a two story white farm house with a brick front and a small open front porch. There was another smaller house behind it over another hill, but he could only see the top of it. The barn was large and beautiful. It was constructed of wood and painted white to match the main house. It was very tall and had two large cupolas on the top. One was near each end of the roof's ridge line. It was a magnificent structure and looked like it belonged in the horse country of Metamora where all the hunt clubs are located in Michigan. Behind the barn to the southwest, was a strand of scotch pines on the rolling field.

Midge decided to engage his camera in the roof before he proceeded up the driveway. The driveway was made of crushed limestone, not asphalt, but it was well maintained and smooth. The van pulled up to the barn. Ryan leaped out and ran into the barn yelling for his friend. Midge took a second to turn his lens toward the house, dialed in the cameras and then hit record. He then got out of the van and stood in front of the barn admiring its huge doors and beautiful corral, or paddock as they called it in English horse country.

A pick-up truck approached from the second house and drove up to the barn. The man Midge had seen picking up Jacob at school got out of the cab. "Can I help you?"

"Yes, I brought my nephew out to see Jacob." The man had a type of military bearing about him.

"Oh, I have seen you drop him off at school and pick him up, but I thought you were usually in a pick-up truck." He looked at Midge as if he was in a line-up of purse snatchers at the station house.

"Yes, that's right, and you are usually in a dark red Ford Expedition." He watched the tall man with gray and black hair closely.

"Yes, that is correct." He grinned but did not really smile, only slightly nodded.

"Are you Jacob's father?" He was a little old, but you never know.

"No, I am a friend of the family who helps out on the farm and with the Nassire's businesses." So he did not call himself a chauffer or employee, but 'friend'.

"What business are they in?" Just passing time, Midge did not really care.

15

"I am afraid his father and grandfather are not home at the moment." So he was avoiding the question.

"That is okay, we just came to see Jacob." He would not push him for information.

"I am afraid that Jacob ………." Just then Ryan and Jacob burst from the barn yelling that a camel had chased them.

"Kia, my friend Ryan is here and the camels have been chasing us. Can we play in the barn with the camels for a little while?"

"I suppose it is alright for a few minutes. Your father will want you bathed and in bed before he arrives home, little one." Kia talked slowly, but with a voice that seemed to command respect, or demand it Midge thought.

"Thank you Kia, we will stay in the barn and play." He and Ryan ran back into the barn to find some more animals to play with.

"Jacob told Ryan that someone killed one of your camels." Midge was now curious about the reaction of this 'friend of the family'.

"Little boys tend to exaggerate, I am afraid. One of our camels was caught in the wire fence and cut himself. It is all fixed now, I am glad to say." Good level sounding answer. But Midge wondered why a boy would say the word killed, if the camel was only wounded and had been fixed.

"I am glad to hear that. If you don't mind, it is a little chilly out here in the shade of the barn. Would it be okay if I wait in my van to stay warm until the boys are done playing and then I can take Ryan home?" He wanted to do some recording anyway.

"That would be fine with me. I will return to the house until they are done and then I will gather Jacob for his supper and bath. Good day, sir." Kia even walked like a military man.

Midge reached out and shook Kia's hand and then went to the van. Kia returned to the pick up truck, drove back to the large main house and disappeared from view.

Midge closed the door on his van and went right to the rear computer console. He selected the camera controls and focused on the main house, then zoomed in the first window on the first floor. It was covered with heavy curtains. He panned all the first floor windows and saw nothing unusual. As he started to look in the second floor windows, in the very first window on the left, he saw Kia with a pair of high powered binoculars viewing his van. He seemed to be scanning the road also. That was strange since he was right with him a minute ago. In the next window, Mitch saw another man with binoculars scanning the rear of the barn and the attached corral area. He moved the 3D camera to the other windows and to his amazement he saw another man with binoculars who seemed to be scanning the highway.

Midge continued to record the views of the windows. He next decided to scan the barn and its paddock or corral. He zoomed in on the siding, the cupolas, and the fence posts and rails making up the corral. He decided he would go out and walk around the barn to see how long it took Kia or his boys to come out of the main house to the barn to check on him.

He refocused on the pick-up truck parked at the side of the main house. He zoomed in on the driver's door so he could review Kia getting in the truck later when he got the film home. With that he went to the front of the van and exited using the driver's door.

He walked directly to the front of the barn with his head looking up surveying the barn. He was particularly interested in the cupolas on the roof. As he walked along the front side of the barn, something caught his eye on the ground by the edge of the barn. He reached down and picked up a brass colored shell casing. He slipped it in his pocket and kept walking. He then reversed his direction and returned to the east side of the barn where his van was parked. Right on cue, Kia pulled up in the pick-up truck, got out and came toward Midge.

"Is there anything wrong, Mr. Gregory?" Kia was surveying the van, then him, then the road, it seemed.

"No, just stretching my legs and admiring the beautiful barn. It is taller than anything I have seen in the area." This man was not comfortable with him being at the farm.

"Yes, the camels require more head room than horses and more food. A full size camel can weigh in excess of 1500 pounds and can eat their weight in oats and wheat some days. It requires a lot of food to be stored." The man seemed to know something about camels, but compared to Midge anyone knew more about camels than him.

"Midge smiled and walked to the south side of the barn where the corral was attached. He noticed that the second post from the barn was very dark on the top third and flies were gathered all over it. "I bet you can almost see Lake Superior from the top of those cupolas,"

Midge said pointing up to the roof of the barn.

Kia just smiled but said nothing.

"Hello Uncle Midge and Kia," Ryan yelled down from the cupola nearest them.

"Hello Ryan and Jacob, are you boys about finished playing yet? It is getting late you know." Midge shielded his eyes as he spotted the boys in the cupola closest to his van.

"Please come down now Jacob, it is time for your supper. Then we must get you bathed before your father comes home." The guy sure had a deep and commanding voice.

"Yes Kia, we will be right down." The boy's heads quickly disappeared from the open area of the cupola.

A couple of minutes later the boys came running out of the large barn door opening in front of them.

"Mr. Gregory, Ryan says you are going to try to find out who killed Kourosh. Is that true?" The boy had big eyes that were the funniest shade of pale green or maybe even yellow, if that was possible.

"Only, if your family asks me to do so Jacob." Midge glanced toward Kia for a confirmation.

"I am afraid it is late Jacob, and we must go to the house now. Say good night to Ryan and Mr. Gregory and get in the truck." No confirmation, no recognition, no sale.

"Good night, and please see if you can find out who killed my camel, Mr. Gregory. I am sure my father and grandfather will be grateful for your help." Jacob turned and ran for the truck.

"Little boys and their stories," Kia raised his eyebrows and held his hands upward at his sides, shrugged his shoulders, then turned and left for the truck.

"Let's go Ryan, we have to get home." With that Ryan and Midge jumped in the van, turned around and headed for the highway. The pick-up did not move until Midge had pulled onto the highway and was headed back to the Sault.

Chapter 4

That was an extremely strange and interesting visit, Midge thought. Why were those men looking at him with binoculars and what were they so worried about? It would be interesting to review the film he had recorded today.

"Did you have fun playing in the barn, Ryan?" Midge could already see he did.

"I sure did. I really had fun playing with the camels and goats. Those camels are so big and the goats are fun to play with. One of them butted me in the stomach, but it didn't hurt, he was just a baby." Ryan wished he had some animals, but he knew his Uncle Midge did not want any at all.

"I saw you and Jacob in the cupolas, how did you get up there?" Midge remembered climbing around in his aunt and uncle's barn when he was a boy. It was a great adventure for a city kid.

"What is a cupola Uncle Midge?" He wondered why his uncle was always using words he did not understand.

"Those tower things in the top of the barn roof." He never would have known what a cupola was either except for playing Scrabble with his mother every Sunday afternoon she could trap him into it.

"That was fun. Jacob showed me a hidden door in the third stall. It led to a stair case that split off into two separate stairs. One went to each tower. It was like playing fort or something. You can see the lake from up there, it was fun." So you could see the lake. That was a tall barn.

"Did you notice anything unusual on the way up the stairs or in the towers?" Now he was curious.

"Like what, Uncle Midge?"

"I don't know. Like anything on the floor or on the walls?" The boy was no detective. He was not very observant of anything.

"Not that I can remember, except there was a lot of really black and crunchy dirt on the floor of the towers, not like the sand in the fields around here or at a beach. And there were green bags filled with something which were all around inside." Sandbags Midge thought, why would you carry sandbags all the way to the top of a barn roof?

"Anything else you remember, Ryan?" Why have sandbags lining a cupola out on a farm, Midge wondered?

"Yeah, I could see all around from up there. It was really high. I could see Brimley and you with Kia down on the ground and the airfield over the hill past the trees." Why was his uncle asking all these questions?

"An airfield, how do you know it is an airfield and not just a long driveway?" Who needed their own airfield up here? He guessed the father or grandfather must be a pilot.

"Well it is straight and long and has a building near the middle off to the other side. It had a long funny red flag on a pole with the wind blowing it. But the biggest reason is there was an airplane parked in front of the building." Like he could not tell an airfield from a driveway or road! Really Uncle Midge, get a grip!

"What kind of airplane, Ryan?" Midge wished he had been in that cupola now that his curiosity was peaked.

"I don't know, but it is red and white with a green tail. It has two propellers and some kind of emblem on the tail with numbers near the front of the plane." He wasn't looking at airplanes, he couldn't remember that much.

"What kind of emblem, Ryan? Could you read it from the barn?" The numbers would be its registration numbers and would start with 'N' if it is registered in the U.S. Maybe the emblem is a company logo or something. Too bad he could not see the airplane from where he had been parked, but the hill and trees were in the way.

"I was too far away Uncle Midge, but it looked like maybe a cat or something and it seemed to be holding something in its front paw. I did not really study it very much. Why are you asking me?" Uncle Midge always had a reason he asked you anything.

"I was just curious is all, Ryan." Red, white, and green with a cat on the tail. Was that significant he wondered?

"I had fun and Jacob said I should come over again. We can ride the camels when his father is home. He is going to get permission from his father and grandfather, he said. Then I can go back and play in the barn with the animals."

"What about his mother?" For some reason it looked like that farm was an all male operation to Midge. He just had a funny feeling.

"I don't know. He never said anything about his mother."

Ryan pulled a small paper from his pocket and held it up. "This is Jacob's phone number. He said it is unlisted so if I call him, I am to use this number."

"Did you give him our phone number?" He bet that Kia did not know Jacob had given Ryan his phone number.

"Yes I did. Was that okay, Uncle Midge?" What is the big deal with their phone number? He had seen Uncle Midge give it to some dumb girls before.

"Sure, I just wondered is all, Ryan." He didn't really mind anyway.

"Ryan, did you see any fences around the farm from the roof?" Midge had not seen anything to fence except maybe the camels and they had a corral to live in.

"Fences? Well just around the airfield I guess, Uncle Midge. I think it is real high, but I did not see any other fences that I can remember, except the big corral behind the barn which is really neat."

"They probably fenced the airfield to keep the deer and bear off the runway. Those things could be a big problem for an airplane trying to land or take off." Odd place for an airfield, he thought.

"Can we stop and get something to eat, Uncle Midge?" Ryan knew he would get something for supper, guys hated to cook usually.

"Okay, but don't spill anything in the van, deal?"

To Ryan 'stop to get something to eat' meant fast food. Burgers, pizza, chicken, or anything he could eat in the van. Midge did not like fast food anymore, but he always bought the kid something to eat when he thought he needed it. His mother would not approve, but why did she leave Ryan in his charge anyway? She knew how he was. He had been her favorite uncle and he did those same things for her when she visited him when she was a young girl.

Midge pulled through a McDonalds and got Ryan the special with two double cheese burgers and a large fry. He also ordered him a frozen Coke because Ryan begged so for it. He hoped he did not wet the bed from all the caffeine and sugar. Ryan attacked the French fries in the bag with gusto. Ryan was a skinny kid, but Midge wondered if that would hold up later in life if the kid kept eating all this junk food. What was he saying? He considered the main food groups cookies, candy, pizza, and milk. Milk was the healthy part.

Midge was anxious to get home and get Ryan to bed so he could study the tapes he had recorded at the farm. It sure was a strange place to raise camels. Actually it was a strange place to put such a modern new farm, if that place could be called a farm. When he was a boy, his family would go to Reed City and visit their aunt and uncle's farm. That was a working farm with cows to milk, chickens to feed, and an old horse to ride. The farm they visited today was more like those equestrian horse farms north of Detroit where everyone dressed like old English ladies and gentlemen. They rode around with their noses up in the air on their overpriced horses with fancy bloodlines. What a bunch of phonies those people are, he thought.

"Uncle Midge, can we rent a movie tonight?" He knew he was pushing his luck now.

"No Ryan, it is a school night and we won't have enough time to finish one before bed time." A kid had to try.

"Please, I will get up on time for school." Maybe he could persuade his uncle he would change instantly and actually get up on time, if he rented a movie on a school night.

"No Ryan, but we can rent some great monster films and pull an all-nighter on Saturday, if you are good in school." Midge was using the old bait and switch game.

"An all-nighter! Okay, I'll be good. Can we rent all the Tremor movies? I love those Graboids." Ryan loved an all-nighter as much for the food he got to eat as the movies he could pick to watch.

"Sure, those are real classics in the movie world. I wonder why they never were mentioned in the Oscar nominations." He is a typical kid that is for sure.

Chapter 5

They pulled into the driveway right next to the house and unloaded the cooler and food from the van. Ryan ran into the house and jumped on the couch, finishing the last of the fries and frozen Coke. Midge returned to the van, ejected the tape from the recorder and pulled the CD from the computer. He would look at the information later tonight after Ryan was asleep.

Midge had purchased this house two years earlier. It was a small three bedroom bungalow with a bath and a half. It was on a double lot with room to park next to the house. The yard was bigger than most on the east side of Sault Ste. Marie. He was not sure when it was built, but someone said it must have been around the late 1800's. All Midge knew is it was close to downtown and cheap. There was not a square corner in the place. It was a low profile bungalow with white clapboard siding. Once he bought the house, he completely gutted the interior. The total electrical, heating, and plumbing systems had to be removed and replaced. He also ran new sewer and water lines to the road. When he rebuilt it, he completely insulated the walls, ceiling, and floor. He did almost all the work himself except for the addition to the kitchen, the expanded second bathroom, and a small laundry room. He did all the wallboard, cupboards, light fixtures, ceramic tile, painting, decorating, and that type of work himself. It was now a modern house inside with state of the art CAT7 coax and home theater equipment in the open living room where he could watch his football games in big screen comfort. The kitchen was beautiful with granite counters, cherry cupboards, and state of the art stove, microwave, dishwasher, and refrigerator. The bathrooms, kitchen, and laundry

23

room had light ceramic tiles on the floor with the rest of the house covered by dark blue carpets. Midge liked to bake just like a real chef when he got the urge. His kitchen was equipped with all the tools to enjoy it.

Being an ex-cop, he was security conscious. He installed steel doors with triple deadbolts that would require a bazooka to knock them out. He chose small bullet proof glass windows. He had two of the bedrooms and office lined with bullet proof ceramic fabric like the army vests worn in Iraq. He just felt safer that way in case any of the ex-cons he had put away might remake his acquaintance some day.

He had small high tech cameras mounted inside small domes under the overhang on every side of the house. He could monitor the outside of his home day or night with the use of infrared cameras connected to his computer room. His alarm system was state of the art and could be set for sound, motions, entry, etc. One of the three bedrooms he had converted into an office and made it his operation center. He could even select to record events when he was gone, like the convenience stores did to monitor everything that went on inside their operations.

Midge was happy with his home inside now. He left the outside unchanged to avoid attracting any local burglar attention. He didn't want it to stand out in the neighborhood.

Next spring he thought he and Ryan would rebuild the old garage. It would be good training for Ryan and let him exercise his mechanical talents. He may even tear it down and have a new one erected if the frame was too bad. He would see how his funds were next year.

He did not have a steady girl friend, but would go to the casinos when the tourists were in town and find some company. With Ryan living with him now, he sometimes would take a room at the hotel at one of the casinos. He knew the desk clerks and management and they gave him a good deal if they had rooms available.

Midge did not like to fish, but Ryan did. They would go out with some of the local fishing boat captains once in a while. Midge would just sit and drink with the captain while Ryan would catch fish. They never kept any of the fish they caught, but released them. It was just for fun as far as Ryan was concerned.

Ryan had his own bedroom, and he used the bathroom near the kitchen as his own. Midge tried to make him responsible for keeping it clean, but Ryan was not very good at it. He picked up his towel and washcloth and took them to the laundry room, but Midge cleaned the tub, shower and commode every week. He was a typical messy kid.

Ryan was a collector of junk. Ryan kept old bolts, pieces of wire, stones that caught his eye, sticks he made into walking staffs, old holiday cards, and every other thing that was the least bit sentimental to him. Midge figured he got this from his mother who had saved everything too. When Midge took over the estate after she and her husband died, he tried to go though it with Ryan to decide what to throw away. He soon found out the kid did not want to let anything go.

Midge understood, but finally had to come up with a different plan. He had Ryan identify his favorite things and put them in big boxes for movement to Midge's house. The boxes were carefully selected by size to fit in the closet and dresser of Ryan's bedroom. Once these were filled, Midge took Ryan to Disney World for a week. While they were gone he had an auctioneer sell everything he could and give the rest to the Salvation Army. When they returned from Florida, they went straight to Midge's house in the Sault. All of the boxes were waiting for Ryan to put away in his own bedroom. The old house was sold and the proceeds added to Ryan's trust fund. The plan worked like a champ.

Ryan loved his new room. For a few weeks Midge and he explored the Upper Peninsula and had a great time. When they came back to the Sault is was late summer and time to find Ryan a school.

Ryan had been home schooled for the last three years. He could read at a high school level and his math skills were excellent. His big issue was he hated to write anything on a piece of paper. He could tell you about every character in Lord of the Rings, but if you asked him to write it down, he was done. You could make him sit at a table for hours, threaten him, bribe him, it made no difference. He wrote nothing.

Midge put Ryan in the public grade school, but soon found out he had to see the teacher everyday about Ryan. It finally wore him out.

He talked to some friends until one finally suggested he put him in St. Joseph school. It was a small Catholic school run by the nuns. They only took children with learning disabilities. Even though he was not Catholic, the sisters accepted Ryan. The only condition was Midge could not interfere with his education. That was fine with Midge, he was not getting anywhere with the kid anyway. It was only about four blocks from their home and the children were a diverse looking bunch of white, red, yellow, and even a couple of military black kids. Ryan seemed happy and adjusted well to the school. He even developed some friends. Jacob became his best and closest friend.

Ryan came out of his bathroom. "I'm going to bed, Uncle Midge."

"Good night, Ryan. Do you want me to take you to school in the morning?"

"No thanks, it is nice out and I want to walk with Toby from the next street."

"Did you brush your teeth?"

"Of course, I always brush my teeth."

"Okay, I'll get you up at six-thirty for breakfast. Don't forget about the all-nighter this weekend."

"I won't, Uncle Midge. Good night."

"Good night."

Chapter 6

Midge left the kitchen with a diet Pepsi and headed to his office. He was interested in viewing what his tape and CD had captured at the farm.

He inserted the tape into the "S" VHS and rewound it. He had it on record while they were out of the van, but he did not expect to learn a lot. While it was rewinding he fired up his Dell desktop. He opened the CD drive and inserted the CD. He next logged onto the internet which was hooked up to his satellite dish. It was not as fast as cable, but a lot faster than a regular phone line. Up in northern Michigan, as in much of rural America, the satellite dish is a godsend.

He logged onto his email and checked his messages. Just some notes from old police buddies with jokes and messages attached. Why did people send some of this stuff to him? If you were on their mailing lists, they forwarded everything funny or politically charged they thought you might like to read. Midge actually opened very few of the attachments. He had anti-virus and spy ware software to protect his computer from attack, but why take too many chances that a new virus could get through?

After he was done with the email, he turned his attention to the screen and selected "S" VHS on his input screen. At first the rear of an SUV came on the screen and then a bar in a town a little south of here. It was from his last stakeout. He fast forwarded the film until the white farmhouse they had visited came into view. He hit pause and looked at the screen.

The front of the farmhouse was where he had the camera start when they left the van and then it slowly panned the farm in a 360 degree arc. He saw the corral and then the front of the barn came into view. Next he saw the field and then the driveway come into view. He hit pause. Beside the driveway were square posts on both sides. They had the house number on the outsides of each post so traffic could read the numbers from both directions. These were modern looking posts, not old wooden posts, but they looked like those small posts you see with underground telephone service. Yes, of course, the Nassire farm had underground phone lines. He rewound the tape a little and played it again. There it was, more underground phone line posts, but why? In this tape he could see three other posts on the camera panning. As he came to the driveway entrance, he paused the tape again. What was different about those posts? They were the right size and shape. They were even that pale green brown color phone companies across the country like to use. No, there was something a little different about them. What is it? Then he saw it. Each post had a little round globe on the top of it. He let the tape play on again and noticed the farm had these telephone posts about every hundred feet as far as his camera could see. It was no wonder the farm lacked any fences. It was monitored by electronic cameras around the total perimeter. He waited for the tape to return to the house and stopped it. On the under side of the roof he saw the domes on the front and one side the of house. They were a lot like the ones for his home security system. He next waited for the camera to pan the barn again. Sure enough, there were the domes. This place was wired for sight and probably sound, just like it was Fort Knox or something.

But why? Were those camels that valuable? What did these people do for a living? It is not unusual for the big lake front summer homes up here to be plush and extravagant, but a farm is highly unusual.

Midge finally came to the part of the tape he had filmed when he had returned to the van. In the main house it showed three different men peering out the windows with binoculars. They were checking out his van and one of them was scanning the road out front. It was as if they were expecting an attack or something to come in from the highway at any moment. The way they were watching his van, he felt like they thought he was smuggling illegal aliens onto their farm or something. And he thought he was paranoid.

Studying the corral posts he had panned in on, he was certain the second post had been soaked in blood. The flies all over it was the confirmation.

He hit stop, rewound the VHS and selected computer on the video selector. He logged onto his skip tracer program icon and brought up his federal crime database. His company had access to all public record crime data base for everything from child molesters to driving violations.

He typed in the name Nassire, selected all, and hit enter. This would take a few minutes so he got up and used the bathroom. He retrieved another soda from the kitchen went back to the console and sat down.

"No matches found" was on the screen when he returned. That was a relief. At least they were not wanted felons as far as the FBI and police were concerned.

Next he tried the immigration and INS data bases he could get access to. He entered Nassire and restricted it to prior to 2000 calendar year. This time the computer had five hits. Starting in 1975 it showed a Yahya Nassire, from Tehran, Iran on a student visa. The US listed address of record as Ann Arbor, Michigan. In 1979 was a Jalil Nassire, from Tehran, Iran shown on a visitor visa to Ann Arbor. There were three other Nassire listings but in New York and California. So it seems the Nassire farm is owned by Iranian, better know as Persian, immigrants who seemed to have come to this country around or before 1979.

Now he understood why they did not want to involve the police. Immigrants, both legal and illegal, often had a bad experience with the police in their old countries. He saw that on his job in Detroit. He had a hard time getting Hispanics, Arabs, Poles, and Slavs to be witnesses for the police. They did not trust the police and were afraid of them for the most part. They kept to themselves and were easy prey for street hoodlums and con artists.

Well, in the morning he would go by and talk to his friend Tom, who was a Captain with the Chippewa County Sheriff Department. Maybe he could get the Nassire family some quiet help on the sly. This was starting to be a very interesting "non-investigation".

At 6:30 am, Midge got Ryan up and herded him into the bathroom to shower. After some yelling to keep him moving, Ryan finished, went to his bedroom and got dressed. Midge fixed two eggs and a pancake for Ryan. He ate quickly, got his coat and backpack and headed for the front door.

"It is late Ryan, so go straight to school and don't be late." The boy was always late, Midge thought.

"I won't be late. Bye, I'll see you tonight." What is the hurry anyway? He is only going to school after all.

"Okay buddy, have a good day." He knew he should quit worrying about the boy, but he had been a cop and that is how a cop was in life.

Midge wanted to go for his morning walk, but would wait a half hour so Ryan would be in school and would not be embarrassed by his uncle following him and his friends. He cleaned up the dishes, changed into his tennis shoes and windbreaker and headed out the door. He locked the door, set the alarm and started toward downtown.

It was a brisk morning but he warmed up quickly as he walked. He walked down to where he could see the water and turned left on Portage Avenue, the one the locals now called 'Fudge Avenue". This avenue followed the same trail that the native tribes used for centuries to portage their canoes between the great lakes by the St. Mary's River. Now he went toward the Locks the big ships pass through as part of the St. Lawrence Seaway. As he came to Ashmun Street he turned left and went up a couple of blocks. He stopped at the Chippewa County Sheriff office to see his friend Tom Molten.

"Hey Tom, how is the day going?"

"Good Midge, what brings you in here today?"

"Well I thought I'd stop by and buy you a coffee."

"I have the time if you have the dime."

"Okay Tom, why don't we run over to Rita's?"

"Sounds good to me, pal. Hey Jack, I'll be at Rita's if you need me and I'll have my radio on."

"Fine boss, we'll hold down the fort."

Midge and Tom walked about a block and went into Rita's. They took a table in the back where Tom usually sat. The waitress, Lennie brought a carafe of coffee and mugs with a crème pitcher and sugar. Tom poured them both a cup of coffee.

"How is the kid doing, Midge?"

"Pretty good my friend, but one of his school pals has a problem."

"What kind of problem?"

"Well, I want to keep this off the record. His family are immigrants and they do not seem to like to have police involvement, if they can help it."

"I understand. This will be just between us." Tom was an old friend. He and Midge had been patrolmen in Detroit together years before Tom moved to the Sault.

"Good. Someone killed the boy's pet and he wants me to find out who did it." Midge watched him for a reaction.

"A pet? Sounds like a problem for animal control, not the police." Just what Midge had thought he would say.

"That's what I said until I found out it was a camel." Let's see what he thought now.

"Did you say a camel?" Tom was listening more intently now.

"Yes I did, but it gets thicker. It seems someone cut the camel's head off and stuck it on one of the fence posts in the corral next to the barn." Tom was hooked now for sure.

"Kind of sick, isn't it?" Tom stirred his coffee a little more.

"The boy goes to school with Ryan and asked me to look into it." Midge knew he would get the straight scoop from Tom.

"Are you going to do it?" Tom watched Midge closely now.

"I told Ryan to have them call the police, but they do not want the police involved. They live on a farm about ten miles out of town toward Brimley. So I do not know if that is under your jurisdiction or Brimley, or whoever."

"Is it that big farm that has a couple of houses and a big barn that sit way back off the highway on the south side of the road?" Tom had passed it a hundred times on M-28.

"Yes, have you been there?" Midge was not surprised since it is in Chippewa County.

"The answer then is whoever." Tom knew this would confuse Midge.

"What do you mean whoever?" Was Tom playing word games?

"I mean that is tribal land and falls under Tribal Police or BIA." It confused Tom when he first found out too.

"How can that be, it is a good ten miles off the reservation as far as I know." This was news to Midge.

"Yes, but under the treaties with the Ojibwa, who we call Chippewa, in 1836 and 1855 that land belongs to the tribe and comes under their jurisdiction."

"How do you know this?" This did not seem right to Midge.

"We had a poacher call over that way about two years ago, by some of their neighbors. We went up to the farm to see if they had any problems with the poachers. Well, it did not take long before the Tribal Police pulled up behind us and told us we were on tribal land. They pulled out a map with a State of Michigan stamp on it. They showed me several parcels that were tribal land and said we had no business there."

"Is that true?" What kind of treaty put reservation land ten miles outside a reservation?

"Look Midge, these tribal rights things are always in the courts. Hunting rights, water rights, ceremonies on national forest land, and any other thing someone claims the treaties cover. I don't need more area to cover, so I say let the tribal police handle it."

"Do you mean Ken Telway down on Skunk Road?" That is next to the Kewadin Casino isn't it, Midge thought.

"Yeah, Ken is the guy, but I would be careful about approaching him concerning those people. They seem to be well connected with the Tribal Council." Tom was hoping to warn Midge off this case.

"How can they be connected, they are not even Native Americans. They are Persian and only came to this country in the 1970's." He was going to show Tom that he had at least done a little homework on the Nassire family.

"I don't know about that Midge, but they are part owner in nearly every Indian casino in Michigan, as I hear it." All Tom knew for sure was they were rich and every cop in world knew not to mess with rich guys. They always had connections that could make your life miserable.

"So that is what they do for a living?" Midge was getting interested now.

"Yes, I would say they have a little bit of money."

"Well I'll go by and see Ken anyway. He is a pretty good guy. I have played softball with him and I like him." Midge did not understand why all the different reservations had different names. They were all Chippewa and they all came under the jurisdiction of the BIA in Washington, didn't they?

"Don't say I didn't warn you, just do not cause those high rollers any trouble. An ex-Detroit cop should know better than to help people who don't want his help." Tom knew the 'once a cop always a cop' syndrome Midge was going through.

"I hear you Tom, I better get going. It is a long way to Skunk Road. Have a great day. I'll pay the bill on the way out. Thanks for the help." With that Midge turned and left the restaurant.

What in the world were Persians doing living on tribal land? Those property records were not part of the official county records. He had repossessed trucks from the reservations, but he used their credit applications to establish addresses and relatives' relationships. The Tribal Police had always been cooperative. He guessed they did not want car dealers refusing credit to the Chippewa. That would be bad for all of them, if they wanted to purchase anything on credit outside the reservation.

Midge walked fast to get his legs stretched out and build his wind. He walked home first and picked up his pick-up truck. He drove to the Tribal Center where the Tribal Police Station was located.

Captain Ken Telway was in his office working on some papers when Midge came in. He looked up when he heard the door open.

"Hello Ken, I wonder if I could talk to you for a minute."

"Sure, are we forming another softball team?" It was strange to see Midge out on the reservation unless he was playing at the casino.

"I hope so, but this is a problem my nephew came to me with and I just found out it may involve tribal people or land."

"Well, have a seat and let's talk." What could this be about, a repossession gone wrong?

Midge filled Ken in on the situation, everything that had happened to this point and the reluctance of the Nassire family to report the incident.

Ken listened politely until Midge was done. "I understand why the Nassire family did not call the police. Being immigrants, they are not trusting of the police. Of course, I am familiar with Jay and John Nassire as they are often in the Tribal Center here for meetings of both the Council and Casino boards. I will quietly approach John and see if he needs my help. Thank you for bringing this to my attention, Midge. Please leave everything to me. I would appreciate it if you would drop any inquiries on your part."

"Sounds good to me, Ken. It was their ten year old son, Jacob who

33

got me into this mess. I will be glad to leave it your hands. Thanks for listening."

They shook hands. Midge left the office and headed home.

Something was strange about this, but the best advice was to forget it. Still, there did seem to be something odd about that farm with the camels in this cold country. He just could not put his finger on it.

Chapter 7

Midge arrived home about two hours before Ryan was due. He reached into his pocket to put his loose change away and pulled out the shell casing he had picked up in front of the Nassire barn. He had forgotten all about this until now.

It was a 7.62mm round, mostly used on NATO weapons like the M-14 US army rifle and M-60 machine gun. It is also used by the Russian and Chinese army in the AK-47. It made the ammunition interchangeable with the armies in Vietnam and allowed the Viet Cong to steal US ammo for use in their AK-47 rifles and machineguns. The US changed to 5.56mm to support the smaller M-16 used by the US army later in the Vietnam War and still use it today. The weapon is much lighter to carry and just as deadly at close range. This round came from a US manufacturer. He examined the letters and found it could be purchased at any gun or sport shop in the US. Not much help, but not a deer hunting rifle either.

Why was it in front of the barn? Who would stand and fire from there toward the highway? That would not be safe, so why do it? Maybe it came off the roof and landed on the ground. What was it Ryan said? Was it something about black crunchy dirt in the cupolas and lined with green sandbags? Maybe it was gunpowder from repeated rounds being fired from up high. He could tell if he could get in those towers and grab a sample. Those high vantage points would be a shooter's dream, but not a smart place for target practice.

He thought about where he had picked up the casing and it did seem to line up directly under the cupola. Yes that could be true, but so what? There are so many 7.62mm rifles available, who could trace them? Most counties in Michigan do not register rifles unless they are automatic. The metropolitan counties record ammunition sales over a certain number of boxes, but that was easy to get around. No, pistols did most of the murders and that is where all the law enforcement efforts were concentrated. Who ever heard of a 7.62 mm pistol? No this came from a rifle, but why was it found toward the highway and not toward the corral? The M-14 rifle ejects to the right, so the shooter would have had to be leaning out the cupola or aiming to the left to guarantee the casing would have landed in the front of the barn and not the back. Of course, the casing could have hit a piece of the cupola framing and ricocheted to the front of the barn. No, Midge was a 95% guy. If his theories fell in the 95% probability range, then that was what had happened. He was a detective, not a spin lawyer who would make you believe rocks could roll up a hill on their own one time out of a billion, and it had happened to his client. Sure it could. All lawyers were liars and had no scruples as far as he was concerned. He had seen them in court and wondered how they could sleep at night. Midge had no use for them at all.

He sure would like to take a few hours and explore that barn, but he better just mind his own business and stay away from that entire farm.

Ryan came home about four in the afternoon. He put his back pack on the kitchen table and asked his Uncle Midge to come out and play catch with him. They went out front to throw the ball around. They were both left handed so they could exchange gloves to play. Midge bought Ryan a new glove last year. He did not like Ryan using his old glove. It was perfectly broken in from forty years of use. Midge took care of his things and Ryan did not. The old glove was oiled and kept in a box. The new glove could be found on the floor, in the yard during a rain storm, or in the driveway. Midge had to be frugal when he was young, a trait Ryan did not share with his uncle.

"How was school today?"

"Great, the sisters read us a story and it was really funny."

"What was the story?" Midge remembered when he was in grade school and the teachers would read to the class. He liked that a lot.

"Alibi Ike. It was about baseball."

"I have read it. Does that guy remind you of anyone you know?"

No kid ever pictured himself as giving excuses.

"No, I don't think so." What did Uncle Midge mean?

"How about yourself, kid? You are always making up excuses for not doing things." Now he would watch the boy defend his actions.

"I don't make up excuses. Problems just keep getting in my way and you always say to me, 'I'm not buying that story'." His Uncle Midge was one of those, 'yeah I did it guys'.

"That's right. I am not buying any stories kid, just the facts and results." He loved to make Ryan squirm.

"You sure are hard on a kid, Uncle Midge." Best just end the argument right now.

"Did your friend Jacob come to school today?"

"Yep, and he invited me to come over Saturday and ride a camel. Can I go Uncle Midge? Will you take me?"

"Listen Ryan, I found out today that is Tribal land and the Tribal Police are going to look into the camel situation. I can take you and pick you up, but I can't be working on the camel thing. Do you understand?"

"Yes, I understand. I will call and find out what time he wants me there. I still have Jacob's phone number in my pocket."

"I'll drop you off and then go over and hang out in the casino in Brimley. I will only be ten minutes away and I will carry my cell phone."

"Okay Uncle Midge," said Ryan as he threw one wide and into the street. His uncle chased the ball and returned it straight on one hop to Ryan who dropped it. Ryan liked to play catch, but was not much of a ball player.

On Saturday morning he drove Ryan to the farm about eleven o'clock. Jacob was waiting with Kia at the barn. Ryan jumped out of the pickup truck and Midge nodded to Kia, who returned the nod. Midge turned the pickup around and headed to the highway. He then turned left and headed west toward Brimley.

When Midge was a kid, his uncle lived in Brimley and ran a gas station and convenience store. It had a couple of motels, two gas stations, and a Laundromat. There were only a couple hundred people who lived there year around and they all did their main shopping in the Sault. Outside the town was the Bay Mills Indian Reservation. Every time his mother came there she brought used clothing and school supplies for the young Indian children. She also gave men's and women's clothing to the mission at the reservation. That was in the fifties and sixties. Things sure had changed. Somehow the tribes became independent nations again and were able to open all these casinos. They were now the ones giving the white man hand outs. Strange world we live in.

There are two casinos in Bay Mills. The newer one is on the shore of White Fish Bay near the mouth of the Waiska River. It is not nearly as big as the ones in the Sault or Mt. Pleasant. He knew one of the bartenders in the lounge and he liked to see her whenever he came over this way. Her real name was Brenda Benton, but she called herself, Little Turtle, when she worked at the casino. He looked more Native American than she did, but she claimed to be a quarter or more which was enough to get her a tribal job and a yearly stipend check from the tribe. Mitch did not understand it, but she was cute and nice to be around. They were not an item or anything, but they had gone out a few times and slept together a couple of times. A man had needs after all.

Midge actually met her when he received an assignment to find and repossess her car. Midge tracked her to the casino and found out she had just started working there. It was a red Mustang Convertible and she loved the car. Instead of snatching it, he went in and talked to her and told her he was here to take her car. She begged him not to take her car. She said now that she had been declared a Native American and had a job at the casino, she could catch up the payments really fast. He told her he would tell the company he could not locate the car, but after a month he would take action if she did not make the payments.

She made up the payments and they have been friends since that time.

"Hello Little Turtle. How are you today?"

"Midge, it's good to see you. Will you be staying long?"

"My nephew is at the Nassire farm for about four hours. I thought I would come see you and kill some time until I have to pick him up."

"You hang out with big shots, eh?"

"I don't hang out with them. Ryan and their boy just go to school together and are friends. I have only met their caretaker, Kia is all."

"Their caretaker? Kia is their body guard. Be careful around him.

He has roughed up some of the tribe members, especially if they oppose Mr. Jay or John on any issues at the Council. He is a bad dude around here."

Jimmy Two Shoes came up to the bar. "Give me a beer and make it a tall one."

"What's the matter Jimmy, you don't usually drink this early in the day." Little Turtle turned and filled a beer mug for him.

"You know Sam Case?"

"Yes."

"Well, he rented a car from me last week. It just got returned with a bunch of bullet holes in the trunk and the back window has been shot out. The worst part is I borrowed it from the Sault agency and they are going to kill me."

"It is not your fault, Jimmy. We have insurance don't we? Sam is responsible, not you."

"Tell that to the boss. Sam is a friend of mine and he did not have a credit card, so I took cash as a deposit. He was supposed to have it back unscratched in two days. No, I'm in big trouble. Sam does not have two nickels to rub together."

"The boss is going to fire you for sure, Jimmy." Little Turtle stated the obvious.

"What did Sam say happened to the car?" Midge asked.

Jimmy turned and looked at Midge.

"Jimmy, this is Midge. Midge, this is Jimmy. Midge is an old friend of mine and can be trusted. Believe me, I know."

Midge reached out and shook Jimmy's hand.

"He said he got sick so he could not return it. He said he drove it to the lake to go fishing and a bunch of white guys were target practicing in the woods and the bullets hit the car by accident."

"Do you believe his story?"

"I would need to have a lobotomy to buy his story. He could have robbed a bank for all I know, and he drove the getaway car."

"I haven't heard of any bank robberies around here. How many miles did he put on the car?" Midge was curious again.

Jimmy just stared at him. "I don't know, I did not check. I was too upset looking at the bullet holes to think."

"Is the car here now?" Midge would not hire this guy to run his rental fleet.

39

"I parked it out at the back of the lot on the west side of the building." Jimmy did not like white men asking him questions.

"You want me to come take a look at it? I used to repair cars and I could give you an estimate of the damage, if you like." Midge could see Jimmy was sizing him up, but with Brenda's introduction he seemed to be coming around.

"Yeah sure, let's go. I can use any ideas I can get."

It was a typical rental car. It was a white Impala with Michigan plates and an Enterprise sticker on the back. Jimmy had backed the car up to some trees with the nose sticking into the parking lot to hide the damage. From that angle, the car looked pretty good, but the back was a different story.

Midge went around to the back and what he saw confirmed his suspicions about the car. There were bullet holes in the trunk or deck lid, and a couple in the roof. The window disintegrated and was all inside the rear seat. The strange thing was all the bullet holes were in the top of the deck lid and roof. By the angle of the holes inside, the gunmen must have been shooting from a tree or something high. The car had a lot of superficial damage but it was not a total.

"What do you think, Midge?"

"Strange angle holes, like the guy was shooting from a plane or a tree."

"Yeah, I saw that myself. This was no target practice accident like Sam told me."

"No, it wasn't. Does this Sam have a lot of enemies around here?" Midge pulled some papers out of the glove box.

"Well he does belong to the Bahweting Blood Braves."

"What is that?" Midge had seen the Bahweting Gallery in a casino, but never thought much about it.

"They are full blood Ojibwa who are fighting the elders and leadership for control of the tribes and all their assets. They oppose any council member who is not a full blood. They are considered radicals by the tribal leadership. Some people say they are dangerous and may even carry guns."

"So he would have lots of enemies inside and outside the tribe."

"Sure, but I know him. He is not a bad guy. I have never seen him carry a gun."

"Is he smart and a leader, or can people manipulate him?"

"No, he is not smart and guys get him to do all kinds of dumb things they do not want to do themselves."

"So it is possible someone got Sam to rent this car for them, and then they used it for something bad?" This felt just like detective work again.

"I guess so." Jimmy knew Sam was lying to him.

"Do you know where Sam is right now?" Midge seemed to have Jimmy's trust now.

"Yes, he is at my house." Jimmy knew he had to confront Sam about the car.

"Let's take the car over to him and ask him some questions."

"He doesn't like white men. He may not answer any questions with you around."

"Where do you live?" Midge knew he probably lived on the reservation.

"I live here on the Reservation, in Bay Mills." Where the hell else would a Chippewa in the Upper Peninsula live, he thought.

"Come on, hop in and we'll go talk to Sam." Midge wanted to know about this car damage himself.

They arrived at Jimmy's house in less than ten minutes.

Jimmy went in, got Sam and brought him to the car. He introduced him to Midge, but they did not shake hands. Sam eyed him suspiciously.

"Sam you drove this car for only eighty miles. Where did you say you went?" Man, this guy did hate white men. It was written all over his face.

"Ah, up to the lake and back. I just drove around." Sam was glaring at him now.

"Do you own a car?" Midge pushed on.

"Yeah, he's got an old Buick." Jimmy jumped in. Sam was getting pissed.

"Then why did he need to rent a car?" A detective pushes on.

"I had a date and wanted to impress her," Sam replied still glaring at Midge.

"What was her name?" Keep pushing Midge thought. This was getting interesting.

"Ah, ah, ...you know, I don't got to answer your questions." Sam glared even more intently at the white man.

"No you don't. I will have the Tribal Police talk to you instead." Just like the natives in Detroit Midge thought, only they were from an African tribe.

"Wait, no, let me talk to him, Midge." Jimmy was a peace maker.

Jimmy took Sam a few feet away. After a couple of minutes, they both walked back to the rental car.

"Okay, I rented the car for a couple of guys the braves introduced me to. They also wanted me to show them where Mr. Jay and Mr. John lived. They weren't from around here. I think they might have been Arabs or something. They were not Ojibwa, or native, I know that much."

"Who are Mr. Jay and Mr. John? You mean the Nassire men?"

"That's them. They are stealing the money and power from the braves and the tribe. This is not right. These strangers seemed they did not like them either, so I helped them."

"What do these men look like?" This was getting a little more interesting now.

"I told you. They look like Arabs to me, but they look mean too, like they could handle themselves."

"Where did they pick up the car from?"

"At this house, last Thursday evening around eight, I think."

"When did they bring it back?"

"It was early Friday morning."

"Then where did they go?" The brave was cooperating now.

"The braves took them back to Canada in a fishing boat through Sugar Island."

"Canada? How did you get them through customs?" Midge knew that Sugar Island was one of the easiest places to cross from Canada to the United States from talking to his Border Patrol friends.

"We are not bound by white man borders or laws, the Ojibwa own this land. The white man has even given us a paper they call a treaty here and in Canada. It is the Ojibwa who should be issuing treaties to the white man. They stole our land, not the other way around." Yes, a real racist Midge thought. He defined a racist as anyone who promoted his own race at the expense or exclusion of all other races.

"Okay, then why don't these Arabs, as you call them, pay you for the damage?"

"You got me on that one. Maybe one of the braves can get them to help pay for the damage."

"So these men do not exist in the US according to the INA or our customs people?" Midge knew the answer to this question.

"No one but the braves know they were here." Stupid white man question both the braves thought.

"Do you think these men wanted to harm the Nassire family?"

"I hope so." Another stupid white man question for sure.

"What has the Nassire family done to you, Sam?"

"They have taken over the Tribal Council and the board of our casinos. The full bloods have little say over our own people and its land. The Nassire are buying our tribe and taking millions out of our casinos and tribal funds. They are not Native, Ojibwa, or even American and that angers us."

"Were these men armed?"

"I don't know. I only got the car for the braves."

"Jimmy, I would advise you to drive this car to Detroit and leave the keys in the ignition down near the VA hospital. The locals will steal it and chop it in one day. The company is insured for that and they will recoup their loss. Sam can say he went to Detroit to gamble at the big casinos and the car was stolen while he was in the casino. It happens every hour in Detroit. The boss will be mad at Sam, but if you keep him out of sight, the Tribal Police will soon forget him."

"Sam, keep the car here and we'll drive it to Detroit tonight. Give us a ride back to the casino in your car. I will be off work in three hours and we'll get started." Jimmy seemed relieved to at least have a plan.

Sam took them back to the casino. They parted with Midge returning to the lounge and Jimmy to his post behind the concierge counter at the hotel.

"How did you do, Midge?" Brenda had just served a couple down the bar.

"I think we have a solution, Little Turtle. I guess I better go pick up Ryan and head for home. What time do you get off tonight?"

"Why, you want to go out? " She liked him and always had fun on their dates.

"Can't, I promised Ryan an all-nighter of monster movies. If you have nothing else to do, we would love to have you."

"I'll pass thanks. I think I'll go see my mother instead. Maybe next time, Midge."

"Okay, but you don't know what you'll be missing. See you next time." Having your nephew live with you put a crimp in a man's love life.

"Bye, come and see me again." She would date him again. He liked her for sure.

"I will, Brenda. I mean, Little Turtle." Too bad, she was looking hot tonight.

Midge got to his truck and sat there for a moment. That brave, Sam, sure had an attitude toward the Nassire family. He wondered how many other braves, as they called themselves, were part of these Bahweting Blood Braves? Midge knew even the Ojibwa who called themselves full bloods probably had mixed blood in them. French, English, American, Ottawa, Sax, or any other number of people had mixed with the Ojibwa for centuries. In America, almost everyone was of a mixed race in some way. It was the same for the Ojibwa tribe as well, but not in the eyes of Sam and the blood braves.

He wondered if the Persians were mixed bloods. He was not sure, but he was sure of one thing. Persians hated to be called Arabs. They took it as an insult and could not understand how anyone could not distinguish a Persian from an Arab. It was the old "they all look the same to me" syndrome. He heard it about blacks, Orientals, Indians, and any number of other people someone was not familiar with. He even heard it from black police officers who said that all whites looked the same to them. Any thing unfamiliar to someone seemed to fit in that category, he guessed. Well, he better get back to the farm and pick up Ryan.

He drove the pick-up truck south and then went east on M-28 to the farm. When he pulled into the farm and up to the barn he saw a dark haired man and a slightly taller gray haired man standing near the corral.

Midge pulled the truck up to the barn and parked it. He saw two men talking beside the corral. He exited the truck and said, "Hello there, is Ryan ready to go yet?"

"Hello, you must be Uncle Midge. My name is John Nassire and this is my father, Jay." He walked toward Midge and extended his hand. They shook hands and then Midge shook his father's hand. Midge noticed they were both tall and slender with short cut black straight hair. They had light green or brownish eyes, no he thought, the eyes were actually yellow. He had never seen anyone with yellow eyes he could remember, but for sure they did have yellow eyes. Their complexions were a little pock-marked as if they had both had acne or some type of pox when they were young. Midge wondered if the condition was hereditary or not.

"It is a pleasure to meet both of you. I have been here only once before and have met Kia, who I knew from picking up Jacob at school. I hope Ryan has not been too much trouble today." Both men exchanged a quick glance, but it was so subtle Midge barely caught it.

"He has been no trouble at all. He and Jacob have been having a grand time. Are you a Michigan fan?" John looked him in the eye.

"What? Oh the hat. I like football and have followed Michigan for years. Some of my relatives went to U of M so I follow them more than MSU. I have been to the big house several times for games when someone gave me tickets." Midge liked the look of John, if that was his name. He had an easy confidence about him, not arrogant but sure of himself.

"I am a graduate of U of M and I have season tickets on the forty yard line on the booth side. Maybe you and Ryan would like to go sometime."

"That is kind of you John, but it is a long drive to a game from here."

"Yes, but it is a short flight. Perhaps this fall you and Ryan would accompany Jacob and me to a game. It would be great fun for the children."

"Yes, that sounds nice John. I am not sure Ryan has ever flown in anything but in a commercial jet before. He would like that I'm sure."

"Then it is a date. When I get the schedule we will pick a definite date. I know Jacob will be excited too." John gave him a Hollywood type smile.

"Great, I think Ryan will love it too." Midge returned the smile with his ex-cop type tight grin.

Ryan and Jacob came running out of the barn covered in hay or straw. All eyes turned to the boys who were laughing and tugging at each other.

"Children, be careful not to fall and hurt yourselves," the Grandfather said. He spoke with a deep bass type voice.

Michael James Ball

"We won't Grandfather, we are just playing tag." Jacob was bouncing up and down with excitement.

"Ryan, are you ready to go home yet? We have to get to the video store and pick out some great monster movies for our all-nighter."

"Uncle Midge, can Jacob spend the night with us and watch the movies with me?" Ryan was tugging at his arm.

"It is okay with me, but he will have to ask his father's permission." Midge turned and looked at John and Jay.

"Can I Father, please, please? I have never been to an all-nighter. It will be so much fun." Jacob was all eyes looking at his father.

"Well, I don't know Jacob. You have never been away from home before." John glanced at Jay with a look of wonder. Midge could sense some hesitation. He was not sure exactly what it was, but there was definitely something there.

"I know, and it sounds like so much fun, Father." Jacob was like every other kid trying to convince their parents that everyone did these things.

"Please, I don't mean to put you on the spot John, but all we do is watch movies on the big screen television. Of course, we eat lots of junk food and the kids try to stay awake until dawn. I will be there, but will doze on and off while I watch the corny monster flicks. They will be supervised and safe I can assure you." Midge watched his face carefully for a reaction.

"Thank you Midge, but I think ..." The grandfather pulled John aside and whispered in the son's ear. They both looked up at the house for a moment. John nodded and then looked at Jacob who was watching him with big eyes and anticipation.

"Very well Jacob, if Uncle Midge and Ryan will have you, you may go."

Jacob ran to his father and hugged him and then to his grandfather and did the same. Ryan was jumping up and down and laughing and ran to Uncle Midge and hugged him.

"What shall he pack for the evening, Midge?" John did not seem to know what a young boy needed to stay overnight. Maybe they should ask the servant, Kia.

"Just whatever you think, John. I will make Ryan get ready for bed and put on his pajamas. I have two sleeping bags they can use on the living room floor. That is the best place to watch monster films in the dark." John seemed to process this information and nodded, then looked at Midge.

"Just one thing Midge, we are Muslim and do not drink alcohol or eat pork. I hate to even mention it in America, but I feel I must bring it up in case that is a problem for you." John seemed open and ready to understand if Midge found this to be a problem.

"No problem, I rarely drink alcohol and never around children. They will only be eating pizza, chips, cookies, candy, pop, ice cream, and anything else that is not good for them. I will make sure there is no meat on the pizza so he won't eat any pork."

"Then I think it would be fine." John hugged his son and tousled his hair.

"I can bring Jacob back tomorrow, but he may be pretty sleepy after an all-nighter."

"We can pick him up if you like." John looked at his father for consent it seemed.

"You decide. I will be happy to do it either way, John." Midge noticed they kept watching the house as they talked.

"Then, shall we say noon tomorrow at your house, Midge?" John was smiling again.

"Fine, John. Well Jacob, you better get your things together so we can get to the video store and buy some junk food for tonight." Midge waved his hand toward their house in a 'let's get going' gesture.

"Can Ryan come up to my room and help me pack, Father?" John looked again at his father and then at the house. A worried look, Midge thought. You could not be a police officer for a quarter of a century and not notice little things about people.

"It is alright with me son, but he must get his uncle's permission." Jacob and Ryan looked at him.

"Sure go ahead Ryan, and don't cause any trouble, kid."

The three of them walked toward the big farm house with the boys laughing and jumping around as they went. The grandfather stayed behind with Midge.

"This is a beautiful farm you have here, Jay."

"It is my son's farm, not mine. It is beautiful, but a little cold for my blood."

"I love the look of the barn. It looks well built."

"Yes, John only hires quality builders. It was built by a company out of Chicago." Jay seemed guarded and a little uncomfortable talking to Midge.

"How many acres is the farm?" Midge was taking in the landscape.

"We do not really farm it, but it is a full section, a six hundred and forty I think you would call it."

"Did John know this was Indian land when he purchased it?" Midge watched Jay for a reaction.

The grandfather seemed a little uneasy for a moment. "Yes, I think he did. He made the arrangements with the tribal council, I think."

"It must have taken some convincing. They are funny about non-natives owning tribal lands, I heard." Midge knew these men were connected with the tribe, but as of yet he was not sure how.

"John did some legal work for the Sault and Bay Mills tribes, so I am sure that entered into the picture." Jay was being very vague, and the truth be known, Midge did not really care about their money or connections. He was just making conversation.

"Is John a lawyer?"

The grandfather seemed sorry he had allowed himself to be drawn down this path of conversation. "He graduated from the University of Michigan Law School, but now he is a businessman and no longer practices law, per say." Jay avoided much eye contact with Midge.

"So when did you come to this country to live, Jay?" Now Jay really looked pained. His brow was furrowed down as he seemed to think about the question.

This questioning was really starting to bother the grandfather. "I had visited my son here in 1978, but I was forced to leave Iran in 1979 when the Shah was overthrown by the Islamic clerics. I have lived in this country ever since and became a United States citizen in 1990."

Just then they heard the boys skipping and chattering down the driveway followed by John and Kia. Jacob was carrying a back pack and Ryan had a soccer ball in his hands. The grandfather smiled and seemed relieved the conversation had ended, but a new worry seemed to enter his facial features. The father and Kia trailed the boys by about ten feet.

"Okay boys, jump in the truck and let's go party down." Midge opened the door to the pick-up.

"I will pick Jacob up at your house tomorrow at noon, Mr. Gregory," Kia said. The Nassire men just looked at Kia and nodded their heads. It seemed rude for the chauffer to interrupt, but the Nassire men did not say a word.

Ryan ran for the truck while Jacob ran and hugged his father and grandfather, then ran to be with Ryan. Midge stopped Ryan and told him to thank Mr. Nassire for letting him play at the farm today. Ryan did and then he and Jacob jumped into the cab.

"Okay Kia, they will be ready by then. Nice to have met you both John and Jay, I will take good care of Jacob tonight with Ryan." He shook both their hands and got into the truck. They all waved at the father and grandfather as Midge turned the truck around and headed for the road.

"This is a boys all-nighter guys, so let's go get everything we need on the way home and have a great party."

"Yes, yes, yes," the boys shouted.

Chapter 8

They stopped at the video store and picked out five movies. Ryan selected all of the Tremor movies he wanted. Jacob selected a giant snake movie and one of the killer spider movies. The boys were into fantasy, not thrillers like Halloween or Friday the 13th type stuff. Midge thought that was good. Next, they went to the grocery store and Midge let the boys select their own snacks. The cart was filling with cookies, candy bars, ice cream bars, chips, cheese corn, soda pop, and gum. From there they went to the pizza store and Midge ordered two extra large pizzas. He made sure not to get any meat on it because he was not sure what pepperoni was made of. He feared it may have pork in it. He and Ryan would put some pepperoni on their pieces at home and Jacob would not have to have any on his.

When they arrived at home, they had a lot of junk to unload. Ryan and Jacob helped carry in the groceries while Midge took the pizzas to the kitchen. After setting the bags of groceries on the counter, Ryan asked if he and Jacob could go outside and kick the soccer ball around. Midge said sure, but to stay in the yard. They agreed and ran out the door. Midge lined up the junk food and pizza on the counters and put the ice cream away. He went to the closet, pulled out the sleeping bags and laid them on the living room floor. He took the pillows from Ryan's bed and threw them on the floor, right on top of the sleeping bags. Finally he decided to go outside and play goalie for the boys while they kicked the ball at him.

He set up the simulated goal between the trucks and the house. He told the boys if they could kick it past him in that roughly ten feet area, it would be a goal. They were small boys so he was able to block a lot of the kicks, but he made sure they got some past him so they could win. After they scored, he would make them go back near the road and start the rush again. This gave them exercise and him a little rest until the next kick. As he watched them rush at him kicking the ball back and forth, he noticed a black Suburban drive up the road past the house. He thought he had seen the same vehicle ten minutes before, but he wasn't sure. Not many locals could afford the big Chevy on his street. Most of those were seen on I-75 going north or south to Detroit pulling boats or snowmobiles. It was almost dark when they went into the house.

The boys washed up, put their pajamas on and went to the kitchen. They grabbed some pizza and pop and headed to the living room. Since Jacob was a guest, he got to pick the first movie. He selected the giant snake movie and both he and Ryan started giggling and acting frightened. They asked Midge to turn out all the lights as they crawled into their sleeping bags. The fun had begun.

Midge went to the front window and peaked out to check the road. There was no traffic to speak of, but he watched anyway. Shortly, he saw the same black Suburban pass slowly in front the house. It had dark tinted windows and he could not see into the vehicle even if the light had been better. It kept moving but slowly until it was out of sight. Midge decided to lock the doors and turn on the alarm just in case. He went to the bedroom and checked his revolver, a Smith and Wesson .44 Mag. with its six inch barrel, the one he carried as a cop in Detroit. He still preferred it to an automatic. Maybe it was just that he was used to carrying it for so many years. The boys were into the movie and had not noticed him at all.

"Uncle Midge, come watch with us. We are getting scared!" The boys were getting into the mood now as it was getting dark.

"Okay boys, I'll be right there." He went into his office and selected the outside cameras on his console. He would just leave them on the screen in case he wanted to see around the house in the dark. He thought after the boys fell asleep he would rewind today's tape and see if he had any visitors while he was gone. Then he went out to the living room, closing the office door behind him. It was time for some pizza and junk food and fun with the boys. It was great to be a kid and watch scary movies when someone was there to protect you.

Half way through the third movie the floor was strewn with pizza crusts, wrappers, an open bag of chips, four empty bottles of pop, or soda as the southern people called the soft drinks, or even tonic as he heard the New England people call it, and rumpled napkins. The boys were asleep. It was well after midnight and they were flat out dead asleep. He thought about turning off the movie, but decided against it. If the boys woke up, they would claim they weren't asleep, but merely resting their eyes. Or as he used to say, I was just inspecting the inside of my eyelids. He would leave it on and slip into his office quietly. He turned the sound lower so he could hear the boys if they stirred.

Midge moved the mouse to clear the screen saver from the monitor. He looked at all the images, but the infrared cameras showed no one outside his house at this time. He sat down and selected the tape drive, rewound the tape to 10:30am this morning and then stopped it and hit play. The tape was in real time with the date and time shown on the film in the lower right corner. Midge let it play for a few minutes and saw Ryan and himself get into the pick-up truck and back out of the driveway. About ten minutes later a black Chevy Suburban pulled up where his truck had been parked behind his van. A man got out, walked up to the door and pulled something out of his pocket. He was wearing a dark suit, white shirt, and dark tie. A fed for sure. Those guys must take a course on how not to blend into a neighborhood or something. He had never met an FBI agent he could not spot from a hundred yards away in a crowd. Those guys would not last a week on the streets of Detroit. They could not blend into the neighborhood even if the agent was black. No wonder they never caught anyone but white collar criminals who were high profile celebrities and not going to run. The camera could not see his hands well as he kept his body between the door and the camera. After about three minutes he gave up, returned to the Suburban and took off his suit jacket. He was wearing an underarm shoulder holster with a 9mm of some type in the holster. He then amazingly brought out a blanket and flashlight and proceeded to the van parked in the drive. He shook the blanket out and spread it under the rear of the van. The agent then lay on the blanket, removed something from his pocket and slid under the van. Midge could see him use the flashlight as both hands disappeared under the van. A couple of minutes later the agent came out and stood up. He shook out the blanket, folded it, and took it back to his Suburban. He put on his suit jacket, climbed in the vehicle and backed out to the road. Unbelievable! He must be headed to the dry cleaners to have the blanket cleaned and pressed. Where did they find these guys?

What were the feds doing at his house? He had been retired over three years and had no murder cases open when he left that involved federal jurisdiction. It was good to see his triple deadbolt locks were as 'unpickable' as advertised.

It paid to buy quality. The doors, windows, and locks had been expensive, but the security features had been well worth the price in Midge's mind.

He now fast forwarded the tape looking for other visitors. Sure enough about 4:10pm a white Ford Focus pulled up and a tall thin man with dark hair got out and tried the door. He only rang the bell and did not try to pick the locks. After about two minutes, he returned to his car and left. There were no other visitors shown on the tape today. Maybe the second guy was a salesman or something, but he did not think so. There was something about the way the man carried himself and his watchful awareness of his surrounding. Was he a cop? He certainly was not a fed. He was dressed like the locals and that was anti FBI code book behavior. No, he was not a cop, but he seemed to be investigating something or someone. The cameras did not reveal the license plate numbers, but in the case of the FBI agent, it was not needed. He would continue to drive by the house thinking he was blending into the neighborhood of five year old rusty and dirty pick-up trucks and cars. The least he could do was go get the Suburban dirty so it did not shine so much.

Midge decided to lie on the couch and catch some sleep. The boys would wake up in the morning tired and cranky, but claiming they were up all night. That was okay with him. He would fix them all some of his famous pancakes. He actually just made them from the Bisquick box, but the boys did not need to know how easy it was to fix them. He would have to skip the bacon with Jacob here, but they would love the pancakes just the same. He would clean up after they ate and be able to take a nap after Jacob left. He figured Ryan would sleep the afternoon away also. He turned the television off, pulled the comforter over his shoulders and went to sleep.

Michael James Ball

He woke up to the sound of gunfire. Oh my god where is that coming from? He bolted up and looked around. The boys were laughing and the television was playing loud with some guys shooting the big monsters with a 20mm cannon. That was the end of that graboid. So that was the gunfire he heard. He got up, used the bathroom, splashed water on his face to wake up, then he returned to the living room. Jacob and Ryan were now in the same sleeping bag with a pillow at the back of each of their heads propping them up to see the movie.

Midge checked the clock. It was barely 5:30 am. These boys would be whipped by the afternoon. He asked the boys if they wanted him to make his famous super duper pancakes for breakfast. He then asked them if they needed to use the bathroom and they said they had just used it. Ryan said Jacob had an accident in the night. Hence both boys in the same sleeping bag. Midge checked the other bag and sure enough the boy had wet his pants and the bag. He picked it up and took it to the bathroom. He washed it with soap and rinsed it out in the bathtub. He then turned off the alarms, took it out the back door and hung it out on the clothes line. He would have it cleaned professionally later. It was his best bag. The price of raising kids he guessed.

He made his flapjacks and the boys asked to eat in the living room which was agreed to since it was a mess anyway. The giant spider movie was on by the time he handed the boys their plates. He was smart enough not to give them milk to spill at least. The boys ate the buttered pancakes with gusto and asked for seconds. Midge gladly complied and then made himself a cup of tea. Being of English parents, tea was the drink of choice, not coffee at his house. He kept coffee for visitors, but usually drank tea when he was alone. One of his favorite treats was a cup of tea with fruitcake. You know that type of cake everyone hates to receive. Not Midge, he loved fruitcake, but always bought the best and only kept it at Christmas time so he would not eat it year around.

After the boys ate, he cleared and cleaned the dishes and picked up what mess he could in the living room without disturbing the movie. He loaded the washing machine with yesterday's clothes and towels and started the load. Midge liked to keep his laundry done up everyday if he could. It made it easy to do even with Ryan's extra load.

By eight o'clock the boys were asleep again. He grabbed his flashlight, left the movie playing and decided to stretch his legs and look around the house. Being spring there would not be any snow to check for tracks, but the ground was soft and may reveal a footprint or something. Midge walked slowly around the house looking for anything unusual or out of place. He did not really see anything but a cigarette butt around the back. He did not smoke, but people were always throwing butts out at the road. They did not see them as litter or trash, he supposed. Smokers were an inconsiderate lot. He saw it in Detroit when smokers emptied their ashtrays in the street while they were stopped for a red light, then wanted someone to make sure their streets were cleaned. He could never figure their mentality. He checked the butt. Was it the meter reader who left it there? Maybe, but the meter was at the other end of the rear wall and meter readers did not like to walk extra. No, someone had at least walked around his house smoking, or stood behind it watching the road, or examined his exterior.

He then went to the back of the van, slid underneath the rear bumper and looked up as he turned on the flashlight. As long as he did not touch anything, nothing would fall in his eyes. He scanned the rails, cross members, and crevices with his beam. There it was, a nice new shiny black and chrome round disc. It must be a tracking device. The new wonders of GPS tracking equipment, he thought. He had used them himself in Detroit, but he had to get a warrant to track a suspect, at least if he wanted to use it as evidence in court. He clutched it firmly and pulled it down hard. It took quite an effort to break the magnet loose from the floor panel. He examined it. Pretty fancy little toy, those FBI boys did have a lot of money to spend. He wondered what the tracking unit looked like. Probably it was one of those new small color GPS screens with a map of the area. Pretty sweet even for a government man, he thought.

Midge decided he may as well check the pick-up truck while he was at it, even though it did not show on his tape. Sure enough, two minutes later he had a mate to the one from the van. When did they plant that? He wondered if they bothered to obtain a search warrant. Probably not he figured since they did not send in a team to search his house. No, this was something not authorized by any judge. Agents did not work alone normally, so where was this guy's team? Who is this guy and what is he tracking Midge for?

Now Midge had an idea. He checked the road and looked over at his neighbor's house. Old Elmer's truck was parked next to his house as usual. Elmer worked for the highway department and traveled all over the UP and sometimes to the Lower Peninsula. Many times he stayed away all week and came home to his wife on the weekend. Joni, his wife, was a homemaker. She did not drive far usually. Just to the church to volunteer to feed the hungry. Midge placed one tracking sensor, or transmitter if you called it that, under Elmer's truck and one under Joni's old car. That should keep the fed busy for awhile. He may end up in Calumet with Elmer on Monday. Now that would be funny.

After checking the front of his house, Midge returned to the boys. They were still dead out so he locked his doors and lay down on the couch. He turned off the movie and hit the satellite button. Saturday morning had on good cartoons. He liked the old Looney Tunes. They were cleverly written. Some people did not understand how much writing and imagination went into each cartoon. He fell asleep during a Bugs Bunny cartoon.

When he woke up, it was after eleven. The boys were still out cold. He remembered camping out when he was a boy. He would cook breakfast on a campfire and how good it tasted burned and all. Then he and his brother would head for home and sleep all day, if their mother let them. They were beat, but loved every bit of it. Those were good memories and did not cost any money to have fun.

He gently shook the boys awake. He told them Jacob was going to be picked up around noon so they better get cleaned up. Ryan got up and used Midge's bathroom while Jacob used the other. Within about fifteen minutes, the boys were changed out of their pajamas and into street clothes. Jacob packed all his stuff into his overnight bag, which was made of that expensive looking leather, and placed his soccer ball on it near the door. The boys then turned on another graboid movie and sat on the couch to wait for Kia to pick Jacob up.

Right on schedule, the large red Ford Expedition pulled into the driveway. Kia came to the door and knocked. Midge invited him inside while he got Jacob's things around.

"Oh Kia, can you stay until this movie is finished?"

"No, young one, I am afraid not. Your father wants you home as soon as possible. He misses you."

"Yes Kia, but can you at least see what a graboid is for a second?"

Kia came around the front of the television and watched as a brownish gray giant slug like creature came out of the ground and was blown to pieces by some wacko gun toting guy wearing a ball cap. The boys squealed and yelled at the screen happy to see man triumph over monster. Kia just shook his head, picked up Jacob's things and headed for the door.

"Please, tell Ryan and Mr. Gregory thank you for allowing you to spend the night with them, Jacob."

"Thank you Ryan and Uncle Midge for having me over. It was fun. I have never seen monster movies before and I wasn't scared one bit. Well, only a couple of times in the dark, but it was lots of fun." His hair was a mess and his eyes looked puffy, but he was all smiles.

"Glad you came over, Jacob. You and Ryan will have to do this again sometime. Jacob was very well behaved, Kia. Please tell his father how well he did." Midge watched Kia stare at him coolly, he felt.

"Thank you Mr. Gregory, I shall. Now Jacob, let's be going. Good bye Ryan and good bye, Mr. Gregory." He turned and held the door open for Jacob.

"Midge, please call me Midge, please Kia."

"Yes, well thank you Midge, I am sure Mr. Nassire appreciates it very much. Good bye." With that he turned and took Jacob to the truck. Midge and Ryan went outside to wave goodbye.

Kia backed the big vehicle out onto the road and drove off to the west. Midge noticed down the block in the other direction was parked a familiar black Suburban. He glanced over at his neighbor's house and noticed that Elmer's truck was still in the driveway. It was Sunday after all and Elmer liked to stay home on Sunday if he could. Midge wondered what time he would leave for work tomorrow and how far his highway job would take him. He hoped it would at least be across the Mackinaw Bridge and into the Lower Peninsula so Mr. Fed would have a nice ride. They waved until the Expedition was out of sight and then went back in the house.

"I sure had fun, Uncle Midge. I love all-nighters, they are really fun. Jacob said he never even saw a monster movie before and had never stayed all night with anyone. My tummy hurts a little and I feel sleepy. Do you mind if I lie down for a little while, Uncle Midge?"

The kid looked beat all right.

"No Ryan, go right ahead. When I stayed out all night as a boy, I slept most of the next day. That is part of the fun of it. I was always useless the next day, but my friends and I sure had fun." He was happy Ryan was getting to enjoy part of the growing up experience like he had.

"Me too. I want to do it again sometime." With that Ryan crawled into his sleeping bag and turned on the movie again. He didn't last ten minutes before he was out cold. Mitch turned the television off.

Midge went out to the street to fetch his Sunday paper. As he glanced to the left he noticed that the black Suburban was gone. Probably followed Kia back to the farm he thought.

He got the out state edition of the Detroit News. It was the largest paper in the state and had the most reporters. He liked to sit and read at his kitchen table while he watched the national news interview shows and drink his tea. It was his quiet time for the week.

Chapter 9

Monday morning came as usual with Midge trying to get Ryan out of bed and ready for school. Ryan never liked to get up. Midge was the same way when he was a boy, but his mother didn't take any guff. If you did not get up within five minutes of being called, she would bring in a glass of cold water and pour it on your head. That got you up fast. You learned pretty quickly it was better to get up when called the first time. Midge was never late for anything his whole life and he did not want Ryan to get in the habit of being late either. It was because of his upbringing. Things like "it is just as easy to be five minutes early as to be five minutes late" stuck in his mind forever. He tried to instill this in his family. Of course, his two ex-wives did not see it the same way. They would be late for their own funerals if allowed. Maybe he was too hard to live with, but he hated being late for no reason. It tore him up inside and made him angry with himself and others. He knew in today's world, everyone thought being late was okay, but he was not like that and never would be.

"Ryan, let's go, you are going to be late for school. Am I driving you or are you walking. It is a nice morning out."

"I am walking, so can I have a cookie to eat on the way?" Ryan just moaned liked a wounded lion.

"No, but you can have a piece of toast and an orange juice." That kid was always trying to eat cookies for breakfast. If the truth be known, Midge liked them for breakfast too.

"Okay, I'm ready." Ryan ran out of his room, put on his coat and back pack and headed for the door. Midge shoved a piece of toast and a fruit juice box at him and opened the door. He went outside and watched Ryan as he went down the street.

Midge noticed that Elmer's truck was gone and the black Suburban was not in sight. He smiled thinking of the nice trip the fed was having this morning.

Midge went in his house and put on his jacket. He locked up, set the alarm and started walking for the Locks. A good walk was just what he needed this morning. The sun was shining, and though the temperature was in the low fifties, it was warm enough when he was walking at a fast pace. He walked to the waters edge and turned down Portage Avenue along the Locks. There was a large freighter entering from the Superior side going south. It rode low in the water so it was probably loaded with ore headed for Detroit, Cleveland, or some other city along the St. Lawrence Seaway. He enjoyed watching the huge ships travel through the Locks. The engineering involved to lift and lower a ship weighing that much simply amazed him. He had taken a boat tour of the locks once and learned there were no pumps in the Locks at all. This amazed him, especially when he found out the Locks used lake water pressure and a simple valve to raise and lower the ships with water. It only took a few minutes and there were no moving parts. What an amazingly simple form of engineering genius.

Midge decided to stop for breakfast at Rita's, his favorite restaurant in town. As he entered he saw his Chippewa Sheriff friend, Tom Molten in the back of the restaurant at his regular table. He was already eating when Midge approached the table.

"Mind if I join you, Tom?" Tom seemed to be alone and engrossed in his food.

"Not at all Midge, pull up a chair." Tom gestured to his right.

Midge ordered his usual coffee, two eggs over easy, bacon, American fries, and whole wheat toast with apple jelly.

"How is the world treating you this morning, Tom?"

"Fine, I guess. Did you hear what happened out at Bay Mills yesterday?" Tom kept on eating, but he had succeeded in raising Midge's interest.

"No, I have been out of touch this weekend. Ryan had a little friend over Saturday and we pulled an all-nighter with some monster movies and a lot of junk food. Then Ryan and I kind of slept the day away on Sunday. It was fun though, and the kids loved it."

"Sounds great, I remember how much I loved that kind of stuff when I was a kid."

"So what happened out on the reservation yesterday, Tom?" Tom had his full attention now.

"There were three Indians found murdered." Just spoken easy like a squad room briefing back in Detroit about dead drug dealers.

"What did you say? Murdered on Bay Mills? I have never heard of such a thing up here. Fights and drunken brawls yes, but murder, what happened?"

"I do not know really, we just heard the call to the Tribal Police on the scanner. They did not want our help so we stayed out of it."

"Three dead, that is unbelievable. Do you know who they were, have any idea of what happened, or any of the circumstances at all?"

"No, just hearsay really, Midge."

The waitress, Lennie brought his breakfast and coffee. Midge fixed his coffee and then dipped his toast in the runny yokes. It may not be good manners but this is the way he had eaten them all his life and he loved fresh yoke on his toast. After soaking up the yokes and eating them with his toast, he cut up his eggs, mixed them with his potatoes and ate the mixture. It looked like something you would cut up for a little kid, but Midge had fixed it that way all his life. His ex-wives hated the way he ate his breakfast, but at least he was consistent every time. Midge would not care if the President of the United States was eating with him, this is the way he ate his eggs and potatoes. Midge ate in silence and just tried to think what were the braves thinking out there to kill there own people?

"Do you know any of the names of the victims?"

"I heard them but I only knew one of them that rang a bell. A young guy we had arrested a couple of times for DUI, a kid named Sam something or other." Tom kept eating.

Midge stopped in mid-bite. "Did you say Case, was his name Sam Case?"

"Yeah, I think that's it. Kind of a wild driver when he has had a few too many, I guess. But we never picked him up for anything violent that I can remember."

The Bay Mills Reservation was home to the Chippewa tribe. It was a desperately poor area for many years, but with the coming of the casinos, many of the tribe were pulled out of poverty. They had good paying jobs as well as monthly tribal checks to native people whether they worked or not. Of course, alcoholism still ran wild with the male population on the reservation. While the Indians, or Native Americans as they now like to be called, were under tribal law while on the reservation, they were still subject to Michigan and Federal laws when they left the reservation. Drunk driving was one of the major charges they faced a great deal of the time. A little auto theft and some petty B&E's were the bulk of their run-ins with the law. Violence against others, except for wife beating, was very rare in the Sault area and murder was unheard of.

"I know that guy. I met him Saturday morning at the casino in Brimley. He knew a friend of mine and she introduced us through another brave who worked there."

"So you saw him alive on Saturday morning?" Tom stopped eating and watched Midge closely.

"He was alive alright. He did not seem to like white men very well, as I remember. As a matter a fact, if I remember correctly, he was not too fond of some of the tribal leaders either." He picked up some egg and potato and shoved it in his mouth.

"Hey Midge, maybe you should go down and see Ken at the tribal police and tell him about it." Tom took a sip of coffee as he eyed Midge.

"Well I don't see how that can help, Tom."

"Look, you were a detective and you know Ken may not get anything from it. This early in the investigation, anything about the guy could be helpful."

"Yes, you are probably right. I just do not want to get in his way is all."

"Why don't you go over and at least tell him you saw Sam Case on Saturday and see if he is interested in what you have to say."

"Yep, I think that's a good idea Tom, I'll do it this morning. The worst that can happen is Ken Telway can tell me to mind my own business."

"I don't think he will do that. He knows you well enough to know you don't stick your nose in police business unless we ask for your help. I know I have appreciated your help before. This far from Lansing does not get a lot of attention from the State boys and resources unless we have a big case that gets in the papers. We can use all the help we can get, my friend."

"Thanks for the kind words, Tom. I think I'll head over there right now." He smiled at Tom and drank the last of the coffee in his cup.

Midge paid the bill and walked home. He would take his truck over to tribal headquarters and see Captain Telway. He remembered Ken asked him to stay away from the camel incident at the Nassire's farm. He half wondered if he would be told to mind his own affairs again, that this was tribal business and not his affair. Well, nothing ventured, nothing gained.

He drove out to the tribal council headquarters where the tribal police are located. When he pulled into the parking lot, he knew something was going on by all the cars in the lot on a Monday. It was usually empty during the day since almost all the tribal council meetings were in the evening. Also, all the police cars were parked instead of being at the reservations or the casinos. They must be putting their heads together to try to piece together some theories behind the crimes. Maybe he should come back another time, he thought.

Midge noticed a BIA, Bureau of Indian Affairs car and a black Ford sedan which could only mean FBI up here. While the reservation is independent tribal land as far as the state and county are concerned, he knew the Federal government had jurisdiction over tribal lands in some ways. He knew the Bureau of Indian Affairs kept a tight control on tribal affairs. He also knew since the Federal government was involved, the FBI must have some jurisdiction in this case. Midge did not really know the rules since in Detroit he had never been involved in such things. He knew if the BIA and FBI cars were in the parking lot, it was a good bet they at least thought it was in their jurisdiction.

Midge parked his truck in the back of the lot and walked through the double doors to the tribal council headquarters building. He turned right and headed down the hall to the tribal police offices. As he approached Ken Telway's office, he could see he was in a deep conversation with two of his officers and two FBI agents. That is all those guys with dark suits, white shirts and dark ties could be. He looked at the other office and saw the other tribal police officers sitting around a table talking and taking notes. Maybe it was better if he just turned around and left. He could always come back in a few days when Ken was not so stressed and busy.

Just as he was about to leave, the door to Ken's office opened and two tribal police officers left at a fast pace down the hall to the main door and exited the building. The two FBI agents talked to Ken for a minute and then left. As they passed Midge in the hall, they were looking him up and down. They always looked down on people as they went by as if their own shit did not smell and everyone else's did. He hated working with those arrogant assholes. Ken was sitting at his desk reaching for the phone when Midge walked in.

"Hello Ken, do you have a minute?"

"I'm afraid not Midge, I am up to my ass in alligators right now. Maybe next week, hey pal?"

"It is about one of the murder victims, Ken."

Ken put the phone down and motioned for Midge to take a seat. Midge closed the door behind him as he entered. Ken sat back down and folded his arms across his chest in a manner that said 'okay, this better be good'.

"I met Sam Case at the casino on Saturday morning while I was over visiting my friend Brenda, the bartender."

"What time did you see him?"

"It was before 4:00pm because I had to pick up my nephew Ryan at the Nassire farm then."

"What were you doing at the Nassire farm?"

"I told you, I was picking up Ryan who was there playing with his friend, Jacob Nassire. As a matter of fact, we took Jacob to our house to stay over night and watch monster movies with us." Ken eyed him with suspicion.

"You did not go there to investigate that camel incident did you, Midge?" Now it was Midge's turn to roll his eyes and shake his head.

"No Ken, I have only gone there with my nephew to visit his little friend. Look, do you want to know anything about my seeing Sam Case or not? I am not sure I have anything that can help you, but at least I will tell you my experience with Sam. You can decide if it can help you at all in the case. If not, fine then I'll forget about it and go home and mind my own business. I'm not trying to cause you any more trouble than you already have, Ken. Believe me, I have investigated dozens of murder cases in Detroit. I was always glad to hear anything recent about a victim that may at least give me a hint of his activities near the day of the murder." He stared Ken right in the eyes.

"I'm sorry Midge, it is just everyone is on me with these murders. The tribal council, BIA agents, FBI agents and the families of the victims are all on my case. I only have a dozen officers and none with homicide experience. This is the first murder we have ever had on one of our reservations in northern Michigan. The FBI wants to come in and investigate, but I hate those guys. They talk down to us like we are stupid 'injuns' or something. They just piss me off." Ken's face looked drawn and tired.

"Tell me about it. Those credit grabbing creeps never solved any of my cases, but wanted to be kept in the loop on everything. That was only so they could arrange a press conference if we solved the case and they could take the credit. I know just how you feel, Ken." Ken's face softened now.

"Please Midge, go ahead and talk to me about Sam Case."

"Well first of all, Tom Molten told me he thought three Ojibwa were murdered. Is that true?"

"Yes Sam Case, Jimmy Two Shoes, and David Briner."

"Did you say Jimmy Two Shoes?" Midge's face registered surprise.

"Yes, why do you ask?"

"Because I met both of those guys for the first time on Saturday morning and that seems like an awfully big coincidence, don't you think Ken? I do not recognize the Briner name, but it is strange I should meet two of the victims for the first time and they were found dead within a day or so. It seems mighty strange if you ask me, Ken." Midge did not believe in coincidence, not at all.

"Yes, it does. Why don't you tell me the details of what you talked to them about, Midge." The police captain placed a pad of paper on his desk, removed his pen from his shirt pocket and started to jot down some notes. Midge had his undivided attention now.

"Well, like I said, I went to the casino in Bay Mills to kill some time before I had to go and pick up Ryan at the farm at 4:00pm. I was talking with my friend Brenda Benton or Little Turtle as she likes to be called, when Jimmy Two Shoes came up and asked for a beer. It must have been about noon or so. He was all upset about a car he had rented to Sam Case that had come back damaged. It seems that Sam had no credit and could not afford to pay for the damage. Jimmy was afraid he would get fired for renting the car to Sam if he could not get it repaired right away."

"One thing lead to another and Jimmy asked me to look at the damage to determine how much it would cost to fix it. I went out into the lot and looked at the rental, a white Impala. I told him it would cost a fortune to fix it. Jimmy then drove me out to the reservation to meet Sam."

"No offense Ken, but Sam sure hates white people. He also had a lot to say about the tribal council members and the non-full bloods as he called them, running the council and the casinos. He seemed like a pretty angry young man if you ask me. After telling them what it would cost to fix the car, Sam drove Jimmy and me back to the casino. I went inside and saw Little Turtle. I said goodbye to her, then left to pick up Ryan at the Nassire farm. That was the last I ever saw Jimmy or Sam." Midge left out the part about telling Jimmy to take the car to Detroit and leave it on the street with the keys in it so it could be stolen. It did not seem to have anything to do with the homicide since they were not killed in Detroit.

Ken was taking notes furiously. He was no shorthand expert, so he was struggling to get everything down on paper.

"Why did Jimmy ask you to go see Sam with him?"

"I think he wanted Sam to hear someone else tell him how badly the car was damaged and how much the repairs would cost."

"How bad was the car damaged, Midge?"

"It was damaged pretty badly. The trunk, or deck lid as they call it in the car business, the roof, the rear window all were damaged. I would guess over three thousand dollars at least to repair it." Midge hoped this would satisfy Ken as he did not want to get involved any deeper than he already was.

"How did the trunk and roof get damaged?"

Midge did not want to mislead Ken, but he knew he was getting sucked in. Why did he come here anyway? This was a tribal matter and he was a white man. He now knew how the blacks in Detroit felt about talking to the police. When they came forward to talk to the police, the criminals threatened them. The police questioned them and many times found out they had open warrants for them and arrested the witness. It did not pay to help the cops sometimes, but he was here now and he would try to help Ken, if he could. "They had bullet holes in them."

"Bullet holes? How many bullet holes, Midge?"

"I don't recall exactly, but at least six overall and the window was certainly blown out by a bullet, I would say."

"This changes everything I was thinking. It looks as if the troubles started before Saturday for these braves."

"It looks that way. When and how were the 'braves' killed, Ken?"

"The coroner estimates the time of death was early Sunday morning like around three or four o'clock. It is hard to pin down exactly. The coroner has never seen anyone beheaded before so he seems quite rattled." Midge shot forward in the chair as Ken described this method of death.

"Did you say beheaded?" Why would three Native American men have been beheaded? That was not a typical method of death between the tribes. Even drug dealers do not do that. The Colombians do not even do that, intense violence yes, but not beheading. It was very unusual.

"Yes, and they look as if they had been tortured before someone removed their heads. Their hands were bound behind their backs and several fingers had been removed. All three bodies were found at the Mission Hill Cemetery. An old man found them when he went to the cemetery to visit a grave on Sunday morning."

"Do you think they were killed on the reservation, or killed somewhere else and their bodies dumped on the reservation?"

"At first glance, it seems they were dumped there, but my officers are checking the reservation right now. It is really too early to tell. Why do you think the rental car was shot up, Midge?"

"I don't really know, but Sam claims he rented the car for some Arabs he loaned it to and they returned it to him in that condition."

"Arabs, what do you mean Arabs? Where are these Arabs now?"

"Sam said the braves, as he called them, took the Arabs back to Canada by boat that morning. He said they called themselves the Bahweting Blood Braves, for whatever that is worth. Have you ever heard of them?" Midge watched the concern come over Ken Telway's face. He was good at reading reactions and Ken looked as though someone had hit him right between the eyes with a baseball bat.

"Yes, I know them well. They claim to be full blood Ojibwa and they give the council and mixed bloods a lot of trouble. They think they should be in total control of the tribe and all its resources. I myself am only a quarter Ojibwa, so I am the type of Chippewa they hate the most." Ken seemed to stare into the air for a moment and then jolted as he looked past Midge.

"Thanks for coming in, Midge. I appreciate your help. Would you mind if I call on you later for more details? Maybe I could send one of my deputies out to interview you when we have sorted the situation out a little better." Ken seemed nervous and in a hurry all of a sudden. He rose, shook Midge's hand and opened the door to the office.

"Fine Ken, I will be happy to help out in any way I can." Midge turned to leave and then he saw the reason for the Captain's concern.

"Hello John and Jay. Good morning to you." Midge crossed the hall where the Nassire men were standing along the wall. They all shook hands. They were both dressed impeccably in expensive dark suits with fancy white embroidered shirts, but without ties. The gray haired grandfather, Jay had the air of an aristocrat who had been trained to stand at attention for formal reviews. The son, John while certainly professional looking in everyway, was more relaxed. More Americanized, if you would, and not so regal looking. Still John looked like he was used to being in charge and having people follow what he said.

"Midge, it is good to see you. Jacob is still chattering about those monster movies and the junk food he and Ryan ate. Thank you for giving him so much fun."

"He was great, John. He and Ryan get along so well. I am glad Ryan has such a nice boy as a friend. That is important at their age, I think."

"Yes, Ryan will have to come to the farm to play again some time. Jacob and he really seem to enjoy the animals." Midge wondered how these rich guys always had such perfect white teeth and perfect hair cuts. He had his front teeth knocked out seven times in sports and fights. His mother said there was only a week between a good and bad haircut. She had never seen these guys.

"That would be great, John. Good to see you, Jay. I better be going, but I look forward to the boys getting together soon. Bye." Midge put his hand out in front of his chest and shoved it forward just a little in a subdued goodbye, then turned and walked down the hall toward the front doors. A wave told a lot about a man. Someone that waved back and forth was either feminine or used the gesture only when waving at a baby or young child. You had to put strength in the wave, but not so extended that it looked like a Hitler salute. Some guys shook a bunched up fist, but that seemed too macho to Midge. Those guys were trying to make people think they were tough or cool. No, an opened handed extended finger wave with just the right amount of tension in the fingers seemed about right to Midge.

"Goodbye, Midge," John said as Midge saw both he and his father entering Ken Telway's office and closing the door. Now that was an interesting event on a day such as this.

As Midge headed across the parking lot to his truck, he noticed it was starting to cloud up like it was going to rain. Maybe he should plan on picking Ryan up at school this afternoon. He would go home now, check his email messages and review his meeting with Sam and Jimmy in his mind to see if could remember anything special that had been said or he saw that might help the police.

As he reached his truck he saw a piece of paper was folded and placed under the driver windshield wiper blade. He reached over and removed it. It was from Brenda. "Midge, meet me at the bar where we first met. I am in trouble. Brenda."

He remembered it well. It was down in Kinross in Jim's Bar. He was looking for her car and found out she worked in a little restaurant near the ex-Air Force town. The town had almost died when they closed the air base, but it still had the bar and restaurant open for business. When he first saw Brenda, he liked her. She had a nice smile and pretty face with a great looking body. Although she did not dress very sexy, you could still tell she had all the right equipment. She must be scared not to put the name of the bar on the paper. Maybe she thought someone was following her and this was her way of protecting him and her from a set-up. The note did not say when he should meet her so he figured she must mean right away.

Checking his watch, it was almost noon. Ryan got out of school at three-thirty so he had time to run down there and get back home before school let out. He could go after Ryan got home, but he thought Brenda must really be in trouble or she would not have left him a note. He was surprised she knew which truck was his. Or had she been in the parking lot when he pulled in and he had not noticed her? No, he would have noticed a Mustang Convertible for sure. Midge always was aware of the people and things around him. It was part of being a cop and just a way of life for him.

He jumped in the truck and fired up the engine. Actually he just turned the key on, but he liked to think of himself as a race car driver and that is what they always said at the track. For some reason he had the sensation he was being watched, like all of us feel at times. It could mean nothing, of course, but a sixth sense told him it was real. He scanned the parking lot, but nothing stuck out except the large red Ford Expedition that belonged to Nassire. The windows were so darkly tinted he could not see into the vehicle, but he had no doubt that Kia was sitting behind the steering wheel waiting for Jay and John Nassire to come out of the building so he could sweep down to pick up his masters at a moments notice. Kia did not strike Midge as the type of chauffer who would sleep in the vehicle while his employers were inside the building. Actually he did not really strike Midge as a chauffer at all. More like a cavalry officer at the head of a troop of some kind. No, Kia would be scanning the building, parking lot, access road, and maybe even the sky for planes when he was on duty.

As Midge scanned the lot he could see many plain sedans and pick up trucks, which were plentiful in the U.P., but did not spot anyone watching him from a vehicle. He pulled out of the lot and headed for I-75. It was only a few miles to Kinross and the bar where Brenda would be waiting for him. He kept an eye on his mirrors and scanned the sides of the road ahead, but noticed nothing out of the usual. It was hard to follow a vehicle out here. Not enough traffic and few buildings and parking places to hide in. The absurd thought of the Nassire family building a farm out in this country was starting to make sense to Midge, but for all the wrong reasons.

He exited the freeway and headed toward the airport. Chippewa County International Airport was the old United States Air Force base that had closed many years ago. They had built a beautiful terminal, but the long runways were the ones that served the big bombers in the cold war era. The old base itself also now housed five correctional facilities. The town of Kinross was about three miles west of the old base. It was a booming little town when the base was operating with a bank, grocery store, gas station, and library to service the base men and women. Now, it was almost a ghost town with just the gas station combination convenience store and across the road was Jim's Bar and Grille still in operation. Midge checked for a tail again and put his truck in the lot at the side of the bar. He did not see Brenda's Mustang anywhere in sight. He locked his truck and went around to the front door and entered.

Jim's was a typical bar with a dark brownish red exterior and the old dark paneled interior. There was a long bar with stools on the right with the bottles of liquor lined up on shelves behind the bartender. Tables were on the left with four chairs at each one. For larger parties, you just moved the chairs and the tables together. There were two pool tables in the rear with a juke box in the middle against the left side wall. It had been modernized to play CD's now because the records were not easy to get anymore. There were two small restrooms at the rear down an aisle leading to a rear door that was used to unload supplies from the back.

The word grille in the name was a stretch. There was no kitchen, but just a flat stove grille and a large commercial double door refrigerator. Jim, or the waitress on duty, would grill you a hamburger to go with your beer, but no fries, forget about a salad, vegetables, or anything roasted. Hamburger, cheese sandwich, hot dog, or on Friday a fried fish sandwich was as fancy as Jim got. All things considered though, Jim made a great bar hamburger for the money.

Midge scanned the bar and saw only two guys seated together near the middle of the bar. There was no one else other than Jim that he could see. He pulled up a stool and asked Jim if he had seen Brenda today. Jim was looking older every time he saw him. He must be in his mid seventies by now, his eye site and hearing had not improved in the last couple of years, and he wondered about his memory.

"Have you seen Brenda today, Jim? I was supposed to meet her here, but I don't see her car in the lot or her in here." The old man looked him up and down.

"Who are you?" He sounded gruff but not threatening.

"Midge from the Sault, she told me to meet her here today."

The old bartender squinted at Midge hard as if trying to recognize his face for the first time.

"Oh Midge, hey it's good to see you. What can I get for you?" The old man seemed to know him now, but was still a little confused as far as Midge was concerned.

"I am looking for Brenda, you know, Little Turtle."

Jim studied him for a second with his head tilted slightly askew then smiled, reached in his pocket and pulled out a note which he handed to Midge. Midge unfolded it and moved down the bar to hold it up near the Budweiser sign. It told him to walk across the street to gas the station, go to the cashier and ask for some ladyfingers. Strange, but he thanked Jim and left the bar. He crossed the street diagonally and went in the convenience store with the gas station.

"Do you have any ladyfingers, miss?"

"Butterfingers?" The young lady looked at him very carefully. She looked around the store quickly and then scanned the pump area outside.

"No, I said ladyfingers." He watched her face and knew she had understood him the first time.

"Yeah, I think we do, follow me. I think you will find what you are looking for back here." The woman turned and walked to the back of the store past the restroom to a door on the left that looked like the storage room.

"In here, please."

Midge went through the door and looked around. Just a storage room then he saw movement. He pivoted back fast and assumed an attack stance from old habits as a cop, but then he saw Brenda come out from the back row.

"Midge, you came." She ran forward, threw her arms around him and squeezed his neck as she held on to him for dear life. The young woman who had escorted him there, had closed the door and left them alone.

"What is the matter, and why all the secrecy? You could have just come by the house, you know."

"I'm scared, Midge. They have killed Jimmy, Sam and David, and I think I am next on the list." She started sobbing and buried her head in his neck. Midge hated women crying.

"It's okay Brenda, I will help you. We can go to the police and they will protect you." He could feel the fear in her as she jolted her head up.

"Not the police, they are part of this. They will kill me." Her face said it all. Her eye mascara was streaked from crying, but the eyes shined pure terror in them. He had seen this before in victims who had survived a drug killing and were being asked to testify against the murderers who had just killed their loved ones.

"Okay, okay Brenda I won't take you to the police. But why should anyone be after you? You have not done anything to anyone have you?" She buried her face on his shoulder again, relieved they were not going to the police, he guessed.

"I followed Jimmy and Sam to Detroit to drop the rental car off Saturday night in my car. I drove them back to the reservation and left them at Sam's house. David was waiting for us there, and they were all found dead the next day in the Mission Hill Cemetery with their heads removed." She started crying again and could not get any more out.

Midge knew better than to try to reason and talk with her anymore right now. She needed time to think and a place she felt safe. He did not know what else to do but take her home with him, if she trusted him well enough to go. He held her for a minute stroking the back of hear head and hair. He had dated her for a couple of years off and on, but neither one of them wanted to settle down. They had slept together a few times and it was always pleasant, but nothing he could not do without. He just liked her a lot and enjoyed her company sometimes. He wondered how Ryan would react with the new house guest staying in his room. Well, she needed help and Midge was going to help her.

"I am going to take you to my house, Brenda. You will be safe there until we can sort this all out. Now where is your car? I did not see it at the bar."

"I traded my mom and I am driving her old white Corsica. I can give my cousin the keys and she can take it home." So the cashier was her cousin. He thought they had a slight resemblance.

"Fine, why don't we go then? I need to get home in time for Ryan when he gets out of school. Let's go."

"Why don't you pull your truck around the back of the store and I'll come out that door and get in." Fear was still on her face, but she looked much better than before.

"Fine, I'll be back in two minutes so be ready." Midge exited the front of the store and made a beeline for his truck, though he scanned the road as he went. He pulled his truck around the back of the store and Brenda jumped in quickly. He headed out of the gas station, back to the expressway and then to the Sault.

As he entered his street, he noticed the black Suburban parked near the other end past his house. He pulled into the driveway right behind his white van. He and Brenda entered the house quickly and he locked the door. Midge went to the front window and looked through the blinds out on the road. He could see no other cars on the street, except the fed as he closed the blinds. He wondered if the fed had a nice ride following Elmer this morning. He kind of chuckled to himself as he could picture the fed at 4:30am hearing the tracker beacon go off, jumping out of bed, trying to catch up and find out where the vehicle went. Midge wondered if he put on his suit and tie before jumping in the big black Suburban and racing south to the construction sight with Elmer. Now that was funny.

"Brenda, now listen to me. You can have my room and I will sleep on the couch. My room has its own bathroom so you should feel comfortable and safe. This house has a full alarm, triple deadbolt steel doors, and bullet proof windows. I have enough weapons and firepower to hold off a small platoon for a day or so. You are very safe as long as you stay inside. We can monitor the outside with an IR camera system I have installed."

"This place is like Fort Knox." She looked around and seemed to like what she saw. She had never stayed in his house before, but always at a motel or hotel room when they had been together.

"No, I don't have any tanks backing me up, but it will do for a house to live in."

"Midge, I don't want to take your bed. I can sleep on the couch, I'll be fine." Her eyes were red and she looked tired.

"No, you take my room. You will have a secure place to sleep with your own bathroom and you will have your privacy. I will use the other bathroom."

"Midge, don't take this wrong, but I am too upset to sleep with you right now. Maybe later I will feel better." Midge was amazed how a woman's thought process was always suspicious that every man just wanted to get in her pants, no matter what the situation.

"I don't want to sleep with you Brenda, just give you a safe place to stay until we can figure out what is happening." He looked sternly at her.

She came over and hugged him and kissed him on the cheek. "Thank you so much for helping me, I don't know who else to trust." She started crying again and held him tight.

Midge went to the front window and looked out again. The clouds had cleared some so he decided Ryan could walk home from school.

He checked to his left and the fed was still parked on the street down near the end. Maybe the guy was not trying to hide. If it were Midge, he would have tried to use someone's house and set up a telescope with a clear line of sight to his house. Why was he under surveillance anyway? Were they watching him, or someone who may come to his house? And who was the tall guy in the Ford Focus the other day? Now that guy looked like a military man if ever he saw one.

"Listen, how about I fix us some tea?" He thought it might sooth her a little.

"Tea? Do you have any beer?" She was no tea broad, just a plain old beer babe, he guessed.

"Sure, I keep a few on hand for visitors in the fridge." He went into the fridge and pulled out two Budweisers. He did not buy any of the light stuff, just the full fat beer. If his guests did not like it, they could bring their own beer. He did not allow smoking inside the house, but he did not care if guests smoked outside. If they wanted to kill themselves, be his guest, but he was not going to breathe all that smoke if he could help it. He took two glasses from the cupboard and placed them on the table.

Brenda grabbed the bottle, twisted off the cap, put the bottle to her lips, tipped it up and took a long pull. "That feels better." She sat down with a sigh. Yeah, a real beer broad, he thought.

Midge was not much of a beer drinker, but he did not want her to feel funny about dinking alone at a time like this. He poured his beer into two glasses and pushed one toward Brenda.

"I'm sorry Midge, I have been just so stressed I forgot my manners. Thank you for the beer. I know you are not a big drinker and believe it or not, neither am I, normally I mean."

"I know Brenda, remember I have known you for a couple of years. Are you calm enough to talk about why you are so frightened yet?" Midge just shut up and watched her face while looking straight into her eyes.

She fidgeted with her beer, took another big drink and then looked back up at him. "Three of the braves were killed after I dropped off Jimmy and Sam. I am afraid someone saw me and thinks I am involved with that rental car and put me on a list to die. They did not just kill the braves, but chopped off their heads and fingers. It is all so horrible, Midge. I'm scared to death."

75

"Do you have any idea who would do such a thing?" He watched her closely.

"The full bloods have been trying to take control of the Tribal Council, but I do not think the elders and mixed bloods would do anything so horrible. That is not the way of the Ojibwa. A knife or gun, yes, but never ever would they sever a head. That would not allow the spirit to enter our heaven. No, this was not an Ojibwa type killing. It is not my people's way."

"Then who up in this country would do that to someone. Even the animal drug dealers in Detroit don't do that to their victims."

"The Nassire's man Kia is who I suspect. Sam talked about those men, Kia especially, and the power they wield on the council. No one opposes them but the Bahweting Blood Braves and they are very careful to protect themselves."

"Why would the Nassire men or Kia want to hurt the full bloods? Those guys are rich and have too much to lose by getting involved in petty tribal politics."

"There is talk they are more than they seem. They provided the Chippewa with the funds to start the casinos. They handle all the money from the slots and games and control the books the full bloods claim. There is even a rumor there is a vault under the Brimley casino where they keep vast sums of money. No one is allowed past the counting room to the vaults except the Nassire men. I have never even been in the counting room which is under the main casino and very well guarded." She was drinking the glass of beer now.

"Sam was a racist. He thought only full bloods should run the tribe. You are a mixed blood in his eyes so you would have been his enemy too. He hates the Nassire men because they are foreigners, not even mixed bloods or Americans."

"Yes, Sam was a racist in the fact he promoted his own race over others. That is the definition of a racist, but he was not against mixed bloods, just non-native people who are draining the tribe's resources and not helping the Ojibwa enough. He did feel the full bloods should have a greater voice and power on the council, but he would never have done violence against the elders." Her voice and eyes were clearing now.

"What about the Nassires? Would he have done harm to them?" He watched her face carefully.

"Yes, I think he would have if given the chance." She spoke calmly now.

"I think so, too. What about Jimmy and David? Would they have been violent if given the chance?"

"Jimmy no, but David absolutely. He had just been released from Marquette for armed robbery. He was an angry brave. He thought the casinos should pay the tribe a lot more each month, but he did not want to work with the tourists, just have the tribe pay him."

"Did Sam talk about his involvement in moving some Arabs in and out of Canada and loaning them the rental car?"

"Yes, he talked about it on our way back from Detroit. He said they took them through Sugar Island both ways."

Of course, thought Midge, it made perfect sense. Sugar Island sat in the middle of the St. Mary's River due east of the Sault between Canada and the United States. It has a Bay Mills Reservation on it and is only accessible by boat or ferry. The Ojibwa fish the waters around the island and pay no attention to the international border between Canada and the United States. Native lands and fishing and hunting rights are protected by both countries. Many people think the most porous border in the United States is with Mexico, but they are wrong. The easiest way to cross into the United States is via Canada. The reason people do not recognize this fact is, unlike the Mexican population, the Canadians have no reason to want to enter the States illegally. They have a high standard of living and love their country, so why would they leave. However, the Canadian government has very liberal immigration laws and visa permits. Some of the 9/11 terrorists entered the US from Canada, but they used the border check points. Another reason there are not a lot of drugs or illegal aliens entering from Canada in northern Michigan, Wisconsin, Minnesota, and other northern border states, is these are almost totally white population areas. Black, Latino, or Oriental people would stick out like cow pies on a dance floor. Native Americans are part of the population, so if you could blend in with them, it would be easy to cross the borders. Besides, there were not enough border patrols to catch anyone anyway, especially Ojibwa.

"So those two Arabs, as Sam called them, were smuggled in from Canada. And wherever they went, they were met with gunfire, as the holes in the rental car prove."

"I think so. But I had nothing to do with any of that." She was really looking tired now.

"No, Brenda but you did deliver Sam and Jimmy back to Sam's house and you may have been seen by someone."

"That is why I am so frightened. And the way in which they were killed, they may have mentioned my name and others when they were tortured."

"How do you know they were tortured?"

"A brave who told me how they found them said they had round burns all over there bodies, their feet were nothing but pulp, and some of their fingers had been removed as well as their heads." She lowered her head when she talked now.

"That would classify as torture to anyone." Midge mulled this over in his mind. The only reason to torture someone is to obtain information from them. It was certainly not over a simple car lost. It was insured after all. No, whoever put the bullet holes in that car wanted to know where the men were who were driving that car. They wanted them bad enough to torture and kill the braves to get that information. But who was the question. Was it the Nassire family or a rival faction of Braves in a tribal dispute? No, Midge thought. Beheading was alien to the Ojibwa culture, but not to Muslims. The Arabs used beheading as a standard method of killing. Repugnant to the Western mind, but not to the Oriental mind he thought. Middle East or Asia used torture and beheading as the will of Allah or Karma. What hypocrites the Muslims are, but maybe it was only the radicals who believed all infidels should die. He was not sure, but did not like those bastards anyway after watching them behead hostages on television during the Iraq War. This was a Muslim killing style, but who were the Muslims who did this foul deed? Surely it was not Jay and John Nassire, but maybe some of their men? What about Kia, could the chauffer be that savage? It was something to think about.

"Let's assume for a second someone did see you and the killers are after you. Where can we go to get help for you? You say you do not trust the Tribal Police, the Michigan State Police, and Chippewa County Sheriff have no jurisdiction on Native Lands, so I am not sure they would investigate anyway. They will protect you at your home in Kinross, but I have no confidence they would do an adequate job of keeping you safe with the limited manpower they have available."

"Me either Midge, that is why I came to you."

"I am not a policeman anymore, Brenda. I can protect you in my home with no problem, but on the street is another issue. I have a CCW to carry my pistol, but against this type of determined men, I would be heavily out gunned."

"Well then, what should I do? If I leave here, I know they will kill me." She broke down and started to cry and shake again. Midge put his arms around her and rocked her gently.

"You will stay here until I can think of something. I will keep you safe until we can figure something out." He knew she had no other option right now.

"Thank you Midge, I knew I could trust you." He held her for a few more minutes until he heard a banging on the living room door. Brenda jolted up until she heard Ryan's voice yelling, "I'm home Uncle Midge, let me in." He kept banging.

Midge looked though the peep hole, opened the door and let Ryan in. Ryan crossed the living room, threw his back pack on the couch and headed for the kitchen to get a snack. He stopped dead when he saw Brenda with her red eyes and a beer in front of her sitting at the kitchen table.

"Ryan, you remember Brenda don't you? She is going to stay with us for a few days. She will be sleeping in my room and I will be sleeping on the couch."

"Hello Brenda, why are you crying?"

"I just have a few troubles, Ryan. How was school today?"

"Fine, but my friend Jacob had to leave early, so I did not have anyone to play with at second recess."

"Aren't there other boys to play with?"

"Yes, but they don't like Jacob or me."

"That is too bad, I am sure you can make them your friends if you try hard enough."

"Maybe. Can I have some milk and cookies, Uncle Midge?"

"Sure Ryan, just be sure to clean up your mess, rinse your dishes and put them in the dishwasher when you are done."

"I will, Uncle Midge. I don't want Brenda to see what a slob I am. Could I eat in the living room and watch cartoons?"

"Okay, but keep the sound down so you don't bother Brenda and me while we are talking."

"Okey dokey, Uncle Midge." Ryan poured himself a glass of milk, grabbed a bag of cookies and headed for the living room.

"One more thing, Ryan." Ryan stopped in the doorway and turned to look at both of them. "While Brenda is with us, we are in maximum security mode. That means all the doors locked and the alarm system on while we are in the house. You know what that means, right?"

"Sure Uncle Midge, but why? Are we in trouble?"

"No, Ryan but Brenda is scared of something and we need to make her feel safe, okay?"

"Sure, I understand." Ryan turned and went into the living room to watch his favorite after school cartoons.

"He is a good kid and he understands the importance of security when I tell him."

"I hope he does not resent me staying here."

"He won't. Play some games with him and watch monster movies and he won't ever want you to leave. Now let's get back to you and your problems."

"I can't think of anyway out of this for me. The sad part is I am not even sure I am a target, but I can't take that chance after what happened to those braves."

"I agree. In the short term, like a week or two, staying here is fine, but you have a life and you can't hide out forever. Let's just relax tonight and give me some time to think about it. Maybe we can think of something in the morning after a good safe night's sleep."

"Your are right. I have not slept in two days and I am exhausted. Maybe things will become clearer tomorrow. If you don't mind, I am going to clean up and turn in. I know it is the afternoon, but I am exhausted. I hope you don't mind."

"Not at all, Brenda. Let me get some things from my room and bathroom and then it is all yours. There is a lock on the bedroom door. Use it if it makes you feel better."

"Thanks Midge, I owe you big time." She leaned over, kissed him on the cheek and headed for the bedroom with Midge following close behind her. Rest was a weapon Midge knew very well they may need in the next few days.

Chapter 10

Midge woke to the smell of bacon. What time was it anyway? The only clock in the living room was in the television. He glanced at the window, but it was dark outside. He could see the kitchen light was on and Brenda could be seen scurrying around. She must be cooking breakfast. Well that was good therapy, Midge thought. She was a basket case yesterday. It is amazing what a good night's sleep will do for a person.

Midge pulled the comforter off himself and stretched. He usually slept in the nude, but thought he better not with Brenda staying with him and Ryan. He even slept in his jeans to not embarrass himself and Ryan. He stood up and went out to the kitchen rubbing his eyes.

"Good morning Midge, breakfast is ready." She smiled but kept her eyes on the stove.

"Let me use the bathroom first." Midge headed to the bathroom he and Ryan now shared.

After about twenty minutes Midge returned to the kitchen, shit, showered, and shaved, dressed in clean clothes with his hair combed.

"You look nice in the morning." She was still puttering with the food and then he saw her flip a pancake.

"Not until after I shower. What is all this?" He did like the smell of bacon in the morning.

"Well I woke up and felt so good I decided to fix breakfast for you and Ryan." Her black hair was pulled back into a pony tail and she was not wearing any makeup. It looked as though she had showered recently.

"What about you?" Midge watched her rear end outlined in his bathrobe. She had a cute figure alright and she was adorable in his oversized bathrobe.

"I like breakfast sometimes, but I just felt like cooking. I hope you don't mind." She was now taking a steel flipper and turning over some fresh fried potatoes in his big fry pan.

"Not at all, but I usually eat out other than some cereal for Ryan." He was leaning against the counter now with his hands between his back and the edge of the counter top.

"Well you certainly have enough food to fix." She swept her hand in a motion that said, "look at all this stuff I fixed."

"A bad habit my mother gave me. Always be prepared with enough food to last for a year in case of trouble or something. She never did explain what 'or something' meant, but it is a hard habit to break. I guess I am all set if a war 'or something' comes."

"I'll say, but not knowing where everything is kept, it took me awhile to find everything."

"You look like you did okay to me. What time did you get up?"

"About half past four. I was wide awake. It took me a lot of effort to find your coffee-maker. It was way up in the back of the cupboard above the refrigerator. I didn't think anyone used those little cupboards above a refrigerator. Don't you make coffee much?" She pointed to those little doors up above.

"No, I only make it for company. I mostly drink tea, but when I worked as a cop I drank lots of coffee."

"Well I am a coffee freak. This is the second pot, would you like a cup?" She held an empty cup up in front of her.

"Sure, I'll have a cup, but I would rather sit with you and talk. I don't want to eat breakfast until Ryan gets up around seven or so, if that is okay with you."

"Fine with me. We can warm up the pancakes and potatoes when Ryan is up. I will cook your eggs fresh and to order."

"He will love that, Brenda." He pulled a chair out for her to sit in and then took a chair across from her so he could see her face well.

They sat quietly for a few minutes drinking their coffee. It seemed like he was married again, except for the lack of tension. He was enjoying his coffee for a change. He looked at Brenda and her eyes looked clear. Still a little red from crying, but much improved from yesterday. He also felt better now he had some time to think about the problem. He at least had an idea now. He would see if it would work or not soon, but he wanted to run it by Brenda first.

"So, are you feeling better this morning?" You look great and I love the bathrobe on you."

"I hope you don't mind, but I was cold and it felt good." She wrapped her arms around herself and pretended to shiver.

"No problem. I said to make yourself at home and I meant it."

"Thanks, I feel so safe here with you. I just hope I do not drive you nuts. I know guys like their space and you are a neat nick who doesn't like messes. A girl can tell when everything in a medicine cabinet is lined up perfectly." She raised her eyebrows and inclined her head a little toward him.

"Guilty as charged. I even line up the cans by size at the grocery store check out counter." He was nodding because he knew he was a nut about organization. It seemed natural to him that all people would want to be organized, but his ex-wives did not see things the same way. Excessive nut case was the term his second wife had used on him after he lined up her make-up in their vanity one time.

"I guess there are worse vices." She sipped her coffee as she watched him.

"Brenda, I have been thinking about your situation. You don't want to go to the Tribal Police and I don't think the State Police or Sheriff can help you much either. That only leaves us with the Federal authorities. The BIA and the FBI do have jurisdiction on Tribal lands for certain crimes, so they may be a possibility."

"Do you think the feds can help me?"

"I don't honestly know yet. But you will stay here and be safe and sound until I am sure I can trust them. There has been a fed following me for the last few days. As a matter of fact, he is usually parked at the end of the street every day."

"They can't be that stupid, can they?" She arched her eyebrows in a questioning manner.

"Please don't ask. That does not mean they can't help you. I saw the FBI visiting the Tribal Police yesterday. They know something is up, but I am not sure what it is yet. I'll check around today and see what I can uncover." He found himself shaking his head no, as much in disbelief as anything when he thought about the feds' stupidity.

"Be careful. The men who killed the braves are very dangerous."

She looked worried even now.

"That is for sure." He finished his coffee, got up, grabbed the pot and refilled their cups. It felt nice being with her in the early morning quiet.

Ryan got up and around about seven. After he got dressed, Brenda fixed him two fresh eggs to go with a pancake. Ryan was only allowed to eat eggs once a week by his mother, so this was a special treat. Midge ate two eggs chopped up with his pancakes. He loved them that way and even did it when he ate in a restaurant with his friends. They laughed at him but he didn't care. He was eating the stuff, not them. Brenda enjoyed watching the men eat her cooking.

Midge decided to drive Ryan to school today. It would give him a chance to check out the fed. He was curious to see if Kia brought Jacob to school today. He told Brenda to keep the house locked and the alarm set. He also gave her a loaded pistol, an old .38 Colt Cobra short nose, but told her not to shoot him when he returned. She promised, then Ryan and Midge left for school in the pick up truck, turning right to avoid the big black Suburban at the other end of the road. It would be interesting to see if the fed followed him.

"Ryan, did you notice anything funny about Jacob yesterday at school?"

"Like what, Uncle Midge?" Ryan was staring at the houses as they passed them. Not a care in the world, just like a boy should be.

"Was he nervous or upset or anything like that?" Midge scanned the road ahead and his rear view mirrors to see if anyone was following them.

"No, I don't think so. We played tag at first recess and he seemed fine. Why are you asking me?" Ryan was looking at him now.

"Just curious that's all, Ryan." He glanced quickly at him and then to the road ahead.

"Is he in trouble? Why did Kia pick him up early from school yesterday? Do you know why, Uncle Midge?"

"No I don't Ryan, it is just something happened on the reservation a couple of days ago. I thought his father or grandfather might be upset or something."

"Why should they be upset about the reservation stuff? They don't live there." This questioning was getting a little too deep. Midge thought he better back off.

"Yes, you're right Ryan, here we are at school. I want you to wait for me at school tonight. I want to pick you up. Do not go home with anyone but me. Do you understand, Ryan?"

"Sure, I'll wait for you after school. Do you want me to wait inside or outside?" Ryan had his hand on the door handle, but was waiting for an answer before opening it.

"Inside. I will come in and get you. Have a good day at school, kid."

"Oh sure I will." Ryan rolled his eyes and opened the door, then slammed it too hard as usual and went into the school. Midge scanned the school parking lot, but he did not see the big red Ford Expedition this morning. Maybe the Nassire boy had already been dropped off at school.

Midge pulled out of the school lot and headed for home, but he went the opposite way to drive by the fed's SUV this time. It was time to find out what this man wanted.

Midge pulled his pick-up next to the fed parked at the side of the road and rolled down his passenger window. He waited for the fed to roll his down and acknowledge him. It took a minute or two, but the dark tinted window came moving downward slowly. Midge was looking at a white man in his late forties or early fifties maybe, in a dark suit with white shirt and dark navy tie. A fed uniform if there ever was one.

"How was your trip yesterday?"

"Very funny, Mr. Gregory. I followed the truck all the way to St. Ignace and found it parked along side the highway near some road construction out on US 2. I thought you had given me the slip until in the afternoon, the old guy got back in it and drove home." The fed did not seem all that amused.

"You were lucky fed man, sometimes Elmer stays over night at a hotel, if it is too far to come home." Midge was chuckling to himself now.

"Yes, I was very lucky, I am sure." The fed stared straight at Midge.

"Who are you and why are you trying to follow me?" Midge decided the direct approach was best at this point.

"We need to talk, shall we go to your house or my place."

"We better go to your place. If the neighbors see you, it might sully my reputation." Midge was having fun with the guy now.

"Follow me, I am staying up by the water." The Suburban pulled forward and turned right at the first street. They headed toward the Locks to a motel right on the water. It was the most expensive in town. The fed could afford it, Midge thought.

They parked at the far end of the lot. The room they entered was on the second floor with a great view of the St. Mary's River mouth where it entered the Locks. You could watch large freighters getting ready to enter the south bound Locks headed for Lake Huron from the balcony. The agent's room was a large suite and very nicely furnished. The Detroit cops never had a room like this when he traveled with them.

"My name is Jim Featherston, it is a pleasure to meet you finally, Midge Gregory." He extended his right hand and Midge shook it while looking the man straight in the eyes.

"Are you FBI?"

"No, I am with the Secret Service from Treasury. I am on special assignment here in Sault Ste. Marie."

"You are either here to protect the President or looking for counterfeit money. Which is it, Jim?" Midge knew they could draw other assignments, but counterfeiting and personal protection is what the Secret Service did most of the time. He liked to call them the SS boys. They certainly did not like to be called that very much. It was a slight toward the Nazi regime Storm Troopers.

"Neither. Do you know some men named Jalil and Yahya Nassire?" Jim motioned for Midge to take a seat in one of the leather chairs in the suite.

Midge knew Jim already had the answer. He was just trying to see if Midge would lie or cover for them. Well, two can play this little game.

"I have never heard of a Jalil or Yahya, but I do know a Jay and John Nassire." This was going to be fun.

"Yes, of course, their Americanized names." Jim took a seat in a leather chair facing Midge.

"So why are you following me? I can tell you where they live and you can go see them yourself." He knew the answer to this parry.

"I know where they live. I am curious how much you know about them." Jim was watching him intently now.

The Camels Eye

Midge really did know very little about them. His search had turned up their visas and immigration status, but he would play dumb and see what the fed told him. "My nephew Ryan goes to school with their son Jacob. That is how I came to be at their farm a couple of times. They seem nice to me."

The agent looked Midge over sizing up the man. He already had a file on Midge, so he knew his police record and his current job as a skip tracer. This man was not going to be bullied or frightened. As a matter of fact he had that old cop look that says, 'try me asshole and I'll show you what tough is.' No, he better just lay everything out for this guy, give him what help he needed, and appeal to his patriotism.

"Why don't we have a little talk and I'll make us a pot of coffee. I have a lot I need to tell you about the Nassire family." Jim went over to the kitchenette and started making the coffee. Midge got up and looked out on the water, then went to the street side window and checked his truck. No one was around so that was good. He looked at the road and then the restaurant across the road. Along the road facing the motel, was a white Ford Focus. Was it the same Focus that came to his house a couple days ago with the military looking man driving it?" Maybe it wasn't even the same car, but he did not believe in coincidence. That car was not parked there when he and the fed entered the motel, of that he was sure.

"Come pour yourself a cup, Midge. The sugar and cream are on the counter."

Midge poured a cup, added cream and sugar and again sat in one of the two arm chairs in the reading area. Jim joined him in the other.

"Tell me Midge, what do you know about Iran?"

"Well I know it was called Persia. It is now run by some Islamic law fanatics and was at war with Iraq at one time. The Shah was replaced by an Ayatollah and they took over our embassy when Carter was president. Some say they are the leading supporters of terrorism in the world today. I don't much like them. That is all I need to know about them."

"Yes, what you say is true, but let me give you a little more background on Persia. Persia is an old civilization that has existed for centuries. At one time, they ruled much of the known world. They built a great civilization many centuries before the time of Jesus Christ. In 539 BC the Persians conquered Jerusalem from the Babylonians.

They ruled from Africa to Europe with much of Asia in their grip also. They were a powerful and prosperous nation with many riches, some captured and taken to Persia and others created by their own artisans. They had one of the most extensive jewel collections in the world. They put the Queen of England's jewels to shame and that is saying something. For centuries, the jewels and crowns were handed down from one king or Shah to another. They also had an extensive museum and antiquity collection for centuries before the Greeks and Romans ever thought about having such things."

"In about 1100 BC the largest emerald ever discovered in the known world was found in the area later known as Cleopatra's Mines, which are located in Egypt about two hundred miles south of Cairo near the Aswan Dam. It is said to be the largest and most perfect cut emerald the world has ever known. The stone is said to be as large as a camel's eye. Emerald is actually a Persian word meaning 'green gem'. Well, just like the lands of Egypt and Palestine, the stone changed owners many times. The name of the stone changed also, but it is still the largest and most beautiful cut emerald in the world and priceless beyond money. Names such as the 'Adder Eye' as the Egyptians call it, or the 'Soul of Jerusalem' as the Jews call it, and other exotic names made the legend grow over the centuries. In the fifth or six century BC it is claimed the rulers of Persia obtained the stone. It is not known if it was stolen, conquered, or purchased, but it became the center piece jewel of the kings and queens of Persia. For many years the emerald remained locked away in the palace or museum, protected and admired by royalty and the people as the most beautiful emerald in the world. The Persians renamed the stone the Camels Eye. Did you know that emeralds are by far the most expensive jewels in the world, Midge?"

"No, I thought it was diamonds." Midge found himself listening with great interest to this story of the Camels Eye.

"Well anyway, in 1972 the last Shah of Iran commissioned Harry Winston, the great jewelry house, to create a royal necklace for Queen Soraya. The centerpiece of the necklace was to be the Camels Eye. The Winston jewelers created a magnificent piece of art said to be the most expensive necklace in the world. Besides the world's most perfect emerald, it consisted of twelve large cabochon emeralds, white, yellow, and pink diamonds set in pure platinum. The center piece was

The Camels Eye

of course, the Camels Eye. Here is a photograph of it taken in 1978."

Jim passed the color photograph to Midge. It was stunning. It made the Hollywood stars' jewelry look like trinkets from a Cracker Jack box. "Wow, what a necklace, I have never seen anything so stunning!"

"Yes, it really is breathtakingly beautiful. I can see why men have killed to possess it over the centuries." The agent took the photo back.

"This is a great piece of history Jim, but has this to do with me?" He could feel himself being railroaded.

"I am on special assignment from the highest authority in our government. I have been charged with recovering the Camels Eye and I need your help, Midge."

Highest authority, what did that mean? God, a supervisor, his wife, or any other unnamed source people like to quote when they wanted to impress you. He was not buying any of the bull. "My help? I don't know anything about the Camels Eye or any kind of jewelry. The only jewelry I have ever bought is engagement rings and I lost both of those to my ex-wives, so I think you have the wrong guy." The agent just stared at him for a minute.

"You know the Nassire family and have been to their home, so that makes you the expert in this case." Midge knew that was coming.

"I have met Jay and John Nassire and have only been to their farm twice. I never got any farther than the barn and was never in their house. Their son Jacob spent the night at my house with my nephew. He is a ten year old kid and we did not discuss emeralds, just junk food and monster movies. I think I will go now." Midge started to rise from the chair. He had told Agent Featherston most of what he knew so it was time to get out of here.

Jim put his hand up in the stop signal motion. "Please, give me a few more minutes to explain what I need. If you then decide not to help us, you are free to go and I will not bother you any more. What I'm about to tell you is top secret, so you must never repeat anything you hear today." He and Midge stared at each other for a moment.

"Alright, I will listen, but I am not making any promises." Top secret, who was this guy kidding? Why would this guy tell him anything top secret?

"Let me tell you about the Nassire family. Don't you find it odd that an Iranian family immigrated and settled in this cold northern

Michigan area and are involved with the Indian casinos?" Jim seemed to be shaking his head in a negative manner.

"Hey, I came up here so they can't be that nuts, right?" Midge raised his eyebrows and opened his hands like in a question.

"And somehow they end up as members on the Chippewa Tribal Council?" Now Featherston had a smirk on his face.

"I figured they must have money in the casinos and the elders need their resources or something. It really is not any of my business."

"Let me lay it out for you, Midge. The man you call Jay Nassire is actually Jalil Nassiri of Tehran, Iran. He is the son of the notorious General Nematollah Nassiri, head of the SAVAK, the Shah's Secret Police. The official name was Sazamane Etelaat va Amniiate Kechvar with headquarters in the Komiteh Building in Tehran. He was trained and supported by our very own CIA, but more ruthless and cruel than any other person in Iran at that time. The General, known as old yellow eyes, was said to have a pock-marked face and was a sadistic killer." Midge was paying attention now. Did he say yellow eyes?

"Jalil was born in 1940 and educated in England at a school called Cambridge. He majored in economics and mid-eastern art history. Jalil means great in Persian. When he returned to Iran in 1967, he went to work in the Ministry of Antiquities in Tehran. With his father's connections and position, and outright intimidation, he rose quickly through the ranks. By 1976 he was the head of the Ministry of Antiquities and responsible for all the museums, art, historical papers, statues, and display of the royal jewels in Iran. In 1978, under direction of the Shah, he put together a traveling display of some of Iran's greatest treasures to tour the royal houses of Europe. He was responsible for the movement, display, and security of everything himself. In January of 1979, the Shah called for him to return from Europe with all the national treasures to Tehran. It is believed most of the SAVAK security agents assigned to protect the treasure were called off by his father, the General. While a great show was made of shipping the treasure back to Iran, Jalil and a SAVAK colonel by the name of Kia Ashad and a few of his men, it seems, did not return to Iran with all of the treasure.

By the end of January 1979, the Shah was in the process of being overthrown. The country was in such chaos, the crates were placed in the lower museum vaults unopened to protect them from the riots of the people in the streets. In February, the Shah was overthrown and the Ayatollahs took power in Iran. Jalil's father, General Nassiri was set upon by the mobs attacking the Komitech Building and dumping the SAVAK files and instruments of torture into the street. The General was trapped on the roof. One of the people's Islamic Revolutionary Guards shot him off the roof and he landed in the crowd where he was hacked into little pieces. Many of the Shah's people were executed by the Guards for crimes against the people. Chaos reigned for many months until the American hostage situation was resolved. Finally things returned enough to normal to reopen the museums of the country.

Upon opening and finally inventorying the priceless works of art for display, it was discovered some of the jewelry, crowns, tiaras, and scepters were missing along with some priceless jade and ivory carvings. There was also countless Iranian government money transferred from London banks to numbered accounts around the world just before the Shah fell from power. But the biggest national treasure missing was the Camels Eye." The story now made a lot of sense to Midge why the Nassire men got involved with the casinos. The tribe needed money and Nassire needed a place to invest or hide it.

"And they think Jalil took it? If so, why don't they have the British or Americans arrest him and return him to Iran for trial?"

"Simply put Midge, because Britain and the United States have severed all diplomatic ties with the Islamic Republic of Iran for many years." Midge knew this, but money always made for compromises.

"So fine, then why is it an American problem now? He has committed no crimes here as far as I know. He and his son are now American citizens." He knew these men could not be treated as foreign combatants or terrorist since they were citizens.

"So it would seem. Times change and war makes for strange bedfellows. With the Iraq war and the overthrow of Saddam Hussein, many American and British soldiers and civilians have been killed or kidnapped in the insurgency that has followed."

"So, what has that to do with Iran?" Where was the agent going with this?

"They are not called a member of the axis of evil for nothing. Some of the hostages who were taken and reported killed are actually being held secretly in Iran for ransom. Some of the executions filmed on television were staged for world opinion and to scare countries into leaving Iraq to the Sunni's and other scum who want to control the people. Some of them were actually smuggled into Iran and are being secretly held by the Ayatollahs in the dungeons of Iran." The agent could see Midge's mind mulling this over.

"You're kidding right? If that is true, let's go bomb the hell out of all the Islamic holy sites until they give them up. Make me president for a day and we will take all those assholes out." Midge actually would do that in a New York minute. Of course, that is why he would never be elected president.

"I am sure you would, but my orders are to help the Iranians recover the Camels Eye in exchange for the hostages' lives. Will you help me Midge?" You mean your orders from the highest authority, Midge thought.

"That is hitting below the belt. I don't like the feds and I hate that damn Muslim scum in Iran and the rest of the Middle East. I am a veteran and ex-cop and have always tried to protect American lives. What has John to do with any of this? He was in this country attending the University of Michigan when all this took place." He knew he was getting sucked in fast and was trying to logically get out before he got in too deep.

"Yes, that is true. I see you have done a little bit of homework on these people after all." The agent knew he had him now.

"Hey, what can I say? I am an old homicide detective, so I get curious."

"Well, John was born in Iran in 1970. He was sent to the United States like many Persians and expected to be educated in the American economic system and law, then return to Iran and serve the Shah. Of course, all that fell apart when the Ayatollah took over, but he did complete his education and received his JD in law from the U of M. After graduation and passing the bar, with the help of some money from an unknown source, he was able to help the Sault and Bay Mills Tribe of the Chippewa establish the first casino in Michigan on Tribal lands. He helped them to lobby Lansing and the federal government to accept a little known interpretation of the Treaties of 1836 and 1855 which recognized native sovereignty on their lands. He has since used the treaties to help the Chippewa create casinos all around the State of Michigan and Canada. His advice is much sought after by all the tribes around the country who want to establish casinos or other legitimate businesses."

"I always wondered where the poor Indians got all that money to start those casinos when they did not have enough for food, clothing, or shelter. But what John did does not sound illegal." Midge could still remember taking clothing and food to the Bay Mills Reservation when his family visited his aunt and uncle in Brimley. The people were so poor back then he could not believe it.

"That is not illegal. However, he somehow manages to find the funds to build and operate the casinos in exchange for a percentage of the profits. He also structures most of their bank accounts and investments and takes a fee for that service. He and his father have made millions of dollars from their relationship with the tribes and wield much power on their tribal councils. There is also a suspicion the Nassire men are using the Tribes' Casinos to launder money for the criminals of the world. Everyone from drug cartels, the mob, and even certain terrorist organizations use their services, we suspect. They are rumored to charge a two percent fee to clean the cash and transfer the clean funds to banks around the world. What better place to convert cash than a casino? And a Tribal casino is basically outside the reach of the State and Federal government enforcement. "

"No wonder the full bloods hate the Nassire family so much." It was mind blowing to think how much cash these guys would have needed to build such an empire. How did they get in the country and invest without our government knowing about it? Of course, he had seen money corrupt everything in Detroit. Today theft of public funds and favor buying is a standard of the mayor's office. It is sad to watch, but that is what the people left in the city want from their officials, he guessed.

"Not as much as the Ayatollahs in Iran it seems. They are willing to forget about all the crowns, jewels, money, and everything else Jalil Nassiri and his men took from them, except the Camels Eye. They are willing to exchange all twenty-three hostages they are holding in exchange for the Camels Eye. Now all we have to do is find it. That is my special assignment and it comes from the President of the United States, the highest authority. I need your help Midge, in finding and returning the Camels Eye."

Midge just sat staring at the agent. This is unbelievable. He could not even comprehend how much money the Nassire family was handling. It was not about the money that would make him help this Secret Service Agent, Jim Featherston. It was about the hostages, his fellow Americans, his fellow human beings with families to come home to. He never took a bribe his whole career in Detroit. He knew lots of cops who did, but mostly small time stuff to help supplement the meager salary the city paid them to risk their lives every day. He would do this for the victims, not for money or recognition. "What do you want me to do?"

"First, tell me everything you know about the men, farm, business, friends, enemies, or whatever else will help me understand these men." Jim went and got a legal pad of paper from the desk and sat back down now ready for whatever Midge had to tell him.

Midge started with the boy asking for help to find who beheaded his camel. He told about the barn, the 7.62 mm shell casing he had found, and Ryan telling him about the spent gunpowder from the cupola in the barn. He mentioned he had taped his first visit with his spy van and he had the tape and a disc at home. Then he told the agent about meeting the braves at the casino and inspecting the rental car with all the bullet holes in it. He told him about Brenda, what she told him and the look on Ken Telway's face when he saw Jay and John standing outside the Tribal Police office. He mentioned a white Ford Focus at his house, but did not mention he had spotted it about an hour ago across from this very motel room window.

"That is about all I can think of right now. Do you have any more coffee?" Midge got up and fixed himself another cup, then brought the pot over and poured Agent Featherston another cup. He pondered why this agent was alone and not with a big task force with lots of agents ready to jump on these guys if they had to. Was this thing really so secret the President did not want many people to know about it? He could believe that, because as a cop he did not tell anyone about his investigation for fear they would sell the information or tip the suspect off for a little cash.

"That's great Midge, you know far more than I do right now. The family is now American citizens, so I will have to be cautious. They also have powerful political friends who would come to their aid in a hurry if asked. I would like to review those tapes with you. We do think the Arabs Sam gave the rental car to were agents for the IRGC, the Islamic Revolution's Guards Corps, sent here to recover the Camels Eye, but not to assassinate the Nassire family. However, if they do not recover the jewel, they are not beyond killing the whole family. That would mean no one would be alive to tell them where the jewel is. That is why they want to capture Jalil and Yahya, or Jay and John as you know them, and maybe torture them in order to reveal the location of the emerald. After listening to you, I think there were only two or three agents this time. It is hard for them to get too many across the border at one time with our crack down on terrorists anymore." Midge knew that was a fantasy. He could probably transfer a full regiment of Chinese coolies across the Canadian border in some spots.

"I would say the Nassire clan knows a little about torture themselves judging from the condition of the Chippewa braves they killed." They had proved to him how ruthless they could be, Midge thought.

"Yes, Kia Ashad was one of the most sadistic bastards in the Shah's SAVAK. We think he is the enforcer of the group and may have three or four of his old agents with him at the farm." Jim sipped his coffee in quiet thought.

"That is what Brenda said before any of this started when I talked with her at the casino. He had a reputation with the tribe members that you did not want to get in his way or else." He did not think much of it at the time, but it seemed very true now.

"I think next, I would like to review the tapes with you and prepare a plan of attack on how to approach the Nassires." Form a plan and attack, just the two of us? Who did this guy think he was the Lone Ranger, and Midge was Tonto, his faithful companion?

"Wait a second Jim, there are only two of us unless you have someone else hiding in the closet or somewhere. I am willing to try to help, but I think we need a few more resources. I also do not want to meet at my house, Jim. I want to keep that place pure so I keep the confidence of Jay and John through Ryan with their son Jacob."

"Good idea. You must have been a good cop. On the being alone issue, you are right for the moment, but I am not without resources when I need them, trust me on that one." That made Midge feel a little better, but not too much.

"Ex-cop as in 'has been'. I am just a private citizen trying to help his government free some hostages. Let's don't get carried away for right now, Mr. Secret Service Man."

"One who carries a pistol under his jacket I might add." The agent could see the bulge under the jacket from the moment he came in.

"I have a CCW in this state to carry it." Midge looked him straight in the eyes.

"Just commenting, not criticizing Midge." Jim cracked a little smile.

"Good, I'll meet you back here tonight after 8:00 pm, if that is good with you."

"Yes, but I don't have any video equipment here to work with." Jim gestured around the suite.

"I do, I'll bring my van." With that Midge stood up, shook Jim's hand and headed for the door. "Oh and by the way, lose the big Black Suburban and get an old beater car to drive if you are going to do any surveillance on anyone up north here." He turned and left the room.

As Midge went down the stairs to his truck, he glanced across the street and noticed that the Ford Focus was not there. Smart move on that guy's part. At least he was better at surveillance than the feds.

Midge drove home and unlocked his front door. He opened it slowly and called to Brenda. "It's me Brenda, do not shoot." He had his hands up and was peaking into the living room from around the door.

"I won't Midge, come on in," he heard her say.

He slowly stepped inside and saw her sitting on the couch with the pistol beside her, but not pointed at him. That's good, she is not one of those people who panic.

"How are you feeling, girl?" She looked pretty good to him.

"A lot better now. I even took about an hour's nap on the couch here." Her eyes were clear now and she had on some make up and lip stick.

"Good, how about some lunch?" He was thinking about taking her out so she could at least get out of the house.

"How can you be hungry after that big breakfast I fixed you and Ryan this morning?"

"Hey, I am a growing boy. How about I take you out or at least I can make us a sandwich?"

"Not for me thanks, but I will have a beer with you." She got up and headed for the kitchen.

"Fine, but I am drinking a diet Pepsi myself. I only have about two hours before I have to pick up Ryan from school. You can come with me if you feel safe enough. I will bring you up to speed on what the fed told me this morning. There is a lot about the Nassire men I did not know." He went into the kitchen, but she was ahead of him. He talked as he fixed a sandwich and handed her a Budweiser. She listened intently as he hit the high points. For some reason he avoided the part about meeting Jim again tonight. He would tell her he was meeting a man about a tracing job, if she asked. He did not know why, but he just had a funny feeling and he always listened to his instincts.

"Now I know I was right to be scared. I am never going back to that casino to work again. What are we going to do, Midge?" He was finishing his cheese sandwich and just shrugged his shoulders. He wondered what she meant by the 'we' she used.

"Well, for the next hour before I have to go get Ryan, I am going to stretch out and catch a nap, if you don't mind." He got up and went to the bedroom, removed his holster and weapon and put it on the night stand. He kicked off his shoes, stretched out on the bed and closed his eyes. In a minute or so he heard some rustling at the foot of the bed. He opened his eyes to see Brenda standing there removing her blouse.

"I'm sorry, I forgot this is your room. I'll go out and lay on the couch." He started to get up, but she put her hand on his chest and gently pushed him back down.

"You are just fine right where you are. I have been under so much stress and tension lately I need some relief myself. I know just the thing to relax me, and I know it will help you too." She then reached behind her back and undid her bra. She took the straps, pulled them off her shoulders and let the bra drop to the floor. She crawled up beside him, wrapped her arms around him and kissed him deeply. She could feel him respond instantly. Good she thought, she still turned him on.

"We don't have time for this before I have to pick up Ryan at school, Brenda. Maybe we can do this later."

"Lover, don't make me laugh. You have twice the time you need. Remember I have been with you before, now let's get going." She put his hands on her breast. He was a goner for sure now.

He knew she was right because he did not get sex very often anymore. She could satisfy him in record time, but the next time he wanted it to last a lot longer. They got lost in each other for a little while and then held each other for a few minutes. A little bit of peace and pleasure in a crazy world.

Midge went outside to move the pick-up so he could get the van out of the driveway. He parked the pick-up way past the house, opened the front door of the house and yelled for Brenda to come out. He locked the door, set the security system and then climbed into the van with Brenda.

"You women take too long to get ready. My ex-wife used to drive me crazy with waiting for her."

"Well I guess the honeymoon is over. Give a guy what he needs and then he treats you like this. Well, what do you know?" She smiled big at him and sat back in the seat feeling safe and happy for now.

They arrived at the school a few minutes later. Midge parked the van at the far end of the lot away from the entrance door. They still had a few minutes before school let out, so he got out, walked to the main door and stood outside. He locked Brenda inside the van so no one could see her and turned the monitor cameras on so she could keep an eye on him and the rest of the parking lot.

While he was standing outside the main door, the dark red Ford Expedition pulled into the parking lot. After a couple of minutes he saw Kia get out of the SUV and walk toward the main door.

"Hello Kia, how are you today?"

"I am just fine, thank you, Midge." Kia extended his hand and Midge shook it. It was a firm and strong handshake.

"Mr. John Nassire has asked me to invite you and Ryan to lunch on Saturday at the farm. Would you be available that day?" Kia looked him straight in the eyes. He could be quite intimidating, Midge thought, if you were a weak person. He could see him bullying some of the tribe members if he put his mind to it.

"Sure, I guess so. What should we wear or bring?"

"Wear something comfortable and bring nothing. Mr. Nassire is a great cook and a fine host."

"I am sure he is, Kia. Tell him we will be happy to have lunch with them. What time should we be there?"

"Why don't you plan on noon, Midge." Kia was taller than Midge and seemed to look down at him when he spoke.

"That's fine, please thank John for inviting us." Just then the bell rang and even though the school was small, children began to push through the front doors. Jacob and Ryan were in the second wave and chattering as they came toward him.

"See you tomorrow, Ryan," Jacob said as he ran toward the big Ford.

"I will convey your acceptance to Mr. Nassire, Midge." Kia turned and started toward the SUV with Jacob.

"Good bye, Jacob. Don't forget our homework tonight."

"I won't, bye Ryan," he yelled as he entered the vehicle. He was waving with one hand and holding his coat in the other as he was trying to remove his designer backpack to throw it in the truck.

"Come on Ryan, I have Brenda with me. Maybe we should have dinner out because I have to meet a guy tonight. We can stop by the grocery store and get you and Brenda some snacks for later, if you like."

"Can I go with you, Uncle Midge?" he asked as they walked toward the van.

"Not tonight, kid. This is business."

"Okay, but can I have hot dogs for dinner?"

"Only, if you eat a salad too."

"Gee, I hate salads."

"You know the rules. Some health food before you can have junk food."

"Fine, but can I have onions on my hot dogs?"

"I guess so, they are vegetables, I think." Midge pulled the side door of the van open and Ryan leaped in throwing his backpack on the floor.

"Hello, Ryan."

"Hello, Brenda."

"How was school today?"

"Boring, just like it always is." Ryan was reaching for his Gameboy he kept in the seat pocket of Brenda's seat.

"I hated school too, but now I wish I had studied more. There is so much of the world I do not know about."

"You can take my place. I'll stay home with Uncle Midge."

"Quiet kid and buckle up." Midge put the van in gear and headed out of the parking lot.

"I told Ryan we would go to the grocery store, Brenda. Do you want anything special to eat or something for yourself?"

"I need some different deodorant. That stuff you have burns my arm pits. How do you stand it?"

"It must be a guy thing. Why don't you come in with us and you can pick anything you want to eat, wear, or use."

"I don't have any money, Midge." She looked at him with her big eyes.

"You are my guest, you do not need any money for anything. By the way, does your mother know you are alright?"

"I called her on my cell phone. She knows I am safe, but not where I am. I thought it was safer not to tell her in case her phone is tapped." Phone tapped, did these guys have that type of resources?

"Good idea. Until we know if you are really in danger, you better not tell anyone where you are staying." He pulled out of the parking lot and headed for the store.

"I agree. It might ruin my reputation." She smiled big at him now.

"I'm not that bad, Brenda." He shook his head and kept his eyes on the road.

"What were you and Kia talking about in the parking lot?" She said it low key like, but he wondered if she was just a typical nosey woman or was she really prying into his business.

"He invited Ryan and me to lunch on Saturday at their farm."

"And you are going?" She looked a little shocked.

"Sure, I think it will be fun for Ryan. I hear John Nassire is a great cook."

"Are you crazy ....?" Midge tossed his head toward Ryan in the back and held his first finger to his lips in the universal quiet sound. Brenda caught the hint and immediately fell silent.

"Yeah, maybe I will take some ham sandwiches to pass." Midge smiled and rolled his eyes not knowing if Brenda and Ryan would understand his little joke.

Midge noticed a white Ford Focus about four cars behind his van. Could it be his new friend again? He would keep an eye out for it tonight. He decided he would turn on his surveillance camera and recorder when they parked.

After they had stopped and shopped at Wal Mart they went over to the Big Kettle Restaurant and had dinner. Ryan had his salad and hot dog while Midge and Brenda ate Lake Superior Whitefish. It was fresh and delicious as always.

It was a little after seven when they headed for home. There was no sign of the Focus, but that did not mean it was not out there somewhere. When they got home, Brenda helped unload the groceries. By the time they got everything put away it was a quarter to eight and time for Midge to go meet with Agent Featherston.

"Ryan, you get ready for bed at nine and be in bed no later than ten. And don't forget to brush your teeth. Brenda, if he gives you any trouble, just call me on the cell phone. I'll come right home and box his ears. Okay?"

"He won't be any trouble for me, will you Ryan?"

"No, I won't but can I watch Fear Factor tonight, Uncle Midge?"

"Fine, but you still have to be in bed by ten, do you understand?"

"Yes sir, I will." Ryan gave Midge a hug and hurried to his bedroom to get ready for bed.

"I hope I won't be too late, Brenda. If you need me I will have my cell phone turned on."

"Midge, how long do you think I will have to stay here?" He turned and held her in his hands with his outstretched arms. "Are you getting lonely already?" She looked like a little girl now, not a woman.

"No, it's just I do have a life you know, and I don't like being a burden to you."

"You're no burden, but I understand if you need to go sometime. My house is yours as long as you need it, but you are free to come and go as you please. No strings, okay?"

"Thanks, Midge." She came to him, put her arms around his neck and kissed him deeply. After a couple of minutes Midge held her at arms length again and told her he had to go before he changed his mind.

"I should not be too late. Lock the door and set the alarm. You still have the pistol I gave you, right? You and Ryan have a nice evening." With that he left the house, pulled his van out of the driveway and headed out to meet with the Secret Service Agent.

As he entered the main highway, an old rusted blue pick-up pulled

101

out of a side street and started following him. To give it a check, Midge drove north to Portage, turned right, drove about three blocks and turned right again. Sure enough, the pick-up kept following him. Midge involuntarily put his hand inside his leather jacket and felt the reassuring handle of his revolver. It was habit, but it made him feel safe.

Midge slowed the van down to let the pick-up pass. The pick-up pulled up beside him and started waving for him to pull over. He thought he recognized the guy but he wasn't sure in the dark. He cautiously pulled his van up in front of a couple of houses in the neighborhood and put it in park. He undid the hasp on his holster and watched as a man in a Detroit Lions cap got out of the truck and walked toward him. As the headlight beams struck the man's face, Midge recognized him at last. He ran the drivers window down and waited.

"Hello Ken, I did not recognize you in civilian clothes."

"Good, I hope no one else did either." Out of his uniform, Ken looked like a typical dock worker or maybe a lift truck driver.

"Why are you following me?" Midge removed his hand from his revolver.

"I want to talk to you, but not here. It is too dangerous. Tomorrow night be at the Hilltop Bar on Sugar Island. There will be a brave at the Hill Top Bar to meet you at nine and bring you to the ceremony house. He will be wearing a Cleveland Browns hat turned backward. Please come alone. This is very important so tell no one, especially Brenda Benton, that you are meeting me. I have to go now. Be there Midge, it may save both of our lives." With that Ken Telway, Chief of the Tribal Police trotted back to his truck and quickly disappeared.

What in the world was that all about? What did he mean it may save both their lives? This was crazy. Go to Sugar Island, at night? No one went to Sugar Island at night. The ferry ran from about five in the morning to maybe one the next morning. It now ran seven days a week instead of five, but no one went there at night, except maybe smugglers and residents. A brave would be waiting? They better make sure none of the patrons saw them. Still Ken seemed frightened or upset and that was not like Ken. Maybe the murderer of these braves had him spooked. What had he discovered? Midge would go, but only because Ken was an old friend and seemed to really need his

The Camels Eye

help.

As Midge drove to meet with Jim Featherston at the motel, he thought about Sugar Island as a meeting place. For a Chippewa it made good sense. There were very few roads and no bridges on and off the island. A ferry transported all the visitors and residents to and from the island on the American side. Sugar Island had belonged to Canada and was called St. George as late as 1840. Before that is was called Sisibakwato Miniss in Chippewa, which meant Sugar Tree Island for the sugar maples that had once covered the island. There had been a lengthy debate whether the island belonged to the U.S. or Canada for years. The St. Mary's River was mentioned in many treaties, but not St. George Island or Sugar Island. The term navigable channel was used to determine which islands belonged to which country. After the dredging of the St. Mary's River west of the island, the water was so deep ships up to eighty feet deep could pass. This moved the navigable passage from east to west. The passage to the east called Lake George, was so shallow it could not handle the larger ships and it was determined Sugar Island would belong to the United States.

In a little known piece of trivia, when the United Nations was searching for a permanent home in 1946, Sugar Island was one of the twelve U.S. sites being proposed to build the assembly building on instead of New York City. Isn't it strange how things work out sometimes? The island had full bloods, half bloods, and white men on it for a hundred years. Today there exists a small Chippewa reservation on the western side of the island. It is part of the Bay Mills Reservation system, the same as the one near Brimley. Midge liked the island, but he did not pretend to understand all the treaties that went into settling it and who owned what.

He would go there tomorrow, but he would be armed and wear a vest just in case. He was not worried about Ken, but who or what was scaring Ken? Things were starting to get pretty crazy for the Upper Peninsula. This was starting to feel more like he was back in Detroit again. Why did Ken say not to tell Brenda? What had Brenda to do with this? It was obvious Ken did not trust her, but why? She was staying at his house and had shared his bed. But she was afraid and on the lam, wasn't she? Three braves were tortured and killed, so she had good reason to be afraid, didn't she? Had he told her too much already? He would be careful what he told her until he was sure where

Brenda stood.

He saw the motel ahead. He pulled into the parking lot and parked up near the sidewalk leading to the main building where the agent was located. He took the time to set his cameras for surveillance and record while he was in visiting Featherston. He got out of the van and locked it while he set the alarm. He would go get the agent and bring him to the van to review the tape he brought from home.

He took the stairs to the second floor and proceeded down the corridor about half way to the agent's suite. He knocked on the door and heard a voice say, 'Come in its open." Midge opened the door and went in closing the door behind him. As he looked straight ahead he saw Agent Featherston seated in one of the leather arm chairs, but something did not look right about the agent to him. He had his arms on the arms of the chair with his feet together flat on the floor, like he was posing for a school picture, or something. It did not look natural for some reason. More stiff like when your mother used to make you sit still in a chair on Sunday or when company was there.

"Good evening, Mr. Gregory. Please do not move until I tell you and then very slowly," a deep manly voice off to his right in the dark area of the room said in accented English. "Now very slowly turn this way with your hands up in the air. I would not try to be a hero if I were you. I just want to talk to you and Agent Featherston. I will not hurt you, if I can avoid it." The man sounded calm which was good. In his years of police work he had learned to like calm and measured over emotional and panicked. Nervous people made too many rash decisions. He turned slowly to his right.

"Now if you would, please zip up the front of your leather jacket. All the way to the neck and do it very slowly if you please. If you attempt to reach for your pistol, I will kill you even though I don't want to." Midge slowly zipped his jacket all the way to his neck. He then put his hands back in the air.

"Very good Midge, you can now put your hands down and sit in the chair next to the agent. Do not make any move for your weapon and I will not shoot you. I just need to talk with both of you. I apologize for the method I am using to get your attention, so let me say I am sorry, but I do not have enough time to do it any other way."

"You're the white Ford Focus." Midge had seen this man on his surveillance tape at his house.

"Touché Midge, you are observant." The man was now leaning against the window sill with his pistol in his hand extended downward in front of him, not pointing at them but ready for any surprise. He was a professional for sure.

"What is this all about, Midge?" The Secret Service Agent Featherston asked.

"I don't know, Jim. I only know he has been following us for a couple of days. He was at my house while I was gone last Saturday. He is the one I have on camera and I saw his Focus parked across the street from your room today." Midge kept his hands on the arms of the chair the same as Jim.

"Very good Midge, you are better prepared than I expected in this rural town. Allow me to introduce myself, gentlemen. I am Liam Hertz with the IAA. That is the Israeli Antiquities Authority. I am here to retrieve the Soul of Jerusalem and return it to its people in Israel." He spoke very good English, but with a British accent the same as all the people of the Middle East, it seemed.

"You mean The Camels Eye?" Midge watched his reaction.

"Some Arabs call it the Adders Eye also, but the fact is it was mined by Jewish slaves in mines in Egypt. It was taken from Cairo to Jerusalem after the Jewish people revolted and Palestine became our nation. It stayed there for over four hundred years before the Persians sacked Jerusalem and took the emerald back to Persia a few centuries ago. It belongs to the Jewish people who mined it and shaped it with their very blood and I am here to retrieve it." His dark eyes seemed on fire now.

"Well, we don't have it, so why are you busting our chops?" Jim asked him.

"We all know the Nassires have the jewel. What I want to know is why you are helping the Iranians get it back? Why is the Secret Service involved in this matter? I thought you were only involved in executive security and counterfeiting." He was looking right at Jim Featherston now.

"It is complicated Liam. Shall we say that the U.S. government has a vested interest in this matter and it does not include the State of Israel. Who sanctioned your mission here on American soil, Liam?"

"I will ask the questions here, Agent Featherston. Why would you want to help this murdering bunch of bastards hold on to something that was not even theirs to begin with? It may interest you to know I received a communiqué yesterday that said an assault team led by the Mullah Seyed Habibi arrived in Canada yesterday and are on their way to the Nassire farm. Why are the Americans aiding these killers?" He was starting to get emotional and Midge did not like that idea.

"You are Mossad, aren't you Liam? One of their hired killers sent out into the world as a type of 'Sword of Gideon' for the wrongs against Jews, right?"

"I am with the IAA, I am not Mossad. Now why are you aiding these criminals?" His voice was getting louder.

"Okay Liam, I'll tell you and you can convey this back to Israel, but not until we have made the exchange. I am on a secret mission, under orders of the President of the United States. Trust me, he would not understand if the Israeli Mossad or the IAA, or whatever you call yourself, mucked this up for us. The Iranians are holding American hostages from the war in Iraq in Iranian prisons. Some of these hostages are the ones who were supposedly killed in the Iraq war and executed on television, but they were not really killed. They are being held by Iran for ransom or political advantage. The price for their lives is the return of the Camels Eye to Iran. They will be exchanged for the jewel."

"You can't trust that Muslim scum. When will you people learn the only thing those asshole Shiites understand is force. They will take the jewel and then behead your people on international television just for fun. These Mullahs have no honor, my friend. I know from personal experience. I spent three long hard years in a Muslim jail. No, Israel understands how to deal with these fanatics better than anyone." He was really hostile now, but at who or what?

"Of course we agree, and that is why we require the hostages to be out of the country on one of our aircraft before we give them the emerald necklace. No exceptions." Jim talked calmly to the man with the gun.

"Now I understand why the Secret Service is in on this. The FBI or CIA would splash it all over the television. You are acting on secret orders from the President himself. He has not even informed the Congress or his own staff. But how in the world can a single agent expect to stop this Islamic assault team from acting or escaping from the U.S. if they are successful in obtaining the Camels Eye?" Americans seemed weak with their political pressures all the time.

"I have a Delta Force team ready to land at Kinchloe as soon as I call them in from Grayling. There is a Seal One team on a boat out in Whitefish Bay right now." Now Liam was impressed. He had no respect for the American politicians and the liberal laws they passed to protect the criminals in their land. But Delta Force and the Seals were a different story, these men were deadly. The strong arm of a very weak republic, he thought.

"Yes, now that is some firepower. They can handle the Mullah's team with ease. That is the only thing those Shiites understand. But why do you not just go in and take the necklace yourself?"

"First of all, these people are American citizens and are now protected under our constitution. Next, we do not know where the Camels Eye is located exactly and the Nassire farm is well defended. Finally, the farm is on Native Land, not U.S. soil, and we have no jurisdiction there." Now Liam just shook his head. Constitution, native land, rights, what a bunch of nonsense it is. These Americans were a powerful country made weak by a few politicians who sold their souls for money.

"So where does Midge enter into the picture? He is a retired police officer, not CIA or Secret Service." Midge was impressed the Israeli had such data at his fingertips. Not Mossad my ass, he thought.

"Midge has been on the farm with his nephew and has the trust of the Nassire family. He is also an ex-police officer and knows how to handle himself." Yes, an ex-homicide detective the Israeli thought.

"So you know Jay and John Nassire, Midge?" Liam Hertz asked.

"Only through my nephew and their son, Jacob, I have met them both but have never even been in their house yet." Midge felt a little better talking to a man who knew a little bit about him.

"What do you mean, yet? Are you planning to get into their house, Midge?" Jim asked the question this time.

"I don't know, but I am invited there for lunch with my nephew on Saturday. Now will you put that pistol down? You are starting to piss me off!" Liam lowered the pistol onto his lap, but still in his hand.

"I would not want to meet you when you are pissed off. I have read your file and you have assaulted many criminals according to the complaints filed against you in Detroit." Yeah Midge thought, but only assholes who deserved it.

"Criminals always complain when someone catches and stops them." Liam knew all about that having served in the occupied territories for a couple of years.

"You stopped some of them alright. You stopped some of them permanently." Midge had killed two men when his life was threatened. He went through hell because both of the scum, who were convicted murderers out on parole, were black. Their crooked lawyers wanted him convicted of murder, not self defense. So many witnesses backed him up that he was found innocent and returned to duty. He retired as soon as he was eligible after the last shooting. He no longer cared if the citizens killed each other off in Detroit after that. It was a lost city for sure in his mind. It might be wrong, but that is how he and many other police officers felt.

"All justified shootings in the line of duty." Both other men seemed to understand.

"Yes, you did win but not without trials twice. The criminals were glad to see you retire." Midge knew that was true. Every cop who gave up trying to defend the citizens because it was too much hassle was a victory for the criminals and their lawyers in the City of Detroit. But what had they really won, he wondered?

"Not as glad as I was to retire. Now what is it you want, asshole?" His cop training was taking over now.

"Asshole? Well the report did say you were extremely direct. No beating around the bush with you. Fine, this is what I want. The Soul of Jerusalem must be returned to Israel. We will not take it from the Iranians until after the American hostages have been released. We will take out the Iranian assault team if it survives the hit on the farm. We will take them out once they are in Canadian territory. U.S. forces will be faultless and not have to withstand the left wing investigation of the Kennedy types in the Senate." He seemed sure of himself now.

"You are forgetting one thing. We do not know where the jewel is any more than you or the Iranians do. And you are only one man, not exactly a force to be feared." Jim watched this tall man carefully for a reaction.

"Yes, while like you Agent Featherston, I have ready access to some talented people at a moment's notice." His team was assembled and waiting for him in Canadian waters.

"So, they are in this country already?" Jim was probing now, but he knew he would not receive an answer.

"They are available within the hour is all I can tell you. We do not wish to tangle with your Delta Force or Seal One teams I assure you. Of course, if pushed I am sure we will give a good account of ourselves." The commandos at his disposal were world class warriors. He had used this team before with lethal results.

"I am sure you will, but why chance it?" Jim knew they would not fight Delta Force or Navy Seals if they could avoid it. The Iranians may be fanatics, but are a much softer target than the well trained and equipped American forces.

"Exactly, we are lovers, not fighters normally. The team has been assembled to protect the safe return of the Soul of Jerusalem to Israel. That is our only interest." Unless he had an excuse to kill these Muslims, he thought.

"How do you expect to find the emerald, Liam?" Jim was posing a question that Hertz had tossed over in his mind for the last week.

"That is the question for all of us, isn't it?"

"The Iranians plan to capture and torture the men at the farm, I think." Jim knew a little more about the Iranian commandos than he was letting on, Midge thought.

"Yes, but that will take many hours with no guarantee of success, Jim." The Israeli was right, there had to be a better way.

"Well I was hoping Midge would help me with this problem." Jim turned toward him.

"How would I be able to find it any better than you, Jim? All I have been to is their barn and have not seen very much of that." He knew he was going to get sucked deeper into this than he wanted.

"Let's cut to the chase, as you Americans like to say. I am in full sympathy with making sure your hostages are safe before I make a move on the jewel. Since the Iranian strike team thinks you are going to cooperate with them, they will be willing to listen to you more than others. They will actually be rather arrogant as long as they are holding the American hostages. I propose you volunteer to obtain the jewel and hand it over to them. Contain them and do not let them go to the farm. Once the hostages are confirmed safe of course, you hand over the jewel to them and wish them God speed. It will be up to my team to retrieve the jewel from them before they reach Iran. Would this not satisfy all parties?" Liam knew this would satisfy the Secret

Service Agent.

"All but the Nassire family, you might say. They may not be quite so willing to give it up." Midge watched the IAA agent carefully.

"Perhaps, but they are, after all, business men. These Shiite dogs who are chasing them and the jewel are just blind sheep following some old religious men's words. They would have no appreciation of this priceless piece of history and what it has meant to the soul of our people for thousands of years. No, the Nassire family is practical and understand they can never show the Camels Eye anywhere in the world. They have too much respect for antiquities to break up such a priceless work of art. We can deal with these men, I think." Liam seemed in control of his emotions now.

"With what Liam, money?" Midge knew these men had more money than they could ever spend.

"There are bigger things in the world than money, Midge. There is safety, access, security, recognition, movement, and many other very valuable things to men such as these. As your famous Godfather would say, 'we will make them an offer they cannot refuse'. " He was a fan of American gangster movies. They seemed to have a certain justice in them even with all the violence.

"Look, I am not authorized to promise anything without talking to my President." He knew he had carte blanc to do anything necessary to save the hostages, but he needed time to think.

"Agent Featherston, you Americans make me wonder how you ever win at anything. I know you are on a black ops mission for the President of the United States of America, not sanctioned by the FBI, CIA, Congress, or any other oversight committee of any kind. Once we know what they will take for the Camels Eye, we will be in a better position to understand if we can meet the demands. Unlike field officers of your government, Israel authorizes its representatives to think creatively and arrive at a solution on the spot." Liam knew he was stalling, but it was time to take action.

"They will never deal with Jews, I am sure." Jim used his last excuse.

"Perhaps, but these are secular men who happen to be Muslim, not sanctimonious Ayatollahs who know what is best for all the people on earth as long as they follow the same view of Allah. Still, it is safer if neither of us, you nor I, deal with them directly. Midge will be our emissary. We will put our trust in him to negotiate with the Nassire family." They both turned to Midge for his reaction.

"Leave me out of this. I don't work for anyone now. I am retired and like it that way." He knew he was screwed, but would put up a good front.

"Midge, you agreed to help me free the hostages held in Iran. Remember?" Jim was boring into him now like a school teacher lecturing a kid who did not do his homework assignment.

"Yeah I remember, but I don't like being pushed around." There, he had at least resisted for awhile.

"Would you feel better if we said please, Mr. Gregory?" The Israeli smiled as he looked at Midge.

"I would feel better if you took that pistol and put it back in its holster, smart ass. Then maybe we can get down to business." The IAA agent pulled back his jacket and slid the pistol back in his holster.

"Fine, now Jim how about getting us something to drink from that mini bar behind you? I am sure your expense account can handle it." Midge got up and stretched and went to the bathroom. Guns made him want to piss a lot.

They all grabbed a drink and went to the table to start forming a plan of action. Midge wondered how he ever got into this thing so deep over a simple dead pet, even if it was a racing camel. He was starting to feel like a cop again and that was not a good thing, he knew.

Chapter 11

It was well after midnight when Midge and Liam left the motel room. Midge did not see the vehicle the Israeli came in as he went around to the other side of the motel, walked up the road and disappeared into the night. Midge reached his van and decided to check it out very carefully. He reached into his glove box and pulled out a small high intensity flashlight. He checked under the frame, the engine compartment, and wheel wells. He did not check inside the van as that was very secure from entry with its security system and special door locks, but not the outside. He was especially worried about tracking devices. Finding nothing obvious he headed for home. He watched his mirrors and scanned the roads ahead, but he did not spot a tail. There was almost no traffic at night, so it would be hard to follow him.

Anyway, he was just headed home to be with Ryan and Brenda. Yeah Brenda, the person Ken Telway told him not to tell about their meeting Friday night. Why did he say that? What did he know about Brenda that Midge did not? He had dated her a half dozen times and now had sex with her what, three or four times? She was not his girlfriend or anything. He was just trying to help her. Protect her, but from whom? Was the Nassire family after her, or the full bloods maybe? He was not sure what was really going on, but she did seem genuinely afraid to him. Wasn't it natural for her to call him? She knew he was an ex-cop after all. He also helped her keep her car from being repossessed so they had some kind of bond. Plus the sex wasn't too bad, but it seemed more of a relief from fear than some kind of love.

He did not believe in love anymore. It was all nonsense anyway.

Just some other way to steal a man's assets without using a gun. No, there was sex and that was all. If they both enjoyed it, then so much the better, but he was never going to get married again. Two ex-wives had cleaned him out and he was not giving some other female beauty queen another shot at him or his assets.

He pulled up to the house and noticed the light to his office window was on. That was strange, but maybe it was the light from the living room shining through. No, the living room light was not on. Maybe he or Ryan left it on. He pulled up next to the door and turned off his lights. All the curtains were closed in a defensive move by Brenda, no doubt. As he went to put his key in the door, Brenda opened it wide and flew into his arms hugging and kissing him tightly.

"Where have you been, I have been so worried about you." She squeezed his neck hard and it hurt some.

"I was working. I had to meet with a man about a car. You know, I am a skip tracer and repo man. That is how I make my money. After all, that is how we met." She released his neck now.

"I am just so scared, that's all. I am frightened to stay in this house alone." She grabbed his hand and tried to pull him inside, but he had to get his key out of the lock first.

"Ryan was with you, right?" He watched her face for any sign that something was wrong, but could not detect anything as he closed the door and locked it behind them.

"Sure, but he is only ten. I like a big strong man around like you." She was smiling at him now and rubbing the side of his arm.

"Well, I am home and we are all safe now. I'm tired and ready to go to bed. What have you been doing all night?" He walked across the living room to his office to turn out the light, but when he opened the door he found the light was off. That's strange he thought, I could have sworn the light was on, something wasn't right, but he let it go.

"Can I fix you something to eat? I am really getting to know my way around the kitchen now." She looked wide awake now. She must have taken a nap while he was gone.

"No thanks, I just want to shower and hit the sack, I'm bushed." He grabbed some things from his bedroom and headed for the bathroom.

He took a quick shower and threw on his pajamas. He never used to wear anything to bed, but since Ryan moved in Midge started wearing pajamas sometimes to make Ryan feel better about his having to wear them. He went out to the couch, pulled a comforter over him and lay down for the night.

"We can share the bed you know." She bent over him giving a full shot at her cleavage out the front of her partially unbuttoned shirt.

"No, I'll just sleep here. You take the bed, Brenda."

"Sleep is not what I had in mind." Her hair was brushed out and hanging at the sides of her face. She was actually very pretty in a cute working girl type of way.

"I appreciate the offer, but I don't want Ryan to see us in bed together." Her cleavage was starting to have its affect on him. Damn women anyway.

"He is asleep and you can return to the couch when we are through, lover." She smiled slyly and licked her full red lips.

"No, I am just going to sleep, thanks. Good night, Brenda." His resistance was weakening, but he was determined not to get in bed with her. If he did, he was a goner for sure. His male hormones would take over and that would be that. He often wondered how many rapists had been lured into the act by some female strutting her stuff and then called it rape when he refused to pay whatever price she tried to extract. It happened more than people want to believe. At the trial, the woman was always portrayed as a snow white virgin who was attacked by this vicious one horned monster. The guy never had a chance. No, he was not getting near what the Chinese philosophers called the 'triangle that drives men wild' tonight. He was going to sleep.

"Well, then I will sleep with you here." She unbuttoned her shirt, let it drop to the floor, removed her pants and stood there completely naked. "I am freezing out here can you let me under the covers please?" That was it. Two minutes later they were in the bedroom doing what comes naturally between a man and a woman. Some will power, Midge thought. No wonder my two ex-wives took everything I owned. It is not fair. Why are they called the weaker sex? After they were satisfied, Midge returned to the couch for the night. He must admit he did sleep better after a little exercise, and it totally relieved his tension.

The alarm went off at seven and Midge got right up. He used the bathroom and made a pot of coffee. Brenda liked it in the morning.

He could put up with it instead of tea to make her happy.

He woke Ryan up and pushed him toward the bathroom. The kid was hard to get moving in the morning, but Midge insisted he get up in time to shower and eat breakfast before he went to school. Brenda was still out cold in bed. The little exercise they had last night seemed to do her in.

Midge decided they would have cereal for breakfast. He had to pound on the door to make Ryan hurry up and get out of the shower. He missed having the use of his own bathroom and bedroom. Brenda had taken over the vanity and sink now. It looked like a major operating table with bottles, combs, brushes, curlers, bags, hair dryer, make-up, and every other type of female apparatus piled on it to help her appearance. Why did they need all that junk? Women were complicated, yet very necessary sometimes, like last night. No wonder they always got so much alimony. They had to buy lots of stuff just to survive every day.

After Midge and Ryan ate breakfast, Midge told him he wanted to walk with him to school. He needed the exercise and he wanted time alone to think. As Ryan got his back pack and lunch together, Midge plucked a hair from his head, licked it and stuck it on the closed door to his office near the floor on the jam of the knob side. He would check it when he came home to make sure it had not been broken from its seal.

They locked the door and set the alarm. Ryan asked his Uncle Midge if he could walk behind him and on the other side of the street so his friends would not tease him. Midge told him he would give him a block's head start and just keep an eye on him until he arrived at school. He would then walk down to Spruce Street and see if he could have a cup of coffee with his Sheriff friend, Captain Tom Molten. A couple of boys joined Ryan on the way, and Midge watched as they pushed and shoved each other all way to school. Just boys acting natural he thought. He turned west and headed toward the Locks.

He stopped by Rita's and found Tom alone in his regular booth eating breakfast.

"Good morning Tom, mind if I join you?"

Looking up from his eggs and potatoes he saw Midge and motioned for him to take a seat in the booth. "Morning, Midge."

"Could I have some coffee and a piece of cherry pie, Lennie?" talking to the waitress, as he slid into the booth opposite Tom.

"How is the world treating you, Tom?" Tom looked tired this morning.

"More feds in town this week than state or local cops, I think." The waitress brought Midge his pie and coffee, set them down on the table, then left them alone.

"Is it because of those braves who were tortured and killed on the reservation, do you think?" He was adding cream and sugar to his coffee.

"Who said they were tortured?" Tom looked up a little surprised to hear that.

"Everyone does, Tom. You must be the only guy who hasn't heard that." He searched Tom's face to see if he was kidding him or something.

"Well, it is not my case, but I don't like people spreading rumors if I am not sure of the facts." He went back to eating his eggs and bacon.

"I'm not spreading rumors, just talking with my friend is all, Tom." The waitress arrived with a pot of coffee to give them a warm-up. Tom held his talk until she had left.

"I'm sorry, Midge. It is just the feds are all over my office and have just about run my men and me out of there. These guys think they own the place." He did not seem happy this morning.

"Why are they using your office instead of the Tribal Police Station?"

"Because the Tribal Police threw them out, that's why. My boss wants us to cooperate with the FBI. He thinks he is going to get a promotion from Washington, I guess."

"I worked with suck-ups like that my whole career. Just take solace that some day you will be able to retire and tell them all to kiss off, Tom." Midge hated suck-ups but they were part of life everywhere. The key to being a successful suck-up was to not be too obvious about it. Those people were called politicians, not suck-ups and always were the ones who got promoted.

"If I didn't have my kid at Lake Superior State, I would retire now. Some day, as soon as I pay off these college bills, I will retire just like you have." He looked resigned to work until he was very old, if you asked Midge.

"Don't wish your life away, Tom. You will retire when it suits you. Don't let others determine what you want to do with your life. There are other jobs out there instead of being a cop, believe me I know."

"I guess you're right, but being a cop is all I know." That is what keeps most people in jobs they hate until they are too old to do anything else. He hoped that Tom would not be forced into that trap.

"Do you ever patrol Sugar Island?" Midge was very curious about this since he would be going there tonight.

"Sugar Island? We try to go out there and circle the island once or twice a month if we can. It is not exactly a hot bed of activity, Midge."

"What about smuggling? I heard that is an entry point for booze and cigarettes from Canada." Tom looked at him as if he had lobsters coming out of his ears or something.

"Yes, but they don't sell it on the island. They cross the St. Mary's and load it on trucks that are headed for Chicago or Detroit. So we watch for trucks headed south or west and bust them on the highway if we get a tip. It makes it a lot easier than taking a ferry to the island or chasing the braves around in a boat while the freighters are steaming up and down the waterway. That is more like Coast Guard work than police work."

"Why do you say it is braves? Aren't there whites on the island who could be running cigarettes and booze?" Tom seemed to give it a little thought.

"Sure, but most are retired and lucky to make it to the ferry to go get groceries let alone smuggle cases of booze and cigarettes on to the main land." That put Midge in his place, but answered his question about police patrols.

"Then why do you even patrol the island?" Midge figured he would play this game.

"Because it makes the old people feel better. Call it preventative medicine if you like." Tom finished his coffee.

"So you don't spend a lot of time on the island?" He was pushing it now.

"We cross on the Island ferry and make the circle up to Payment and then south to Homestead. We stop at all the stores and homes we can to be visible. Then we drive back to the ferry and come back to the mainland in about half a day. That is what we call a patrol and is about the extent of our coverage."

"What about boats or aircraft?" Midge was starting to get on his nerves now.

"We do not have anything up here. The Coast Guard patrols the water with a cutter and the Border Patrol has nine agents for patrol. They mostly watch the official crossing near the ferry and the waterway. They also have one boat, for whatever good that is. Homeland security is said to have a plane, but they are not using it to watch Sugar Island. Why should they? The U.S. and Canadian border is the most porous in the world. Homeland security has increased the coverage, but most of the resources are applied to the trucks, ships, and planes that cross in Detroit and Windsor, not in Sault Ste. Marie." There, that should stop all the questions, he figured.

"So has there ever been much crime on the island?" Midge did not want to quit the game yet.

"Not reported to us. Sometimes a tourist borrows a boat to go fishing, but they always find it somewhere on the shoreline later on. We have never had a violent crime reported on the island." What was this interest in Sugar Island all of a sudden?

"What about the Bay Mills Reservation? Do the Tribal Police have an officer on the island?"

"You're kidding, right? The whole island has less than five hundred people on it. There are probably only a hundred or so living on the reservation, but I am just guessing really. Ken does not have that many deputies to spare so I can't see him having a regular patrol on the island." Why in the hell was he asking him anyway? Why was he so curious about police activity on that island? Maybe he was planning to rob a bank, but of course, there was no bank on the island, was there?

"So once you are on the island, you are on your own." Midge figured he had Tom on the edge and decided he better be careful not to raise suspicion.

"Well, a lot of the people on the island hunt and fish so they are armed I guess. We have just never had an assault. The DNR has ticketed fishermen for no license, but that is the big crime over there."

"Does the DNR ticket Chippewa for fishing?" Another question Tom probably did not know.

"Don't ask me. They claim to have a right to hunt and fish according to some treaty, but we don't get involved with that nonsense. Why do you want to know about Sugar Island anyway?"

"No reason. I have been out there with Ryan, but never saw any police presence. I guess it makes sense now." He knew Tom was not buying this story, but what choice did he have?

"Well, I better get moving. I have to meet a plane coming into Kincheloe with a BIA agent aboard and I am stuck with picking him up." Everyone still called the airport Kincheloe, even though it became Chippewa County International Airport years ago.

"That should be the Tribal Police job, shouldn't it Tom?"

"I know, but they refused to help the guy. It all pays the same, Midge."

"I hear you Tom, have a great day." Midge paid his bill and followed Tom out. Tom turned and left for the station and Midge went straight a few blocks, then turned and walked back home.

As Midge approached his house, he thought he saw a car pull out of his driveway. He was still over two blocks away and he was not wearing his glasses, so he was not sure. When he reached his front door, he did not notice anything unusual. He put his key in the door and let himself in. He checked to make sure the alarm was not on, closed the door and relocked it. The light was on in his bedroom and he could hear a hair dryer whirring in the bathroom. As he crossed the living room he checked the telltale to his office and sure enough, it was broken. That was interesting.

"Brenda, are you in there?" There was no reply so he went to the bedroom door and looked in. She had her back to him in the bathroom blow drying her hair. He walked into the room and said, "Brenda?" She let out a scream and dropped the hair dryer on the sink top, but it did not break.

"You scared me to death. Don't sneak up on a girl like that. You just took ten years off my life." She put her hand over her heart and took a couple of deep breaths.

"Sorry, but I kept calling you. The hair dryer makes such a racket you did not hear me." She turned it off and turned around and hugged him.

"I'm glad you are back. I did not know where you were when I woke up." She didn't get up until after nine anyway.

"I walked Ryan to school, well sort of, and went down to Rita's for a cup of coffee and a piece of pie. I wanted to go for a walk. You were asleep so I did not want to disturb you." Her hair was all fly away from the blow dryer.

"After last night, I was just out cold this morning. But I feel great now, so what do you want to do today?" She turned and started to brush her hair.

"Was someone here this morning?" He watched her face in the mirror but did not notice any reaction.

"Not that I know of, why do you ask?" She now started to apply her make up. A daily reconstruction project for most women and Brenda was no exception, it appeared.

"No reason, I just thought I saw someone pulling out of our driveway when I was walking home just now." He wondered why he used the term 'our' driveway. This was not going in right direction.

"I didn't see anyone, but maybe someone turned around in our driveway or something." There was that word 'our' again. She was saying it now too.

"Do we need any groceries or toiletries from the store?" It was a rhetorical question he did not really expect an answer to.

"I could use some Massengill and we are out of flour, almost." They always needed something, he thought.

"I don't even want to know what Massengill is and I don't use much flour." How could he run out of flour?

"I want to make some homemade cookies for Ryan. The other stuff is for females so you don't need to know, smarty pants." She now started to apply her lipstick and would be looking for someplace or someone to blot it on.

"Okay, let's jump in the van and run to the store." He turned and left the bathroom.

"I'll be ready in ten minutes." A woman can't just jump in a vehicle and leave. It is like someone will spot them without their hair done and make-up on and they will get a ticket or something, he thought.

"I am going to log on to my computer and check for my messages. Call me when you are ready to go." She said something but he did not really hear it.

Midge opened the office door, went in and closed it behind him. He pulled up to the console and looked at the desk top. He did not notice anything out of place, but he knew someone had opened the door since this morning. That did not mean they had entered the office and used his computer necessarily. He moved the mouse and his screen was instantly on. That is strange. Did he leave his computer on for the last couple of days? When he was working, he had a habit of doing that sometimes, but he had not worked on it in a couple of days. He always left the camera and recorder on so he would check it. He selected video and rewound the tape two hours as he viewed the outside of his house. He fast forwarded it until he saw a dark blue car appear on the screen. A dark haired thin man he did not recognize got out of the car and came to his door. The door opened and he went inside disappearing from the cameras. In just over ten minutes, he reappeared from the front door, got into his car and left. The clock insert showed it was 11:06 am, just about the time Midge was coming home. What was going on here?

"Midge, I'm ready to go. Where are you?" He quickly exited the video and brought up his email. Just seconds later Brenda poked her head into the office. "So there you are. I'm ready to go, are you?"

"I was just checking my emails. I got another job for a car to locate. I can check it when we get back." Midge turned off the monitor and headed for the door. Brenda just leaned against the door and spread one arm across the entrance.

"You know, Ryan isn't home, we could stay here and find something fun to do, if you know what I mean." Her hand was now rubbing her left hip in a slow and sensual way.

"We're out of here. You are going to wear me out, girl. I need to get home early and take a little nap so I can stay awake on the stake out tonight." He better get on the road before his male hormones overwhelmed him again.

"Can I go with you tonight?" She was looking at him funny, he thought.

"Not tonight Brenda, I need you to stay with Ryan because this one is in a bad area and I can't take him with me. Maybe next time, let's get in the van." He did not want to discuss this anymore.

They left the house, got in the van and drove to Wal Mart which passed for a high level department store in the Sault. Midge started thinking about the keys to his house. How many did he have anyway? He had one, Ryan had one, but he was not sure where the boy kept it. He thought he also had a couple of spares. He knew he had one out in the old garage under an old lemonade can filled with nuts and bolts. He kept it there in case he locked himself out, but he never told anyone about it, not even Ryan. And what about the alarm? Did Ryan know the code? Yes, he decided Ryan knew the code, but Midge had told him to never tell anyone the numbers or let anyone see what it was. Was he becoming paranoid? Who was that man who came to see Brenda and went into his house? Was he a boyfriend she did not want him to know about? He didn't care about that. He wasn't married to her or anything. He was just helping her out is all. And why was she giving him so much sex? Not that he was complaining, but was that girl over sexed or what? He was not naïve by any means. He was no movie star and Brenda had to be ten to fifteen years younger than him. Why was she making such an effort to keep him satisfied? If his ex-wives had been that attentive, he would never have divorced them. Well, that was not really true. He just didn't like the first bitch, but he had to admit, she was a looker.

"What are you thinking about?" Women always wanted to know how a man feels about something. What the hell was the difference how someone felt? Men never want to talk about feely and touchy things.

Another reason he got divorced. Did all the women of the world do this, butt in on a man's thoughts? Probably so he figured. "Nothing, just daydreaming is all."

"Do you think those Nassire men are really after me?" She was just not going to shut up, he figured.

"I don't really know. It just seemed safer to keep you out of sight until they find out who killed those full bloods." That should satisfy her.

"Who are *they*, Midge?" Here we go again with the questions.

"I don't really know. I guess the Tribal Police, maybe. There are an awful lot of feds in town right now wanting to help them. FBI, BIA, Homeland Security and that type of guys."

"Why is Homeland Security involved?" She had a million questions stored in her brain.

"I don't know, but I think the FBI, INA, Coast Guard, Border Patrol, and a bunch of other groups all think the reservation falls under their jurisdiction. I do not really understand all the rules and games that go on today." Man he hoped they got to the store soon.

The Camels Eye

"When do you think I can go home, Midge?"

"You can go home today if you want, Brenda. It is up to you when you feel safe or comfortable with it really." He would drop her off right now if she said the word. The sex was great, but he did not like sharing his house with a woman.

"I feel safe with you, but I am afraid I am getting on your nerves. I am not sure Ryan likes me staying in the house either." She knew men did not like women taking over their bathroom or bedroom and she knew she was not as neat in the kitchen as Midge.

"Ryan is fine, and you are not bothering me. I'm just old and set in my ways, but I want to make sure you're safe before you leave." A little white lie never hurt.

"Thanks Midge, you don't know how much I appreciate all you have done for me. I am trying to be good to you, too." She turned toward him and smiled big.

"You don't have to try to be good to me. I am helping because I want to, not because I think you will be good to me. Please don't feel you have to do me special favors." So that is why he was getting so much sex. He did not want her to be laying out her body for him if she did not want sex.

"Midge, I like you and I am not giving you sex because I owe you. I am having sex with you because I want to. It is as much for my pleasure and tension relief as yours." A little white lie never hurt.

"Thanks Brenda, that makes me feel a little better." He better change the subject.

"Where were you last night, Midge?" She knew he was not on a stake out that was for sure.

"I told you I was with a client. He wants me to do a job for him." She knew that was not the truth either.

"I thought you got all your jobs from the internet." She had him now.

"No, just my repo jobs. I also do work for local attorneys and businessmen." He did not like this type of questioning about his work.

"Not for the police or government?" Where did that question come from? The fact was she knew he had met with a fed probably.

"I never work for the cops or government, but I sometimes listen to their cases and give an opinion or two if they ask me." Why was she so curious all of a sudden? Was someone feeding her information about him?

They were at the Wal Mart, thank the Lord. Midge pulled in and parked about twenty spaces up the third row to the right of the door.

"Why are we parking so far away? I see a parking spot in the middle row only five cars from the entrance." A typical woman, they hated to walk.

"I like to walk and that will save the spot for someone who needs it because they can't walk so well." Why did women fight so hard to park close to an entrance? His ex-wife would cruise around a parking lot for twenty minutes to move up ten spaces. He could park, shop, check out, and be back in his truck by the time she got the perfect spot. Go figure.

"You are just like my ex-husband. That man would park two miles away just so no one would hit his car when they opened a door. You should have seen the piece of junk he was driving. It wasn't like he had a Lincoln or Cadillac or some fancy car. He still was ready to make me walk even if it was raining out." Midge was starting to see the female flaws coming out in Brenda. Yep, all women were the same once you got past the sex, he thought.

They shopped fast. Brenda got her Massengill, some other female type items and Midge put it all on his credit card. They filled the cart with the sacks of groceries and headed outside for the van.

"We need to get home before Ryan gets out of school. I also want to catch that nap I told you about." As they were pushing their cart in the lot up the lane, Midge heard a squealing of tires behind him. He grabbed Brenda and pulled her between a car and an SUV on his right. The dark sedan flew toward them and hit their shopping cart sending food and female products flying into the air. Midge pulled his police revolver from its holster and took a shooters stance with his hands on the roof of a car, but the speeding dark sedan was racing to the road. He did not dare to take a shot from here. He saw the driver for only a split second. Dark clothes, dark baseball hat, sunglasses, wearing a dark jacket. Some description he thought, he couldn't pick out Al Pacino in a line up with what he had seen.

"Are you okay, Brenda?" He helped her up from the asphalt.

"Yes. Who was that and which one of us was he after?" That was the same thing Midge was wondering.

"I don't know who it was and that's a good question. Which one of us was he after?" Yes, a very, very good question, Midge thought. He retires to the peaceful north country and it is starting to feel more dangerous than the Motor City. Who would want to hurt him? A lot of people he could think of, but most of them were still in prison. Besides, none of them knew he lived in the Sault, did they? Maybe they were trying to kill Brenda, but why? Was it because they thought she knew something about the full blood braves who were murdered? Did she know more than she was saying? Someone seemed to think so or at least was not willing to take a chance that she knew too much. He was going to have to go into Detroit mode and start protecting himself and the others around him. Shoot first and ask questions later, if they were still alive to answer his questions.

They picked up as many of their items as they could that were not too damaged and put them in the shopping basket, then headed for the van.

"At least the parking lot will be pure now." She made a smart ass remark.

"What do you mean?" Midge was still thinking about the car that tried to hit them.

"The guy broke my bottle of douche and it ran all over the lot." She was smiling now.

"What?" He was trying to hear her this time.

"My Massengill, it is douche to keep me clean down there. You know?" She had him smiling too.

"Oh, that is what you bought. Let's get in the van before anything else happens to us." They hurriedly loaded everything into the van as Midge kept a wary eye on the parking lot.

They drove home without further incident, but Midge kept a close eye on the road and his mirrors. He also decided he better pick Ryan up at school, considering he was not sure who the target of the attempted hit and run was.

They took the groceries and what was left of Brenda's female supplies into the house. He left her there to put things away while he drove to the school.

Midge pulled into the lot and was a half hour too early. But that was okay he would set up his surveillance equipment. He would record the passing traffic and the surrounding scenery to see if he could spot anything interesting or out of place later when he reviewed the tape.

His head was swimming with questions, but not answers. He started to think what a week this had been. Three braves killed, Brenda coming to live with him, a secret service agent seeking his help, an Israeli holding him at gun point trying to make a deal with him and Jim, the Tribal Chief of Police wanting to meet with him tonight on Sugar Island, and being invited to lunch tomorrow at the Nassire farm. That should be an interesting lunch, if he lived that long he thought.

Who had tried to run him down in the Wal Mart lot? What did Brenda really know and what was her real agenda? Who was the man Brenda let in his house and why had she denied it? Who was in his office and what exactly did they do in there? Why were so many people able to be where he was going before he got there? Was his house bugged? Was his van being tracked? Was Brenda calling and informing someone about his plans? Why was she asking so many questions? What about the plan Jim Featherston and Liam Hertz were working on for him to try and carry out with the Nassire men? How could he possibly get the Nassire family to give him the Camels Eye? What reward would be great enough to make them trade for such a treasure?

Midge noticed the big red Ford Expedition pull in and park. Jacob's ride was here. With its dark windows he could not tell who was driving, but he was pretty sure it would be Kia just like always.

The bell rang and the boys started pouring out of the front doors. Ryan and Jacob were the last to come out as usual. The driver's door to the Expedition opened and out stepped, not Kia, but a younger man, much in the same cut as Kia. He was tall and dark with a moustache and short cropped black hair. He wore a dark suit with an open oxford white shirt with no tie. The man had a military bearing like one of those parade troops who marched in parades or at the Tomb of the Unknown Soldier. All the lines of their body straight with narrow hips, flat stomach, big chest and tight jaw line. They looked the same the world over. No short stubby guys in the public eye, no those stubby guys were used to fight and die in countless encounters over the centuries. Parade soldiers would always be on the recruiting posters. He opened the rear door for Jacob who turned and yelled, "I'll see you at lunch tomorrow, Ryan."

"Is it okay if I bring my BB gun?"

"Sure, I have one too and maybe we can shoot some cans. Bye." Jacob waved and disappeared into the Expedition.

The Camels Eye

"Bye." Ryan yelled as he opened the front passenger door, threw in his backpack and jumped into the front seat.

"Hi Uncle Midge, are we still going to Jacob's tomorrow for lunch?" The boy seemed excited about it.

"I should say we are, kid. How was school today?"

"The usual I guess, only Sister Margaret told us it was a sin to covet thy neighbor's wife. What does covet mean, really Uncle Midge?" Boy, did Midge know what that meant, but in reverse. Someone had coveted both his wives. While he was pissed at the time, they sure got the rotten end of that deal. It reminded him of two drunks fighting over some bar fly broad. After losing half an ear and having a broken nose and shiner, he declared himself the winner. Then he got a good look at the old hag in the morning light, and wondered why he had fought so hard to win. Sometimes you have to be careful what you wish for because you just might get it.

"It means to want what someone else owns really bad even when it doesn't belong to you, I guess." That should keep it clean in Ryan's mind he figured.

"You mean like Jacob's farm and animals?"

"Do you covet his farm, Ryan?" He knew the boy loved animals, but he did not want any more.

"I would like to live in the country sometimes and have horses and goats, I guess."

"Then you wouldn't live near the school or Locks or stores. And you would have to feed, water, and clean up after those animals all the time."

"We could hire servants like Jacob does." Oh here we go, now he wanted to keep up with the Joneses or should he say the Nassires?

"That costs a lot of money Ryan, and I am retired. Besides I like my house and where it's located. I also don't want to take care of any more animals, kid."

"How does Jacob's family get all their money, Uncle Midge? Maybe you could do it too." Great, now the kid wanted him to go back to work.

"I don't know how they get their money Ryan, and I don't care. Remember to be happy with what you have and not be envious of what others have. What they have has no bearing at all on what you have, kid." But Midge had been wondering that very same thing about the

Nassire family for the last few days.

"What does envious mean?"

"It means jealous, desirous, resentful, or covetous. Yes, that is what the Sister meant when she said not to covet." There, that should end it. He never had kids, but he would have been the kind of dad who said 'go ask you mother' to a lot of these questions.

"Okay. I sure think I am going to have a lot of fun at the farm tomorrow."

"I hope so Ryan, I really do." He hoped he had an interesting time too.

They were at the house now. They pulled into the driveway and pulled up near the door to the house. Midge unlocked the door as Ryan ran around the van and into the living room. Brenda was in the kitchen when Midge got there.

"What are you making?"

"Homemade pizza, it's my specialty."

"I could have picked one up if you had let me know."

"Not like this one you can't. My mother taught me to make it and it is my favorite, even if it is a lot of work."

"Did I have the right stuff to make it in the cupboards?" He did like homemade pizza himself, but it was too much work for him anymore.

"I bought what I needed at Wal Mart today. Fortunately all of the necessary ingredients made it home with only one can dented." She was proud to know how to make homemade pizza that tasted great.

"Sounds good. My ex-wife used to make a pretty mean pizza herself, so I will be interested in seeing how yours compares." He knew it was wrong as soon as he said it. He was no smooth talker, but even a blunt ex-cop knew not to compare one woman's cooking with another's. No wonder he was not married. Well, he did not really care anyway.

Ryan burst into the kitchen. "Hello Brenda, what are you cooking?"

"I'm making homemade pizza Ryan. My specialty, dear boy." She held her head up slightly and smiled while she was spreading Crisco on a round pizza pan with her hands.

"I'll bet it is not as good my Mom's. She made the best pizza in the whole wide world." Wow Midge thought, this kid is going to end up divorced in life for sure just like his smooth talking uncle. Brenda's eyes narrowed, but she did not say anything. It was easier to accept from a boy than a man, Midge thought.

"Come on Ryan, let's get out of here and let her cook. I'll play goalie if you want to kick the soccer ball at me."

"Yeah, come on Uncle Midge, let's go." He turned and ran out of the house.

"Call us when the pizza is ready, can you Brenda? I love to eat it hot from the oven before it cools too much."

"Are you sure it will be good enough for you two fine connoisseurs to eat?" She turned and removed a bowl from the sink that was covered with a towel. It had been sitting in some hot water letting the dough rise. This was a good time to leave, Midge decided. She would call them and they better say they loved it if they knew what was good for them. He would tell Ryan to praise the pizza when they got outside. No sense in putting Ryan on her shit list too. He spun, left the kitchen and went into the yard to play with Ryan.

After kicking the ball around for about a half hour, Brenda called them in to eat. After washing up, they all sat down to a big slice of homemade pizza. Midge had to admit it was fantastic. Extra sauce, extra cheese, mushrooms, and ham and cooked to perfection. No commercial pizza parlor could afford to make a pizza like this without charging a premium for it. The problem is the chains would have such a lower price, that very few people would buy the premium one. A pity really, Americans talked about quality all the time, but not many were willing to pay for it.

"This pizza is just like my Mom's, Brenda," as he took another big bite with sauce now lining both sides of his cheeks near the corners of his mouth.

"Now that is high praise indeed." She reached her hand over and patted Ryan on the top of the head.

"He's right, but it is better than my ex-wife could ever make." A poor attempt to compliment her, but it should work. Women are easy when it came to praise. They will take all they can get.

"Thank you Midge, it is sweet of you to say so." She smiled coyly at him and while he was not sure if she was mocking him or not, he decided that the compliment had its effect and she now truly believed him. Peace on earth, good will to men, or something like that.

"That was a great supper, Brenda. I hope you don't mind if I go take a nap. I'll be out late tonight and want to be alert for it."

"Where are you going tonight, Midge?" Here we go with the questions again.

"I'm going down to St. Ignace. A construction worker is behind in his payments on his truck." That should satisfy the woman. He hated to criticize the woman who just made them a nice pizza, but it really was none of her business. Or was she asking for someone else, he wondered.

"When will you be leaving?"

"In about two hours or so, but not later than eight o'clock. I want to set-up before the guy gets home if I can." It was less than an hour's drive from his house to the Mackinaw Bridge. This would give him plenty of time to make a rendezvous at the bar on Sugar Island.

"Okay, would you mind if I use the van to run over to my sister's house for a few minutes. I'll clean up the kitchen when I get back."

"I didn't even know you had a sister."

"Yep, she lives in Rosedale. Can I use the van?"

"How about you use the pick-up instead? It doesn't have all the equipment in it that I will need tonight."

"That would be fine. Can I get the keys and have you pull the van out of the way?"

"Sure thing Brenda, I'll move the van out of your way. Can you be sure to be back by eight because I don't want to leave Ryan in the house alone tonight."

"I should be back before then easily. Does the pick-up have any gas in it?"

"I just filled it a couple of days ago and haven't used it much."

"Good, let me get out of here." They both went outside and Brenda was on her way to her sister's house. That is, if she had a sister. She was really starting to worry him.

Midge went back inside and stretched out on the couch to grab some sleep. He did not really need it for tonight, but he would tomorrow which might be a pretty full day after a late night. He put in a Star Wars DVD for Ryan and laid back and went to sleep.

Chapter 12

"Wake up Midge, it's a quarter to eight." He felt someone shaking his shoulder. He opened his eyes to see Brenda's face right above him talking to him.

"You said you wanted to leave no later than eight." She seemed a little agitated or was it just he had been shaken awake and was still a little confused?

"Yeah, thanks. I'll use the bathroom and then get going." He stretched and yawned and then sat up. He rubbed his eyes and noticed Ryan was still watching Star Wars. He must have started it again, that little rascal. He loved those Lucas films. Midge got up and headed for the bathroom. "Is everything all right?"

"What do you mean?" She was looking kind of funny at Midge, he thought.

"With your sister. You said you were going to check on your sister, didn't you?"

"No, I did not say to check on her. I said to run over to see her, I believe." She was eyeing him now in a defenseive posture like a woman can get when she develops an attitude. He had seen a lot of those expressions just before both his wives left him.

"I was just concerned is all. I hope everything is all right."

"She's fine. I just wanted to visit my sister, okay?" She rolled her eyes and headed to the kitchen.

He used the restroom. The older he got, the more often he had to pee. He did not go to doctors, but either his kidneys had shrunk, or he better give up candy and pop and start exercising more. It was hard to

131

do when you were on surveillance all the time. After washing his face and putting on a dark sweater, he cleaned his glasses with soap and water. It was better to get all the body grease off and start fresh for the night. He had greasy skin like an Italian even though he was about as English as you can get. He put on his high top Duckbill shoes that were dark and light brown and waterproof. These might come in handy trudging around the island, but only if he did not end up knee deep in some water tonight. He next strapped on his shoulder holster and put his nickel plated Smith & Wesson .44 Magnum with its six inch barrel and Safariland grips securely in place. Why he didn't carry a 9mm automatic like the hoods he didn't know, but this baby would never jam. He just had to make sure every shot hit its target. He did not have ammo to waste in a fight. Finally he took his leather jacket from the closet and put it on, then zipped it up. He checked his image in a mirror and decided he looked like some hit man from a Ludlum novel. He was satisfied and ready to go now.

"Bye, Ryan. I want you in bed by ten, do you understand? We have a big day tomorrow at the farm." He hugged Ryan and patted him on his head.

"Bye, Brenda, thanks for watching Ryan tonight. I will try not to be too late." He turned and started for the door.

"Bye, Midge, be careful out there tonight. I'll lock up and set the alarm when you leave." She did not look angry with him at least.

"Okay, good night." And with that Midge left the house, got into his van and drove off.

Midge turned west out of his driveway as if heading to I-75 for St. Ignace. He quickly turned right and headed toward the Locks and Portage Avenue. He paid particular attention to the traffic behind him. He did not notice anyone following him, but he would be extra careful tonight. He liked watching the big Great Lakes freighters moving up and down the St. Mary's. What an engineering marvel the Locks were, so simple, so massive, yet precise. There were no water pumps in the Locks, just valves that moved lake water in and out of the Lock. Americans did not appreciate enough their ingenuity and ability when it came to harnessing Mother Nature. He parked along the road and watched a freighter proceeding through the locks. He wondered how much it weighed, eighty or maybe a hundred tons, and yet the water in the Lock lifted it like it was nothing. How big of a chain and crane would it have taken to do that, and then how much damage to the hull would result? He had no comprehension of how physics worked most of the time, but he knew he was watching something awesome right now.

He was to meet a brave at the Hill Top Bar parking lot on Sugar Island. His van would be easy to spot, but he did not know what the brave looked like with the exception of wearing the Cleveland Browns hat backwards. Up here most people wore a Lions, Red Wings, or Packers hat. Even though the Packers were a Wisconsin team, most U.P. men identified with the rugged Packer mystique. No one wore a Cleveland Browns hat in the Sault, so it should be easy to spot. The bar should be busy on a Friday night, but it was almost all local people from the island. The Sault had plenty of bars, so there was no need to cross over to the island to drink. It was about a quarter to nine when Midge pulled out and headed southeast on Portage to the ferry.

He pulled into the line to the ferry facing the water. It did not take long for the ferry to come across and discharge the cars and trucks from the island. The ferry was the only way on and off Sugar Island, except boat or aircraft. Midge would know that no one was following him, unless they were on the same ferry trip with him. It would take a half hour or more for the ferry to reload on the mainland and take the next cars to the island.

He paid his fare and drove on to the ferry. It could carry about fifteen vehicles in the four lanes on the deck. Of course, it depended on the size of the vehicles. It was only about a three minute trip across the water to One and a Half Mile Road, which was the main road on the island.

Sugar Island was a little over seven miles wide at its widest part and about twenty nine miles long. The Bay Mills Reservation was on the west side of the island near the center, facing the mainland.

They did not want him to drive onto the reservation for fear of discovery. The brave would meet him in the bar parking lot and take him to meet Ken somehow.

Midge drove about three miles to the top of the hill, parked around the side of the bar in the gravel lot and waited. He turned off his lights, but left the van running to keep it warm inside. He went to the rear console, turned on the IR cameras and started recording. It would be hard to sneak up on him tonight with all the equipment he had at his disposal.

Midge watched as a brave scanned the area and proceeded slowly toward the van. He had a hat on backwards, but Midge could not see if it was a Brown's hat, or at least not from this angle.

The brave circled around to the rear of the van, avoiding the lights of the bar, not wanting his silhouette to show. As he moved down the side of the van, Midge moved back up to the driver's seat and let the window down.

"Who are you?" Midge watched him approach in his side view mirror.

"I am called, Neka, it means Wild Goose in English." The brave had long black hair tied in a pony tail in the back.

"Let me see the front of your hat." Midge had unzipped his jacket and had his hand on his revolver.

"I am to take you to meet with Kiwidinok." He grabbed his hat and rotated it so Midge could see the Browns logo above the bill of the hat.

"Are you really a Browns fan?" He watched the lot for any other braves that may be with Neka, but saw nothing.

"No, they had this on sale for two bucks at Wal Mart." Leave it to Wal Mart to move discount merchandise any way or anywhere they can, Midge thought.

"I have a boat on the south part of the Island. Pull back on the road and go left. I will tell you when to turn until we get to the boat. We will go in by water. That will stop anyone from following us."

"I agree with that idea. Are you packing?" The brave patted his jacket.

"Yeah, are you?"

"Yep," Midge said patting the left side of his jacket.

"Then let's go see the man." The brave jumped in the passenger seat and they headed out of the parking lot. They drove east about two miles and then turned south. They drove right through the reservation, four more miles and then Neka pointed to a one lane gravel drive. It was more like a fire trail running down to the water. He had Midge drive down to the water. There was a rundown cabin with no lights and broken windows on his left. Midge stopped the van and he and the brave walked down a path to the waterway, which is called Lake Nicolet on this part of the river. Midge could see a boat tied on to a tree riding in the water.

Midge did not know much about boats, but he could tell by the way it tilted up in the nose it had a big outboard mounted on the rear for its size. They would have enough speed to avoid any large ships in the channel, he thought. But who the hell was Kiwidinok? Was that Ken's Chippewa name? He hoped it was because he did not know many other Chippewas, except Brenda maybe.

They headed north along the western shore of the island. They proceeded north slowly against the current until they reached the small Bay Mills Reservation near the center of the island. That made sense to Midge. Ken Telway would want to meet on his turf in order to feel safe and make sure he was not followed. He was not sure what had Ken so spooked, but the man was not taking any chances, that was for sure. The temperature was below fifty degrees, but there was no wind tonight so he felt plenty warm. The brave slowed the boat and ran them into a bank. There was no beach here, only a jagged dirt shoreline with trees coming almost to the waterline. The engine died as they bumped along the shore. The brave jumped from the boat pulling a line with him and tying it off on a stump.

"Welcome to my village. Be careful getting out so you don't fall in the water."

"Thanks, I'll be careful." It was dark and Midge felt his way to the front of the boat to where the brave had gotten off. He carefully stepped high and wide onto the shore.

Neka led the way through the trees to a dirt road. No, more like a fire trail for a truck through the woods. After about ten minutes, they followed a foot path to the south. Neka stopped and made a bird sound like a robin, it seemed to Midge. A return sound came back, but it was not a robin. Midge was not sure of his bird sounds even though his ex-wife had bought one of those bird clocks where a different bird song played at each hour. Drove him nuts at first, but he got used to it after a few months. She took it and everything else with her when she left him. So much for community property, he thought.

"Okay, let's go." They approached a dark low profile cabin like structure. At least they weren't going into a tepee, though Midge had never seen a tepee in Michigan. It might be a Plains Indian tribe that used tepees, he thought.

As they approached the door, he saw Ken Telway. He was not

wearing his uniform, but was dressed in jeans and a dark shirt with no hat or coat. "Hello Midge, I am glad you came."

"Why all the mystery, Ken? Couldn't we have met in the Sault somewhere?" He watched the police captain carefully.

"No we couldn't, it is too dangerous." His eyes dropped a little but not too far.

"Do you mean for you, or for me, Ken?"

"For both of us, my friend. Please come in, there is someone I want you to meet."

The interior of the small cabin, no, he would call it a hovel or hut was dark. It was clean even though it had a dirt floor. This was no tourist cabin in the woods. He could see an old pot belly stove in one corner with the glow and warmth of a log fire inside. The room was thick with the smell of sweet hardwood smoke. There were two other people sitting with their backs to him on the floor near the stove. There was no other light in the room. On the opposite side he could see a plain wood table with six wooden chairs. This must be a meeting house of some kind since he saw no beds or sleeping mats of any kind. Neka had remained outside, probably with his bird calling friend, Midge thought.

Ken went forward, bent down and said something to one of the people sitting near the stove. Ken stood up and looked at Midge. "Midge, let me introduce you to Kiwidinok, the Medicine Man of the Anishinabe and also one of our elders. His white man's name is Robert and he is a member of our tribal council."

Midge was confused because they did not rise to shake hands or even acknowledge him. Ken moved his arm and pointed at a spot on the floor so Midge figured that is where Ken wanted him to sit. He wondered what was wrong with the table and chairs. Ken took a place next to him near the stove. Ken put a couple more sticks in the fire. As the flame lapped around the new wood, the place was illuminated. He noticed they were all in a semi circle now and could see each other quite well. The two Chippewa or Anishinabe were watching the fire and barely moving at all. They were both very old and looked like full bloods to Midge, as if he was any judge of such a thing. They both wore their long black and gray hair straight back with a leather braided band around their foreheads. They had long ear lobes and the wide Indian nose with a pock-marked complexion. They were wearing leather shirts with some bead work under the blankets they were using to keep them warm. No one said a thing for a few minutes. They brought him all this way for this?

"So you two are not Chippewa then?" They just continued to stare into the fire and did not seem to even acknowledge his presence.

Ken spoke, "Chippewa is the name the white man gave us. It is the official name used on every treaty with the United States. It is what we call ourselves when we talk to whites or non-Native people. Ojibwa is what we call ourselves to other Native people. It is also the name we used in all treaties with Canada. Anishinabe is the name we call ourselves among our own people. I hope this clears up your confusion."

"Perfectly, I never knew and I am sorry if I offended you." Midge had called Native American people Indians, injuns, red-skins, chief, and every other politically incorrect name his entire life. He was in the army with some Navajo and he called them Chief all the time, not understanding they did not like it. Everyone had nick names then, like wop, guinea, Mick, or any other slur. He never thought much about it. They called him Limey because he was English by decent.

"Do you know a man named Kia Ashad?" The speech was slow and halting like most old people who were in no hurry to talk to you, but deep and scratchy like a deep base country singer.

"I know a man named Kia, yes I do. He is the chauffeur for the Nassire family." The man, this Kiwidinok, was still staring at the fire. Maybe it was impolite to stare or look at one another during a pow-wow or whatever they called this meeting.

"He is no chauffeur, but he means to do you a great evil, as he did to our Anishinabe braves." He seemed to be talking to the fire.

"How do you know he did harm to your braves, Kiwidinok?" He remained silent.

"We have a witness who was at Mission Hill and saw the whole execution that night." Ken was speaking now in a low slow voice. "Two witnesses actually, but the second one is too frightened to say anything."

"If you know Kia Ashad was responsible, then why don't you arrest him or have Jay Nassire hand him over to you?"

"It is not that simple. He is very powerful and controls the actions of the Nassire family. Besides, the Nassire family is very connected both within the tribal council and with the state and federal authorities. They have spies within the council, much of the tribe and even in the Tribal Police."

"Then bring in the FBI with the BIA and take them out." The old men had weathered faces, almost like leather, signifying a life lived outside.

"Let me tell you a story about my childhood. We lived on the big bay and we hunted and fished the land and waters. We were poor but proud and well fed. The white man came and put us on a reservation and took possession of much of the bay and the river front. They then told us we could only hunt and fish by their rules, not when our families needed food. My people went hungry. They gave us cheese and rice and powdered milk. They made our men idle or put them in jail as poachers according to white man laws. They introduced us to alcohol and made slaves of our men to the liquid devil. We cannot go back to that." The old medicine man just stopped speaking.

Now Robert took up the story. "Many years ago, about the year 1980 in white man time, the Nassire men and Kia came to the Bay Mills Reservation and told us they had a way to rid our tribe of poverty. I was one of the tribal council braves then and welcomed any ideas that would end the poverty and depression our people were suffering. They offered legal and financial aid in the form of establishing casinos to bring revenue to our nation. It would take millions of dollars and many hours of treaty negotiation and enforcement, as well as lobbying the state and federal politicians to gain the rights we were granted by the whites in treaties. We, of course, did not have the financial resources, or the legal expertise to pursue such a bold action for our people.

The Nassire men offered all of these things for us in exchange for twenty-five percent of all profits, some tribal land to build a home, and membership on our tribal council. We did not understand who Kia Ashad was at that time. There was much debate among the council. After analyzing the jobs, housing, food, income, and hope it would give our people, the council voted unanimously to accept the generous offer. The Nassire men also set up all the bank accounts and would handle all the cash in the casinos and tribal government funds. They managed well and our tribal income is one of the highest in America. Even though we are fully in charge of our physical operations, the

Nassire men still hold all the financial controls, Chippewa men and women received jobs. Some even manage many of the casino and hotel functions and earn a good living. The casinos and hotels have given our people pride of ownership, even though the money is actually controlled by the foreigners." He stopped speaking and stared at the fire. Ken threw two more sticks into the fire.

"Some of our full blood braves, who call themselves the Bahweting Blood Braves, after our ancient drumming ceremony, have decided they want to take control of the council and oust the Nassire men from our tribal affairs. Some of the elders don't like the braves, even though they also would like to see the foreigners give up so much control," Ken told him.

Midge watched how calm the three men were, yet they were here in secret on Sugar Island because these men feared something or someone. "So the full blood braves are the ones who attacked the farm and tried to kill the Nassire men?"

"No, but they provided the transportation, weapons, and intelligence for the other foreigners to attack them."

"The ones Sam called Arabs he and the others smuggled back and forth to Canada for the attack?"

"Yes." Ken was carrying the conversation now.

"And you say you have an eye witness to the beheadings, maybe two people even?"

"Yes, one of our braves was at the Mission Hill Cemetery that night with his girl friend. He saw two vehicles pull into the cemetery and the braves were dragged out into the field. He pushed his girlfriend down behind the gravestones and crawled forward to see what was happening. There was not much he could do to stop them as the men were heavily armed and he had no weapon."

"Did he see them actually beheaded and can he identify the men who did this crime?"

"Yes, he said the Braves had already been badly beaten from the way they were on their knees swaying. Their hands were bound behind their backs and they were barefoot. He saw a man bring a large curved sword from the truck and hold it high above their heads before he brought it down in a fast stroke and severed the heads of the Braves, one at a time. Then they cleaned the blade, got back in their vehicles and left."

"Ken, you said he recognized the man who did the killing."

"Yes, it was Kia, the Nassire enforcer. Jay and John Nassire were with the group and watched the beheadings. They were in another vehicle that brought the other men to the cemetery."

"Why do you think they killed the braves in this way?"

"Two reasons, first it is their custom to kill their enemy this way. They consider it just and merciful. Next was to send a clear signal to our young braves that if they help the Persians enemies, they will be killed in the same manner and they can not enter the nether world of their ancestors. You see, we must have our heads to enter our holy place." Ken spoke slowly and never let his eyes leave the fire, as if reading the flames.

"So these braves can never enter the holy place of the Chippewa?"

"Now they can, we sewed the heads back on and buried them that night in a traditional ceremony at Mission Hill overlooking the bay. If the foreigners had removed and hidden the heads, the Braves could never be at peace."

"So you have an eye witness to murder and you are afraid to arrest the murderers and bring them to trial. What is stopping you from going out to the farm and arresting the whole bunch of them?"

"Two things, first they are better armed than we are, unless we bring in the feds. But more important, as Robert explained earlier, they hold the strings to all the financial systems the tribe operates. It would cause great harm and suffering for Chippewa all over Michigan and Canada." Ken picked up two more sticks and threw them in the fire.

"So how do I fit into this mess? I am not Chippewa, did not help the killers who attacked the farm, and I did not witness any crime."

"You talked to the Braves about the damaged car and showed up at the Nassire farm snooping around their barn. The Nassire family have information that you are working with a fed who wants to do them harm."

"How would they know that?" He was interested now.

"They have a spy who tells them everything." Ken still speaks to the fire.

"Brenda Benton?" Midge couldn't believe his ears.

"Yes, she has worked as an informant for John Nassire within the tribe for almost a year now." Ken turned and looked at Midge.

"So you are telling me, she is not in any danger from the Nassire family? I am keeping her in my house while she is stealing information from and about me?" What a chump he was he thought. Give a man a little sex and he loses all logic.

"She may be in danger from Kia, but not John and his father, but yes she works with John Nassire and is having sex with you also. Your house is being monitored." Monitored but how? They must have planted bugs in his house since Brenda came, or she planted them he thought.

"Those hot damn camel humping slimy turtle shits. And whatever other names that offend them I can think of. Monitoring my bedroom activities?" He was just flat out pissed now.

"They are quite professional about it. They probably had Brenda feeding them information after she began staying with you, Midge. How else are they getting such information about you?" Ken was now looking at him with his eyebrows raised as if waiting for confirmation, but he new it was true. It actually answered a lot of questions about the last few days.

"So what are they going to do, try to kill me?" He would put nothing past these guys now.

"They are more controlling and subtle than that. We have learned they are going to make you an offer to work for them and not against them." In a pigs eye they would, he thought.

"I don't want to work for them or anyone else."

"They will not let that get in their way. Are you working with the feds against them?"

Ken looked directly at him.
Midge was cautious now. Was Ken Telway working for the Nassires or Kia or was he really against them? And why had they decided to tell him all these things unless they wanted him to help them somehow? "Let's cut to the chase here men, what is it you want from me?"

"We want you to get rid of Kia Ashad and his four thugs and become our new chief of security for the Tribal casinos." So that was the game.

"Why don't you do it yourself? You don't need me to provide or supervise security for your casinos." Midge now watched all three men. The two old ones eyes never left the fire.

"We want you to free our people from these men. You were a po-

141

lice homicide detective and a Detroit street cop. You would know how these things are done. We do need protection from the mob and you have better contacts than we have. You are an honest man and would be fair with our people." The old medicine man spoke slowly and clearly. If they knew about the fed, did they know about the Iranian hit squad that was in transit and the Israeli also? No he decided, they did not know.

"I will not kill Kia and his thugs for you. I was a policeman, not a mob hit man. I suggest you get your tribe together and throw them off your council and out of the casinos if it is so important to you. They don't have enough men to take out your whole Tribal Police force."

"We did not say kill them, we said get rid of them. How you do it is up to you. We need your help, Midge. You will be well rewarded for your work."

What other way was there, Midge thought? Kill, buy out, threaten, persuade, what the hell did he mean persuade? "Let me sleep on it for a day or two, I'll get back with you, Ken." It was time to get out of here. Why did he even agree to come here? Of course, he did confirm his suspicions about Brenda, but the Kia thing was news to him. He had let his sense of adventure get him in trouble again. That had caused him a lot of problems in his life. "Is Neka going to take me back to my van?"

"Yes, he will help you get back, but do not speak of this meeting with him. He knows we are talking, but not what about. I will call you on Sunday, Midge. I hope we can work together." Ken reached out and shook his hand. The two old men did not take their eyes from the fire which was just deep red coals now. They said nothing as Midge bent over and passed his hand slowly in front of the medicine man's face.

"Blind?" He whispered to Ken. Ken just nodded slowly.

Chapter 13

Midge returned to his van and took Neka back to the Hill Top Bar where he got out and disappeared into the night. Midge walked around his van, but did not see anything that struck him as out of place. He unlocked the van and slid into the driver's seat. The console in the rear had its small green light shining on the monitor indicating it was on. He would just leave it on for the night.

Midge started the engine and pulled out his cell phone. He dialed his house but after six rings was transferred to his answering machine. He hung up. Must be in bed asleep, he guessed. He would swing by the fed's hotel on his way home and check on the plan before he went to the farm tomorrow.

He drove back to the ferry crossing and waited to return to the mainland. He drove onto the ferry, crossed the water and pulled back on to Portage Avenue. As he pulled out onto the road, he did not notice an SUV pull out a couple of minutes later. It was only a few minutes to the motel on the water. He was tired, but not so much he would skip meeting with the fed. He was not sure if or how much he would tell him about the meeting on Sugar Island. He hoped the fed was not asleep and the IAA guy was not around.

He reached the door on the second floor and knocked.

"Who is it?" a voice from inside said.

"Midge Gregory, I want to talk to you."

He watched as the glow of light disappeared from the peep hole. Then the door slowly opened about three inches and stopped as a face appeared in the slot.

He had his foot flat on the floor against the door as a door stop thought Midge, and his pistol was in his right hand, ready to act, if something did not go right. "Kinda late isn't it, Midge?"

"Yeah, well let me in, I don't like talking through a door crack from the outside."

Jim was in a bathrobe with his pistol in his right hand. What kind of a guy wears a bathrobe on the road? How many suitcases did a fed travel with? Detroit cops only took one carry-on. Shaving kit, socks, underwear, and a couple extra shirts, that was it, because who cared what they looked like, the criminals? A bathrobe? He wondered if it was monogrammed. He grabbed a chair while Jim locked the door; a careful sort of guy.

"I'm going to the farm tomorrow, well I guess today, you could say. What is the plan?"

Jim poured himself a glass of ice water. He never offered Midge anything. "What did you go to Sugar Island for tonight?"

So the man had eyes out and about. "Fishing, just fishing."

"In the dark, without lights?" Jim just looked at him as he took a sip of his ice water.

"We were using a net, the smelt were running." Midge didn't know a smelt from a whale, but he went with some buddies one time when he was a kid. They got drunk and his buddy heard someone yelling the smelt were running, grabbed a net and raced into the water with all his clothes on. They did not catch anything that night but a cold.

"Smelt running in the main channel of the St. Mary's?"

"Well, we didn't catch anything anyway. Why were you spying on me?" That should end this conversation.

"I wasn't spying on you, but they were." He pointed to a scanner on his night stand.

"FBI?" Midge said as he looked at the scanner.

"Yep, and they have followed you here." Midge went to the window and parted the curtains. He could see a black SUV across the road in the restaurant parking lot.

"They aren't with you?"

"No, I am on my own, a black ops as they say."

"Why are they following me? I have not done anything to get the FBI on my case."

"The Nassire family has, and I don't mean murdering those braves. No one cares about the dead braves in the FBI."

"What would give the FBI jurisdiction over Tribal affairs?"

"Money and tons of it. The DEA is looking for drugs, but the FBI has been following the money. That is about the only thing they are good at and they want those funds."

"What funds? I thought all this was about the Camels Eye and hostages in Iran."

"For me it is. I am on a special mission for the President of the United States to get the hostages home safely. I do not care about drugs, money, prostitutes, hijacking, or any other crimes these Nassire men may be involved in. I just want the jewel so I can get the hostages home safely. Period."

"Then what is the problem? Call the FBI and ATF off and let's see if we can get the necklace."

"I am working a black ops, but they are not. I found out from my control in Washington, that the FBI has been working this case for over a year. They could find no drugs or weapons so the ATF is out of the picture. They are just hanging around hoping something turns up. The big issue is money, millions upon millions of it. You see I found out these little Sault and Bay Mills casinos take in more cash than the big Las Vegas casinos some weeks."

"These little operations? No way man. I know of some speakeasies in Detroit that probably gross as much business. I don't believe it."

"Neither does the FBI. What it does believe, what it knows, is the Indian Casinos in the Sault area are laundering money for the mob in Chicago, Detroit, and Cleveland. They are banking it as player dollars and paying no tax on it, since it is Tribal land, not U.S. soil. They put it in their bank and then ship it offshore to a number of banks where the money can be used legally. They do pay the State of Michigan about one percent of the gross to help the schools, but they don't have to. They are just trying to be good corporate citizens, I guess. These guys have the best money shop going. That's why the FBI is on the case. I just happened to stumble into their investigation."

"So tell them to get out of the way until you are done."
"I would have to bring the White House in on it, and that may jeopardize the hostages' lives if the FBI leaks it."

"Then what do we do?" Midge was really getting confused now.

Too many players to keep track of and this thing was spinning out of control.

"I'm thinking on it, Midge." He was kind of staring out into space.

"Jim, let me lay out some facts for you. The Iranians are in Canada on the way to take out the Nassire family and reclaim the Camels Eye. The FBI is getting ready to crash in on the Nassire farm and the casinos, but they aren't sure how to proceed yet. The Israeli is after the Soul of Jerusalem and the Chippewa are ready to throw the Nassire men out of the game. I'm going to be at the farm in less than twelve hours and you are '*thinking*'?"

"Look, I need the Camels Eye, and that is all my mission here encompasses. I don't give a shit about the FBI, mob money, tribal control, or anything else. Now shut up and let me think." He placed his head on his clasped hands under his chin.

"Fine, you can think all you want. I'm outta here, asshole. I am not going to the farm tomorrow or any other time. It's all 'urine', as they say on the farm." Midge got up and headed for the door.

"Wait. Okay, I'm sorry, but this thing has gotten way out of control. I don't really have a plan, at least not a workable plan. It has to be tomorrow. The only way I can hold off that Mullah and his team is to give them the necklace or kill them. If I kill them, the hostages are dead. The FBI won't move until next week. They don't work on Saturday and Sunday because they can't call for the press to cover them on the six o'clock news. Too many cooks are working on the soup and who knows what that Israeli has up his sleeve."

Midge sat back in his chair and looked at Jim. He really was in a heck of a jam. "Look, we need to work on one item at a time. The Nassire's have the Camels Eye and that is what we must have to save the hostages. Is that right?"

"Right." Jim nodded his head.

"Then let's work out a plan to get the jewel and forget all the rest of the nonsense for now. Okay?"

"Okay."

"We don't know where the necklace is at, so the only people who can put their hands on the Camels Eye are probably the Nassire men. Now what could we offer them in exchange for the jewel?"

"Money?"

"If only half of what the FBI and the Tribal elders believe is true,

The Camels Eye

these men already have more money than they can ever use in ten lifetimes. No, money is not a motivator for these men. Freedom and security is what these men need. They have an Islamic government that would like to kill them and an Indian tribe that wants them out of their business and life. They have a mob that won't take kindly to them saying they can't launder money for them anymore. So no Jim, they will not give us the Camels Eye for money."

"Then what can we offer them?"

"Let's talk about the value of the Camels Eye to them. They can't sell it because it is too well known. They could bust the jewels out of the necklace and fence them all separately. That would make a fortune to most people, but they won't."

"Why do you say they won't, Midge?"

"Because Jay Nassire is a lover of art and in his own way a patriot, be it to a fallen Monarch and his people, but a patriot in his own mind. When the Shah fell, Jay had only two choices. Return to Iran and be executed by the Ayatollahs like his father was, or take what treasures and money he could and flee to where the Islamic Guards would have a hard time chasing him. He had to get to the United States, because Europe was too friendly with the new regime and he would be an easy target there. What Jay Nassire wants the most in the whole wide world is protection for his family and U.S. citizenship for himself, his son and grandson."

"They are already citizens."

"But they obtained their citizenship under false pretences. We could revoke the citizenship papers due to fraud and deport them to their country of origin under the law."

"That would be Iran and you know they would be executed. No immigration law judge in this country would sign such an order."

"The President could sign such an executive order to be carried out immediately due to national security reasons. The courts would be powerless to act in time to prevent their deportation. It would be too late for the Nassire family by the time the court system got involved."

"If the President would sign such an order, that is."

"If he didn't, he would be signing the death warrant of every American hostage in Iran."

"He would sign it, but would they give up the jewelry for such a threat?"

"Not entirely I suspect, but it would make them stop and think about it. We of course would guarantee their safety and freedom from prosecution for any crime committed to this point, even the money laundering charges."

"But, what about the FBI?"

"The FBI doesn't prosecute cases, the Attorney General does that, and who does he work for?"

"The President of the United States." Jim was getting into it now.

"Right, so that is easy, but what do we do about the mob? Those guys don't like people who quit working for them, especially if they are making them tons of clean money," Jim continued on.

"Yeah, so we have to get the mobs attention on something else. Like maybe we raid all their drug, prostitution, and extortion shops at one time. We arrest all the Dons and Capos and make it rough on their runners for a day or two." Midge was starting to like the plan now.

"But, how would we find them, Midge?"

"You dumb fed. The local cops know all the mob operations. They just can't use the evidence in court because of the way they have to operate in our legal system. All of those ACLU bullshit rules are made to keep the mob and crooks powerful. The mob is one of the largest contributors to those commie fags at the ACLU and people don't even know it. Don't get me wrong, they will all get off in a couple of days. But we hit the cities that are laundering their money through these casinos, and they won't have any money to wash for a few days."

"I don't know if the Attorney General will sign off."

"What he will sign off Jim, is the lives of the American hostages in Iran if he refuses to act. Finally, we put the Nassires in a federal protection program if we have to and relocate them to wherever they want to live. If we can offer them all these things, they may give us the Camels Eye and save the hostages."

"It will take time to get approval for all this."

"There is no time. You make your call to your so called 'control' and tell him or her I have promised them all these things. They have to act immediately. If they say no, then you can kiss the hostages goodbye."

"What are you going to do tomorrow, or should I say today?"

"Pretty much promise them what we just said, but I may have to improvise a little as I don't really know all the facts yet. I will tell them about the Iranian hit team, the FBI, the Chippewa, and the mob crackdown if I need to. I will try to show them we are their only hope for survival. Just wish me good luck, I am going to need it." Midge got up and started for the door.

"Good luck Midge, I will have my cell phone on if you need me. I hope this works, for the hostages' sake."

"So do I Jim, so do I."

When Midge arrived at the house, he was not quite sure what he would find. He opened the door and turned off the alarm. Everything looked in order, but he put his hand inside his jacket anyway. The feel of his old police revolver always made him feel a little more secure. He walked through the living room noticing that his office and bedroom doors were shut. He passed them and went into Ryan's bedroom, whose door was open. He found the boy asleep in his bed with his clown nightlight on. He went back to his bedroom and opened the door. He pushed it slowly until he could see his entire bed. There was Brenda with her head sticking out of the covers, fast asleep. Now that surprised him, as he did not expect her to be there.

He went into his office next and checked out his computer. It was still off. He felt the monitor and it was cold. For some reason he did not expect that either. What was going on? Well, he would grab some sleep and worry about it in the morning. He would sleep with his revolver tonight just to be on the safe side.

It was ten o'clock when the noise from the Saturday morning cartoons woke him up. He slept longer than he thought he would. Ryan was sitting on the floor watching some superheroes action. He could smell coffee and thought he could hear Brenda stirring in the kitchen. He put his arms above his head and stretched and groaned for all he was worth.

"Good morning, Uncle Midge." Ryan said to him without turning his gaze from the television.

"Well, look who is awake. How about some breakfast, sleepyhead?" She had her head in the kitchen doorway smiling at him.

"No thanks, Ryan and I are having lunch at the farm today. How about I shower and shave and then we have some coffee?" He rose and headed for the bathroom.

"Fine with me, I just made a fresh pot." She went back into the kitchen.

After Midge was cleaned up, he poured a mug of coffee and sat down at the kitchen table. He looked at Brenda in a different way now, like she was a suspect he was trying to get a warrant to arrest.

"I tried to wait up for you last night, but I gave up and went to bed. I didn't hear you come in." She sounded so normal it made him wonder if he was wrong.

"You and Ryan were out cold." He could sound natural too, he decided.

"Did you get it?" She looked directly into his eyes.

Midge looked up from his cup which he was holding with two hands. "Get what?"

"The car or guy you were looking for?" She held his gaze.

"Oh no, no he didn't show." He was blowing his own cover story.

"Too bad, you don't get paid if you don't find him, right?" She was on to him for sure he thought, but did she know where he really went last night?

"Yeah, that's the way it works. But I'll find him, I always do." He had to dig his way out of this hole.

"What time is lunch today?"

"They said to be there at noon."

"What vehicle are you driving today?" Why was she asking him that?

He was suspicious now. "The van I guess, why do you ask?"

"Would you mind if I borrow the pick-up truck this afternoon?"

"Need to go see your sister again?" He watched for her reaction.

"No, I want to get my hair done and do a little girl shopping, if you don't mind." A little girl shopping spree, sure she did.

"No problem, it should still have plenty of gas in it. But here is some money in case you need it." Midge gave her a hundred dollars.

"I have money Midge, here take this back." She pushed the money across the table to him.

"No, I insist. My treat for all you have been doing for Ryan." He pushed it back to her.

She smiled and picked it up. "If you insist, I'll buy something nice and sexy with it." She batted her eyes at him. Like a serpent lulling its next victim to sleep, he sensed.

"Sounds good. Let me get Ryan around to go. What do you think

I should take as a gift for lunch?"

"Well, if there was a woman, I would say flowers or wine. But being Muslims, I don't think that would be a good choice. How about a dessert of some kind? That is always a safe bet."

"Good idea. I'll swing by Marge's bakery and get a fancy cake. Thanks for the idea." He got up and told Ryan to get dressed and ready to go.

He handed Brenda the keys to the pick up and house as he was leaving. He hoped he would find his stuff still all there when he got home tonight.

Ryan picked out a German black forest cake with those cherries on top. They pulled out of Sault Ste. Marie headed west on Nine Mile Road. Midge had put his police revolver under the driver's seat in a special compartment. It had a door hinged on the bottom with a secure latch on the top. He did not lock it, as he may have to get at it in a hurry.

Ryan was excited to spend time with Jacob on the farm again. He loved climbing around the hay in the barn and playing with the goats and camels. He liked animals and missed living on acreage with his parents. Uncle Midge was good to him, but he missed his mother who had been his anchor in life.

It was a bright sunny day. A perfect day for a picnic, if that is what they were going to have. Ryan had brought his soccer ball and his BB gun in hopes he and Jacob would get to play.

They pulled into the driveway and up toward the barn. Midge was scanning the area. He thought he saw some kind of a reflection in the cupola closest to the driveway, but he could not see anyone up there. Perhaps it was a piece of window glass or something. He wondered if he should drive up to the house or not, when Kia stepped out of the barn and put his hand out for Midge to stop. He stopped and put the passenger window down.

"Park right here, beside the corral, Mr. Gregory." Midge pulled over near the posts. He could see three large camels in the enclosure. He did not see Jay or John Nassire anywhere in sight.

"Is this okay right here, Kia?" he asked as he exited the van.

"That is fine. The lunch will be held on the patio behind the main house." Sounded like a state dinner or something, Midge thought as he told Ryan to hand him the cake.

It was almost another four hundred feet to the main house on the hill. Luckily Kia pulled a golf cart with a surrey top on it out of the barn. "This will be much easier men," Kia said looking at Ryan and Midge. They jumped on with Ryan in the front seat next to Kia. Midge sat backwards watching where they had come from. He had an uneasy feeling that he was being watched. He pulled his key FOB out and locked his van. He watched the lights blink as the security system engaged. You couldn't be too careful in these bad neighborhoods, he chuckled.

As they crested the hill, passed the pine trees, and turned toward the house, Midge got a look at the private airfield on the west side of the property. Nice hanger, fuel pumps, wind sock, a big transmitter antenna, three small overhead doors like in an auto garage, two giant wide and tall doors, and a long wide runway that ran northeast to southwest. A White aircraft with a green, red, and black tail with dual engine props sat next to the hanger. Strange, they didn't make the runway perpendicular to the road, he thought. Then he wondered if the wind direction was important to taking off and landing. Maybe so, he was no pilot.

The place had pine trees on the slope, like many of the hills in this area south of the big great lake. At one time this land was cleared and homesteaded by farmers betting their lives against the government promise that they could make a go of the farm against all odds and receive the deed to one hundred and sixty acres. The soil was sandy and fragile and the growing season short and cold. It was a bad bet this far north, but people came and tried anyway. The American dream to own your own land, no matter how poor the land was Midge thought, was a powerful pull. Who knows how this piece ended up as tribal land? Of course, the whole state had been tribal land originally he reasoned.

As they pulled up behind the house, Jacob came running out the back door.

"Ryan, Ryan you're here. Come on, let's play." Ryan jumped off the cart just before it stopped. He ran up to Jacob and grabbed him as they started jumping up and down on the patio. Midge stepped off the cart holding the cake and turned to see John Nassire coming out of the house holding a few skewers of meat and vegetables that looked something like kebobs the Greek restaurants made.

"Hello Midge. I hope you and Ryan are hungry. It will take a few minutes to barbeque the lamb kebobs, but everything else is prepared. Come join me for some fresh squeezed lemonade. Father will be out in a little while." Kia nodded at John and went into the house. What was that nod all about, Midge wondered?

The patio was beautiful. The ground was covered with paving stones of a light reddish brown color. They were laid in sweeping patterns and shapes as if an artist had drawn them in free form. There were six trees in raised white block structures that Midge thought looked like maples, but they were too small. Maybe they were those Japanese dwarf trees he thought. His ex-wife would have known. They had beautiful flower beds on the patio with bright red, yellow, blue, and purple tulips. Someone knew what he was doing with these flowers. Midge couldn't grow weeds, but his ex-wife could. He always said she was so dumb she couldn't pour piss out of a boot if you put the instructions on the heel. But she knew how to grow things he had to give her that. They had a nice big wrought iron table with a thick glass top, large comfortable chairs with bright blue pattern cushions and a big matching umbrella to sit under. The barbeque was a big stainless steel unit with six burners, a top with gauges in it, and a big rotisserie unit. John had mounted the lamb on long stainless steel skewers like for a Greek Shish Kabob. It was a beauty all right. That baby would put his little two burner Char Broil propane grille he bought at Wal Mart to shame.

Midge was drinking his lemonade when the door opened and Jay came out with a large dish of something that looked like some kind of salad. There were already some dishes on the long glass topped table. John had taken the Black Forest cake and set it in the center of the table. Another man, who was dark like Kia, but younger, placed two more dishes on the long table.

"Hello Midge, we are so glad you came to lunch with Ryan today. I hope you do not mind we are having a traditional Persian meal today." Jay stayed busy arranging all the dishes. He took a large platter over to the grill where John was still busy grilling those long kebobs of lamb. They were making Midge's mouth water.

"Boys come, it is time to eat. You may play with camels after we have finished lunch." John was smiling as he yelled to them. Midge wondered if Kia was going to join them, but he seemed to be staying in the house. He kept looking out the door to see if they needed anything, he guessed. Where did one find such dedicated servants? It must be a Persian thing.

The boys joined them at the table, but did not bother to wash their hands. This was a picnic after all. "Let me introduce you to the foods we have prepared for our honored guests today," John commented. He placed a large platter of kebobs on the table. Midge was really hungry now.

"I will use the Persian or Iranian name and tell you what it is in English. First, in this bowl we have Assh-e Gandom known as soup to you. It contains wheat, spinach, peas, beans, and lentils. It is my father's specialty." Jay smiled and nodded his head toward Midge. "For our main dish we have Kabab Barg or barbequed lamb kebobs. Very tasty, you will like them. For our bread we have prepared Naan-o-Pancer-o-Sabzi, which is flat bread with feta cheese and herbs. Salad-e Shirazi is our salad made with cucumbers, tomatoes, onion, and fresh mint. Our side dishes are Maast-o-Khiar made with yogurt, Kookoo-yeh-Loobia Sabz which you may call a type of bean salad, and Pooreh-yeh-Seeb-Zamini or mashed potato." Midge thought all the dishes looked great, but felt even better about eating them now that John was explaining them.

"Now for dessert, we have two fine dishes today. First we have Jacob's favorite, Baamieh, which is a deep fried flat cake like a donut, soaked in homemade syrup. And finally a beautiful cake called a ………"

"Black Forest cake. It is German, and I picked it out myself from Marge's bakery." Ryan was beaming.

"Thank you for that, Ryan. Now gentlemen, may I propose a toast to good friends and good food? Here, here." They all raised their glasses and Ryan and Jacob almost broke theirs knocking them together.

They all passed their plates to John and he filled them with a little of everything. All the different tastes were great thought Midge, but the mint in everything seemed a little foreign to him, which is exactly what it was. The lamb was outstanding and he complimented John on it. He kept noticing Kia checking on them through the open doorway. No one asked him for anything and he never came out of the house.

"How many camels do you have here and are they one or two

humps?" Jay chuckled and shook his head at Midge's question.

"I raise racing camels. They are all dromedary, or one hump as you call them. My father, and his before him, raised the finest racing camels in the Middle East, or dare I say the world." You could tell Jay was very proud of them.

"Can they out run a race horse?"

"That depends on what you mean by outrun, Midge."

"I mean in like the Kentucky Derby or the Michigan Mile."

"Then the answer is no. But if you mean in the desert, then the answer would be yes. If you mean running in the desert for over a week, then the answer is yes. A camel is an amazing creature, built to withstand the elements of his environment. Races designed to test his endurance and speed are huge in our part of the world." He sure knows how to defend his camels, Midge thought.

"An old joke in this country is a camel is just a horse built by committee." No one laughed at the joke. "I guess it works better as a business joke. How fast do they run?"

"They run up to about twelve miles per hour, but can run for hours at that pace. Your race horses can hit speeds of up to sixty miles per hour in short spurts, but don't run much over two miles, do they?" Jay had him on that one. Some of the horses he had bet on in his life could not even run two miles, at least not nearly as fast as the rest of the horses in the race.

"The ones I bet on only run half as fast and never finish." No one got that joke either, not even the boys. He was wasting some of his best material on these guys. There must be a language barrier here.

"A camel weighs up to three quarters of a ton and stands over seven feet at the hump. They can carry up to a half ton of weight, but for long trips we like to load no more than three hundred pounds. Their feet are flat and broad with two toes on each foot. They have leathery pads on the bottom to protect them from sharp objects. They have three stomachs and can carry enough food and drink to last a month or more. Try that with your horses. Most people think camels are not predictable, bad tempered, and spit and kick you all the time. Actually a camel is good tempered, patient, and highly intelligent. They are easy to train and very loyal if you know how to treat them."

"I never saw a camel race."

"That is because you have never lived in Iran or one of the Arab countries."

"No I haven't, Jay."

"Please, let us finish our lunch. Then we will take the children to the barn and I will show you my beautiful animals." All but one Midge thought. That sucker is buried around here somewhere and without a head.

"That is an awful long runway even for your plane, isn't it John."

"Yes it is long, but I built it to handle customer planes that land and want to visit the casinos." This was a subject John liked to discuss.

"They use this landing strip instead of Chippewa County International Airport?" Midge was impressed now.

"Yes, if the weather is good. We have a lighted runway, but no radar or control tower."

"What kind of a plane is that parked by the hanger?" Midge knew nothing about airplanes, boats, racing camels, or much of anything, except cars and motorcycles, he guessed.

"It is a 1980 Cessna 340A. It seats six and can maintain an air speed of over two hundred fifty. It is a nice plane to fly." He seemed to love talking about flying.

"Are you licensed to fly?"

"Yes, but only multi-engine and instrument, not jets." That was pretty good Midge thought, he could not fly any plane at all. He took lessons once at Willow Run, but quit after two lessons. The little Cessna 150 was so slow he figured if he wanted to really go very far, it would be better to rent a seat on a commercial aircraft and let them worry about the flying.

"Do you haul in customers for the casinos with you plane?" He was interested in his answer now.

"No, but I use the aircraft to go to meetings. Sometime I take Jacob or some council members with me. It saves a lot of time over commercial airports, especially with the limited flights available up here at Chippewa International." Limited was the right word. Chippewa County International had only four flights a day. Two in-bound and two out-bound to anywhere you want to go, as long as you want to go to Alpena or Detroit.

"So, do customer's aircraft land here?"

"Yes." John did not seem like he was trying to be evasive on anything.

"How do they get to the casinos from here, call a cab?" Midge really was wondering about this.

"No, we shuttle them back and forth in one of our Expeditions. We have three dark red ones. You see those garage doors in the hanger building? We store them in there."

"Like the one Kia takes Jacob to school in most of the time?" Midge was very curious now.

"Yes, just like that. They are all identical." So they are all bulletproof then Midge thought. Why do you need bulletproof limos in Brimley, Michigan? Maybe the mob guys require it. Now that was interesting. Good to know if you needed to attack one of those trucks.

"Man these little donuts are great, but sticky." Midge was licking the sticky syrup off his first two fingers.

"Baamieh, it is a traditional Persian treat. We do not eat a lot of heavy desserts in my country. It is too hot for heavy cakes and pies, as the Americans are so fond of. Of course, having been a policeman, you are probably an expert on donuts." John was smiling now.

"Now that is a funny joke, John. Cops and donuts, that is funny." Midge smiled and nodded up and down. It really was funny when even a foreigner knew cop jokes.

"I'm sorry if it is offensive to you." John looked serious now.

"No, I really mean it. That is funny. Cops and donuts go together in this country. I was just surprised to here anything funny coming from such a serious guy is all."

"Actually Persian people love to laugh, but our sense of humor is quite different from Americans. Well, shall we go visit the camels?" John and Jay rose and started for the barn.

"Yeah, let's go," and the boys started for the barn on a dead run.

"Would you mind showing me your airplane later, John? I don't know much about them, but I think they are cool." Midge watched John's expression change and glance at his father, then at the house.

"Certainly Midge, if we have time." Kia came out of the house as they started toward the barn. It looked like he had a two way radio in his right hand and he was speaking into it. These guys were security conscious beyond belief. They must think an invasion is coming or something. They just might be right, Midge thought.

John checked over his shoulder and then smiled and said to Midge quietly, "We need your help Midge, our lives are in danger. Do not respond, just smile and keep walking. I will pretend to show you our camels and our goats, so just listen please." They kept walking toward the barn with Kia trailing them by about fifty feet.

What the hell did he just say? Their lives are in danger? From what or who? These guys have security coming out their ass. It would take a major strike force or swat team to hit these guys.

John smiled and pointed toward the corral while he said in a low voice, "you must have Ryan ask for Jacob to spend the night. Make up your all-nighter story if you can, but Jacob must spend the night at your house." He turned and kept walking while still pointing toward the barn and animals, smiling as natural as hell.

Midge's mind was racing. What the hell is going on? His mind was having trouble computing the information he had just received. Here was a rich man with security guards all around, and he needed his help. Why?

They came to the fence of the corral and Jay pulled some kind of grain out of his pocket. It looked like oats or something, but the camels loved it. Jay nuzzled one of the camels and stroked its head. These things were loving and gentle. Midge thought he saw movement in the right hand cupola, the one he had seen a light reflection in as he had driven up the driveway. Kia had stopped about fifty feet away, supposedly surveying the field and driveway.

The boys had climbed over the rails and were chasing a baby goat. Those goats were the cutest things in the world, but he had a friend who owned three of them, and they destroyed everything in sight. They tore the siding off his house, chewed the shingles off his roof, ate the tops off all his fruit trees, and dented the roof and hood on his car and truck by jumping off the roof of his house onto the vehicles. He had gotten them as a 4-H project for his three boys, but they had become so destructive he had to get rid of them. He traded them for two horses, which Midge said were even more care. He said he would trade those goats for two elephants if he had to, and he would be ahead on the deal. He hoped Ryan would never ask for a goat.

In a low voice, John said, "Pet the camels Midge, and then we can go to the airplane. It is important no one hears what I am saying to you. We will leave my father here and force them to split up." Jay did not acknowledge the conversation. Midge knew he had heard John since he was standing right next to them. Jay just kept on loving his camels. The boys finally caught up with the baby goat and were holding him.

"Just say out loud so Kia can hear you, that you would like to go out and see the airplane." John talked without looking at Midge, but instead at the boys playing with the baby goat. What was going on here? This was like being in undercover work again.

"John, would you mind showing me your airplane? Those things really fascinate me," Midge said in a booming voice.

John turned toward the air strip, raised his hand pointing toward the aircraft and responded in a loud voice, "It would be my honor to show my airplane. After you, sir," and Midge started walking across the field and through the pines toward the hanger. He noticed Kia had put the two-way to his lips and began speaking into it. The man seemed to hesitate and then decided to stay and protect or maybe watch the father Jay, it seemed.

They were alone now and John seemed in no hurry to get to the airplane. He stopped and swept his hands around in the air, as if he was explaining something about the farm to Midge. He kept smiling as if he was having a great time explaining things, but all the time talking, even when he was not looking at him. "Midge, please do not talk, just listen. I know about the raid coming on the farm either tonight or tomorrow. I must get Jacob out of here. My father and I are being held prisoner by Kia Ashad and his killers. You must help us, for the boy's sake."

What was going on? Everything is upside down. He is supposed to be asking John to help him. He is the head of this crooked enterprise and he is asking me to help him, claiming he is a prisoner, after witnesses saw him at the beheading of the braves. This did not make sense.

"We don't have much time. Tell the FBI that Kia Ashad is not a U.S. citizen and neither are the killers he employs here. They are all Iranian or Iraqi and all are wanted as terrorists by Interpol and your CIA. I am not afraid for myself and my father, but my son must be safe. Take him to your house and have him put in protective custody until this thing is settled. I am willing to turn states evidence if we can be placed in the federal protection program and relocated to somewhere safe from these killers and the mob, if necessary." He was still smiling, moving his hands around as they entered the trees.

And I was going to offer this guy a deal? Man, is this thing screwed up.

They cleared the pine trees and came out on the other side of the hill. As they approached the hanger, a tall thin black haired man with a goatee came out and lit a cigarette. He watched them with a neutral expression on his face, as John nodded and walked to the aircraft.

In a low voice, with his lips barely moving, he spoke, "Just smile and listen. That is Ali. He is the one who tortured the Indians before Kia took their heads off. He came from Saddam's personal guard. If the military come in tonight, tell them not to use the airstrip. It has barriers like in the rental car lots every hundred feet. Kia also has shoulder mounted rockets to bring down aircraft. It would be suicide for your troops to attack the farm." John opened an engine cover and pretended to show Midge how it worked.

"But you and your father were with the SAVAK! You were part of these killers!"

"No, that was my grandfather. He was as ruthless as they say he was. My father worked in the Antiquities department and I was at the U of M in Ann Arbor for most of those horrible years. Kia was the SAVAK colonel who was assigned to guard my father and the crown treasures. Now it is he who is in control of my family." He climbed on the wing and held his hand out for Midge to join him.

"But you are the banker and the money man for the casinos and the mob."

"On paper yes, but Kia gives us the instructions." He opened the door and climbed into the cabin. It was a six passenger with the four rear seats facing each other, two in the front and two in the back.

"Where is the Camels Eye? My government must have it to save the hostages lives in Iran."

"I will turn it over to you when my family is safely away from these killers."

"I need to talk to my contact. It will have to be soon. There is an Iranian Mullah on his way to torture or kill you to get the necklace."

"Kia knows about it and he is ready. He still has contacts in Iran. But he does not know where the Camels Eye is hidden. Only I know that answer, not my father or my son, only me, and of course, my poor dead wife."

Poor dead wife? Did he even have a wife? If he did, Midge had never seen her. Of course, if she was dead how would he have seen her?

The man he called Ali, was walking over near the aircraft now. Circling it like a wounded lion ready to pounce.

"We better go back now. Take this and do not let anyone see it." He shoved the folded paper into Midge's pocket just as they heard a noise on the wing. Ali was coming to check on them.

John opened the door as Ali was almost to it. "Midge this is Ali. He works as a limo driver for our casino customers." He held the door open for Midge to exit the airplane. Ali had already turned and left the wing without acknowledging Midge's presence. Midge could see the steel grates running across the runway every two hundred feet or so. With one push of a button the big claws would come up out of the grate and puncture any landing tires that rolled over it. Just like those rental car companies used to keep people from driving out with their cars. Those would be lethal to any aircraft trying to land without permission. Midge wondered where the Delta Team and Seals were standing by. Surely they would need to know this information John had just given him if he could get it to them.

They walked back to the barn. John assured him he had all the knowledge about the money laundering and he did have the Camels Eye in his possession. John repeated his plea for help and fast. Kia was talking to Jay as they crested the hill and came through the pines headed for the barn. The boys were on a camel with Jay holding the lead rope guiding them in a big circle outside the corral. They felt like the tallest boys in the world on that camel's back.

"That is some airplane you have there, John. I would love to take a ride in it sometime." He noticed Kia was on alert now.

"Maybe some other time, Midge. Tonight I have to work in the casino in Bay Mills. We are expecting some high roller customers." Was this some kind of a code? Visitors in Bay Mills, but of what kind? The kind with guns and lots of money, he bet.

"Okay, but I'll hold you to that promise for a ride some other time." Kia was watching the exchange, but pretending to watch the children on the camel enjoying themselves immensely.

"Show me the barn, John. This is one of the coolest barns I have ever seen." Without waiting for an answer, he headed straight for the big sliding door near his van. He entered and saw the stalls on each side with tongue in groove pine and bars in the sliding doors for the stalls. He noticed each stall had a water trough in the corner with a float in it for automatic water refills. The stalls were clean with fresh straw on the hard dirt. They reminded him of horse stalls, only taller. About half way down, he noticed a stairway, near the third stall, leading to the roof. Ryan had told him there was a landing and then it split into two stairs, one to the left and one to the right. Midge wondered what would happen if he raced up the stairs to the right. Would he meet one of Kia's killers, and what would he do if he saw Midge? The walls were very thick, too thick for a barn. They were almost thick enough to be a stockade or fort in the old days. Yes, this place would be a swat team nightmare. No cover, secured position, and a well armed target with communications and superior firepower. It would take an armored car or tank to take this place. He doubted that the Delta team or Seals had such equipment with them.

"Do you know much about barns, Midge?" John was just entering the opening of the sliding door with Kia right behind him.

"My friend had a farm, but he built his barns himself and it showed. They were just frames and metal sheeting like most pole barns. His stalls were built out of old pallets stood up on end. Of course, he raised sheep so it was all he needed. Where do those stairs lead?" He was watching Kia squirm now, trying to decide if he had to take control. "Hey, look at the tractor. This is a John Deere. Man I wanted to have one of those so bad, but my ex-wife would never let me get one.

"We use it to clean the stalls and grade the corral. We also use the bucket to clear the runway and drives in the winter." John kept a wary eye on Kia.

"It doesn't have a cab on it, isn't it cold?" Midge's eyes were cataloging everything he saw in the barn for later use.

"The cab is taken off and stored in the hanger after winter." The conversation sounded natural.

"Yep, this is one great looking barn, John. What time do you need to go to Brimley or Bay Mills? Ryan and I will get out of your way whenever you say." Kia pretended to be checking a stall, but Midge knew he heard him.

"Very soon, really. Why don't we go out and see how father and the boys are doing?" John walked past him and exited through the other sliding door on the far end. Midge noticed John patted a storage room door as he went by. It was a thick door with huge hinges on it, and bolts running parallel in two lines across the door like there were reinforcements on the inside. It was mounted in a thick green steel frame. The walls were different too, covered with wood, and bolted every three inches. It was like they weren't bolted to wooden studs at sixteen inch centers, but to steel plates or something. This had to be a weapons and explosives room. He would bet his house it had access to the overhead stairs that ran to both cupolas. Cupolas that were reinforced with armor plating, sandbags, and firing slits. The Delta guys and Seals needed to know this.

They exited the barn into the sunlight, but Kia went the other way around the corral. John was pointing to the ground, and showed him a slight indentation that seemed to run all the way to the airstrip across the fields. "All our power and tunnels are underground to the houses and barns from the hangers, and I do mean *all* the power."

So he was telling him where to take out the power to the facility. He wondered if each building had a separate back-up generator. No, that would be too much overkill even for these guys. The power and its back-up generator were in the hanger building, he thought. It made sense, but why did he emphasize the word *all*? He looked back and noticed that indentation in the earth ran right up to the end of the barn where the armored room was, but why? He would have to think on that a little while.

"Father, we are going to have to go get ready to go to work now. Are you boys having a good time riding a camel?" Kia had rounded the south end of the corral now, and stopped and watched them.

Jay pulled the camel's head close to him, petted his head and then said something to him. The camel bent his legs and lowered himself to the ground so the boys could slide off, laughing as they dismounted. They ran to the camel's head and hugged and petted him. Then Jay had him rise and led him back into the corral. Kia watched as John put his arm around Jacob and started walking toward him.

Midge came up to Ryan and hugged him saying quietly, "ask Jacob to spend the night with us Ryan. We can pull an all-nighter again."

"Can we, can we really Uncle Midge?"

"You bet, if his father would let him." Kia was not watching him now. He was concentrating on John and Jacob.

"Hey Jacob, can you spend the night at my house? We can have another all-nighter. It will be fun. Come on, my Uncle Midge says it is okay with him if it is okay with your father." John stopped and looked at Jacob. He deliberately ignored Kia's glare.

"Do you want to spend the night with Ryan, son?" John knew the answer, but this was for Kia's benefit.

"Oh yes, father, it is so much fun, can I please? You have to work tonight anyway and we have so much fun together." Jacob was bouncing up and down and pulling on his father's arm.

"Well, I guess it is okay with me as long as Mr. Gregory agrees." He looked at Midge as if the answer was going to be a surprise.

"Sure, the boys can pick out the movies and the junk food. They are no trouble really, if it is okay with you. "I can even bring him back home tomorrow morning, if you would like."

"I will pick him up in the morning, Midge. It is the least we can do." Kia was smiling as he took back a little control. "Come Jacob, I will help you pack your pajamas and toothbrush." Jacob and Kia headed for the main house on foot.

"Hey Jacob, can you bring your BB gun too?" Ryan shouted.

"Can I father? Ryan has one too."

"Fine, then you may take your air rifle if you wish. Wait for me. I will help you pack too. Thanks for coming today Ryan and Midge. If you want to pull up by the house, Jacob will be ready shortly." He and Midge shook hands. They did not see Jay because he was in the barn putting the camels in for the night.

Midge went to the van and hit the unlock button. As soon as he got Ryan in and seated, he went to his console computer. He turned on the cameras, shut off the monitor and started the van engine. As he drove slowly to the house, he had the feeling several eyes were watching his van. He turned around near the house and pointed the van nose toward the road. He got out and went around to the sliding door, but he did not open it. He would put Jacob in the front seat, as he did not want to give Kia a very good look into the van.

Jacob came out of the house carrying his designer leather backpack he brought to school everyday and his air rifle. He was followed out the door by John and then Kia.

"Jump in the front Jacob, you can ride shotgun today." He opened the front passenger door and Jacob climbed inside, removing his backpack as he entered and throwing it behind the front seats. Midge closed the door. "What time will you be coming to get him in the morning?"

"About ten o'clock, I think," Kia said looking at John, but not for confirmation Midge could see. More like an order or something even more sinister. Midge could tell Kia did not approve of this overnight stay.

"Well, see you guys in the morning. Thanks again for a great lunch John. Bye." He went around, climbed in and pulled out onto the highway. He noticed a man in the cupola this time as the sun was illuminating the space. He didn't even seem to be hiding now. He had a lot to accomplish tonight, so he had to hurry and get the boys home. He wondered if Brenda would be there when he got home. He also wondered if she was working for Kia or John. He had forgotten to ask John about her. Well, he would know soon enough.

When Midge arrived at the house with the boys, they unloaded the groceries, pizzas, and movies they had picked up. They put their air rifles in Ryan's room. They had more graboids and some giant ant movies to watch this time. Brenda was not home. That did not actually surprise him. He put everything in the kitchen and loaded a movie right away to keep the boys busy while he called Jim Featherston on his cell phone. He had a lot to tell him.

He dialed the phone number Jim had given him. Three rings and he heard, "this is Jim who is this?"

"This is Midge and I need to talk to you ASAP."

"Not on the phone, where are you at right now?"

"I'm home, but I don't want to meet you here. I have a problem because I have the boys with me and Brenda is not home to watch them. I will call you back as soon as I can find someone to take care of the boys. Bye." He disconnected and started to think who he could get to stay with the boys that he could trust. His neighbors, Elmer and Joni, they were dependable people. Maybe he could get Joni to sit with the kids while he ran out to meet with Jim for a few minutes.

He looked out the window above the kitchen sink and could see both of his neighbors vehicles were home. He would just go over and see if he could talk Joni into helping him out. The boys were deep in thought with the giant ant colony on the screen. As he went outside to visit his neighbor, his pick-up truck pulled into the driveway. Brenda was driving and she was alone. As she got out of the truck, she smiled,

165

"Where are you going, Midge?"

"Over to see if Joni could watch the boys while I run an errand." Instead of a pretty girl, he now pictured a shifty game playing female. It is funny how your mind works.

"What do you mean, the boys?" This seemed to be news to her, so her sources were not that up to date.

"Jacob Nassire is staying over night again." She looked concerned now, Midge wondered why. Maybe this was going to get in her way somehow, but he had no idea why.

"Jacob is here, but why?" Her brow was furrowed. This was not part of her plan, he guessed.

"They are watching movies and eating junk food. Why do they need a reason? I am going to see if Joni will watch them." He turned and started for his neighbor's house.

She looked at him silently now. She was judging his mood or his motives maybe, but she was judging him, that was for sure. "I can watch the boys now that I'm home. I don't have any other plans tonight."

Could he trust her? Who was she working for, John or Kia? He would just flat out ask her. He had no time for any more games. If she would not answer his question, or said it was Kia, he would throw her out right away. He must get an answer now and keep the boys safe. "Who are you working for Brenda, John or Kia?"

She put her hands on to her lips, "Kia, that slime, I wouldn't spit on that man's grave. I am trying to help John and my people get rid of that trash and his band of killers. He is trying to kill me. Do you know that, Midge? How can you be so stupid?" She sounded convincing to him. If she was acting, she should get an Oscar for her performance.

"Have you planted microphones or tracking devices in my vehicles? And if you haven't, then how do the Tribal Police know you and I have been having sex?"

"Because I told one of my friends, that's how, but not in those exact words. I told them I am falling in love with you, I have been staying with you and we have slept together, you big jerk." She started crying now, but that was no gauge. Women could cry on command to get their way. They have been trained by their mothers since they were babies to use it to get things. But somehow he bought her story, maybe because he wanted to believe her, but more like the way she said it. It was positive like, all the way."

"Okay, I'm sorry, but you have to admit it looked strange."

"I'm sorry. I wanted to tell you, but I thought you were trying to get John in trouble some way and he is the wrong guy to be after. John is a good and decent man who helps my people. He is as much a victim in this mess as anyone."

"I know that now, but I have to hurry. Things are going down hill fast. I need to go see a fed. Can I use the truck?"

"Sure, it's yours, just let me grab my purse." She reached inside and pulled out her oversized brown leather purse. Too overfull as far as Midge was concerned. He could see the outline of a pistol, a 9 mm it looked like to him. "I will lock the place up and wait for your call or return. Don't worry about the boys. No one will get in this house with me here." She had stopped crying now and looked in control.

"Thanks, I have to go, but I will call you later." He grabbed the keys from her and jumped in the truck, throwing gravel as he left the driveway, using his cell phone as soon as he was on the road.

"Jim, I am on my way. I should be there in five minutes." The signal was clear today in the Sault.

"Not here Midge, I don't want to tip our hand, in case we are being watched."

"Okay, then I'll meet you at the Chippewa Sheriff's office. Do you know where it is?

"Sure do, I'll see you in five minutes."

Midge turned right instead of going straight ahead. He should beat the Secret Service man to the Sheriff's office easily.

He waited for the big black Suburban to pull into the lot. He could see his friend Tom was still on duty with only one other deputy in the building. There were no other cops or police cars in the lot. Jim pulled in fast and jerked to a stop. He leapt out of the SUV followed by a tall thin man wearing a black military jump suit with a black beret. Midge jumped out of his truck and headed for the building, watching both of them closely. They would ask to use Tom's office. He was sure Tom would agree, he had a lot to tell Jim, or them, and did not want any other ears listening to his conversation.

"Where's your van?" Jim asked.

"At home, we can go get it later if we need it."

"Midge, this is Colonel Eric Stormer, he is the Delta Force Team A

167

commander and he is here to help us. How did your meeting go with John and Jay? Are they going to give us the Camels Eye? Time is running out, you know."

"Let's wait until we get inside and have some privacy." Midge held the door open for them and quickly followed them inside.

"Hi Midge, what brings you in here on a Saturday?" Tom was surprised to see Midge and the two other men he did not know.

"Tom, would you mind if we use your office for a few minutes. I need to talk to these gentlemen and we need some privacy." He was already heading toward it.

"Sure, go ahead. I'll go in the dispatch office and give you some privacy. Everyone else is out on the road, so there is no one here to bother you. Take your time." Tom looked both men up and down before turning and heading into the dispatch room. A fed and a military guy, that was for sure, but what was Midge doing with them? Maybe he did not want to know that much. No, he would just mind his own business, life was easier that way. Midge and the two men entered his office and closed the door.

"Yes, they are willing to give us the jewels, but it is not like we thought. John and Jay Nassire are not in charge, Kia Ashad is in control. They are virtual prisoners in their own home. Let me bring you up to speed." He quickly described John's plea for help, the deal he made to keep Jacob safe at his house, and the formidable defense system the farm presented. Jim and Colonel Stormer listened with deep concentration, not interrupting at all until Midge was finished.

"So to attack the farm would mean suicide for some of my team, and may not result in the return of the Camels Eye anyway. Since John is the only one who knows where the jewel is, we must protect him at all cost," the Colonel said.

"I think that's right, but I have an idea that may work. It would require some people to pull it off." Midge was thinking as he was talking.

"I'm all ears. I don't have anything else to try that I can think of off hand." Jim Featherston was looking at him very intently now.

"I was thinking, if we could separate Kia and his men from John and Jay Nassire, we could take out Kia and his men without any concern over the loss of the jewel. Kia does not know where it is located anyway."

Jim looked concerned, "I'm with you, but how can we do that when

Kia never lets them out of sight? He does not sound like a man who will be easy to fool."

"I think the casino in Bay Mills is our best shot. Listen, Kia or his people are the ones who actually handle all the money in the counting room and in the secure vault in the secret third level under ground. I am told no tribal people have ever been allowed in there. John and Jay work the floor and take care of the high rollers and the guys the mob sends in. When they come out of the building to the employee parking lot, Kia usually comes out first with his people and the money. Once they are secured into those armored Expeditions, John and Jay come out. It is a good security procedure, since the Nassire men can't get out of the casino lot without being seen by Kia."

"What about other people in the parking lot? It is risky if they open fire on us." The agent was already thinking about collateral damage.

"Yes it is, but not too risky if you take out Kia, the head of the snake, before he reaches the vehicles. They come out the employee lot side, but there are a lot of cars in that lot." Midge was thinking like a SWAT team guy now.

"Those guys are not going to surrender without a fight and we do not want any collateral damage to civilians." Midge thought that was typical Washington blabber coming out of the soldier's mouth. This Colonel would take a hundred civilian casualties if he had to, just as long as there were no television reporters or cameras around.

"I agree, but if I am taking Kia down, I blow him away immediately and call it self defense. He is not even an American citizen and he is on Tribal land, not U. S. soil." Take that logic, soldier boy, Midge thought.

"Yes, but he will still receive legal protection when we arrest him," the Secret Service man chimed in again.

"You mean *if* you arrest him. Only in America can a group of Arabs attack the World Trade center and have the ACLU yelling for their protection. They would try to make the victims at fault. Those same scum lawyers will defend Kia and his thugs and try to convict you guys and the President for not reading them their Miranda rights. Only in America can the ACLU exist to destroy the country that feeds and protects them." Midge hated those lying bastards and all they stood for --- or against, like America.

"I know, but if we don't do something, the hostages are going to die and I can't have that on my conscience. If we take them out at the casino, it is safer than assaulting the farm. If they get to the farm, it will take some casualties or tanks and gun ships to get them out," Jim said.

"You're right. Now what resources do we have available? We only have about four hours or so to move on them." Midge heard the paper noise in his pocket. The paper John had given him was wrinkling and he heard the noise of the paper creasing. He reached inside, pulled the paper out, then unfolded it.

"What's that you have there?" Jim was eyeing the paper with suspicion.

"It's a paper John Nassire slipped to me in the airplane we were looking at when one of Kia's killers was checking on us." He looked and saw it was actually two pieces of paper folded together.

The first paper was a rough diagram of the farm with the hanger, main house, the second smaller house behind it slightly to the east, and the barn. It also contained some dotted lines running between the barn, hanger, and houses labeled tunnels. So that is what John was trying to show him behind the barn. That is why the indentation in the ground ran to the weapons room in the barn. They used that secure room to escape if there was a big attack they couldn't handle. They could move to the airstrip and get out of there by airplane. Man alive, these guys were prepared. It must have cost millions to construct and now Midge was thinking they may have vehicles down in the tunnels to move fast in case of attack. Maybe golf carts with electric power so they did not get gas fumes in the tunnels, like the one Kia used to drive them to the house, for the picnic. The paper also had five foreign looking names written across the bottom of the paper. Kia Ashad was the first one. He bet the others were his band of killers' real names, not their false passport names.

"Well, what the hell is it?" Midge passed the first sheet to Jim. Jim studied the paper in detail, understanding immediately what he was holding. He laid it on the desk and shared it with Colonel Stormer.

"I bet those names will show up on someone's wanted list. Can we fax it to your control or to NSA and find out who these guys are?" Midge was taking control now.

"Get me to a fax machine and I'll get some help ASAP." Jim was heading out the door to the dispatch room to see Captain Molten. He returned in under three minutes. "They are working on it." Whoever "they" are supposed to be, Midge thought.

The second sheet was a diagram also, but this one had written Ojibwa Mills Casino on the top. It was what engineers termed a plan view, as if looking at it from above, and a separate side view sketch. The plan view took in the casino, hotel, golf course, and an RV park. It is the only casino in Michigan built on the water. They call it Waishkey Bay, but it is really a cove on Whitefish Bay near where the Waishkey River runs through Brimley. The hotel had 114 rooms attached to the casino, which was one large floor with slots, games of chance, and other gambling except poker. The poker room was by invitation only for some reason. On the water side was a dotted line drawn from the casino to the water and labeled 'tunnel'. Another dotted line, labeled 'tunnel' went out to the power building to the south of the casino parking lot where all the water pumps, sewers, power and heating systems were housed for the complex. This is where all the employees parked and the equipment was stored. The customers used the north lot that ran beside the casino and in front of the hotel. Midge bet there was a secret elevator in the building somewhere behind some of the machinery, a false wall, or something. Now that was news to Midge. The tunnels must have been dug secretly under the casino during its initial construction he thought, using underground water pipes or power cables as an excuse.

The side view sketch was even more revealing. It showed three levels to the casino. First was the casino floor for gambling, next was the usual casino lower level or basement with the counting room and safe in it, serviced by an elevator. But what was unusual was the third level down that was serviced by another elevator with no stairway access. That was not to code, but he doubted this room showed up on any building plans anywhere. It looked like a secret and highly secured room. This must be the one the Indians and Brenda told him about that only the Nassires' men, like Kia were allowed to enter. No Indian had ever seen inside the room. They wondered what it had in there that was so secret.

So Kia was safe when he was in that room, almost invincible, but with access to the escape tunnel to the bay, or across the parking lot to the utility building. He wondered how much firepower was available to Kia and his men in the third level down room. He would bet it was heavy duty shit with body armor and at least machine guns and grenades and maybe even some shoulder fired missiles.

"Look at this, Jim. This is a diagram of the Ojibwa Mills Casino. Looks like John was thinking like us, that it would be the best place to take Kia out and free the Nassires, but only if Kia doesn't get to that third level room first."

Jim and Colonel Stormer studied the paper for a few minutes and then the soldier put a strange looking phone up to his ear. It was one of those large satellite phones with a large strap the military use. Americans saw them on the evening news when soldiers were calling in air strikes against the Taliban in Afghanistan.

"Team Leader One, this is Charley One with Rose Garden, do you copy? Over," Stormer spoke slowly and clearly into the telephone.

"Charley One, this is Team Leader One, we copy. Over," came the reply.

"We have a go. I say we have a go. Launch code four-one-niner, location three-zero, do you copy? Please confirm. Over."

"That is launch code four-one-niner, location three-zero, ETA fifty minutes. Confirm, over."

"ETA fifty minutes confirmed. Out." Stormer set the phone on the desk. "Well there is no turning back now. Let's get to the vehicle and you can follow us to Chippewa County International Airport in Kincheloe. That is the staging area for this operation."

"I know where it is, I'll meet you there." Midge was talking to their backs as they left the building.

Midge was right on their heels.

"Everything okay, Midge?"

He spun around to see Tom coming out of the dispatch office. "Sure, Tom, everything is fine.

"That full bird looked like he was in a hurry and so did the fed. A strange combination for an ex-cop to be hanging out with on a Saturday evening, in Sault Ste. Marie, Michigan if you ask me, Midge."

"Yes it is Tom, good night, and thanks for the use of your office." Midge turned and headed for his truck. This could be a long and interesting evening. He just hoped everything would work out well for the hostages' sake, the ones both here and in Iran.

Chapter 14

The Mullah, Seyed Habibi, and his team of six Islamic Revolutionary Guard Corps commandos, sat quietly in the small repair shop in the Village of Parker River. It lies on the Canadian shore just east of Sault Ste. Marie and Sugar Island. He had arrived by car yesterday from the Iranian Embassy in Ottawa. The other members of the team had come from different routes through Canada and had arrived yesterday and today from Montreal, Toronto, Windsor, and Hamilton. He and his six man team were in position and awaiting night fall. A fishing boat was to arrive at the pier outside to shuttle them to Sugar Island on the American side. They would speak only English on this mission to avoid raising any alarm among the locals, if overheard.

Seyed Habibi was no stranger to dangerous assignments. He had infiltrated Iraq, Jordan, Syria, and even Israel on two occasions. He had fought against the Americans in Afghanistan with the Taliban. He was trained for this work and spoke fluent Arabic, Hebrew or Yiddish, French, and English, as well as his native Western Farsi in Iran. Eastern Farsi, called Dari and some Tajiki spoken in the 'stans' and Ukraine were also part of his language inventory. His English had only one defect in this part of the world. It had a British accent because he had learned it from a British school master. It had proved impossible for him to totally Americanize it for some reason.

He felt naked without his beard, but a beard would call undo attention to him and his men. His hair was cut short which accentuated his large ears and gaunt face. His eyes were dark brown and seemed to smolder when he talked, which wasn't often. He also missed his Qur'an, which was his constant companion in Iran, but he was to appear a non religious infidel on this assignment. He and his men were now dressed in brown Carhartt jackets and blue jeans with brown hunting boots and brown baseball hats. They carried only large fishing knives trying to look like Native American hunters or fishermen. This would provide the perfect cover for them tonight when the braves took them across. They would pick up their weapons, which had been dropped two weeks earlier from a great lakes freighter near the Bay Mills Reservation on Sugar Island in U.S. waters. The weapons had been picked up by a Chippewa fishing boat. Seyed's team would then be transported to the Bay Mills Reservation near Brimley in a work truck for the attack.

Seyed was a Shiite Mullah trained by clerics his entire life. He lived in an Ayatollah's orphan school and then in a Tehran mosque. His father and mother had been tortured and killed by the Shah's hated secret police, the SAVAK, in 1978, just before the fall of the Shah. He had been only four years old at the start of the revolution, but had spent his entire life in the study and service of Islam. He received his training in Islamic religious schools and proved to have a remarkable gift for languages. He was also trained extensively in the use of weapons and explosives in preparation for serving in the Iran-Iraq war. But the war officially ended in 1988 with a UN imposed cease fire. Seyed was never able to report to the battlefield as he was too young to serve in the Islamic Guard at the time. He had since made up for this by volunteering to attack Islam's enemies wherever they lived.

He was the perfect instrument of Islam. He was fearless in his duty and felt Allah would reward him in paradise if he was martyred. That was all a true believer could ask for. He most enjoyed killing infidels and Jews. He had killed many men and women, most infidels, but some fellow Muslims. In Israel once, he took part in the murder of eighty school children under the age of twelve in a desert kibbutz. He gloated in the extermination of so many future Zionists. He had never been with a woman and was immune to their evil wiles.

He spent two years as a religious policeman, and had to punish quite a few women. He could not actually put all the blame on them, for the Shah with his western ideas had allowed them to act as harlots and nonbelievers, by not requiring the wearing of the hejab, the typical form of Islamic female dress. It took months, and unfortunately, some capital punishment on his and some other policemen's part to show the women of his country the errors of their ways. He could not believe some of them not only dared to not cover their heads and bodies, but openly challenged him and his fellow policemen. He normally only flogged or beat the offensive women, but once he found a woman and her teen age daughter wearing red nail polish like in the great Satan magazines from the west. He went crazy and cut off their hands to show the other women of his country the Islamic republic would not tolerate these sins of the west. He nailed all four hands, painted nails facing out, on a post in the town square to warn other women not to mock Allah's law, the Sharia.

When openly challenged by a woman in public the first time, he immediately beheaded her and hung the head from a pole with a sign, telling the other women to obey Islamic law or die. After a few of these incidents, it was determined he was a little too radical and was transferred out of the religious police to the IRGC, the Islamic Revolution's Guards Corps intelligence service. He essentially became a spy both inside and outside Iran to protect the revolution from its enemies. If he was called upon to kill fellow Muslims, even Sunnis, he killed them as fast and painlessly as possible. They were believers after all, but infidels he killed as slowly as possible and inflicted a life time of pain for their sins against Allah before he sent them to hell.

The assignment here was bitter sweet for him. He was to return the Camels Eye to Iran. He would have to get it from the sons of turtles whose mothers had mated with camels, the Nassiri men, westernized to Nassire. Their father, General Nenatollah Nassiri, old yellow eyes, was the man who had arrested his parents. His parents, he was told, had been tortured and killed for supporting the return of the Ayatollah Khomeini in 1978. His mother was pregnant at the time with his bother he was told by the clerics. Hate had burned in his heart all this time and now he would finally meet the sons of the Nassiri line. He would kill them all as slowly as possible.

The last mission to recover the Camels Eye had failed, when the agents retreated under heavy gunfire and returned to Canada. This time would be different with him in charge. The army of the great Satan would capture the Camels Eye for them and hand it over to him for return to Iran in exchange for some infidel prisoners in Tehran. Well, he would call Iran and have their countrymen released before he accepted their ransom. After he had sent the jewel back to Iran, he would find and kill the Nassire family and anyone who served them. He owed that to his father, mother, and unborn brother.

He sat looking at his men as they shared some cold rice mixed with lamb. They drank only water, but some of the men looked very tired and worn. He knew it was from staying up late drinking and fornicating with infidel women. When his countrymen visited the west, they seemed to forget the Islamic laws they had sworn to uphold. He knew they consumed alcohol, gambled, and had sex with the western harlots. This was the way soldiers away from home always behaved. He did not blame them, but the Americans who were corrupting the world. He did not like the Canadians very much. They were infidels, drank alcohol and their women were whores, but at least they did not try to enforce their ways and sins on the world. As a matter of fact, they were a weak country living in the shadow of the United States. Give him two Islamic divisions, no interference from the U.S. military, and he could capture this country for Islam in a year. These people were weak in the knees. They loved to talk about their armed forces, but they were a sham without guts or leadership. They hid behind the skirts of the United States and claimed to be an independent country, but had never fought anyone for real since World War II.

Sitting here a short way across the waterway from the land of Satan made his skin crawl. He had no illusions as to their backbone, however. He had fought their soldiers in Afghanistan and Iraq and they would flat out kill you. They were susceptible to women and children suicide bombers, but in a straight man to man fight, they would kill you. As much as he hated them, Allah had not given him enough strength to kill many of them. Iran would have to use French and German opinion against them to control them. The French were greedy cowards, but very useful as a buffer to stop the cowboy president from invading them. They could be bought off with a little money and trade. He remembered his military studies and an infidel general named Patton who said, 'I would rather have two German divisions in front of me, than one French division behind me.' Seyed agreed with him. The French were a whiny, deceitful ally who wanted to have a place at the table, but not fight in the war. They were easy to bully, but he could not understand why the Americans even bothered with what they thought. He would never understand the west and their willingness to listen to the opinions of cowards.

When Iran had seized the U.S. embassy, Carter was president, and they handled this weak man easily. The Mullahs talked about Reagan becoming president and had decided releasing the hostages was the best action with him in charge. Without Carter, their negotiating power was gone. They now said if the cowboy Bush was president, he would have bombed and invaded Iran just to prove a point. He hated the cowboy president, but like gladiators of old, he knew the man would do what he said, even if he said he was going to hunt you down and kill you. Seyed would do his business in the U.S. and then get out quickly. He was that smart regardless of his hatred for the Americans.

They sat quietly and ate. His men seemed relaxed, but he did not allow any smoking tonight. Although he did not smoke, it was the one vice his country allowed, but he wanted no light inside the building. When the Chippewa arrived to transport his team across, he wanted everything to go smoothly. By tomorrow night, with the Allah's blessing, he and his men should be on the Canadian side of Lake Superior with the jewel in their possession and the Nassire men all dead and in hell.

He allowed his men to sleep now. Rest is a weapon and it could be a very busy night. He rested his eyes but his ears and mind were alert. He could go days without much rest. He was trained to suffer the way the Prophet had done. It made him feel alive to be hungry and cold, not like the western people who were fat and lazy. Subhaanallah, glory be to Allah. He could hear his men breathing rhythmically and even, they were resting well.

It was dark outside now. The boat would arrive for them soon. He hoped the crossing would be uneventful, at least until they could retrieve their weapons and put up a fight if the U.S. border guards intercepted them. The braves had assured them this was the easiest border to cross in the world, but he was still concerned.

He watched through the window facing the waterway and could see the red marker lights of a freighter going northbound. They were slow but huge, and he would not want to be run over by one of those in the dark. He had not seen any border or coast guard boats today, so he figured there must be very few of them.

Suddenly there was a spotlight shining on the building from the road side. He ducked down and told his men to be alert. They responded quickly and took up positions under the work benches. A few moments later they heard the sound of the front door knob being turned and a little bang, then silence. Seyed breathed slowly and listened, but heard nothing. Then he heard the movement of a car or truck and he slowly crept to the front window from the back room. He peered above the ledge and saw a police car drive to the next building and shine his spotlight all around. The policeman got out of his car and checked the front door to see if it was locked, then moved south to the next building. Just a routine property check by a local policeman, Seyed thought. He wondered how often this policeman made his rounds. Relieved, he told his men to relax. They instantly lay back down and resumed their rest, just like any other battle tested soldiers in the world.

About an hour later, he heard the low hum of some outboards. He squinted out of the water side windows, but could not see anything on the water. There was no moon tonight and they were not carrying any night vision goggles or binoculars. Hunters and fisherman would not have much use for those things, legally at least. He heard a noise out by the dock and his senses went on alert. He could now see a shape coming toward the building, darting low until he reached the door and then knocking lightly. Seyed's men were on their feet in an instant and standing beside him at the door.

"Arab team, let's go," he was saying in hushed tones.

Arabs, what the hell did he mean? They were Persians, not Arabs! Arabs were the low life scum of Islam, but still better than infidels. He opened the door. "How many boats do you have?"

"We have two. Get in and let's get out of here before the OPP comes back. My name is Neka, follow me." He led them to two small fishing boats being held by a rope to the dock by another brave. They quickly all jumped into the boats with their outboards running and were soon headed into the dark waters. Seyed could see some light highway traffic in Canada behind him, but nothing but black water ahead. He hoped this Indian knew where he was going in the dark. In a few minutes he would be in the United States of America, the home of the great Satan. Allah be praised and his will be done.

Chapter 15

Midge and the fed arrived at the Chippewa County International Airport about fifteen minutes later with tires squealing as they approached the terminal. Jim Featherston and Colonel Stormer were on the sat-phone outside the small terminal. This airport had been the Air Force Base Kincheloe. It was an old SAC facility that was closed down many years ago and turned over to the locals to use as an industrial park, correctional facilities, and a commercial airport. It devastated the local economy when it closed just like so many other military towns around the country when a base closed.

The area had never fully recovered economically, but the people had survived. The Agent's support team in Washington had ordered the FAA to have all flights rerouted or cancelled. The airport was closed to all other controllers routing aircraft tonight, which was very easy since the airport had only four scheduled flights a day. Of course, there could be charter flights scheduled, but that would be unusual this time of the year.

The colonel had commandeered the large conference, or as they called it, Meeting Room A, in the terminal. He had evacuated all personnel except the air traffic controllers and their supervisor from the building. They had about twenty minutes until the arrival of the Delta Team. Midge found a copy machine and quickly made a dozen copies of the maps of the casino and the farm John Nassire had sketched for him to give the Delta team.

Ken Telway walked into the conference room. "Hello Midge, hello Agent Featherston, I have my men in position. We have sealed off the airport entrances and are awaiting further instructions." Midge was stunned. How did Ken get in here and why did Jim not seem to be shocked to see him?

"Great Ken, just stay to the side and listen until we have the plan." So he was in on this mission, but when or how had Jim involved him?

A CH46E Sea Knight helicopter landed just outside the east of the terminal and a single black clad Seal leaped out and headed inside. This was the Seal One team leader, Captain Windsmere, USN. He and Jim Featherston shook hands and went to the conference room. Midge was introduced to Captain Windsmere and handed him a copy of the maps of the casino.

"This is our target tonight, Captain", and he handed him a satphone so the Seals could communicate with the Delta team and himself during the operation. NSA was supporting the operation with full satellite and transmission coverage in Washington tonight.

"I will move our boat about a hundred yards to the east of the casino, just outside the State Park. From there we can see the water side of the casino and will await your instructions, sir." He saluted, turned and ran for the Navy helicopter and then was gone.

"That guy didn't waste any time did he?" Midge was impressed with the captain.

"Seal One teams don't waste time, Midge. They are the best the Navy has to offer."

"Let's get my role straight right now. What is it you want me to do or should I just get out of your way?" Midge was getting a little impatient with the waiting. Just then the fax machine rang and papers started to print out. Jim went over to retrieve them, while Ken just watched from the back wall.

"Good, we have photos of the Nassires, Kia, and two of his men. It's a start. Midge, just as soon as the Delta Team lands, you, Colonel Stormer, and I will brief the team and decide how we will use you. I feel like you should go into the casino and signal us when they are getting ready to come out if you can. You are the only person we have who really knows them other than Ken here, and he has other duties." Jim had a plan, but did not want to lay it all out until the total team was assembled.

"Fine, I'll wait." He would not have to wait very long. He saw Stormer coming through the terminal doors from the runway at double time speed.

"They will have touchdown in two minutes, so get the maps ready men." He hustled out the door again and headed for the runway.

Midge and Jim laid the maps around the table. They had managed to find a transparency maker and an overhead projector and had the first map for the casino projected on the pull down screen at the front of the conference room. They were ready for the Delta Team briefing now. They went to the rear doors of the terminal to watch the Delta Team land.

Two helicopters could be seen coming fast and low across the east runway. They were moving with only minimum lights and landed just outside the terminal where Colonel Stormer was on the sat phone directing the pilots. The first one set down. Nine helmeted, fully flack jacketed, black clad and heavily armed troopers leapt from the side door to the ground and jogged toward the terminal with Colonel Stormer in the lead. It was a troupe carrying Chinook and could carry up to forty men or more depending on the equipment they carried. It was not equipped with any weapons systems, but the other chopper was a different story. It was an AH-64 Apache attack helicopter and it carried only a two man crew, but had enough fire power to take out a tank company. Its main guns were 30mm cannons, but it carried 8 Hellfire missiles and 38 Hydra Rockets and was the most lethal helicopter the army had at its disposal. This was a powerful attack force when packaged together.

The soldiers entered the conference room and were handed two map sketches each as they gathered around the table. They had the photos of the targets taped to the wall on the far side. No one sat down, but just turned and faced the overhead screen which already had the plan view map showing.

"Gentlemen, our target tonight is some men who are currently in this casino in Brimley. We plan to take them out, and I mean capture if we can, as they exit the casino and head for their vehicles in the parking lot to the south of the building. As you can see by these dotted lines marked tunnel, they have two alternate routes they may use if they think we have the parking lot exit blocked, so we must stay concealed until the exact moment we receive the go signal. We also need to cover these tunnel exits in case they take one of those routes. There could also be civilians in the casino and parking lot tonight and we do not want any collateral damage, is that clear?"

"Yes sir!" they all answered at once. These guys acted like they all had the same brain.

We estimate there are approximately seven men total with only five being our targets. The other two men must be rescued and protected at all cost, is that clear?"

"Yes sir! Another single voice response to the Colonel.

"The photos on the back wall are the subjects. The first two on the left are the men we need to protect. They have vital information that is the reason for this whole mission. If the choice comes between terminating a target or saving these men, let the target go and protect these men. Now what we do know about the targets is they are well armed, all ex-military, and willing to kill anything that gets in their way. We must take them out cleanly or they will cause havoc for us or any other people in the area." He paused for effect and saw all his men nodding, especially his two snipers.

He next unfolded a map of Chippewa County on the table and used a red marker to circle the casino area, the state park, and then the Nassire farm. Pointing to the state park he said, "this is where our LZ is located tonight, gentlemen. It is less than two miles out from our target. We will land here and deploy to the casino. Snipers, one of you go on the utility building roof on the southeast side of the lot, and the other to the north side of the lot on the roof of the casino. Squad one, you are to take cover in the tree line along the south side of the lot. Squad two, you are to split up leaving one man to cover the tunnel entrance to the water and one in the utility building itself in case they use that exit. The rest of you will deploy south along the drive at thirty yard intervals. I will set up the command center on the roof of the hotel to the northeast side of the parking lot. Any questions?"

There were no questions.

"We will leave the choppers at the state park, but they will be available to us at a moment's notice. Captain Telway, we need the Tribal Police to close the Brimley road at M28 and the local road a mile east of the state park. We need to do that immediately." Ken pulled out his two-way and started barking orders to his officers as he left the room and headed for Brimley.

"Midge Gregory here will be our warning signal. He will come out of the casino just before the targets and radio to us the command,

'Persians Go'. That will mean be ready to launch the attack. The command "Persians Tunnel' will mean the targets are exiting by one of the tunnels so be ready there. The command 'Persians Abort' will mean something has changed and we will not be in position to attack, so move out and reform at the LZ. Does everyone understand the commands? 'Go' means we attack, 'Tunnel' means they have moved to the tunnels and 'Abort' means they have escaped and you are to head for the LZ. Is it clear to everyone? Those are the three scenarios we have planned for tonight." No one said anything, but just nodded in the affirmative. Midge guessed he could remember the three commands easy enough. Stormer handed him a small hand held radio already turned on and dialed in to their frequency for the night.

"One more thing men, if you get a clean shot at this man," he pointed at Kia's picture on the rear wall, "you have a 'go' at any time during the operation and that includes both of you snipers. He is to be taken out first if possible, but only if you have a clear shot. Double tap him. Any other questions, men?"

"Yes sir. What if the targets are successful and escape the casino kill zone, what is our Plan B after we rendezvous at the LZ?"

"Good question Sergeant Major, we follow them to the farm and try to take them out there. We want to finish it at the casino because the farm is their home base and they could be well prepared for us there. Midge, put the farm map up, will you?"

Midge removed the casino map overhead and put the farm diagram on the viewer. "As you can see gentlemen, there are four main buildings on the farm; two houses to the east side, the hanger and runway on the west side and the barn near the middle in front of both of those. These dotted lines are hard to see, but they are tunnels that run between all of the buildings. If the targets reach these buildings, we believe they have heavy weapons and fortifications there. Only Midge has been on the ground there, so I will let him talk about what he saw." Colonel Stormer stepped back and Midge stood up.

"The only thing I am sure of is the barn, as I have not actually been inside the other buildings. There is an ammo or weapons room in the northwest corner here." He pointed to the drawing of the barn. "I do know it is heavily reinforced with steel plate and god knows what else is inside the room. The one tunnel terminates there, but I do not know how deep in the ground it is. In the sunlight you can follow the depression in the grass. I did not notice any vents in the field, so I think the air ventilation is pumped in from the buildings into the tunnels. I also think they have golf carts down there so they can move fairly fast. I do know the cupolas on the barn are reinforced and sandbagged and have a view of the total approach to the farm. I found a 7.62 mm round on the ground there, so I know they have at least light machine gun capability. I might mention the big Ford Expeditions they drive are armor plated with bulletproof glass. I know that for a fact, so if you tangle with those trucks be careful. That is about all I know."

"Thanks Midge, that is a lot compared to anything else we know. Okay gentleman, let's check our com-gear, weapons, grab our night vision head gear and then load up. Midge you will be riding with us, but you will have to hoof it to the casino on your own. Sergeant Major, issue Agent Featherston and myself headsets, microphones, and night vision gear with helmets and flack jackets when we get to the chopper. Let's move out then, ETA ten minutes to LZ, now move!" The team filed out fast through the doors and onto the waiting chopper.

On the way out the door Midge used his cell phone to dial his house. Brenda answered on the third ring.

"Hello?"

"Brenda don't talk just listen. I have a funny feeling about tonight so I want you to take Ryan and Jacob with you into my office and close the door. Do not come out of the office for anything. The room is armor protected and has all the camera links in it. Have Ryan show you how to turn the system on." He had to yell to be heard as he went outside.

"Midge?" She sounded frightened now.

"No more questions Brenda, just do it! Call the Chippewa County Sheriff and have them send a car to the house. Tell them to call Tom Molten if they have any questions. I have to go, just get in the office now!" He was screaming into the phone to overcome the noise of the chopper blades downdraft as he disconnected and climbed into the Huey.

Chapter 16

The hum of the dual tires was giving Seyed a headache. His team was bouncing around in the back of a high cube painters van. It was a large Chevy van with the body cut away just behind the cab where the driver and his passenger sit. A large box van body was mounted behind the cab with a panel and sliding door that opened so a worker could walk from the cab to the back to get materials or tools. The van was white with lettering on the big rear box with 'Tribal Paint and Wallpaper' stenciled on both sides. This was a real working van, not a mobile tactical unit like the police use for their SWAT team deployments. The Mullah was riding into battle in a junk filled painters van. The braves did not even think to remove the paint cans from the last job they used the van for, so the Iranians had to sit on the dirty things. Also it was filled with the white dust from carrying drywall to the job. The white gypsum dust stuck to the Iranians shoes and left white powder on the back of their pants where they sat.

Seyed had been in worse conditions, but this was almost embarrassing to ride into battle this way. At least their weapons had been retrieved from the water drop and were waiting in the van when they climbed in. He remembered entering Israel from Palestine on a mission a couple years ago. He was hidden under the oranges in the back of a stake truck and could barely breathe. They had to go through several Israeli check points and had to keep absolutely still even though it was extremely hot in the Negev.

It was one of the greatest missions he had ever been on, but it was filled with danger getting into enemy territories. It was really harrowing getting out after they had assassinated the young Zionists in their devil worship school at the kibbutz. The Israelis had poisoned world opinion and everyone was calling it an act of terrorism. One man's terrorist is another man's patriot. It was war against the Jews. Just as the Prophet Mohammed slaughtered all the women and children of the non-believers he came across, he also had carried out Allah's will according to the Qur'an as the clerics had taught him in Tehran. The Israeli children were weak. They cried and begged to be let go or not hurt. Young Muslim children would beg to die for Allah. At least the true believers would. If these Zionist children were allowed to grow up, they would arm themselves and enslave more Muslim people. They would do this with the help of the great Satan country to back them. What he did was to draw the world's attention to the plight of the Palestinian peoples' suffering and let the Jews know that nowhere, even deep inside Israel, was safe for the Jews, whether it be soldiers or children.

How they whined and cried as he lit them on fire. They did not know how to die for their cause as his people did. Yes, some of the Arab armies were weak, but that was because their leaders did not follow the true Islam faith, just mouthed the faith. In reality they were not true believes as he and the clerics were in his holy Mosque in Tehran. Even the Israeli soldiers were weak, forgetting their duty to try to rescue the burning children while he and some of his team slipped into the desert and made their escape right under their noses disguised as medical personnel.

That was a great victory for Allah and the world now feared Iran and that is what he called respect. It took over a month to escape the Israeli forces, but even though several of his team were caught, he managed to slip back into Palestine and return to Tehran a great hero to the Ayatollahs. While the world condemned him, he was exalted by all of Islam for striking a great blow against the Jews and their great Satan masters.

He was now on all the infidels wanted lists around the world, but he could still use Canada to operate out of safely. They accepted Arab terrorists released from prison all over the world. The whole world knew terrorists were welcomed there, but so what. The American papers and their right wing journalists were always trying to get Canada to turn them over to the fascist government in the United States, but the Canadian government knew better than to do that. The Canadian government was filled with cowards who did not want to incur the wrath of Islam by interfering with what the world called terrorist activities. As long as he or other terrorists did not commit any crimes against Canada, their politicians would welcome them to stay and operate out of their country with full immunity.

Seyed also had support in the United States from the ACLU and the Kennedy faction of the Democratic Party. Not in obvious words, but in help protecting his and fellow terrorists' civil rights and freedom to operate against their military and authority of the great Satan government. Democracies were so weak he could not understand how they had ever ruled so much of the world. Of course, he had studied history and knew the old world infidel leaders were not the weak kneed leaders of today. With the exception of the cowboy President, Islam could push, bribe, threaten, or bully the European and liberal American leaders into submission. Look at Spain, with one bomb on a train, the election was changed. The people elected who the Ayatollahs wanted and withdrew from Iraq immediately. The people of Spain are still hiding under their beds in fear today. A few gallons of oil or a few dollars of goods purchased and Europeans were eating out of Allah's hand.

But the great Satan cowboy, he must die because he would never be able to be controlled by Islam. He was the devil himself. Seyed only wished his mission was to kill the President of the United States of Infidels, but he would satisfy himself with returning the jewel to Iran and hopefully killing the offspring of old yellow eyes on this mission.

He felt the van slowing down. The sliding door opened a few inches and Neka leaned in. "Police roadblock ahead, keep quiet till I see what is going on." He slammed the access door shut.

Seyed and his men racked their weapons and got ready for an attack. They listened carefully as they heard the brakes squeal to a stop.

"Hey Bill, what's up with the roadblock? Has there been an accident?" he yelled out the drivers lowered window.

"No, just have orders to close the road to Brimley, I'm not sure why, Robert."

"How long do we have to wait? We have had a long day in the Sault," Robert yelled back at him, but Neka did not say a word.

"Not sure Robert, but I would bet it will be a long night. If I were you I'd take a room in the Sault tonight," the BIA officer yelled from the ground. Seyed was listening, but still did not fully understand the situation outside his van box.

"Okay Bill, then I'll turn around and head for the Sault. Goodnight Bill." With that he rolled up his window and made a u-turn on M-28 and headed toward the Sault.

After about a mile, Neka slid the access door open a little again and put his head inside. "The road to the Reservation is closed for the night. This doesn't look good. They never close the road to Brimley. What do you want to do?"

Seyed was having trouble hearing with all the tire noise in the back. He spoke loudly, "Did you say the road to Brimley is closed for the night?" He leaned forward and turned his head slightly to the right so he could hear out of his left ear. For some reason he understood things from his left ear instead of his right. He answered the phone with his left ear so he could understand better. He could hear just fine with his right ear, but he seemed to understand better with his left ear. Maybe he was left brained instead of right brained.

Neka was speaking loudly now also, "Yes, they have closed the road to Brimley. We can either go back to the Sault or go back a few miles, go north to the Six Mile Road and try to get into Brimley that way. That road runs right by the state park. What do you want to do, Seyed?"

"We are not going to the Sault. Take the other road and get us into Brimley as fast as you can. I sense something has gone wrong tonight." He spoke loudly and with force.

"Okay, Robert will take a detour north to the lake road. Sit back and relax, it should take us about twenty minutes if everything goes okay." With that Neka closed the access door and all Seyed could hear was the incessant humming of the dual wheels echoing in the big steel box he was locked in.

Seyed felt the big van turn to the left a couple of times after slowing down and finally start coming to a stop. The access door opened again. "Another road block at the state park. Keep quiet," Neka yelled. The Iranians got prepared for the worst.

"Hey Billy, what's the deal tonight? I just tried to get home using M 28 and you guys have it closed. Now I try the back way and you guys got this road blocked too. What gives with all the roadblocks tonight? We ain't never had a roadblock since I lived here." Robert was yelling out his open window again.

"All I can tell you Robert is that Brimley is closed for the night and there is no way you can get to the Reservation. I would advise you to turn around and head for the Sault." The officer was yelling to be heard over the noise of aircraft overhead moving toward the state park.

"Alright Billy, I know when I'm beat, I'm heading for the Sault. I hope the tribe will pay for my room tonight, since it is BIA that shut down all the roads to my house. Good night." The officer just waved and went back to his squad car. Robert turned the van around in the intersection and headed east toward the Sault.

The access door slid open again. "Something big is going on in Brimley tonight. Did you hear all that noise overhead a minute ago? It was a couple of helicopters going into the state park. We don't have any helicopters up here. Must be FBI or somebody like that. What do you want to do now, Seyed?" Neka was yelling into the back of the van box.

Seyed tried to think. He had planned to make contact with the Americans in Brimley he thought, but now what was he going to do? Why were they blocking all those roads to the town? The Americans had to cooperate with him, as long as Iran still held the American hostages at least. He was not too worried about the police, but he wanted to be in on the action on the Nassire men. He had a blood feud to settle with them and he would not be denied. "Where is the Nassire farm from here?"

"We have passed it twice down on M-28, but we can't go there now. That place is well defended." Neka remembers the last time he and some Iranians had tried to enter the farm. It had cost them a rental car, and later three dead braves.

Seyed was thinking now. He knew he did not want to invade the farm with his men. He could let the infidel soldiers do the dirty work. He just wanted to kill the Nassire family after they were captured. If they were killed by the American soldiers, well that was fine too. He would at least like to take off an ear or something to remember them by. "Head toward the farm, but don't go to it. Let's park beside the road about a mile away and watch the farm to see what happens tonight."

Neka considered this a minute, then told Robert to drive to the hill just east of the farm, park the van and wait. "Okay, we will park near the farm where we can watch without them being able to shoot us." He then slammed the door to the back.

Seyed smiled now with the knowledge what he had waited for his whole adult life was about to be fulfilled. Praise be to Allah.

As the braves and the Iranians were headed toward the farm, a big dark red Ford Expedition was headed east on M-28 for the Sault. The driver had just left the roadblock on the road to Brimley and was on his cell phone talking to Kia.

"Yes, the BIA has totally shut down the road. It is sealed off completely. Something is very wrong, Kia."

He listened to Kia talk to him on the phone.

"Yes, I remember where it is, I went there with you once." Asa listened carefully now.

"Yes, I understand Kia. But what if the boy does not want to come with me or the detective will not let him talk with me?" Another lecture was happening in his ear piece now.

"Yes, I have them in the back of the truck. Are you sure you want me to use those?" Asa had to move the phone away from his ear a little now, Kia was getting angry.

"Yes sir, I will do as you say. I will bring the boy back to the farm, no matter what. Yes, and be careful. There is something very wrong tonight in Brimley. Yes, I will see you at the farm with the boy. You better call the farm and alert the men." He had to pull the phone far from his ear now. "Yes, of course you can sir, I am on my way. I should be there about a quarter to eleven. Good bye." Man, he did not want to call him back again. He was only trying to warn him that something was going on out here. He pushed the accelerator pedal to the floor. He would make it to Mr. Gregory's house in record time. After all, the cops were tied up at road blocks tonight.

Chapter 17

The seniors from the Auburn Hills Senior Center were gathered along the hallway leading from the casino to the hotel entrance where their bus was parked. They were usually in their hotel by this time of night, but the bus had overheated on the way up north and had to stop in Saginaw for repairs. They did not get to the Comfort Inn in the Sault until after eight that evening. After eating, the seniors decided they wanted to go to the casino anyway and that is why they were there so late.

"You know, I like the slots at Kewadin better than these. I have lost too much money here. I think they're rigged." Edith worried about money and with good reason. She had been on Social Security for over twenty-seven years.

"What do you mean Edith, all slot machines are rigged. That is how they make money," one of the ladies seated with the group in the lounge said to her.

"I remember when Delbert took me to Las Vegas. We won on those slots. They were made better." She was smiling now.

"Delbert has been dead at least thirty years. When did he take you to Vegas?" a different lady from the group chimed in.

"It was before my two boys were born. We drove out west in that old Hudson Delbert bought from his dad. That was the best trip I was ever on in my life."

"A Hudson? They quit making those in the fifties didn't they?" An old man in a sport coat and tie jumped into the conversation.

"That was a car, big and cushy with lots of power." The little blue haired lady smiled even bigger just thinking about it.

"Yeah, big and comfortable, but no variable power steering or anti-lock brakes or traction control like we have today. Only a fan for ventilation instead of today's air conditioning, not nice like today's modern engineering and design." The old guy had retired from Ford Motor Company engineering twenty years ago and wanted people to know he still knew his cars.

"Anyway, I lost almost nine dollars tonight and I just want to get back to our hotel and go to bed." She looked tired, but at ninety-two, she always looked tired, but she still went on every trip she could afford. She was not going to sit home and be miserable and die in a rocking chair. If she was going to be miserable, she liked company.

"Did you lose your own money or was it from the ten dollars in nickels the casino gave us when we came in tonight?" June knew the answer but just wanted to make sure any of the new people in the seniors group were not going to feel too sorry for Edith. She had a way of trying to make people feel sorry for her on their trips some times.

"Well it was all my money once they gave it to me. I want to go back to the hotel. It's getting late. Why can't we go back now?" She was starting to get whiny now.

"You know Tony said the bus leaves for the hotel at eleven. If you did not want to come to the casino then you should have stayed at the hotel. Don't ruin it for everyone else just because you want to go now. It is only another half hour or so." Some of the other seniors were glad June was with them. They wanted to tell Edith to be quiet sometimes, but only June had the nerve to tell it like it was. She did not care. She hated people who whined or complained or any other selfish thing they did. She wasn't putting up with any of that nonsense. If people did not like it, they could kiss her ass.

"I don't think I can make it until eleven." She was using her almost crying tone now.

"Why don't you go climb on the bus and take a nap. Tony is out there and he'll let you on. We don't really want you to sit here and bitch until you make us miserable." That was telling her, some of the more timid ladies thought while June plowed into her.

The old engineer stood up and said, "come on Edith, I'll help you to the bus so you can rest." He helped her up and headed for the parking lot where the bus was waiting at the curb.

The Camels Eye

Midge was walking around the casino watching the action. It was actually more crowded than normal, but when he saw the buses outside, he figured it was senior night. These people needed to get out too, but the only big problem was in the buffet and the nickel slots. They would line up and take forever to get their food and sit down. They closed down the bathrooms with their lines and having to change their Depends. They were not usually in the casinos this late at night, but he saw that these buses were from near Detroit. He would normally turn around and leave if he saw the senior busses in the parking lot, but not tonight.

He was looking for John Nassire. It was only a single floor playing area, but he could be at the hotel, in the main office, or down in the counting room. He had picked up some coins on the way in so he would not look conspicuous just standing around the playing floor. It was quite a jog to the casino from the state park where the helicopters had set down. It was only a little over two miles, but it was mostly up a gradual slope. All his walking kept him active, but he was not used to jogging at all.

There were a lot of seniors in the lounge area and along the hallway toward the hotel, but they seemed to be just waiting to leave, not drinking or eating. He moved back to the five and ten dollar machines and wondered if John might be schmoozing some of those customers, but he did not see them.

His cell phone rang. "Hello? What is it Brenda?" Brenda was screaming into his cell phone.

"Did you call the cops like I asked you to? She was saying she did but no one came yet.

"Just stay inside the office, it is bullet proof and keep the steel reinforced door locked". She was telling him that is where she was calling from since someone tried to blow the front door to the house open with some kind of explosives.

"Dial the city cops. Just dial 911 and tell the operator an intruder is firing at the house and you are returning fire now." She said that would not do any good.

"Yes, that will make them respond faster if they think you may kill a criminal. They will take all night if they think a criminal is just going to kill a citizen. Yeah, I am in the casino looking for John.

"No, Kia must have sent him to get Jacob." She was not doing

193

what he said.

"Things could get very hot here very quickly. Just dial 911 and fire a shot in the ceiling so the operator can hear it and they record it." She finally agreed to follow his instructions.

"Good luck Brenda, and keep in touch." Midge closed his cell phone and put it back in his pocket. He needed to concentrate on his job here right now. There was nothing he could do to help Brenda and Ryan or Jacob right now. He wished he had never gotten involved in this whole mess. He would just have to trust his house security would protect them and the police would arrive in time.

Midge spotted John and Kia getting into the elevators by the office. He started that way and then stopped. What good would it do him to chase Kia into the fox's lair? He would have to come back out this way unless he chose to use the tunnels. He did not think they were on to the trap yet. He took up a spot on the other side of the casino nearer to the front entrance doors. He could watch the elevator from here, leave the casino and signal the Delta team that was hopefully waiting in the night for them.

While Midge was watching the elevator, someone was watching him from behind a bank of slot machines. He had on a loud tourist shirt with a Green Bay Packers hat and glasses and stayed sitting down most of the time to conceal his height. This man had also seen Kia and John enter the elevator, but what he saw that Midge missed was the way in which Kia had grabbed John's arm so roughly and was pushing him into the elevator. Something was wrong and he was not sure if Midge was aware of the alarm in Kia's actions. He could not warn him, but dialed his cell phone and spoke to his man in a car in the parking lot telling him to be ready for anything.

Outside the Delta team was in place. The two dark red Expeditions were parked in the first row of reserved parking across the driveway directly in front of the employee entrance to the casino. The sniper on the roof of the casino was covering the first vehicle while the second sniper was positioned on the utility building with a good view of the main entrance doors. Four men were hidden in the woods across the driveway at the edge of the parking lot. They were waiting for the signal to rush the dark red Expeditions. The men along the road as it left the casino lay in wait as a backup if anything went wrong.

The Camels Eye

Agent Featherston and Colonel Stormer were on the roof of the hotel with their binoculars watching and listening. "Listen up team. We have received no word about the targets, so hold your positions and stay alert. Out." Stormer hoped it would not be a long wait. In the army, 'hurry up and wait' was a standing joke since the first army was formed, probably. But they were trained to wait for days if they had to, for the kill.

The tour guide for the seniors, Carolyn had finally found the last man who was still gambling and had persuaded him it was time to leave the casino. About twenty other seniors were seated in the lounge and along the hallway leading to the hotel. "Well we found Roger, so I guess we can go back to the hotel now." Carolyn pulled out a roster with a pen and started to call out names.

"Lillian?" She looked at the group.

"Here." Lillian raised her hand as if she was in grade school instead of an eighty two year old retired teacher. Carolyn put a check mark beside her name.

"Edith?" She did not see her.

"She got on the bus already with old smarty pants. I think his name is Lou," June shouted out for Carolyn to hear. "Hurry up Carolyn I am going to have to take a pee if we take too long to get back." Carolyn wrote 'on the bus' next to Edith and Lou's name to check after they boarded the bus.

"Ina, are you here?"

"Yes, here." Ina had no sooner answered than there was a big commotion across the casino floor near the main office. The elevator had opened and about six guys were coming out of it. People were screaming and pushing and trying to get out of their way. The first two were carrying large duffle bags with the other four leveling machine guns at the patrons and nudging the two tall men in the front to move to the door. A tall man in the middle with gray hair pointed his Uzi to the ceiling and let loose a short burst of fire to quiet the crowd. Some people were already exiting the main entrance and broke into a dead run for the parking lot.

The seniors started to scream and move back away from the action, all but June who was taking her camera out of her big bag and snapping photos of the action. People all around them were running and diving to the floor behind slot machines and anywhere they could hide.

The big tall gray haired man walked up the hallway to the seniors from Auburn Hills and told the tour guide Carolyn, to have them get on the bus with his men in the middle for protection. They started to herd them toward the door with the Nassire men in front of Kia and his men. They were going to use the seniors as human shields.

Midge was near the main north front doors and pulled out his two way and called in "Persians Abort", Persians Abort" hoping they heard the command signal and did not open up on the hostages as went they went through the front door of the hotel to their bus. There was no reply. Midge pulled his revolver out of his holster, went out the main doors and crouched behind a bush next to the building in the corner and waited for the group to reach the hotel front doors.

Outside Colonel Stormer had seen the chaos coming out of the hotel front doors of the casino. He knew something had gone wrong inside, but he had his men hold their positions. "Snipers, be alert. Remember, if we have a kill shot, you have a go, I repeat you have a go, but only if it's wide open. Do you roger?"

"That's a roger," both snipers responded.

"The rest of the team, hold your positions until I give the command to attack."

"Roger", that was the only reply necessary.

Agent Featherston was now watching the hotel door under the portico and did not like what he was seeing. People were fleeing in a panic for their lives. He knew Kia and his men must be causing it.

Then they heard Midge's transmission, 'Persians Abort, Persians Abort' which meant not to fire. They had gotten away. But how can that be when they were still inside the casino? Everything was happening outside the plan now.

The IAA man was behind the action now but could read the situation and knew it was not a time to take action against Kia and his men. He would catch up with them at the next point in the chase. He could take one of them out now, but there would be hell to pay for the civilians in the room. He was not a Palestinian or Muslim and he did not cause innocent lives to be lost unnecessarily. He ducked back down between the Lucky Seven row of machines and watched as they herded the old people toward the hotel main door.

When the group of hostages was almost near the front door, an old woman in the group tripped and fell to floor. One of Kia's men pointed his Uzi at her head, but then decided to kick her hard to the side. He grabbed another woman by the thin blue hair and was propelling her through the door in front of him along with the rest of the seniors' group.

The snipers were watching for a kill shot, but Kia was surrounded with old people and crouching low behind them. As soon as the group exited the doors under the portico, Carolyn led them on to the bus as an Iranian wearing an armored vest held an Uzi to her head. The seniors started to board the bus slowly.

"Hold your fire Delta, they have hostages. It looks like they are leaving here on that senior bus full of hostages. As soon as they exit the parking lot, we will redeploy to the LZ. Do you copy?"

"Roger," was all that came back.

"Bird One and Bird Two get ready for extraction of Delta team. Bird Two, the targets have commandeered a tour bus and will be headed south shortly. Move south about one mile at five thousand feet and monitor the bus when it turns on the highway. Do not engage, the bus is full of hostages. Bird one, be ready for Delta team boarding when we arrive at the LZ. Do you copy?"

The copy response could not be heard as gun fire erupted from the group boarding the bus. A tall man with white hair had broken from the group and was running in front of the bus in what looked like an attempt to escape. Another man quickly jumped from the group, but was running in the other direction toward the rear of the bus. One of the armored vest men carrying an Uzi let fly with a well aimed burst and the gray haired man running north seemed to be cut in half by the fire. The Uzi man quickly spun and started firing at the man racing south away from the bus. The fleeing man was hit and going down, but then bullets went high and right over the man's body as the shooters head exploded against the side of the bus.

The rest of the senior group was on the bus with the last man dragging two large satchels. The bus door closed and the bus started moving right through people running to get out of its way. It ran right over the fallen body of the slain gray haired man without slowing down at all, followed the circle drive to the main road and headed south out of the parking lot along the main road.

The Delta team was already redeploying to the LZ for extraction. They would let local law enforcement deal with the aftermath.

Midge got to his feet still holding his revolver with two spent chambers. He ran to the terrorist, kicked his weapon away and checked the man for a pulse. One look at the side of his head told him it was a waste of time. He next ran to check on Jay Narssire who had just been run over by the bus. He was dead with four closely placed holes in his chest, two going right through his heart. Kia's man could shoot.

Midge started to panic now. There were only two men in the world who could tell him where to find the Camels Eye and one was dead for sure. He now ran to John Nassire who was on the ground about fifty feet to the south. A crowd had started to gather, but they were still in a daze from all the gunfire. He reached John and felt for a pulse. There was one, thank God. He gently turned John over and tried to talk to him.

"John, are you conscious? Can you hear me, John?" John opened his eyes and looked at Midge.

"My father?" his eyes stated in the form of a question for Midge.

There was no time to sugar coat it for him, "dead, John, your father is dead by the same guy who shot you. I killed him as he was shooting you."

John did not nod his head but his eyes said he understood. "Jacob?" his voice was raspy sounding now and he was choking on blood. Midge heard an air leak sound and checked John's wounds. He had taken two to the chest before Midge was able to kill the gunman and ruin his professional aim. That was the only reason John was still alive. One had penetrated his right lung and the other his right shoulder, painful and a lot of blood loss but not fatal if treated soon, but the lung shot worried Midge. He could choke to death before they could get him to a hospital. If he died, so did the American hostages whose lives depended upon the return of the Camels Eye.

"Listen, Jacob is safe at my house. Kia sent a man to get him, but he is with Ryan and Brenda and the police are on the way. He is safe." John was starting to lose consciousness now. Midge shook his head and tried to get him to focus.

"Where is the Camels Eye John, we have to know in order to save the hostages. Please John, tell me where it is at before you pass out. Please"

John's eyes were losing their focus and his lids were closing.

Shock was setting in Midge knew. "Where is it John, quickly? For God's sake, tell me before it's too late."

"Jacob."

"I told you Jacob is safe. You have my word on it. Now where is the jewel? Quickly, John before it's too late to save many innocent peoples lives." John was fading fast.

With one final effort from his pierced lung and blood filled throat he whispered, "Jacob, Jacob, Jac….." and then passed out. Midge could not revive him. A nurse arrived from the casino with a first aid kit. She started to treat John while waiting for the ambulance to arrive from the Sault to provide Paramedic treatment on the way to the hospital. John would be lucky to be alive in the morning.

Midge knew he would not be getting anything more out of him tonight or ever again if John died before recovering consciousness. What a mess, one hostage dead and another on his way if he did not get treatment fast. Kia and his men were escaping the trap, and no jewel to exchange for the hostages. His house was under attack and he had just killed a man with a shot to the head. He was not a drinker, but if he was, this would be a good night to start on a binge for sure. No one could blame him.

John seemed obsessed with his son's safety. Actually he could not blame him. His father was now dead, Kia had killed his wife if his brief conversation with John was true, and all he had left in the world was his son, Jacob. Yes, he could understand Jacob was all that was on his mind. He wanted to leave this world with Jacob on his lips, as his last conscious thought.

He told him Jacob was safe, but he was not sure about that. He just had confidence in his security system and protections built into his house. He had never really thought he would need such things in the quiet peaceful Sault, but being a cop in Detroit he had learned to be paranoid. He hoped it would work. As soon as he took care of John he would check it. But he had to stay with John in case he could wake up for a minute and tell him where the Camels Eye was located.

People were now filing out of the casino to their cars or hotel rooms. A man in a loud shirt and Green Bay Packers hat walked out of the casino and was picked up at the road by a man in a white Ford Focus. They drove south out of the lot like many other patrons who would not be coming back to this casino any time soon.

Chapter 18

Kia had pulled the bus driver out of the seat, clubbed him with his Uzi and thrown him down in the aisle. He jumped into the seat, released the air brakes, put the bus in drive, accelerated through the parking lot and pointed the bus south. While he was driving he pushed the number three on his cell phone and waited for a connection.

"Yes, this is Kia, prepare the airplane. Start it in the hanger and we will take it out from there. Do not put it on the runway to warm up. We should be there in twenty minutes. We will go through the barn tunnel to the hanger. Put all the funds on the plane and be ready, we are going to the island." He did not say goodbye but just disconnected.

Some of the women were crying in the seats. June was trying to help Tony to his feet and put a handkerchief on the front of his forehead to stop the bleeding. Carolyn was trying to calm Edith whom she thought may be having a heart attack. They were all keeping their heads low in the seat in case there was more gun fire in the bus or outside.

As the bus neared the intersection of M-28, Kia saw that two BIA police cars were blocking the highway ahead. The officers were standing beside the patrol cars trying to wave the bus to stop. Kia did not even slow down but split the police cars as the tribal officers dived for cover. While most of the seniors were diving for cover, June was up and watching the action. She may never see anything like this again and didn't want to miss any of it.

Kia rode the brakes, made a 'wheels off the ground' left hand turn and headed east toward the farm. He would be on his home turf in a few minutes.

At the LZ, the Delta Team had reached Bird One and was loading when the earpiece in Colonel Stormer's helmet went off. "Charley One this Bird Two, come in, over." Bird One was fully loaded and lifting off now.

"This is Charley One, go ahead Bird Two."

"I have a visual on the bus. It has just broken through a roadblock and is now headed east on M-28. Over."

"That is a big 10-4 Bird One, they are probably headed for the farm. Do not engage, but hold your position about a mile behind them, do you copy Bird One?"

"One mile behind, Bird One copies, Charley One. Out"

He switched to intercom on his helmet. "Team, listen up. They have a bus load of hostages and are headed for the farm. Remember the layout, and we will have to be careful not to go in and cause too many civilian casualties. Remember these guys do not care who they kill, so we have to be very careful with our approach. Check your weapons and be ready when we land. Out."

Jim Featherson was sitting there thinking this was the worst case scenario they could have tonight. They had a bus full of hostages, going into a well fortified and defended position, two men down at the casino, and no Camels Eye to even show for it. What a mess they were in now. He might as well kiss his retirement goodbye. The President would be having him for lunch, and he would be the main course.

"Charley Two, Charley Two, this is Gregory come in, over," Agent Featherston heard in his helmet.

"Yes Gregory, this is Charley Two come in, over."

"Charley Two, I need immediate evac to my house. It has been attacked and I have an idea where the jewel may be, over."

"What about John or Jay? Over."

"Jay is dead and John may not make it. He is unconscious and seriously wounded. Over."

"Can you get to the waters edge where the tunnel exit is? Over."

"Yes, I know where it is and I will head there immediately, over."

"I will contact Seal One and have them pick you up and deliver you to your house ASAP. Do you copy? Over."

"I copy Charley Two, I will be waiting for a ride, over."

Agent Featherston immediately signaled Captain Windsmere, and asked for the extraction of Midge Gregory from the casino at the tunnel entrance on the bay that was on the Seal One Team map. Windsmere ordered his Sea Knight that was already on battle station stand by into the air. Three minutes later Midge was hauled into the chopper by two Navy Seals and they were airborne for the ten minute run to his house.

The bus arrived at the farm. Kia turned into the long driveway and drove straight for the barn. He turned right and drove right through the open barn doors scaring the camels in the stalls half to death.

Down the road in the painters van, Seyed was watching the action with great interest. The helicopter was hovering down the highway and a large passenger bus had turned and was going into the farm driveway. He had put Neka in the rear with his men and had taken the front seat in the cab next to the driver. He had his AK47 on his lap pointed at Robert, the Chippewa driver. He watched as he saw another helicopter come into view on the north side of the road flying low over the tree line. It was a troop carrying Ch 47 Chinook. He knew this from his days in Afghanistan fighting the great Satan's soldiers. It was their main means of transportation for the soldiers with the night eyes. He could not tell what the other helicopter was from here, but if he knew the Americans it would probably be an Apache gunship with enough firepower to take out a tank or blow a fortified cave to rubble. Those things were lethal to his Taliban fighters and had almost killed him several times, if it were not for the grace of Allah.

"Get ready to move, we are going in as soon as I say."

"Are you nuts? Those guys almost killed us the last time we went to the farm. We were only a little ways up the driveway when they opened up on us."

Seyed pointed his AK 47 at Robert's head and said, "I will kill you, if you don't move when I tell you. Do you understand?" Robert just nodded his head, put his hands on the steering wheel and waited for Seyed to give him the word to go.

Seyed watched the action with interest and was waiting for the right moment to enter the farm. He had no wish to be martyred while driving up to the barn under machine gun fire. He was after the Nas-

The Camels Eye

sire men. He would wait for the American soldiers to take some causalities, then he would take his men in and find 'yellow eyes' children and kill them. He would let the Americans find the jewel and give it to him so he could complete his mission. Then he would call Tehran, have the hostages released and head home with the Camels Eye.

Kia opened the bus door and headed into the barn to unlock the weapons room. One of his men stayed with the bus while the other man helped Kia take the satchels from the casino into the room at the end they had just opened. Now everyone could hear machine gun fire from the top of the barn and most of the people in the bus hit the floor. All except June, of course, who had her camera out, taking pictures of the barn and Kia's man who was left on the steps of the bus. As soon as the gun fire started in the top of the barn, he too leapt off and ran into the end room disappearing on the right.

The Delta team was now approaching the farm from the north, low over the tree line. They were ready to assault the barn, but were not really sure if Kia was using the senior bus hostages as shields or what. The bus was inside the barn and was blind to the Delta Team and their pilots.

Colonel Stormer ordered a pass over to the left of the big barn with landing lights on to try to get a look inside the barn at the bus. As they crossed the highway, the copulas in the top of the barn erupted with machine gun fire. The pilot of Bird One quickly banked the Chinook hard left showing as much of his armored belly as he could as he accelerated to the south east out of range of the menacing fire. The machine guns had hit their mark but the Chinook suffered no critical damage to jeopardize the mission. It did lose one of its landing lights for its effort.

As they climbed out of machine gun range, Colonel Stormer asked Agent Featherston, "How much caution do you want us to take?"

"What do you mean?" Jim asked.

"If we don't take those machine guns out from the air, we will have to assault the barn from the ground. They control all the fields of fire from the top of that barn. I will lose a lot of men and maybe all the hostages. That is not a very good option for my team."

"Take the machine gun nests out, but remember there is a bus full of hostages in there so try not to kill them all." Agent Featherston was sorry he ever heard of this mission.

203

"I can't promise anything for sure, but we will try" The Colonel told him.

"Bird Two, this is Charley One. Come in, over."

"This is Bird Two, go ahead, over."

"We need you to take out the machine guns in the top of that barn, but there is a bus full of hostages inside the barn so we have to be careful, over."

"We copy that Charley One, but if that barn is made of wood, we may start a fire that will burn the whole thing down and kill everyone inside it. Please advise, over." Colonel Stormer had already advised them to be careful, what did the pilot want? Of course he knew, the pilots wanted a direct order from the commander in charge. Since the civilian lawyers of dead soldiers in Iraq had sued pilots for friendly fire deaths, the American pilots were reluctant to take aggressive action against an enemy without direct orders. Better to let the terrorists kill all the hostages than put up with the ACLU lawyers in American courts. They could sue the Arabs in their home countries instead. What a country to be a soldier in. Every body was a critic, but those lawyers did not want to fight America's enemies.

"Bird Two, I am ordering you to take out both machine gun towers in the top of the barn. Use your Hydras, not your Hellfires. Do you copy? Over."

"That is affirmative Charley One, we copy and are moving into position now, over. The Apache moved to the north of the target figuring that would be its best hope for success with the lowest chance for fire in the barn. Of course everyone knew that the hostages were at high risk, but the Colonel had made the decision and he would fry, if this battle field gamble went wrong, not the pilots, they had it on tape.

June saw the guard jump from the bus and head into the end room on the right. She jumped up and limped into the drivers seat, leaving Tony the bus driver holding his head in the seat next to her.

Carolyn yelled at her, "June what are you doing?"

"I'm getting us out of here if I can. This is a bad place to be right now." She had never driven a bus before in her life, but that didn't stop June. The pedals were confusing to her because they both looked like gas pedals. She figured the outside one must be the gas and she pressed it. She could hear the engine rev up some but the bus didn't move. Where was the shift gear? She looked around and found it beside the

The Camels Eye

seat. She moved the lever to drive and felt the bus try to move forward. She pushed on the gas pedal but it wouldn't budge. She was out of ideas.

"Release the brakes," Tony yelled from his seat, but it was useless. June had exhausted her knowledge of operating a bus, after finding the gear shift. Tony stumbled to the front of the bus holding the bloody handkerchief to his head, reached over June and pushed the air brake button in to release it.

"Go June, go now. Get us out of here."

She was not sure what was going to happen, but she stomped on the gas pedal and the bus shot forward. The big sliding barn doors in front of the bus were closed, but she didn't care. She just plowed right through them, knocking them up and to the side while scraping the bus roof all the way into the field, but clear of the barn. She kept driving until she tried to turn the big bus to the right and got stuck in the soft field about three hundred feet from the barn. The people on the bus were taking cover behind their seats as gunfire was starting to hit the roof of the bus. Next they heard a large explosion on the top of the barn and then it was gone. There were boards raining down on the field, but there was no more gun fire coming from the cupolas.

As Bird Two acquired his target, he watched in amazement as the barn doors on his right burst open and a big passenger bus drove into the field beside the barn. It was churning up grass and trying to turn north in a big circle, but sank into the grass about three hundred feet from the barn. The machine guns turned their fire on the bus now. The gunner depressed his fire control button twice and both cupolas exploded into a thousand pieces. The gun fire stopped almost immediately. But as the pilot had feared, the Hydra secondary incendiaries burst the barn into flames. A few minutes later the munitions stored in the barn caused a massive secondary explosion causing the barn to disinigrate into a thousand wooden pieces. It rained down debris as far as where the bus was now parked in the field.

The seniors were still shaking when they heard June asking for her camera.

"Nice shot Bird Two, I am glad someone drove that bus out of there. Bird One is going in. Cover us, over."

"Roger that, Charley One."

The Chinook headed straight for the bus. There was no hostile fire

205

on the approach this time. The Delta team leaped from the chopper as it hovered about four feet off the ground and surrounded the bus. Two soldiers got ready to blow the door and the rest of the team got prepared to storm aboard and take out any terrorists who were still alive.

The bus door opened and a woman sitting in the driver's seat had a camera and told them to smile.

"We're alright, the men with the guns are gone," June said as she smiled, holding her camera. "Come on in if you want, we're okay really."

The Sergeant Major entered the bus first still alert and battle ready, but quickly lowered his weapon. All he saw was a bunch of bruised, frightened, and exhausted senior citizens. The tour guide, Carolyn stood up and told the soldier, "I think we are going to need an ambulance to look after some of our group."

The soldier responded, "Yes ma'am." Then he put his hand to the side of his helmet and spoke, "Charley One, this is Team Leader One come in, over." Charley One and the Agent were still in the chopper.

"Go, Team Leader One."

"The people on the bus need some medical attention. No gunshot wounds just bumps, bruises, and stress, over."

"I roger that Team Leader One, I will send for medical assistance ASAP. Now proceed with caution up the driveway to the big white house, over."

"Roger, I will leave one man with the bus and my team will proceed up the driveway to the white house, over."

"Ten-four, Team Leader One, we will coordinate from here." Colonel Stormer keyed the mike and called Ken Telway on his police radio. "Telway, this is Stormer, we are at the Nassire farm and seek immediate medical attention for the civilians on the bus, over."

"Ten-four, I will dispatch medical and police officers immediately, over."

As soon as Seyed saw the barn explode and the soldiers leap from the helicopter, illuminated by the burning wreckage of the barn, he ordered Robert to drive to the farm. Scared to go, but too scared to disobey Seyed's order, he put the van in drive and floored it causing the heavy vehicle to lurch forward. They reached the driveway to the farm, turned left and drove toward the burning barn where a helicopter was seen hovering near a bus at the far right of the field.

"Charley One, this is Bird Two, there is a large vehicle approaching your position from the north. Do you want us to take it out? Over."

Stormer looked out the side door and saw a big work van approaching. "Negative on that Bird Two, but stay in position and acquire the target just in case, over."

The van pulled up parallel on the driveway near the chopper. One man dressed in a Carhartt jacket with blue jeans tucked in brown rubberized hunting boots, but carrying what Stormer recognized as an AK 47, approached the chopper. The man had short black hair, was not pointing the weapon at them, but was waving his right arm high in the air, back and forth frantically.

"Charley One, this is Bird Two, another vehicle has just entered the drive and is proceeding across the field to your north. Do we engage? Over." It was starting to look like a state fair parking lot all of a sudden, the pilot thought.

"Negative Bird Two, hold your position. Bobby do you copy? Over."

"Go Charley One, I copy, over"

"Bobby, there is a vehicle cutting across the field toward you. Stop it, at all costs, over."

"I roger that Charley One, I am leaving the bus now, over." Bobby came out of the door and held his left hand up for the big SUV to stop. He could tell it had no intention of doing so by the way it was chewing up turf as it barreled toward him. He pushed the safety off his AR15 and depressed the trigger going right for the windshield. His rounds seemed to bounce off the glass like throwing marbles off a Lexan bank teller window. He quickly shifted to its front right tire to take out its steering, but despite several direct hits, the SUV continued on its path. He rolled under the edge of the bus for protection and let a burst go along the side doors as the SUV passed him. To no effect, the vehicle kept moving through the pine trees and over the small hill.

"Charley One this Bobby, the SUV is armored and I could not stop it. Do you want me to pursue? Over."

"Negative Bobby, stay with the bus, over."

"I roger that, out."

"Charley One to Team Leader One, over."

"Go Charley One, over."

"Return to the chopper on the double. We have company. Have

your team surround and take down the van in the driveway, over."

"Roger that Charley One, we are moving north now on the quick, over."

Colonel Stormer had his AR15 at the ready as the strangely dressed man with the AK 47 approached the side door of the chopper. When he got close enough to speak, he stopped and put his AK47 down on the ground.

"I am Mullah Seyed Habibi of the Islamic Republic of Iran. I am here to take custody of the Camels Eye and the Nassire family." He was screaming to be heard over the downwash of the Chinook rotor blades.

"Leave the rifle on the ground and climb in so we can talk." Midge was leading the conversation now.

"I do not follow your orders. You will follow mine or all of your hostages will die." Seyed was having trouble controlling his temper this close to the Great Satan soldiers who had killed so many of his comrades over the years.

As he was talking, the Delta Team had surrounded the van, had the driver out and was opening the back of the box. Gunfire erupted as the back panel door was being raised. Two stun grenades were thrown inside by the Delta soldiers and two loud bangs could be heard all the way to the chopper. The Delta Team then quickly opened the rear door and disarmed the six dazed soldiers and one Indian in the compartment who were moaning and holding their ears. They dragged them quickly to the ground and band tied their hands behind them and then banded their feet together. This force was no longer a threat to the Delta Force.

Seyed watched the action and considered for a moment grabbing his AK 47 and mowing down the infidels. But a quick look at Colonel Stormer with his AR15 and black combat uniform and helmet made him decide against that. He instead climbed into the Chinook for a talk with the infidels. He could hear them making radio transmissions to each other.

"Good job, Team Leader One. Now deploy for defense and hold for further orders, over." His team was superbly trained for terrorist attacks as long as they arrived in time to make a difference.

"Roger that Charley One, setting up defense perimeter now, over."

"Charley One, this is Bird Two, you have emergency vehicles approaching from the east and west. Blue lights from the west and red from the east, over."

"Roger that Bird Two, I asked for them. Hold your position and keep me informed of any other events, over."

"Roger, Charley One, out."

"Team Leader One, set up a flare line to stop traffic from proceeding up the driveway. Direct the emergency vehicles to the bus for medical treatment, over."

"Roger that Charley One, setting up now, over." Three flares burst into flames just north of the van across the driveway.

The BIA police cars and the Sault ambulances arrived about the same time. The Sergeant Major stopped the lead BIA police car and told him the situation. Then the police captain and his fellow officers started directing vehicles toward the bus stuck in the field.

With everything now seemingly under control, Agent Featherston and Colonel Stormer turned their attention to the Iranian Mullah.

"Now let us bring you up to speed on our situation on the ground. Jay Nassire was killed at the casino, John Nassire is dying and currently unconscious, Kia Ashad and some of his men are still unaccounted for at this time. We have not yet been able to find the Camels Eye, but we have a man working on it. That is where we stand right now. Any questions?"

Seyed hated these arrogant Americans. They did not use subtle language at all, just boom and right to the point. They should be kissing his ass and they were acting like they were in charge. He held innocent hostages back in Iran, cooks, mechanics, school teachers, aid workers, and so forth. How would the world like to see a beheading a day on CNN or Aljazeera? How long could the cowboy President last while the left wing Kennedy and Pelosi camps raved for concessions on television? Democracy was a weak form of government, except for this Cowboy maniac who refused to follow UN orders and pay attention to the polls in his own country's newspapers. This was not right to be immune to European opinion or UN controls.

"What about the young boy, was he killed also?" Jim eyed this obvious zealot with suspicion now.

"No, Kia tried to abduct him, but we have him safely in protective custody now."

"You will surrender the boy to me along with the jewel immediately and then take me to my ship." That is how you talk to infidel dogs.

Always show strength to these weaklings.

Jim was pissed now, just about everything that could go wrong tonight had, and now he had this maniac making demands that were not in the agreement with his government. If he lost the hostages, this son of a bitch was going to die. He didn't give a shit what happened to him. "Listen asshole, you will not be getting your shit covered hands on the boy and if anything happens to the hostages in Iran, you and all your asshole assault team will end up in the bottom of Lake Superior. It is one cold and deep ass lake. Do you read me, mister?" Colonel Stormer had to put his hand on Jim's shoulder. He could see murder in his eyes.

The Mullah was taken aback by this attack. What is wrong with these Americans? The French would have given him all their money and their wives, the Spanish an island in the Mediterranean if he promised not to hurt them, and the Germans, they would give him a whole factory of high tech equipment as long as he promised not to commit any terror events on their soil. But no, this infidel man was threatening to kill him and all his men. *These Americans were insane!* No wonder the world hated these swaggering swine. They are the 'bust you in the mouth' kind of people. He did not understand these infidels at all.

"My government had an agreement with your government. That is all you will get and only if I can find the damn Camels Eye. So sit there and shut up or I will bind you like your cowardly men over there that you call an assault team, and leave you to die in the dirt. You couldn't assault a group of old women without getting your ass kicked you dumb ass rag head, so sit there and shut your mouth before I kick all your teeth in." Jim was in a rage and it would not take much for him to pull this asshole out of the chopper and give him a first class ass whooping, American style.

Seyed glowered at the Agent, but kept his mouth shut. One look at his face and Seyed knew this man could not be bluffed. He was just like the camel mated cowboy President he served. If it came to a fight with this American, he knew he would die. He still had a mission to complete, even though he would now not have the pleasure of killing the Nassire family. He had to concentrate on his mission now and get home to the land of believers. He would remember this humiliation and many innocent Americans would pay some day. He would launch a Jihad against their undefended civilians.

"Charley One, this is Bird Two, over."

"Bird Two, this is Charley One, go, over."

"Yes Charley One, I can see the reflection of something moving over the hill from your position, over."

"Is it a threat to us? Over."

"No, it seems to be moving out from a building to your southwest about three hundred yards out, over."

"The air strip, they are going to fly out of here," Jim yelled at the Colonel.

"Bird Two, can you approach and light up the target? Over?"

"Roger that, but it is starting to pick up speed. We are moving to intercept, over."

"Charley One to control, over."

"This is control, go ahead Charley One."

"We have a bandit trying to escape our location. Can you track him? He is moving southwest and going airborne right now, over."

"That is affirmative Charley One, we are tracking on Sat-128, over."

"Do we have any fixed wing assets in the area to intercept? Over."

"That depends which way he turns. Can you intercept on your end? Over."

"What do you think, Bird Two? Over."

"Negative Charley One. He looks like he can do over two hundred fifty knots. That is way out of our league unless he banks and flies our way, over."

"Control, do you read? We cannot intercept with choppers, can you assist? Over."

"We will continue to track the aircraft, and try to rally a couple of jets from Border Security Air Command North, over."

"Roger that Control. Keep me informed, over."

"Will do Charley One, Control out."

Now there was another screw up, Jim thought. While we were engaged trying to treat the hostages and secure the Iranian assault team, Kia and his band of killers were escaping. Did he have any hostages on the plane? No he decided, there were no hostages on the aircraft, just Kia and his men with who knows how much money. Well, he needed to concentrate on the task at hand. Where was the Camels Eye?

"I roger that Control. Keep me informed, over."

Chapter 19

The Sea Night was a stable aircraft used for air to sea rescues. The two seals on board were dressed for war, Midge could tell. They were so much better equipped than he ever was when he was in the army. The communication gear and the protective vest and light weapons amazed him. As a cop for many years, all the protection he had on was his shirt. These Seals were the elite warriors of the Navy fighting forces and he was happy to see them and the Delta Force soldiers on this mission.

He could not stop thinking about his conversation with John Nassire on the pavement outside the casino. Had he been confused or delirious when he asked him about where the Camels Eye was? Of course, he was bleeding to death and going into shock, but all he would keep repeating was Jacob's name. Was it because of concern for his son, or was he really trying to answer Midge's questions and help him? He found it hard to believe a ten year old boy would be trusted with the knowledge of a priceless gem that people were willing to kill for.

They hugged the coast and then headed directly for the Sault, flying by using night vision goggles as it was almost midnight. Midge watched the lights on the ground increase as they approached the city. He could see the waterway and Locks lit up in the distance, so he could get an idea of where his house was located in the dark. As it turned out, he did not need any land marks. There were blue flashing lights illuminating his house from the Sheriff and Sault Police cruisers in his front yard. He pointed at his house for the seals benefit. They relayed it to the Navy pilots who banked the Sea Knight and made a perfect landing on the road in front of his house.

Midge was met as he exited the Sea Knight by Captain Tom Molten, his friend on the Chippewa County Sheriff's department.

"How is everyone in the house, Tom?" He was yelling as they moved toward the house. The Sea Knight was lifting off and heading back to the Seal One team.

"They are just fine Midge, but your house may need a paint job, my friend." Tom was about six foot five and had long lanky legs.

"As long as everyone is safe, I can always repair a house. Are they all inside or what, Tom?"

"Yes, they are inside the house, most of the damage occurred outside. The shooter was never actually able to get inside. We arrived too soon and he fled in a dark red Ford Expedition." Midge glanced at the two police cars as they walked past them. Both the front ends had been smashed and their air bags deployed. They were facing the opposite way from each other and about ten feet apart as if something had crashed into them and split them into two pieces. Those armored SUV's were a pretty tough truck for sure.

"Uncle Midge!" Ryan jumped into his uncle's arms and hugged him tightly. Midge was relieved to see Ryan was not hurt. They hugged as they entered the house where he saw Brenda on the couch holding and stroking Jacob's head, gently rocking him a little bit.

Tom gave the police officer a nod of his head and they both left the house, closing the door behind them. Every light in the place was on both inside and out. He could understand that after the fright they had all been through. They were too frightened to turn the lights out and go to bed right now.

The place did not look too bad inside except for the star burst cracks in the windows and the black charring on the outside of the front door. Once again he was so glad he had installed the three deadbolt door with steel frame and steel cross members imbedded in the wall. He had learned its value in Detroit when they tried to break down the front door in a drug bust. The cops couldn't get inside. The dealer finally came out after a few hours, but not until he had flushed and cleaned up all the drugs and records in his house. Midge knew he wanted a door like that if he ever built another house.

"Are you alright, Brenda? I'm sorry about all the trouble, okay?"

"I am fine Midge, and it was not your fault. Kia was after Jacob, not me or Ryan. I'm just so glad you called me and I was able to get everything locked down in time. There is no telling what he would have done to Ryan and me if he had gotten inside. The police arrived just in time to save us too. I do not know what I would have done if he had gotten inside. I may have shot him or even killed him. I am not sure I could live with that very well."

"Yeah, tell me about it." Midge had not had much time to reflect on the terrorist he had shot to death. He knew it would keep him awake sometimes in the future, but that was then and this was now.

"Is Jacob alright now?" Midge watched the boy cuddling Brenda and he dreaded what he would have to do next.

"He's just upset is all. He'll be fine after he gets home with his father and grandfather again." She kept stroking his hair from the front of his head to the back. It soothed the boy.

Now Midge had a decision to make. Should he ask the boy about the Camels Eye and see if he knows where it is located, or should he first tell him about his father and grandfather? If the boy went to pieces over the news of what happened to his family, and he really could understand that reaction from a ten year old boy or anyone for that matter, then Jacob would be of no use in the search for the jewel. Jacob was all he had left, more importantly the last glimmer of hope for the hostages in Iran. No, he would try to question him first and inform him about his family later.

"Jacob, listen to me, please." He watched as Jacob turned his eyes toward him.

"I need to ask you some questions and it is very important you think very hard if you know the answers to the questions." Midge watched him and noticed Ryan was watching closely now also.

"Where is my father, I need my father. I want to go home, please call my father, I want to go home." He turned his head to Brenda and started sobbing into her chest. This was the last thing Midge wanted right now, a hysterical kid.

"Jacob, listen to me for a minute. If you will stop crying and listen to me and help me find the answer to some questions, then I will take you to see your father." He waited for Jacob to stop crying. Brenda was still holding him and stroking his hair. He seemed to be calming down a little now.

"Midge, can you get him a drink of water and some Kleenex to wipe his eyes and nose? Then maybe we can talk with him about what you need to know." Midge went to the kitchen to get Jacob a drink of water, while Ryan ran to his bedroom and brought back an open box of Puffs. After Brenda had dried his eyes and nose and gave him a couple drinks of water, he seemed to breathe easier, but he still held onto Brenda's hand. Midge had to be careful. He did not want to upset the boy again, but he was clumsy with kids and women. He knew how to question a murderer or thief, but that type of aggressive questioning would not work in this situation.

"Jacob, how about you and Ryan play a game? I will ask a question and we will see which one of you boys knows the answer first. Ryan, come and sit next to Jacob on the couch, will you please?" Ryan jumped on the couch beside Jacob and held his free hand. So far so good, Midge figured.

"Now, let me ask if you know the name of a necklace, called the Camels Eye?" Neither boy responded at all. That told him no one had told Jacob about the Camels Eye. Where did he go next?

"Jacob, did your father ever talk to you about a necklace that may have been in your family for a long time?"

"My mother had a necklace." He seemed to be trying to recall it.

"Was it big and had a large green stone in the middle of it?" Now he was getting somewhere.

"I don't remember, can I go see my father now?" This was heading in the wrong direction.

Midge was trying to think of exactly the words he used with John when he asked him about the jewel. All John said in response were the words Jacob, Jacob, and finally Jacob again. What was he trying to tell him?

"Jacob, is it possible you may have the jewel and not even know it?"

"I don't know." Of course he didn't know you idiot, Midge thought to himself. But there was something about Jacob being involved with the jewel, he just knew it. It was driving him crazy just thinking about it.

"Jacob, do you have a secret hiding place in your room at home or a hidden piggy bank or something where you keep your best stuff?"

"We don't have a piggy bank and we don't eat pigs at my house."

No, they wouldn't have a pig in their house, that was a dumb question.

"I keep all my good stuff in my back pack, I'll show you." Ryan raced to his messy room and grabbed his spider man back pack he carried to school everyday. The others watched him as he dumped its contents on the living room floor.

"Look, I found this on a walk last week." He held up a small stone that was red and gray with some silver flecks in it, as proud as if he had found a diamond. Ryan was a saver of insignificant things. He'd kept an old bubble gum wrapper, a piece of string, a piece of candy he saved that now was not edible, a bottle cap, an old valentine card he liked, some old keys that no longer fit anything, a rusted bolt, a broken piece of blue glass, a steel penny, and a small piece of wood that looked like a horse head to him.

These were just a sample the kid carried around with him. You should see the drawers in his room. Midge was always throwing things away when Ryan wasn't looking. He did some of it for health reasons. Ryan would just as likely save an old piece of sandwich in his room to eat later. Midge would find it while trying to clean out under Ryan's bed. It was all mildew and green. It could attract mice or ants or some other kind of bug, but he could never make Ryan understand being neat and organized helped prevent these problems. A ten year old boy just did not seem to care, and maybe that is how they all are.

"Ryan, that is some neat stuff you have saved." Brenda was trying to praise Ryan, but she could see that Midge did not approve of any of it.

"What's in your back pack, Jacob?" Ryan was on his knees reviewing all his valuable boy treasures.

"I don't know, my dad packs my lunch in it for school. He put some clothes in it for me to stay over night yesterday." Yes, Midge remembered that at the farm. After Midge had Ryan ask Jacob to spend the night, John had gone into the house with Jacob and packed his backpack for the overnight stay.

"Where is your backpack, Jacob?" Ryan asked his little friend.

"I don't know, I think you took it, didn't you?" He looked at Ryan.

"Oh yeah, I know where it is. I put it in my room after we got ready for bed." Ryan jumped up and made a bee line for his room with Jacob jumping up and following him. A minute later, they returned with each of them holding one of the straps to Jacob's leather designer back pack Midge had seen him with at school many times.

"Here it is." They both shook the contents out on the carpet next to Ryan's junk and threw the expensive pack over with Ryan's Spiderman classic backpack.

Jacob started holding his things up the same as Ryan had done, "toothbrush and toothpaste, a pair of blue socks, clean underwear, a clean dinosaur shirt, a comb, some fruit roll ups, and a blue towel." That was it as Jacob waved the towel around Ryan's head for fun. Of course, he was wearing his pajamas, and the clothes he had worn yesterday were in a heap with Ryan's in the bedroom. No bottle cap, stones, wood, wrappers, or piece of blue glass, or any other boy's treasure, and most of all no Camels Eye, Midge thought.

"Jacob, is that the back pack you take to school everyday?" Brenda was amazed anyone would spend that much money on a kids back pack. "You talk about flaunting your wealth at the other parents. That is ridiculous and he would not fit in with the other boys that way."

"Yep, everyday." The boys were examining the piece of dark blue bottle glass up against a light.

"I know just what you're thinking. That baby had to cost a hundred dollars or more just to carry his books to school.

"A hundred dollars, Midge you must not shop for leather purses much." She picked it up and examined the stitching, the seams and hasp on the flap. "This thing cost four hundred bucks if it cost a dime. Feel how thick and heavy it is. It will last a lifetime, but it seems a waste on a kid's school bag. What if the kid loses it or it gets stolen? I would kill my kid if he lost it." She handed the back pack to Midge.

"You or I would never spend that much or give a kid that much responsibility just to take to school. I never even cared what clothes I wore to school." Midge had to admit it was some fantastic leather work. He cared about how his baseball glove was made and knew a quality short tight stitch from a long cheap stitch. "This thing is so heavy though, I would hate to take it on a long hike. Good thing it was only being carried in and out of school from the parking lot."

"I don't care how heavy or light it is, that bag is way too expensive for a ten year old kid. John must be crazy." Brenda threw her hands up in the air.

Yes, it was way too expensive for a ten year boy to use, but someone always picked him up and dropped him off and kept track of all his things. The boys were playing with Ryan's junk and seemed lost in a boy's world for now. Midge grabbed both of the back packs and carried them to the kitchen table. He at least did not have to bother turning on any lights, they were all on. Brenda followed him and started to make a pot of coffee as she watched him.

He laid both the bags flat and next to each other. He went to a drawer near the dishwasher and pulled out a tape measure. He first measured the Spiderman back pack. It was typical for a ten year old. He never really looked for size because Ryan was picking out by picture or superhero on the packs. No boy would want Cinderella on his backpack because the boys would tease him to death. But now he examined the backpack carefully, he could appreciate the design effort required to make a good kids product.

The Spiderman pack was basically in three main colors, red, black, and blue and the zippers were surrounded with light gray cloth. Spiderman himself had white and black on his suit and the blue letters across the back of the bag were shadowed a little bit with white.

The bag was sixteen inches long and thirteen inches wide. If you pulled the bag out in the front, it was six inches deep at its biggest point. It had one zipper that ran totally across the top and about six inches down each side so you could get wide books in and out easily. There was another zipper across the rear face of the pack all the way across and it was about six inches down from the top. It was a thin compartment that was probably best used to carry thin sheets of paper like homework or small folders. That pocket ran all the way to the bottom of the bag with only the thickness of the material between it and the outside bottom.

On the top of the bag was sewn a black strap that was held on with a strong box stitch with diagonal stitches to help support the weight of hanging the bag on a hook at school. Pretty good engineering, he thought. Brenda brought him a cup of coffee and pulled up a chair to watch.

The shoulder straps were sewn right in the center of the pack at the top of the inside panel. They were each two inches wide and covered with a rubbery feeling nylon just like the rest of the material on the pack. The bottom of the shoulder straps was sewn near the bottom on each side to small triangular ears and secured with the same box and diagonal stitch used for the top strap. The adjustable portion of the shoulder straps were only one inch wide, and over twelve inches long. They were made of braided nylon and threaded through a four bar adjuster so it would hold and not come lose.

The stitches were okay. Most of the bag was molded together at the edges and sealed with a round seam that held everything together. Midge wondered what kind of a machine made those round-rope-like edges that held things together like seats and bags.

"You know, I have a lot of respect now for the guys who design these things. Other than the pictures on them, there is a lot of planning that goes into making a product for kids. I just never looked at it that way before."

"Or gals."

"What? Oh yeah, or the gals who designed this bag." Women's libber for sure, he thought.

"Now let's check out the designer bag here." Right off the bat it was two inches longer and one inch wider. Big deal, he thought. It was seven inches deep instead of six so he would give it that.

It was made of beautiful leather instead of rubberized nylon of some kind, but it was only going to carry books and paper and junk anyway.

It had the same top zipper opening going down six inches on the side also, but the zipper was made of stainless steel. It looked like satin and worked smooth as silk, not hard to pull like the plastic one on the Spiderman bag. Score one for high fashion.

The front compartment was all the way across also, but the inside of the pouch was lined in silk and had the same high quality zipper as the top.

The shoulder straps were wider and more padded, but a kid would need that to carry all the extra weight.

But the biggest difference came when you tried to stand them up on the bottom. The spider man pack would fold into a clump of rubber covered nylon, while the premium leather pack would sit flat on the floor so you could look into its silk lined compartment for you stuff. It must have a wire frame under the leather to hold its shape. The bottom was flat and weighted so it would not tip over. It must be full of sand or a brick to keep it upright so well.

"It is really nice, you have to admit, Midge."

Finally he measured the inside of the back pack silk lined main compartment. This is where the cheap backpack won hands down. The Spiderman pack had almost the sixteen inch height as usual storage space, while the eighteen inch designer leather bag had only a depth of fourteen inches of usable space in all.

"There you are Brenda, you get more carrying capacity on the cheap pack then the all leather brands. What do you think of that?"

"Are you sure you measured right? That sounds like a lot of space to lose just for the bottom reinforcement and weight." She was feeling inside it now with her hand.

Jacob, was that what John was trying to tell him at the casino? Too much space, too expensive for a kid to use. Jacob, Jacob, Jacob was all he could hear from John's fading voice.

"Hey, I was looking at that." Midge grabbed the leather back pack from Brenda, turned it upside down and carefully examined the bottom of the bag. He could see nothing but close heavy stitches holding the seams of the bag together.

He put his hand inside and could feel nothing. If it had a false bottom like a drug runners suit case he could not feel anything move. He got up and went to his bedroom to retrieve his hunting knife. He always kept it honed razor sharp so it would skin a deer, even though he did not hunt. He checked the kitchen wall clock and it was almost a quarter to one in the morning.

He went back to the table and told Brenda, "move back, this knife is dangerous."

"What are you going to do? Put that knife down. You will ruin Jacob's backpack. I hope you have five hundred bucks to buy another one." She moved away from the sharp knife.

"Look, I am out of ideas and out of time. There are some American hostages in Iran whose very lives depend on us returning this damn Camels Eye. If I am wrong, I will apologize and buy the kid a new one, so step back."

He started in the center of the bottom of the bag that was sticking up and pushed the knife in half way. He used a slight sawing motion to cut the bag across, around the corner and all the way down one side to the table. He then reversed the knife and slit the other side open all

The Camels Eye

the way. When he folded the leather down, it revealed a thick black rubber like block that fell out on the top of the flap he just pulled down.

"Great, Midge, a damn weight just like we thought. You owe the kid a new bag."

It was a four inch block alright. Midge examined it closely. It appeared to be made of two separate pieces of rubber type material glued together to form one piece. He took his knife and carefully ran it back and forth along the seam all the way around the block of spacer until he finally felt it give. It split into two pieces and he lifted the top piece off.

Inside was sealed in a clear thick plastic bag the most beautiful necklace he had ever seen in his whole life.

Brenda gasped as even in a plastic covering the light was reflecting back from all the diamonds and the most perfect emerald she could imagine. "The Camels Eye, no wonder so many people want it," she whispered respectfully.

"Yes, it is the most beautiful thing I have ever seen." He was drawn to its beauty like a moth to a flame. It took him a second to shake himself back to action.

He quickly put the top back on, got some scotch tape from the drawer and taped the two pieces back together. He went into the living room carrying the jewel. He was not letting this thing out of his sight at all, until he gave it to Agent Featherston in person. He picked up his radio and depressed the voice button.

"Charley Two, this is Gregory, over."

"Roger, this is Charley Two, go Midge, over."

"Charley Two, we have found what we need for the exchange, over."

"Do I read you right, Midge? You have found the item? Over."

"That is affirmative Charley Two, I have it at my house right now and it is beautiful, over."

"Roger that Midge, we will be airborne in ten minutes with an ETA of eight minutes after that. Good job, but be careful. Over."

"Charley Two, I will meet you at the Brady Park on Water Street right next to the Coast Guard Station. I will have a police escort and I want to get it to a safe place ASAP, over."

"Roger that Midge, the same ETA, see you there, out."

The boys had fallen asleep on the floor and Brenda was standing next to him now.

"Watch the boys and lock the doors, I am going to get Tom and his men to take me to the park on Water Street. This is almost over Brenda, thanks for all your help." He hugged her and started for the door.

"Be careful Midge, there are men who will kill to take what you have."

"I know, believe me I know." He rushed out the door to Tom and told him to take him to the park and bring his men. Tom asked no questions, but loaded everyone into the two cars that still drove and, with lights and sirens blazing, headed for the park.

Chapter 20

That was great news. Featherston and Stormer were giving each other high fives as Seyed watched in disgust at their childish celebration.

"Team Leader One, this is Charley One, come in, over."

"Go Charley One, over."

"Let's get ready to mount up and move out. Cut the band ties on the legs of the Iranian prisoners, but leave the hands bound for now and load them in the chopper. Turn the Indians over to the BIA to handle and get your whole team loaded up ASAP, including Bobby from the bus. Over."

"Roger Charley One, out."

"One more thing Team Leader One, have Bobby confiscate the camera from that woman on the bus who is taking all those pictures. We don't need any more help from civilians, over.

"Roger, do you copy Bobby? Get the camera. Over."

"Roger, she is not going to like it, but I will take the camera, out."

The Delta Force soldier approached the woman who was outside the bus taking photos. "Ma'am I have orders to confiscate your camera. Sorry but it is a national security issue."

"Nuts to you! It cost over sixty dollars for this camera and you're not getting it." The other soldiers were loading the chopper with the prisoners.

"I must insist ma'am." He was losing his patience.

"No, I don't care what they say. This is not the army's camera and I'm keeping it." June was holding it away from the soldier in her left hand, like she was daring him to try and take it.

"June, give him the camera, it's not worth it," the tour guide Carolyn said.

"Carolyn, you can give him your camera if you want to, I am not giving him this one." She wasn't budging.

The soldier had to wrestle June's camera from her hands and then he turned and sprinted toward the chopper. Mission accomplished, as he keyed his mike. "Charley One, I have the camera and am on the way in, over."

"Roger that Bobby, any trouble?"

"Roger, I had to wrestle the old lady for it, but I out muscled her, out." He was smiling as he raced for the chopper. The Delta team members would have a field day with him for wrestling an eighty-one year old lady out of a camera. Some combat action, he thought.

"There now, see what happened? You lost your camera anyway so all that arguing was for nothing. It does not pay to argue with the military or the police." Carolyn turned and headed back to the bus.

June pulled out her camera from her big bag and started snapping more photos.

"June, you had two cameras?" The tour guide, Carolyn was amazed.

"No, but tell Tony I'm sorry, they stole his camera. He asked me to get him a few pictures. Oh well, too bad," and she turned and took a picture of the big Chinook lifting off.

Bird One was airborne and headed northeast to the LZ at Brady Park next to the Coast Guard Station in the Sault. The Iranians were all seated on one side of the aircraft with the Delta Force team sitting facing them. All the Iranians hands were still band tied behind their backs except for the leader and he was totally disarmed.

Seyed glowered at the Satan soldiers. It was men just like these who killed so many of his Mujahidin brothers in Afghanistan. Take away their fancy communication gear and air cover and his Taliban brethren would have slaughtered these infidels. Once he got his hands on the Camels Eye and the Americans released him and his team for the run to Canada, he would find some way to retaliate against these evil men. But he would wait until he was in Canadian territory, where these killers could not hurt him.

"Control to Charley One, come in, over."

"This is Charley One, go control, over."

"Charley One, we have a change in direction on that bandit we are tracking for you, over."

"Where is the bandit now, over?"

"Bandit has turned north and is headed toward Lake Superior, what do you advise over?"

"Bandit must be intercepted at all costs, over."

"I thought you might say that, Charley One. We are patching you through to Blue Streak Leader who is in position to intercept, over." NSA had contacted Border Air Command North and had two F16 Tomcats moving to intercept position in case the bandit made a run for Canada. They were patrolling just inside the US border over the big lake.

"Blue Streak Leader, this is Charley One, over."

"Blue Streak Leader here, we have the bandit on the screen about ten minutes out. What are your orders, over?"

"Intercept and force back to Michigan, or terminate. I repeat, force land in Michigan or terminate. This operation is authorized by Rose Garden One, over."

"Rose Garden One, acknowledge, over."

"That is affirmative, over."

"Roger, will do, out."

So now it was up to Kia and his men. They could return to Michigan and land and be taken into custody, or they would be shot down over the largest and deepest fresh water lake in the world.

Bird One and Bird Two were over the LZ in minutes and circled as they saw the park was illuminated from the police cruisers flashing lights. They sat down and were greeted by a riot gun toting Sheriff Captain who escorted them into the Coast Guard building. Midge had managed to have the Commander of the station open it, and was waiting there. They had brought along Seyed also to view the Camels Eye.

"Here we are gentlemen, the Camels Eye." Agent Featherston and Colonel Stormer along with Seyed Habibi looked down at the priceless work of art. Even the stark Mullah was taken by the beauty of this magnificent necklace with the world's largest and most perfect emerald as its center piece. The Iranian pulled a piece of paper from his pocket and unfolded it.

"Call your contact and have the hostages released now."

"Not yet, first turn the necklace over so I can verify it is genuine."

"Are you nuts? There is only one of these in the world, call them, now." Agent Featherston was getting frustrated.

"Until I am sure you Americans are not tricking us, there will be no call. Now turn the necklace over so I can see the back. Midge looked at Jim and then the Colonel and they both nodded their heads. He turned it over for the Mullah to inspect.

The Mullah carefully examined some marks on the back of the platinum chain that held all the stones together and then he looked carefully at the paper again. He was satisfied, this was the Camels Eye.

"It is the real Camels Eye. I will make the call." He pulled his cell phone out of his pocket and dialed a stored number. He talked in Farsi and was done in less than two minutes. At the same time Agent Jim Featherston had called a special number and informed his control that the Iranian had made the call for the release of the hostages. It would all be in the hands of both their governments now.

"I will take possession of the Camels Eye now."

"Not until I have confirmation of the hostages' release and they are out of Iranian air space and in control of the US military. But what I will do is release your men to you so you can make preparations to leave my country."

Seyed did not know how much more he could stand to be humiliated, but he was unarmed and out numbered in the land of the Great Satan so he went along.

Colonel Stormer had the Iranians brought into the building, their hands freed and given some water to drink. They then sat cross legged on the floor in the corner of the front room of the Coast Guard building with four soldiers watching them.

"Charley One, this is Silver Streak One, over."

"Silver Streak One, this is Charley One, report, over."

"Bandit refused to return to land so we had to terminate, over."

"Roger, the bandit was terminated and mission accomplished, thanks for the help Silver Streak One, out."

"Silver Streak One, good hunting, out."

So just as Colonel Stormer thought, Kia did not want to spend time in an American jail, or worse be deported back to Iran where the Ayatollahs would kill him slowly and painfully. He may have thought the jets were only bluffing, but this was a new world since 9/11 and this president did not bluff, as some of his predecessors had.

Agent Jim Featherston's sat phone rang. It was his control telling him the Boeing 777 was in route over Iraq and under military escort from the carrier Kitty Hawk. He was to release the Camels Eye to the Mullah and escort him and his men to the Coast Guard dock to board their own ship for Canadian waters. Great job! They would see him in Washington in the morning.

"Alright Seyed Habibi, the Camels Eye is all yours. Give him the necklace, Midge." Midge resealed the package and handed it to Seyed. Seyed said something in Farsi then held the necklace above his head and chanted something about Allah. His men all got to their feet, started hugging each other and chanting words about Allah also. Seyed called a number on his cell phone again to tell his masters that the Camels Eye was now in his hands and he was on his way home. Praise Be to Allah!

"If you will all follow me, we will escort you to your boat, which I understand is waiting at the pier." Colonel Stormer left the building with the Iranians walking in single file behind him flanked by the Delta Force soldiers. Seyed was on his cell phone again communicating with the skipper of the boat that would take his team out.

They double timed all the way to the pier and watched as the Iranians all boarded a sixty-five foot charter boat with a Canadian registration. As they boarded, the Seal One Team was waiting on the north side of the Locks with their binoculars to make sure no one slipped into the water and back into the United States before they crossed into Canadian water.

After the skipper cleared the Lock, the charter boat headed for a small inlet where a secret military airstrip was located just outside Wawa, which is about 90 nautical miles away on Old Woman Bay. There they would board a jet for Ottawa and then directly home.

The Delta Force stood on the Coast Guard pier and watched as the cabin cruiser carrying the Iranians and the Camels Eye moved into the lock to pass through to Lake Superior. They then formed two lines and jogged back to the park where the Chinook was waiting to return them to Grayling.

Standing in the park surrounded by police cruisers with red and blue revolving lights throwing beacons across their faces, Midge and Jim faced each other.

"Well Midge, your country owes you a debt of gratitude. And those hostages owe you their lives. I wish we could give you the Medal of

Freedom, but as you know this was a black operation. You cannot even talk about it legally to anyone. But understand your president knows what you did, and so do I. I salute you my friend."

"Yeah, I know. Just another day at the office. It's like being a cop again. I was glad to help in any way I could, Jim. It was a pleasure to meet you. You're a good man Jim Featherston, but if it is all the same to you, I hope I never work with you again."

They both laughed and shook hands, then Jim turned and headed for the big Chinook where the Delta Force was busy loading up for the return home. Outside the loading door was Colonel Eric Stormer, the Delta Force Team Commander. When he saw Midge standing there, he turned and came to attention, then snapped off a crisp salute, a salute of respect for a fellow warrior. Midge just waved to him. His army and cop days were behind him now. He would leave the defense of the country to men like Stormer and Featherston. He was satisfied with that situation for sure. The country should be grateful such men were willing to serve and risk their lives everyday. He was also happy most lawyers never would be required to do the job these brave men did for the country.

The Chinook would drop Jim off before heading for Grayling, at Chippewa County International Airport where a military jet was waiting to take him to Washington D.C. Then it was on to the White House for Jim to report to his President.

Midge walked over to Tom who was still in shock at what he had witnessed tonight, and asked him for a lift home. He would grab a couple hours of sleep before taking Jacob to the hospital to check on his father. It was a good thing he was retired and had lots of spare time on his hands. He wondered how he ever found time to hold a job. They pulled out of the park road with the bubble gum machine on the top of the cruiser lighting the road ahead. What, no siren Midge thought? He could do without that this morning, thank the Lord. He closed his eyes and put his head against the headrest for the five minute ride home. It had been quite a night, but the hostages were on their way home, and they were the reason he did it. God bless America.

Chapter 21

Far out in the bay in Canadian territorial water was anchored a great lakes cutter. It looked a great deal like a Coast Guard cutter with the large spot lights and siren, but without the deck guns. It also carried some other unusual equipment on board. It was the kind of boat the Coast Guard used to intercept drug runners and other assorted smugglers. It was big, fast, and maneuverable.

It was flying a large red and white flag with a huge maple leaf in the center. This ship had been monitoring all the communications traffic for the last three days in the Sault Ste. Marie area, especially the interesting military chatter tonight. Sitting next to the radio operator was a tall thin man from the IAA. In the next cabin were four Israeli commandos dressed in Canadian Coast Guard uniforms and carrying German made assault riffles, awaiting orders.

The radio operator translated the message from Farsi to English and handed it to Liam, the mission commander. He just smiled and went to check on the commandos.

They were holding in place between Sault Ste. Marie and Wawa in the fishing waters about twenty-five nautical miles across the Canadian border in Lake Superior, playing a waiting game.

On board the charter boat, Seyed and his men were on their cabin floor worshipping in submission to Allah who had made this a successful mission in spite of a few setbacks. The ship was cutting through the night at about twenty knots with all the navigation lights on as required by law. They were outside the main shipping channel now headed north about ten miles off the coast. This area of Canada had very little population except for vacationers. They didn't show up much before the Memorial Day weekend and left for home just after Labor Day in North America.

The Canadian Captain was not sure who these guys were he had onboard, but the man who hired him was on the boat also and had paid him handsomely in cash for this one night charter. As a matter of fact, it was more than he would make for a whole month of fishing charters. Besides, they paid him in US dollars, not Canadian, so depending on the exchange rate, he got twenty to forty percent more and it was tax-free money. The biggest bonus was he would only be gone one night.

He was shocked when the soldiers showed up at the Coast Guard pier to escort them on board in the Sault, but he figured there must be something funny for a foreigner to hire him for a charter at night and pay him in cash. The only thing he insisted on was there would be no guns and no drugs aboard his vessel. He had the only guns on the boat in the pilot deck and he and his mate knew how to use them. They must be some type of Arabs and the Americans were deporting them or something. Maybe they were even terrorists to the Yanks, but Canada welcomed that kind every day to Montreal and Toronto. He did not personally agree with his government's policy. It seemed like Canadians were getting a free ride while the Americans were doing all the dying in defending North America, but that is how things are right now. As long as his passengers stayed in their cabin, things would be just fine.

The first mate brought the Captain a fresh cup of coffee. Even though there was no freighter traffic, they had to watch for fishing boats in these waters. The twin diesels were cutting through the dark waters nicely tonight. The weather was clear, but there was no moon and the water was black. Lake Superior is one of the coldest lakes in the world and the most treacherous in a storm. Waves were known to crest at sixty feet at its worst. Many a ship lay on her bottom that did not head the call to take shelter and tried to plow through the stormy waters. That is why he was staying fairly close to shore, but out far enough not to be hitting moored boats waiting for the dawn to go fishing.

Down below deck they had finished their thanks to Allah. Seyed wanted another look at the Camels Eye. It held a special place for him because it was one of the things the Shah and his followers had stolen from Iran's history. The Ayatollahs would now be able to show the people how Islam had riches beyond belief because of its faithfulness to the one true god, Allah.

He was a little concerned about his men. They had sinned while they were on foreign soil, so that meant they could easily give in to temptations of all kinds. His friend and fellow Mullah, Rasheed had been on the boat when the Americans had escorted them on. This man, he would trust with his life. He had brought with him an airline carry-on pouch, but with an important difference. It was a diplomatic pouch with the Seal of the Islamic Republic of Iran. With this case, no Canadian official dared touch it. It could not be searched under international law, even if he carried a nuclear bomb, if such a thing could be made that small. Thank Allah for the United Nations and the rules that allowed him to cross borders and kill at will with Allah's protection.

Seyed wanted one last look at the Camels Eye before they boarded the airplane at dawn for the flight home. He would risk it because he wanted to show his friend Rasheed this magnificent treasure. He carefully placed the black rubberized block on the cabin's table. He used a table knife he found in the galley to slit the scotch tape on three sides so he could open the protective container. All the men gathered around as he pivoted the top piece back and revealed the Camels Eye.

It was still in its plastic protective bag, but even with just the light from the overhead recessed reading lamps, the necklace spread its wonder. The men were in awe as this was the first time they had cast their eyes on the prize for which their mission had been designed.

Seyed decided he would remove the necklace from the clear plastic bag which had protected it from the elements all these years since the Nassire man had stolen it from the people. He carefully unfolded the top of the bag and separated the sides. He then wiped his hands on his pants to make sure he had no dirt on them and gently, as if touching a woman's breast for the first time, reached in and grabbed the necklace. It felt smooth and cool, yet almost magical to him. His hands trembled a little as he removed it by its hasp from the bag and held it up to the light.

Rainbows projected everywhere in the cabin and across his men's faces. It was like someone had captured the sun and harnessed it to a platinum chain that was for their personal pleasure. Surely Allah must have created such a thing in heaven itself for his hundred virgins.

No one could remove their gaze from the diamonds, rubies, and emeralds for they were hypnotic. But the greatest of all was the centerpiece around which all the other stones were gathered. The Camels Eye, the largest and most perfect emerald the world had ever known. A freak of nature some said, a gift from God others said, but a stone to be viewed was to be possessed. Armies had fought over this stone, or at least been rewarded by their victory with its possession. It first belonged to the Egyptians, then the Jews, and finally the Persians who now had it in their possession where it belonged, again. The Camels Eye would reside in Tehran, the land of the Believers, for ever more.

Seyed was having a hard time controlling his emotions. He had never been in love with a woman, but he imagined if this is what it felt like, then he knew why some men would kill to protect them.

Their trance was broken by a blast from an air horn and the whir of a siren not fully engaged, but the short whoop police often use to get a person's attention. Then they heard a loud speaker blaring in the night. Seyed quickly returned the necklace to its protective bag, back inside the protective black rubber block and into the diplomatic pouch. It was now out of the reach of the Canadian authorities.

Up in the pilot's cabin, the captain was bringing the boat to a stop as ordered by the Coast Guard Cutter. They must think he was running cigarettes or whiskey to avoid the US taxes, but he was going the opposite direction, so that was strange. They certainly did not think he was fishing illegally, not at the speed he was traveling. Well, his papers were all in order and he should be on his way in a few minutes after a cursory inspection. The only thing that gave him any concern at all was the passengers he was carrying. He did not even think about passports or anything when these people had chartered his boat. He hired out to Canadians and Americans all the time and passports were never an issue. He wondered if the Canadian Coast Guard had been tipped off by the US Coast Guard to watch for these men. Well no matter, the Canadians let any one into the country. Half the 9/11 hijackers came through Canada, with their custom officers' blessings.

The huge and powerful spotlights illuminated every part of the charter boat. After bringing the boat to a full stop in the black water, the Captain and his mate stood at the rail on the walkway outside the pilot house and faced the cutter. As it came along side, the Captain could see the huge maple leaf flying from its mast. He still liked that flag better than the one of his youth with the Union Jack on it, when they were so tied to Britain in the Commonwealth.

The loud speaker on the Coast Guard Cutter blared its orders. "Captain, stand by to be boarded. Have your license available and prepare to be searched. Failure to follow instructions will be met with force and the confiscation of your vessel. Have all hands on deck for inspection immediately." He could then see seamen moving in with grappling hooks to secure the two boats together.

"Quickly, get all our passengers on deck and meet the sailors to show them around the ship. I will get the ships log and meet with their officer. Hurry before they get on board."

He hustled down the gang ladder to the cabin door and knocked loudly on the teak wood door. "Everyone on deck, Captains orders!"

A deep voice came back, "No, we will remain in our cabin, leave us alone."

"No, everyone on deck, now! We are being boarded by the Canadian Coast Guard and they are armed. After a quick inspection, we will be on our way. This is all very routine, do not worry just get up on deck. Now!"

Seyed looked at his men and spoke quickly in Farsi telling them not to speak when they got on deck, but let him do all the talking. Do not answer any questions. He would show his diplomatic passport and warn the officer in charge what could happen if he violated international law.

One of his men asked if they should hide the Camels Eye in the cabin. He said, "No." If they were looking for drugs, they would search the cabin thoroughly and may even steal it and claim they never saw it. No, he would keep it in the diplomatic pouch on his person. It would be the safest place.

The Iranians unlocked the cabin door and climbed the ladder to the deck. The mate lined them up and stood next to them as the sailors from the cutter leaped onto the deck with assault rifles at the ready. This was actually standard practice for a Coast Guard Cutter with all the violence in the drug war anymore, so the mate was not concerned. Seyed stood next to the mate and watched the sailors but did not move or say anything.

Once his sailors were in position, a tall thin officer of some type with black and gold braided epaulets on his shoulders came on board.

He went directly up the gangway to the pilot's deck and asked the captain for the vessel's papers.

Two of the sailors went below deck to search the cabin while the other two trained their weapons on the line-up of men on the deck.

After inspecting the Admiralty papers for a few cursory minutes, the Commander said, "Captain, I am Commander Burns, do you know the passengers you are carrying?"

"Not really Commander, just a normal charter. I was hired for today is all. I do not know any of them."

"Just a normal charter, hey? One where you wait at a US Coast Guard pier while seven men are escorted to your charter boat by US soldiers? Is that what you call a normal charter?"

"Well it turned out different than I thought it would, but I have not violated any Canadian laws, that I know of."

"I will not stand here and debate with you Captain. You know you are in violation of several Canadian laws, but I did not stop your vessel for that. I have been ordered by Ottawa to stop this ship, take these men off and deliver them to an air base for evacuation from this country. Do you understand, Captain?" He kept his eyes level with the captain who was as tall as he was.

This was music to the captain's ears. He would turn the passengers over to the Coast Guard and be rid of any responsibility for what they might do on Canadian soil. Best of all, he got to keep all the money they had paid him for his services. "Yes Commander, I fully understand. Let me go with you and explain it to my passengers, if that is what you wish."

"Lead the way, Captain." The tall Commander was pleased this was going even smoother than he had anticipated. He followed the Captain down the gangway to the deck.

Two sailors came out of the cabin and announced in a loud military voice, "all clear below deck Commander. Nothing illegal we can spot, sir." They moved their weapons to cover the men lined up on deck.

"Very good men, stand to." The Commander shouted and the sailors lowered their weapons, but still were alert for any trouble.

"Gentlemen, Commander Burns and his men have been directed by the Canadian government in Ottawa to escort you to your next destination. You will be leaving my boat and boarding the Canadian

Coast Guard Cutter for that purpose. It has been a pleasure serving you and may you have a safe journey home. They are all yours, Commander." The Commander stepped up near the rail with the spotlights shinning in the faces of the Iranians who were squinting to see the officer. He was just a shadow to them really, with a voice coming out of the center of the top of the form.

"I am Commander Burns of the Canadian Coast Guard and I have been ordered from the highest echelons of my government in Ottawa to deliver you safely to your next destination." So Seyed thought his embassy had put pressure on the weak kneed Canadian government. They wanted to make sure he was delivered safely or Iran would unleash terrorists at will on its citizens. He was well pleased with this turn of events.

"Who is in charge of your team?" The shadow asked.

Seyed turned and pushed the mate out of the way facing the shadow with his own face illuminated brightly. "I am in charge. My name is Seyed Habibi and here is my diplomatic passport from the Islamic Republic of Iran. I am carrying a diplomatic pouch that is under the full protection of international law. I demand to be treated as a representative of my government under the protection of the United Nations Rules which your country is fully obligated to obey." He would push these weak infidels around now as if they were women and subject to his will.

The name meant nothing to him, but Liam's blood ran cold as he looked at the lit up face in front of him. It was the eyes and the cold way they flashed as he told the 'Canadians' who he was and how he was to be treated.

No, he had not seen this man in a picture, which he was certain was posted somewhere at Mossad headquarters or in Israeli Embassies around the world. He had seen this man before, in person and up close. As a matter of fact his face had been lit up that night also.

But it was lit by fire, the fire of eighty young helpless school children burning at a kibbutz in the Negev desert.

He was a young paratrooper commando. His unit had been sent to rescue the children from the Palestinian terrorists holding them hostage while the rest of the world stood idly by and watched.

Freedom fighters for Allah they called themselves. He had chased them into the Negev and killed many of them, but not this one. This

235

was the fanatical leader of the massacre and Liam had sworn to kill him one day, if it took the rest of his life.

As his prime minister had told his unit after the funeral, 'Israel will smite the hands that took these young children's lives, no matter where they are or how long it takes. Israel will avenge these children, the flowers of Israel, so help me God'. He would keep that oath he swore that day. The Sword of Gideon, The Sword of God, would strike this butcher down, and maybe then the children would be at peace at last.

He had to get control of himself. He would not allow the white hot rage that burned in his heart to affect his performance now. Breathe deep and relax just like taking a kill shot.

"Yes, Mister Habibi, those are my orders. You and your men are to be afforded diplomatic status and we will totally honor the protection of your diplomatic pouch. Now if you and your men will follow me, we have a plane to catch." He turned, saluted the Captain, climbed over the rails and headed for the bridge on his Cutter.

Seyed was pleased. This is how Islam would take over the world. With stupid rules the infidels had created themselves and would now be their doom. Allah be praised to the highest.

The sailors led them to the Cutter deck and then down below to a small sparse cabin. They untied the charter boat and pushed off the bows and stern. The Cutter then revved its engines and moved out through the night.

The charter boat Captain told the mate, "I am glad to be rid of those guys. Let's head for home."

"Hey Cap, did you notice that the Cutter did not have any insignias on its bow or tower?" The mate had noticed it for a moment. Being an ex-navy sailor he thought it very strange.

"Not really Tim, but maybe with this being kind of a clandestine operation, they did not want too many markings just in case some fishermen spotted them and a television station or something picked up on it. Now let's head for home. You have a thousand dollar bonus for tonight Tim, and I bet you can't wait to spend it."

"A thousand bucks? To hell with the markings, thanks Cap.. Let's get the hell out of here, hey?" They both hurried to the cabin and shoved the throttle lever forward as their spirits were high and their worries were now few.

The Coast Guard Cutter cut a deep wake in the water as her twin engines roared, but instead of heading toward shore, she headed up toward Thunder Bay into the deep water of Superior. Below the Iranians were resting against the cabin walls.

The Commander decided it was time to act now. His emotions from seeing the man who butchered all of the precious young children, including his younger brother, were burning a hole in his very soul. He told one of the commandos to get them all up on deck. Use the pretext that a Navy rescue helicopter would be picking them up in a few minutes and take them to a secret airport so they could be returned to Iran.

Seyed took the news well, but insisted on a few minutes with his men to thank Allah for their deliverance with a prayer. The commando left and waited on the deck with his other team members and the Commander. Liam had to keep his men under control now. All of his men had fought Islamic terrorists around the world, and the men in the cabin were the worst kind of human garbage. Ridding the world of this Muslim scum would be a pleasure.

Seyed and his men filed on deck. The Commander approached Seyed and saluted, "Mr. Habibi, there is a call for you on the ships radio, if you will follow me please."

Seyed grinned an arrogant smirk. Now that was more like it you infidel officer of a weak infidel country. Some day Islam will rule the world and then I will teach you how to bow and lay postrate with your face and head to the ground in my presence. Just give us time and some more help from your liberal rights granting politicians and we will conquer all the western infidel nations.

"Who is it, Commander?" He would push the man around a little bit now. He clutched his diplomatic pouch like a football used in the great American sport.

"He did not say sir, but it is my Admiral who requested me to come get you." It was hard to remain calm now. He could just pull his 9mm Glock from his holster and put a bullet right between his eyes and end this charade. But no, that would not be the justice he had waited for all these years. Just a little more humiliation and then retribution would come.

"Very well Commander, then lead the way and get my men something warm to wear. It is cold on this deck." That would not be a problem soon, Liam thought.

They climbed the stairs to the bridge. As they entered the door, the Commander pointed at the ships radio on the far side of the bridge. As Seyed approached it, the seaman behind him struck him hard with a lead weighted blackjack. Seyed went down like a sack of potatoes on to the floor.

"You could have killed him you fool." The Commander grabbed Seyed's hands, placed them behind his back and bound them with plastic band ties. While he removed the diplomatic pouch from over his head, he hissed at the inert body while holding his head up by the hair. "The Sword of Gideon has arrived, you butcher. You will now pay for your sins, for the souls of the Israeli children, whose lives you snuffed out." He got up, placed the pouch on the map table, and went to the door.

"The helicopter will be here in five minutes. Have the men line up." The commandos moved them all to the front of the bow. They had the Iranians stand facing them while holding on to the rail so they would not be blown over board by the helicopter's wash.

The Commander climbed down the ladder and joined his men. He was holding his Glock in his hand with the safety released.

He had to shout to be heard in the wind, "Gentlemen, it has been a pleasure meeting you. The Prime Minister sends his best wishes for a safe and happy journey. *The Prime Minister of Israel, that is, and your destination is hell!*"

For a second the Iranians were confused and could not equate with the words that the Canadian Commander just shouted. What? Then the commandos opened up with their assault riffles and Liam with his Glock. They were expert marksmen with the bullets all finding their marks in the chest, piercing the heart and both lungs, and then to the mid section to make sure all the stomachs each had a hole in them. It was over in a minute and the Iranians lay in a twisted clump on the bow.

"Bring me the leader. He is the man responsible for burning to death the eighty young school children in the Negev. I was there and I saw this man do it, but until now I could never find him to kill him." He had not told his men this fact before because he was afraid they could not control their emotions. He had barely controlled his own.

Two of his men dragged out Seyed who was just regaining consciousness. They threw him at Liam's feet and stepped back. Seyed

The Camels Eye

had trouble focusing, but a quick kick from Liam to his head cleared some of the cobwebs.

"What is the meaning of this? My government will kill many of your citizens, if you do not release me immediately."

"Shut up you Islamic terrorist scum. I have been waiting years to catch up with you. Allow me to introduce myself. I am Liam Hertz the son of Ethel and Milton Hertz and brother to Stuart Hertz who died in a fire after being dowsed with gasoline in a school in the Negev, many years ago."

Seyed's eyes went wide. Israeli? What did this man say, Israeli? That cannot be, he was in Canada. They would not dare operate here. The UN rules, the protection of international law, world opinion, this was wrong. Where was his pouch, his Camels Eye?

"You are going to atone for your sins tonight, Seyed Habibi. We are going to apply the Sword of Gideon to you tonight. You will pay for what you have done to the children of Israel and the Israeli people."

"I am on Canadian soil, you cannot touch me. Now release me or you will face Islam's wrath as you have never known before." He was shaking with both rage and fear. His life could not end now, not until he had returned the Camels Eye to his people. He was so close, not here, not now. Allah, smite these Jews with your hand, he prayed.

"Or what will you do, pour gasoline on us, and burn us up as you watch in glee?"

This man must have been there that night. He could see it in his eyes. There was more hatred in this man than he had ever seen in his life. There would be no rescue, no mercy from this Jew. Well then, he would die a martyr for Islam. His only regret was he had not completed his mission, but others would follow and they would succeed.

"Do what you will Jew, but I will go to Allah with joy remembering the pitiful cries and pleading from the weak Jew children that night, as their skin melted around their skeletons and they collapsed into burning heaps. *Allah akbar!* He glared at the Israelis in a maniacal way. In his mind he was already on the staircase to Allah, on his way to paradise.

It took every bit of control Liam had left not to blow this man's head off, but no he must take his time. He could never get him back to Israel to stand trial. The Western world would condemn Israel for taking this man prisoner, but he would make sure the families of those children he had burned alive would know that justice was served.

"Bring me some gasoline and a torch he told his men." They quickly found a gas can and matches below and brought them to the deck and put them in front of the Mullah. Seyed's eyes were starting to show a little less defiance and more fear now. Liam took a combat knife from the sheath of one of his men and held it in front of Seyed's right eye. Fear showed in his face now, no matter how much will power the Mullah tried to muster. Was he going to be doused with gasoline and burned to death by these Jews? Liam was getting the effect he wanted on this zealot with the gas can. It was obvious that his bravado was now gone.

"You believe that Allah will reward you in paradise with one hundred virgins or some such nonsense. You tell that to the fools you send out to die for you because you Mullahs are too much the coward to go yourselves."

"Well, you will go to paradise without your manhood. You will not be able to enjoy any of those virgins you have dreamed of, Seyed. Spread his legs and hold his shoulders now men." They jumped on him and Liam expertly cut away his pants. He grabbed his ball sack and penis and pulled hard downward with his left hand. His right hand pulled the sharp combat knife in an arc between Seyed's legs and sliced his testicles and penis clean off from his body.

Seyed screamed in terror, all his bravado was gone from his soul now. He just wanted this nightmare to end quickly. He passed out for a minute, but when he could see again, the Jew was holding his manhood about three feet in front of his face. What a sadistic infidel bastard. He would kill the Jew, if he got the chance.

Liam was an expert at torture. Both receiving and giving, he had learned from the best Syria had to offer. But he was not trying to extract information from a prisoner now. The man had nothing to bargain with now. This was pure revenge. Revenge for his brother Stuart, and all of the other Jewish flowers who perished that night. Pure undiluted hatred and he would not regret one minute of it.

One of the commandos brought a hot iron they had heated with a welding torch and seared the wound shut. Liam did not want him to bleed to death before he was finished.

He now propped Seyed's head up and made him watch as the

The Camels Eye

commandos attached chains to each of his dead men and brought them to Seyed for inspection before packing them in some weighted sacks. They would soon send them to the bottom of the lake. The Iranian bodies were loaded into weighted bags and thrown overboard as the commandos watched them sink into the deep black water.

Seyed was numb now. It was as if everything was happening in slow motion, like in a movie, and he was just part of the audience. He was starting to go into shock. Liam considered shooting him with morphine but did not want to dull the pain for him.

One of the men started to wash down the deck now. He had seen enough of Liam's revenge. He understood it, but could not watch any longer.

Liam now cut the band ties loose on Seyed's hands. There was no resistance left in the Mullah now. Liam removed a fire ax from an extinguisher cabinet and showed it to Seyed. He hissed, "we shall smite the hand that strikes Israel, so help us God."

With that Seyed watched in horror as the tall Jew struck with the ax and cut off both his hands just above his wrists. Amazingly he was still conscious and everything was still happening to him in slow motion. Why did this Jew not end it now? Even he had showed mercy to his victims, sometimes. He did not deserve this much cruelty for just burning a few children. Allah be merciful.

The other Commandos were sick of it now. "Liam, enough already. We know how much you hate him for what he did to your brother, but we have to get out of these uniforms and meet an aircraft in three hours. Finish it, for God's sake. Finish for your own soul, not his. Just get it done."

Liam was numb now. His whole body was tingling like a person who had exhausted himself in a fight. The voices sounded far away as he kept his eyes on Seyed. 'Finish it' was all he heard. How long did it take his brother to be finished as the flames and heat devastated his body. When did a burn victim stop feeling the pain, the intense heat, lose consciousness? He did not know, but he did know it was time to finish it.

Liam looked at his men, but they did not look into his eyes. They were tired of the carnage. These were battle hardened men, but even they had seen enough. It was time to finish the job.

Handless, Seyed stared numbly at Liam as he laid him on his back.

He could remember seeing the curved blade of the ax being raised in the air, above his face and watching, as if in slow motion, the blade race toward his throat. Then nothing, nothing at all, the pain had ended.

As Seyed's head rolled away from his body, Liam collapsed to his knees, all of his rage and anger spent. All the years of dreaming of meeting up with this man fulfilled with a vengeance. He was as exhausted as he had ever been in his whole life. He put his head into his hands and wept. The tears flowed like water and he was not ashamed. He had his revenge, but it was small payment for all the years of pain. It did not seem that revenge was all that sweet, after all. His men did not look at him because they understood, what he was going through, was a private moment between him and his conscience.

It was time to get on with the mission now, to return the Soul of Jerusalem to the Jewish people after all these centuries.

While his men loaded Seyed's body parts into another weighted perforated sack to sink into the black water, Liam picked up the hands and head and washed them down with the deck hose. He then put them in a duffle bag for transport with him on the aircraft. These he would take back to Israel. He would take them to show the families and other survivors of that flaming night in the Negev desert, so many years ago, that Israel never forgets and never forgives such horror. Even more selfishly it would bring closure to a bad chapter in his life. Perhaps now, he could stop waking in the night, seeing the ghostly images as if the blue and yellow flames were still before his eyes. The smell of human beings being seared in the flames was a smell he could never, would never forget. Maybe now his demons would go to the grave along with the children of that wicked godless night. This he would do for Israel, for his brother, and for his own soul, so help him God.

Liam and his men quickly changed into civilian clothes. They put all the uniforms, helmets and boots into another bag and sent it to the bottom of Lake Superior, to rest for ever in its depths like the Edmund Fitzgerald still rests in song for eternity. They tossed the assault rifles, knives, and ammo into the water directly, as none of these items could float and be found by curious ships passing, or even worse, be washed up on shore.

They now brought the real ship Captain up from his state room below. Liam wanted to make sure this Canadian Jew, who so readily agreed to help Israel in her hour of need, was not involved with any of the dirty work. He had risked enough. Like Jews all over the world they would help Israel if they were needed, even at peril to their own lives. It was such a man who had saved his life in France and hid him after he had assassinated two Black September terrorists responsible for killing six Jewish hostages in a failed hijacking. The French Jew risked his own freedom and life to help rescue a son of Israel. This man, whose ship he was on, was a Canadian by choice. But he was a Jew by birth and he could never deny his people in their hour of need.

He told the Captain to take them to the rendezvous point and then went with him to the bridge to retrieve the Soul of Jerusalem from the map table. He vowed it would never leave his person, until he presented it to his government in the land of the Jews, a land everyone in the world did not think they should have. Islam was trying to annihilate its people from this earth, from his home, Israel. They were both headed home, the IAA agent and the Soul of Jerusalem.

Chapter 22

Tom drove Midge home, pulled into the driveway and put the police cruiser in park.

"Is there anything else I can do for you, Midge?"

"No Tom, you have been great. Thanks for helping Brenda and the boys with that Iranian lunatic who was trying to get into my house, and for staying with them until I got home. It has been a hell of a night. I really appreciate all you have done for me and my family." Midge was serious. Being a cop, he knew what a risk Tom had taken. If he ever got a chance to repay Tom, it would be his pleasure.

"They say someone shot and killed one of the terrorists outside the casino last night in Bay Mills. They say the man was killing others with a machine gun of some kind, when a shooter put two slugs through the man's skull. Witnesses say he did it with a pistol. That was pretty good shooting, if that is true." Tom eyed Midge with a great deal of curiosity.

"Sounds like the guy got a couple of lucky shots off, to me." Midge had learned as a child, never admit to anything. The motto he lived by was to deny, deny, deny, even if they had you on national television. Continue to deny and blame someone else. It worked great for O. J. Simpson. He got acquitted and they are still searching for the boogey man who killed his wife.

"Yeah, real lucky. Lucky for me in a way too, Midge. It happened on Tribal land and the Sheriff's Department has no jurisdiction there. So I will not have to find and arrest the poor bastard who killed the terrorist and charge him with murder. You see according to the victim's lawyer, the terrorist was not threatening the shooter so he could not use deadly force and we would have to execute the warrant. A shitty deal all around really, don't you think.

"Yeah, a shitty deal, that's for sure. But after working as a cop in Detroit for over a quarter of a century, I saw a lot of shitty deals. So I guess that is just the way America works. Good night Tom, and thanks again for all your help. Tell your men thanks too, I owe them all a beer." With that Midge opened the door and got out, then leaned in so he could see Tom better.

"No thanks needed, my friend. But as far as the beer goes, now that's a date. Good night, Midge." Midge closed the door to the cruiser and started for his house as Tom killed the flashing blue lights and backed out of the driveway to return to the station. He was happy he did not have anything to do with the shooting at the casino tonight. Thank God, for little favors.

Brenda opened the door before he could reach for the handle. She ran into his arms and squeezed him for all she was worth. She pulled him inside the living room as if he was a man trying to resist arrest or something.

She closed the door and held him by the shoulders at arms length facing him. He could feel the excitement in her body, almost like some kind of human electricity. Her face was actually beaming, yes beaming in the dull light of a table lamp across the living room. Was she really that glad to see him? No other woman in his life ever looked that excited, not his mother, and certainly not any of his ex-wives. "He's alive, he's alive, Midge. I called the Tribal Police station and got hold of Ken Telway. He is alive and in the War Memorial hospital. Can we go see him right now, you, me, and the boys, can we?" So much for a woman being excited to see him, he thought. Well, he might as well have a little fun.

"Who is alive?" He watched her face go from glowing to confusion for a second. You know, from a smile and crinkly eyes to the raised eye brows, wide open eyes and open mouth kind of look. His last wife did that a lot until their relationship broke down. Then anything he tried to tell her was met with that squinty eyed, smirk shaped mouth, with her head tilted down in that 'I don't believe anything you say, asshole' manner. Why do they always tilt their heads to the right? Maybe it is because women are right brained and all the weight on that side of their cranium makes their neck give out and their heads fall to the right.

She finally recovered, let out a gasp of exasperation and slapped him on the chest. "You brat, you know who I am talking about, John ... John Nassire. He is in stable, but guarded condition, so he is off the critical list." His aunt was in a stable guarded condition the night she died of an unknown cancer, but they called it a heart attack on the death certificate. They always say heart attack or pneumonia when symptoms kill the patient, not the cause.

"Is he conscious, and will they let us see him?" Midge really would like to stall until daylight so he could at least get a couple of hours sleep.

"This is really important to me. If I have to, I will go alone, but I think Jacob needs to see his father. Please Midge, can we go now?" Tears were starting to form in her eyes. Those watery eyes that overflow so much, the clear river of eye water would flow down her cheeks right to the corners of her mouth. How did eyes manufacture water anyway? He understood the snot from your nose, but the eye thing was a mystery to him.

"Okay, you get the boys around while I wash up quickly and change my clothes. Then I will help you get us all into the van. I hope it didn't catch any stray bullets or shrapnel tonight." She put a vice grip on his neck, so hard he flinched. Back to being excited about him was she, well maybe not. He grabbed some clean clothes and headed for his bathroom. The boys would need to use Ryan's.

Brenda had a hard time waking the boys up until she mentioned they had to go see Jacob's father in the hospital. Then they were both out of bed in a flash. Jacob was up because he was worried about his father and Ryan because he wanted to go with his friend, Jacob. She made them wash their faces and use the toilet before they got dressed in the clothes she had laid out for them. Jacob was wearing the clothes from his now ruined leather back pack. Ryan wore his alligator shirt from Florida, the same one he had worn for five years. It was his favorite shirt and featured an alligator with its long teeth and mouth open with bright red blood all around. There were holes in the side of the shirt surrounded by red fake blood as if the gator had bitten the boy wearing it. Other boys loved it and girls hated it, just the way Ryan wanted things. She also made him put on clean underwear and jeans with his tennis shoes.

Midge came out wearing a fresh pull over dark blue shirt with a small red pony over his left breast. His jeans were Wrangler with clean socks and Reebok white tennis shoes. No fancy designer stuff for him. He helped the boys get cleaned and dressed and told them they could eat at the hospital after Jacob visited with his father. Jacob never asked about his grandfather and Midge was glad. That was a family matter to handle and he was no good with kids anyway.

Midge went out and warmed up the van while Brenda freshened up. She finally came out wearing a tight red wool sweater that clung to her curves like it was painted on and tight designer jeans that looked new but already had some strategically placed rips and holes in them. Why would anyone pay good money for used clothes, he wondered? His ex-wives and niece would, that was for sure. He could not figure women out for anything. She really finished the outfit off with four inch dark brown leather heels. It not only made a woman look taller, but leaner through the rear end and along the back which seemed to pull back the shoulders and push out her bust even more. A nice touch and she was doing this just for him, right?

One thing he had to admit was this dark haired beauty could fill out a sweater and jeans in all the right places to make some men drool or even worse. She was certainly well endowed in the chest area and her booty, as the blacks called it, wasn't too shabby either. Well, he had seen the real thing, but he still liked fantasizing about it better with her clothes on.

But if he liked how she had dressed her body, he loved what she did with her face and hair. She usually wore her hair in a pulled back pony tail tied with a bow at the top. Now she had let her long hair down and it curved around her face like one of those models who pose for the hair commercials. The only thing she was missing was a fan to blow it up in the air like the models had. Brenda's hair shaped her face as if she was some kind of a Madonna, and he wasn't thinking of the singer.

He had never seen her face so lovely. It had a kind glow to it. Of course the total package helped; the red sweater, the hair, the understated make up, and even the jeans.

Yep, he liked those jeans on her, even though they were a long way from her face. She was a pretty woman alright, not in that emancipated way of the runway models. They were too gaunt, too boney, and too ghostly when you saw them in person, to even make love with them. No, this was a full boned filled out American woman, part Native American actually, and in person, the rival for any of those light and camera enhanced models.

"Well, let's hop in the van everybody and get to the hospital. Put on your coat. It is chilly outside this morning. It will only take us a few minutes to get there." He put his hands and arms out like a man trying to herd people onto a bus.

He finally succeeded in getting them all in the van and then he hounded them until they buckled their seat belts. He closed the sliding door on the side and then took his place in the driver's seat. "Did anyone forget anything? Last call before we pull out, do you hear?" Not a sound was uttered. The pleasure of starting any trip in the wee hours of the morning before the sun came up was the women and children were too sleepy to say a word. Peace on earth, good will to men, oh yeah.

They arrived at War Memorial Hospital, but had to use the emergency entrance because the front lobby did not open until eight. A hospital may be a twenty-four hour operation, but visitors were restricted access to hours most humans were normally awake, not at four in the morning.

They were stopped by a security officer who had some kind of Japanese or Chinese symbols tattooed on the left side of his neck. Midge did not know what it said. It would have been hard to read if he did know Chinese writing because in the middle of two of the symbols were creases in the folds of his neck. This guy needed to go on some kind of a diet.

His blue shirt with his badge on the right and a light blue emblem with the words War Memorial Security embroidered above his left pocket, was so tight Midge thought if he bent down to touch his toes, he would probably rip the shirt right down the middle. As a matter of fact, he wasn't sure how the guy got it buttoned anyway. The buttons were tilted side ways in the holes pulling at the stitching like a Sumo wrestler, and the front pleat holding the button holes was wavy instead of straight. In between each button was an elliptical patch of white skin repeated five times down to the guard's belt line, if you could call that giant balloon lapping over his belt a line. Midge decided to move Ryan and Jacob over to the side while the guard talked to Brenda in case one of those buttons exploded under the pressure. It could put an eye out flying around in the air.

The guard was eyeing Brenda from head to toe and trying to make eye contact in a sultry kind of way. He must be hoping she could not resist a man in uniform. He told her visiting hours did not start until eight am, but they were welcome to use the waiting area until then if they liked.

Brenda explained the situation with Jacob and his father in critical condition. She asked if he would call the nurse's station on the ICU floor and ask permission for his son to see him. The way the guard was drooling and watching her, she could have asked him to call Alaska to find out what time the next dog sled was leaving and he would have done it.

He hung up the phone and said to Brenda, "They said okay, but only the boy and his mother and only for a few minutes. I will be glad to escort you up, if you like." Midge bet he would, if he could walk that far, he thought.

"Oh sweetie, would you? This is so sweet of you. Come on Jacob, we are going to see your father, sweetheart." Midge felt 'Sweaty' would have been a better name for Ray. That was the name engraved on his brass nameplate, pinned below his badge.

"Take all the time you need Brenda. Ryan and I will be in the waiting room right down the hall here."

They were already heading through the double doors that led into the hospital center. She just threw her hand up in the air and waved as if she was leaving on the Queen Mary for England, he thought. He took Ryan to the waiting room where there were already a few injured people and their family or friends waiting for medical attention.

Two hours later with the sun starting to peek into the sky, he was napping in a chair beside Ryan, who was out cold. He had heard ten different horror stories of why people had come to the emergency room today and he just wanted out of there. Then he saw Brenda coming back and she was holding Jacob's hand. Jacob's eyes were red with signs that he had been crying. She put Jacob in a chair next to Ryan and then came and sat next to Midge.

"Is he okay, I mean John, is he going to be alright?" Midge asked.

"He woke up when we were there and he talked to Jacob and me a little bit. He told me you saved his life and to thank you. He will be in here a week or two at least." She was solemn now.

"How did Jacob do seeing his dad like that?"

"He did okay with that part." She kept her voice low and he had to lean over to hear her.

"Then why was he crying?" Midge asked.

"John asked me how his father was doing. He did not know he was killed at the casino. I had to tell him. John and Jacob both took it hard. They both cried and it was hard to keep John from trying to hold Jacob. The nurses had to come in and help me settle them down. It was hard." She put her head on his shoulder now and he stroked her hair. He was not really very good at this comforting stuff.

"I thought he knew about his father, Midge. I was not prepared for that. It nearly killed Jacob to hear it at the same time. I totally forgot about Jacob being behind me and I just blurted it out, like an insensitive oaf. It was terrible." She was crying softly now.

"Well, I never thought, but I knew John did not see his father fall. They took off in opposite directions from the bus. The terrorist shot his father first and then turned and fired at John as he fled. They did not see each other again." Midge was recalling the scene in slow motion as his mind reenacted it.

"John said you saved his life, by taking out Kia's man." She looked at him penetratingly now.

"How would John know, he was running the other way." Midge did not really want to go into this. It was better for him to just forget it. Just part of the job, he thought.

"The Tribal Police told him while they were waiting for the ambulance. Is it true Midge, did you kill that man who was shooting at John?" She was intense now but he did not see why it mattered very much, since John was alive no matter who shot the man.

"I'm not sure. There was so much going on, anyone may have hit him. I took a shot or two at him, but who can say if I hit him or not?" Midge tried to let that be the end of the subject.

"Some witnesses said it was you, but you don't want to take any credit for it, why?"

"You know I have some war medals and some police commendations some where in a trunk, if I haven't lost them, and they are all meaningless. My grandmother said it best when she was dying in our home, 'what good is fame, jewels, accolades, and money when you die, if you do not have your family and God?' and that is how I feel. I don't want any credit or any blame, so let's just drop it, okay?"

"Thanks, Midge." She grabbed his face and kissed him on the cheek as a mother or sister would kiss a brother they were proud of, and of course, they were never going to sleep together again. Midge knew this was the end of a short but happy relationship.

"Can you take Jacob home with you and keep him until his father is better? I am going to stay with John and take care of him until he doesn't need me anymore." She had that 'you're a real friend' look. Oh well.

"Sure, I'll take the boys home and get some sleep myself. Do you need me to bring you anything from the house?" She still looked hot in that red sweater. It was probably why John regained consciousness.

She gave him a big hug, left the waiting room and headed for the double doors. On her way through the door she stopped and gave big Ray a hug and a kiss on the cheek, then literally skipped her way through the double doors and into the hospital. Ray could fantasize about that moment for a month or more.

Midge shook the boys awake then half carried them to the van and headed for home. They all could use some sleep.

They slept until after four in the afternoon, when Midge got everyone up and showered and dressed to go back to the hospital to visit Jacob's father. He left the laundry in a pile as he loaded the boys back into the van. They stopped at Wendy's on the way so Jacob could get a baked potato and garden salad while Ryan and Midge ordered bacon and double cheese burger combos. They ate inside because Midge hated eating in a vehicle anymore, after so many years of eating in the car as a cop. It was after seven when they finished eating and were headed for the hospital.

John had been moved out of the ICU and to a regular double room on the third floor. They got their passes from the desk and went up.

As they entered the room, they found John in the first bed inside the door with Brenda sitting beside the bed, holding John's good left hand. His right arm was taped to his body to keep his wounded shoulder still. You could see his chest was heavily bandaged under his hospital gown.

Jacob ran to hug his father and Brenda helped him to keep him from hurting John. Midge and Ryan stayed back against the wall, out of the way. In the next bed was an older guy who had no visitors. He was watching his television with great concentration it seemed, and paid no attention to John's visitors.

After a few minutes, John spoke to Midge. "Hello Midge and Ryan, thanks for taking such good care of Jacob. I owe you a lot for everything, Midge." He was elevated in the bed some, but it was still hard for him to move very well."

"Forget it John, we enjoy Jacob's visits and it was Brenda who took care of the boys, not me. I am very sorry about your father, John. I know you and Jacob were very close to him." Midge actually hated to bring it up, but it seemed like the right thing to say right now.

"Thank you Midge, and thank you for saving my life. I know you don't want anyone to know, but I know I owe you a debt for everything you have done for me and my son and my Brenda here." Now that was a funny term 'my Brenda'. He wondered exactly what that meant. He should have made her change out of that red sweater before she came to see him.

"Forget it John, you don't owe me anything. It looks like you are recovering faster than they ever thought you could." He really meant it. The color had returned to his face and his eyes were pretty clear considering all the sedatives he had in him.

"I am getting wonderful care. I could not ask for anything better." He looked at Brenda and she squeezed his free hand, leaned over and kissed it.

Jacob and Brenda held conspiratorial conversations while Midge and Ryan kind of hung out in the doorway. Midge was just about to ask permission to go wait in the lobby when he heard the guy in the next bed start to complain.

"Darn President, he's preempting Desperate Housewives. He is on all the channels. What is it now, have we invaded some other country? He better get this over quick, Marcia is after that new hunk down the street and I want to see it." He kept muttering under his breath about how out of whack our country's values are nowadays.

Midge looked over at the far TV and saw the President and his wife at an airport with the camera panning on a Boeing 777 parked with a mobile staircase against the side entry door. There were men and women below assembling in a line being directed by some military personnel in an attempt to get them to line up straight. Some of the people were falling to the ground and kissing it. He could remember doing that himself, when he had landed at Edwards Air Force base in California, on his return from Vietnam.

Midge wondered how long those people had to sit in that airplane, on that runway, so all the politicians could gather to get this photo op on prime time television. He asked Brenda to turn on John's television and turn up the sound, which she did, as she and John were interested in what was happening also.

He listened to the President. 'My fellow Americans, this is a great day for America and a great day for some of our fellow citizens who have long been held hostage in a hostile land.' The cameras panned the welcoming committee including politicians, Democrats and Republicans, army generals, navy admirals, and cabinet members. Midge thought he saw Jim Featherston standing between the head of the CIA and the Director of Homeland Security. 'Today we welcome home twenty-three of our finest citizens. These men and women have endured some unspeakable horrors and long months in captivity in the Middle East. Some were thought to be dead, killed on Arab television to shock America.' The cameras now zeroed in on the twenty-three people assembled in front of the aircraft. Some looked sick and frail, others just looked tired, but they all looked secure and happy on American soil. 'Their families did not know if they were dead or alive, or if their bodies would ever be recovered, so they could receive a decent Christian burial. Many in America had lost hope, given in to despair, and surrendered to their fears. Many called for concessions so the terrorists would leave us alone. The pressure on America to pull out and leave the people we have freed was enormous, but we have stayed the course. Appeasement of the terrorist is not the answer. America will not shrink from its responsibility and we will never forget those who serve on our peoples' behalf. Today I want the American people to join with me in welcoming the former hostages and now free Americans home. This happened so quickly their families did not even know about their release until less than fifteen hours ago. I will read their names one at a time and if each person will please come up and receive the Medal of Freedom, then hold for a few minutes for a group photo. We will then put you on a bus and take you to a medical facility where you will receive treatment and be allowed to contact your families. The first hostage is Nancy Woods, a nurse who was kidnapped on ……..'

The President read off the names and placed a medal around each neck. After they were all recognized, the politicians gathered around for photos. What a public relations coup. This would make news all over the world, except maybe on Aljazeera. Some of the families around the country were finding out on live television, that their loved ones were alive and home in America. They might be angry about not being there, but you had to give the White House credit. It was a Neilson rating smash hit, and even though it interrupted Desperate Housewives, all was forgiven.

The talk shows would be filled for the next two weeks with interviews of the ex-hostages and their families. Books would be ghost written for the hostages and movies made about them and their daring rescue.

Another happy ending for the cowboy president, and well deserved if you asked Midge. He had the courage to stay the course, and send his man, Agent Jim Featherston, on an unauthorized mission with a team of dedicated soldiers who risk their lives every day for no credit at all, to help free the hostages. No one would ever know their story of dedication and bravery.

They had a dedication to America, that many Americans scorned and mocked, until they needed help. Then they demanded someone like Colonel Eric Stormer or Captain Carl Windsmere should risk their lives to save them. And in the great tradition of the American armed forces, they would do their duty, so help them God.

It was over and the news anchors were coming on now to interpret the real meaning of what the people just saw. As if anyone would have trouble understanding the words the president used. They were finding hidden meaning in every word, phrase, pause, or gesture, and then spreading confusion so they could tell the American people the real story behind the rescue. That was the system for job security for the intellectual elite and physically gifted faces of television.

Brenda turned off the television. "Midge, you should have been in Washington with them. Without you, none of this would have been possible." She was holding John's hand, but she really meant what she said.

"No, it was John who was the hero, and paid the hero's price. If he had not had the courage to act, I could not have done anything. I give him all the credit."

"No, Midge, I acted out of fear or maybe even desperation. I had a selfish goal of freedom for my family and yes, even myself. You acted out of kindness and were selfless. You have gained nothing, not money, fame, or recognition. All you did was give of yourself to others and that is the greatest gift in the world. I thank you again and all the hostages, I am sure, thank you for their freedom also." John and Brenda embraced gently.

"Don't get carried away, what is done is done. I hope I never have to do something like that again. I am too old and I just want to relax and retire for good. It is why I moved to the Sault. There is no crime or action up here."

"Sure." Brenda and John both laughed.

"I wish that were true," a voice came from the doorway.

Midge turned to see Ken Telway smiling. They shook hands and then Ken went over to see John Nassire. The two boys were sitting in the chairs bored out of their minds. "I'm glad to see you're doing better, John. Hurry up and get back to work, the Tribe needs you. If it wasn't for Midge here, you may not be alive."

"We know," John said looking at Brenda. Midge guessed he knew who the 'we' were alright.

Ken turned to Midge. "We need to see you down at the tribal headquarters tomorrow, Midge. We have a few loose details we need to ask you about."

"Like what? I don't belong to the tribe. Why do you need me?"

"I can only say the feds have some questions about yesterday and the shooting at the casino. Come by any time, I should be in my office all day." Ken smiled and then said he had to go. He wished John and Brenda the best and left the room shaking Midge's hand again on his way out.

"Well, how about I take the boys home and leave you two alone? I'll bring Jacob up to visit again tomorrow." They were both nodding their heads and Jacob hugged and kissed his father and Brenda. It had the looks of the start of a nice family, he thought.

"Good night"

"Good night, Midge and thanks for all you did for us and the rest of America." Midge barely heard the last, as he took the boys out and down the elevator.

He could only hope they got home in time for the delayed showing of Desperate Housewives.

The End

Epilogue

It had been hectic the last few weeks.
    John was released from the hospital. Brenda took him and Jacob home and moved in with them. Midge had the feeling she would not need her bartender job anymore.
    Midge and Ryan attended an elaborate funeral for Jay Nassire. He was buried in the Bay Mills Reservation Cemetery on Mission Hill in his adopted land. The following week Midge attended a wedding at the Tribal Council Offices in Bay Mills. He was best man for John as he married Brenda, with Jacob and Ryan being dual ring bearers.
    The Tribal Council offered Midge the job as Director of Security of the Sault Tribe Casinos. It was a very generous offer, but he turned them down. He was retired, after all. He did however make a recommendation for his replacement which they accepted.
    He attended Tom Molten's retirement from the Chippewa County Sheriff's Department on Saturday and visited Tom at his new job as Director of Security of the Sault Tribe Casinos on Monday. Tom's boy could now afford to stay and graduate from Superior State University. He loved Tom's new office. Midge thought they would be seeing each other a lot, when he went to the casinos to gamble and meet female tourists at the bar.
    Ken Telway was back to being Tribal Police Captain and a couple of the Bahweting braves were doing community service on the reservations. His men were now making regular patrols on the Sugar Island reservation.
    Jim Featherston was back in his office in the Treasury Building in Washington D.C. He had called Midge to tell him the President had signed a special commendation for service to his country. He would like Midge to come to Washington and accept it privately, from a

grateful President. Of course they could not do it publicly. Midge told him to keep it, but Jim could buy him a beer the next time they met. Jim said he understood and the beer was on him.

Colonel Stormer and his Delta Force had returned to their home base in North Carolina and were training for their next mission.

Captain Carl Windsmere and his Seal One Team returned to California and were working out everyday in case their country needed them.

The Ayatollahs were protesting to the White House and demanding to know where their Mullah Seyed Habibi was being held. They wanted the Camels Eye returned immediately. The cowboy President told them to stick it up their ass. If they could not keep track of their own people, that was not his problem. The Mullah probably stole the emerald and was living it up with some half nude French beauties on the Rivera, he told the Iranian Ambassador.

The senior citizens were still talking about the hijacking of their bus, the black helicopter, escaping from the barn, with June driving the bus just before the barn exploded. Of course no one believed them, not even their children or grandchildren until June's daughter Mary Jean printed out the pictures from June's digital camera. They showed the soldiers, helicopter, and fire burning, but the news services could not verify the events that were a couple of weeks old, so they were not interested. Still the Senior Center in Auburn Hills would never forget that trip, for the rest of their days on this earth.

Midge and Ryan were getting ready to head to the Chippewa County International Airport. It was their first leg of a long day of flying. They would fly from the Sault to Detroit to Orlando and from there take a limo to the Polynesian Hotel in Disney World. He had promised Ryan a vacation and they were going to spend a couple of weeks in sunny Florida.

"Hurry up Ryan, we have to finish packing and get to the airport. We are supposed to be there an hour before departure, and we have to get through security," which was actually a joke at Chippewa County International Airport with only four flights a day scheduled.

Midge had turned on the television and was watching NBC with Katie and Matt and Al with the weather. He especially wanted to know the week's forecast for Florida.

He liked this crew even if Katie seemed to be a little gullible and naïve, she was like everyone's little sister. She was balanced by Matt's cynicism on everything, and Al was the king of the non-offensive one liner.

He heard Katie say, 'and for all you jewelry junkies out there, we have a special report from Jerusalem this morning about a long lost jewel that will blow you away. You don't want to miss it. We'll be right back after this message from our sponsors.'

Midge called Ryan to come quickly, sit on the couch with him and watch the upcoming session on the news. Ryan did not really care about it, but he sat down and watched with his Uncle Midge.

'And now, live from Jerusalem is our Middle East Correspondent, Jim Ellixson at the Jewish National Museum. Hello Jim, what is so special about the jewel on display at the museum today?'

'Well Katie, the story behind this jewel is clouded with history and mystery. The emerald is called the Soul of Jerusalem and people are lined up for over two blocks to get in and see this magnificent piece of history. It is said to have come from Cleopatra's mines area in Egypt, where it was uncovered by Jewish slaves who worked the mines. Its history includes possession by the rulers of Egypt, Babylonia, Palestine, the original Jewish state, and Persia over the last few centuries. It is said to be the largest and most perfect cut emerald ever discovered in the world. It mysteriously reappeared in Jerusalem recently, under some cloudy circumstances.' Yes, very cloudy, thought Midge.

'Jim, can our audience see what the stone looks like?'

'Yes Katie, our cameras are transmitting a close up of it now.' The camera zoomed in on a glass case lined with black velvet on the bottom with tiny spot lights shinning from the four top corners of the protective enclosure. Now the audience could see a gold braided chain of twenty-four carat gold, from which hung a flat gold circle with a Star of David in its center. The star was holding a large multi cut perfect green emerald. The sparkle and multiple rainbows shined for the world to see.

'Jim, that is the most beautiful necklace I have ever seen, and people say a diamond is a girl's best friend. Thanks Jim, for showing it to our viewers and have a safe trip home.'

'Wow, what a treasure. Now we will take you to Al and the weather, right after these messages from our sponsors.'

Midge just sat and stared at the television, not even seeing the commercials. What a beautiful job the Jewish craftsmen had done of packaging the stone inside the gold Star of David. The setting certainly did it justice. He could still remember holding it in his hands. He knew it was something special the likes of which the world may never see again.

"Uncle Midge, I bet the emerald cost a lot, don't you?"

"More than you'll ever know Ryan, more than you'll ever know."

Printed in the United States
36964LVS00005B/1-51